Mary Balogh was born in Swansea, South Wales. She now lives in Saskatchewan, where she taught for twenty years. She won the *Romantic Times* Award for Best New Regency Writer in 1985 and has since become the genre's most popular and bestselling author. Her most recent Topaz historicals are *Tangled* and *Longing*, which have been published to great critical acclaim.

Karen Harper, author of *Circle of Gold, Wings of Morning, River of Sky,* and *Promises to Keep* (all from Signet), taught literature and writing before leaving teaching to write full time. Her work frequently appears in *Good Housekeeping*. She lives in Naples, Florida, and Columbus, Ohio.

Patricia Oliver, who has a Ph.D. in comparative literature and teaches English at the university level, was born in England and now lives in Texas. She has lived for many years in Latin America, speaks Spanish and French, loves horses, cats, and gardens, reads avidly, and is a lifelong fan of Georgette Heyer. Her latest Signet Regency novel is *Lord Gresham's Lady*.

Margaret Evans Porter received the Best New Regency Author Award for 1989/1990. Having studied British history at Oxford University, she completed her B.A. in Theater and English, and received her Master of Arts degree in Radio, Television, and Film in the U.S. She enjoys traveling, and makes a point of returning to Great Britain every year. She and her husband reside in metropolitan Denver. Her newest Signet Regency is *Dangerous Diversions*.

Patricia Rice was born in Newburgh, New York. She attended the University of Kentucky, and now lives in Mayfield, Kentucky, in a rambling Tudor house, with her husband and two children, Corinna and Derek. Ms. Rice has a degree in accounting, and her hobbies include history, travel, and antique collecting. Her most recent Topaz historical is *Paper Roses*.

ANNOUNCING THE

TOPAZ FREQUENT READERS CLUB
COMMEMORATING TOPAZ'S
1 YEAR ANNIVERSARY!

THE MORE YOU BUY, THE MORE YOU GET

Redeem coupons found here and in the back of all new Topaz titles for FREE Topaz gifts:

Send in:

 2 coupons for a free TOPAZ novel (choose from the list below);
- ☐ THE KISSING BANDIT, Margaret Brownley
- ☐ BY LOVE UNVEILED, Deborah Martin
- ☐ TOUCH THE DAWN, Chelley Kitzmiller
- ☐ WILD EMBRACE, Cassie Edwards

 4 coupons for an "I Love the Topaz Man" on-board sign

 6 coupons for a TOPAZ compact mirror

 8 coupons for a Topaz Man T-shirt

Just fill out this certificate and send with original sales receipts to:

TOPAZ FREQUENT READERS CLUB-1ST ANNIVERSARY
Penguin USA • Mass Market Promotion; Dept. H.U.G.
375 Hudson St., NY, NY 10014

Name_____

Address_____

City_____State_____Zip_____

Offer expires 5/31/1995

This certificate must accompany your request. No duplicates accepted. Void where prohibited, taxed or restricted. Allow 4-6 weeks for receipt of merchandise. Offer good only in U.S., its territories, and Canada.

BLOSSOMS

FIVE STORIES BY

Mary Balogh

Karen Harper

Patricia Oliver

Margaret Evans Porter

Patricia Rice

A SIGNET BOOK

SIGNET
Published by the Penguin Group
Penguin Books USA Inc., 375 Hudson Street,
New York, New York 10014, U.S.A.
Penguin Books Ltd, 27 Wrights Lane,
London W8 5TZ, England
Penguin Books Australia Ltd, Ringwood,
Victoria, Australia
Penguin Books Canada Ltd, 10 Alcorn Avenue,
Toronto, Ontario, Canada M4V 3B2
Penguin Books (N.Z.) Ltd, 182–190 Wairau Road,
Auckland 10, New Zealand

Penguin Books Ltd, Registered Offices:
Harmondsworth, Middlesex, England

First published by Signet, an imprint of Dutton Signet,
a division of Penguin Books USA Inc.

First Printing, April, 1995
10 9 8 7 6 5 4 3 2 1

Contents

The Forbidden Daffodils

❦

by Mary Balogh

She stood with her forearms resting along the rough top of the wooden stile, gazing into the woods beyond, wondering if she would climb over to stroll among the trees. Normally she would not have hesitated. It was one of her favorite places to walk, though the country lanes, bordered by ferns and wildflowers, always beckoned when she wanted more brisk exercise, and the wide golden sands were her choice when she wanted solitude but did not want to be cooped up in her room. One could never be low in spirits when one was on the sands, with all the elemental force of the sea just beyond. One could only be uplifted and reminded of the littleness of one's own troubles in the vast scheme of things.

But the woods offered solitude of a different sort. She always had a feeling entering the woods rather similar to the one she had when she entered a cathedral—not that she had entered any for many years. There was quietness in the woods and a sense of the closeness of God. And the woods were in some ways better than a cathedral because they were living and changing.

She loved the woods at all seasons. She loved them when the trees, still essentially bare, were greening with spring buds, and when the ground was colored with bluebells, and when the leaves were so thick on the branches that it seemed almost as if there were a roof overhead. She loved the many colors of autumn, both when the colors were above her head and when

7

they were spread on the ground at her feet, at first a soft carpet and then a crunchy delight. She loved the time of the snowdrops, the first sign of spring, and the time of the primroses that followed after.

But most of all she loved the time of the daffodils.

Aunt Hetty grew daffodils in the flower beds beneath the front windows of the house—vast numbers of them. They provided floral arrangements for the house and the church for several weeks each spring. Aunt Hetty was famous for her daffodils, even in a country famed for them—Wales had made the daffodil its floral emblem. And yet ironically Aunt Hetty was English.

But the daffodils in the woods were different. They bloomed wild there and grew in disorganized clumps. Fortunately no one had ever thought to try to cultivate them, to force them to grow in a pattern pleasing to a rational human mind.

And daffodils growing among trees, splashes of sunshine in the shade, always seemed more glorious than daffodils growing in flower beds.

The snowdrops and the primroses always brought hope with them, the hope of a new year, of a new beginning, of a renewed life. But the daffodils brought more than hope. They were like a blaze of glorious defiance, their bright color and their reaching trumpets and stretching petals bold and vivid in contrast to the delicate pastel shades of spring around them.

The daffodils were a startling reaffirmation of life.

They were beginning to bud now. In a few more days, in a week at the longest, they would burst into full bloom. She had watched them for the past few weeks as their green shoots pushed up through the soil and the grass, at first tentative and then bold and unmistakable. And yet now, on a pilgrimage she made almost daily, she hesitated, her forearms resting on the top of the stile.

Every time she went over it—she must have crossed it more than a thousand times—she was trespassing.

The wood was part of the park belonging to Tŷ Mawr, the Big House, perhaps literally called that in Welsh by some humorist of the past who could think of no other suitable name to give it. Or perhaps no one had tried to give it a name and so it had been called Tŷ Mawr until the name came to be official.

It had stood empty for years, its owner now living in England and apparently not considering this wild and beautiful corner of Wales worth even a summer visit. But now someone had leased it for an indeterminate length of time—a single gentleman, according to local gossip, English of course. And he had arrived. The rector's wife had brought word yesterday afternoon, when she had called to take tea with Aunt Hetty and Aunt Martha, that he was expected at any moment. And the milkman had brought the news of his actual arrival when he made his delivery early this morning and passed the word across the doorstep to the servants, who carried it upstairs with the morning tea. A proper gentleman he was, it seemed, with a carriage grand enough for a duke, and enough baggage loaded onto the accompanying coach to provision an army.

And so the woods were now to be off-limits. They were his, and one did not yet know how he felt about young ladies wandering about there to feel close to God and to observe the changing of the seasons. He might at least have waited until after the blooming of the daffodils, the would-be trespasser thought crossly.

But it was very unlikely he would have the woods patrolled, she thought, tempted again. And very unlikely that he would set foot in them himself, at least today. He had arrived only yesterday. And it was early morning. Early for an English gentleman, anyway. She knew a thing or two about English gentlemen. And about English ladies, too. She had been one herself until five years ago. She used to sleep until noon and dance until dawn.

No, there was no danger whatsoever this morning.

And surely within the next few days she would meet him and be able to guess whether he was the type of man who would resent a trespasser who did nothing but admire the beauty around her. She had never picked any of the daffodils or any of the other wild-flowers. She liked to see them bloom where they were.

She set a foot on the lower step of the stile, throwing back her cloak and hitching the skirt of her dress as she did so.

Aunt Martha had wondered if he would be a young man. She had looked sidelong at her niece and nodded significantly. And a handsome man, perhaps.

Aunt Hetty had said that it was very unlikely that a young, handsome gentleman would be coming alone to this rural corner of Wales at this time of year. Such a man would be in London for the Season.

"But the Season does not begin until April, Hetty dear," Aunt Martha had said. "It is not even March yet. Perhaps Kate, my love—"

But she had not been allowed to complete her thought.

"You know that Kate could have no dealings with a gentleman of *ton*, Martha," Aunt Hetty had said quite firmly.

Or with a gentleman of any rank, her words had implied, though she had not spoken unkindly.

Kate sat on top of the stile and swung her legs over to the other side. Perpetual exile. That was what she was living in. Sometimes she almost forgot. It really had not turned out as badly as she had feared, nor as badly as Papa doubtless had hoped. She would go and live with her mother's sisters in their cottage on the remote Gower Peninsula in Wales, he had told her on that terrible morning after bending her over his desk and whipping her—the only time he had ever done so. He would make them an allowance for her keep, but none for herself. She would live there for the rest of her life.

Five years ago it had seemed like a sentence of

death, or at least like a sentence of transportation to some primitive and dread penal colony. Even after her arrival she had been horrified. There was nothing but the wild, elemental scenery and no one but her aunts and a few—a very few—neighbors.

Now, five years later, she sometimes asked herself if she would go back even if she had the chance. And sometimes it surprised her that she did not want to leave, that she had grown to love this place and the unexpected peace it had brought her. Somehow her surroundings had become part of her, indistinguishable from her. London and all the *ton* balls and routs she had attended and her father's estate seemed unreal now, as if they belonged to a different lifetime—and, of course, they did.

She would consider herself happy, she thought, stepping down the other side of the stile to the forbidden woods, if there were not the loneliness. It was not always conscious. It was rarely a raw pain. Rather it was a gnawing awareness of emptiness—an emptiness that waited to be filled. It was not in itself a bothersome feeling. It became so only when she thought consciously about it and realized that the emptiness would never be filled.

She had been hopelessly disgraced five years ago. It had been very public, quite impossible to cover up. And she had refused to take the only course that might have restored some measure of respectability. Hence the whipping—administered not so much for the offense but for the stubbornness that had followed it—and the exile. The perpetual exile.

But she would not think of it. She rarely did so now. Life for the past five years really had not been bad at all. Aunt Hetty was kind to her and Aunt Martha openly loving. She suspected that they both enjoyed having with them the daughter of their sister, the sister who had married so dazzlingly far above herself. The neighboring gentry—very low on the social scale and in very few numbers—treated her with

respect. Papa would not have given any of them the
time of day. And she had found in her surroundings
all she needed to bring her peace.

But the peace never quite masked the loneliness.

There were more daffodil buds than she could
count, many of them yellow tipped, most of them still
tightly clenched, a few of them beginning to loosen,
to consider the bold move of bursting into the glory
of full bloom. She bent over one such bud and cupped
it gently in her hands. She felt the familiar yearning
that always came with the daffodils—half pain, half
exaltation.

And then she heard a dog barking ferociously and
looked up sharply to see a black-and-white collie rac-
ing toward her. She snatched her hands away from
the bud and took a hasty step back before standing
very still. Her heart was pounding with alarm.

"She will not touch you," a voice called from some
distance away. A male voice. "She is all bark and
no bite."

And sure enough, the collie stopped when she had
bounded to within three feet of Kate and laid her
forepaws along the ground while she wagged her tail,
bottom elevated.

But Kate's attention was on the man who was striding toward them, coming down the slope through the
trees. He was in the shade, though she could see that
he was indeed young and that he was dressed fashionably and elegantly in a many-caped greatcoat and tight
pantaloons and white-topped Hessian boots.

If she could have found a rabbit hole in which to
hide, she would have wriggled into it, she thought.
How humiliating to be caught trespassing!

But the discomfort caused by her predicament fled
when he came closer, together with the excuse her
mind had been frantically composing. For as he approached and removed his hat, she could see his
face clearly.

A startlingly familiar face. Belonging to a man she

had hated passionately five years ago. A man she would always hate.

The Marquess of Ashendon had always known where she was. Lambton had told him—the Earl of Lambton, her father. There had been no reason not to tell him. He was the last person who would have thought of going after her.

Or so it would have seemed.

He had not gone after her. She had refused to marry him, both when they were in private together as he made his offer and after her father had joined them. She had refused icily and quite adamantly when they were alone together, fiercely and passionately when Lambton had urged the match on her. She had stamped her foot at her father and had then turned on Ashendon, her eyes flashing, and told him she would not marry him if he were the last man on earth. She had mouthed the old cliché with conviction.

No, he had not gone after her. Not again. He had done that once in order to save her from a dreadful future, though she would not admit as much, and then had brought her back, spending two nights on the road with her in the process, sharing a room with her each time. And they had been seen together by an alarmingly large number of acquaintances.

Any other woman—any woman but Lady Katherine Buchanan—would have realized that she had no alternative but to marry him. None whatsoever. Even though she hated him. Just as he had had no alternative but to offer for her, even though he loved her and knew this was an appalling way in which to enter marriage with her.

She had refused him.

Her father had summoned a servant to escort her to his study and then to go out to the stables to fetch his whip.

"I would rather you did not hurt her," the marquess had said stiffly to Lambton, clasping his hands very tightly behind his back. "It is surely enough punishment that she is ruined."

"She might have been yours to discipline, Ashendon," the earl had said, fury vibrating in his voice. "She has chosen to remain mine. She will feel my whip on her backside until she can do nothing but lie on her stomach while I arrange to send her away."

"Back home?" the Marquess of Ashendon had asked.

But Lambton had laughed harshly. No, not home. She would be sent to live with her maiden aunts in the small village of Rhos in South Wales. To live there for the rest of her life.

She had been Lambton's treasure, the only daughter after six sons. He had doted on her, given her everything she had ever desired. His wrath when she finally defied him was correspondingly harsh and unyielding.

Ashendon had shuddered as he walked away from Lambton's house. He had had no doubt that Lady Katherine was about to feel a whip for the first time in her eighteen years and that the beating would be a prolonged and vicious one. But it had been out of his power to help her. She had taken away any such power by refusing his offer.

No, he had not followed her to Rhos. It would have been pointless to do so. Her hatred was too strong. But he had a retired lodgekeeper and his wife living on his estate. He delighted them by sending them each summer on a holiday to Wales, and each summer they spent a few days at Rhos, where they became familiar faces, dutifully walked the sands and took the air until it was time to come home and report to the marquess that Katherine was still there and that she was in good health. The aunts at least appeared not to be mistreating her.

And he discovered soon after her leaving that there was a large house and park—indeed it was called the Big House in Welsh, Tŷ Mawr—on the outskirts of Rhos that had stood empty for years. It had taken him some time to discover to whom it belonged. But even when he knew, he held back. He would wait for three years, he had decided at first. He would give her time to grow up, time to allow the passions of that incident in her life to cool, time for her hatred to fade. Time for her exile to have made her desperately unhappy. Rhos must be in one of the wildest, remotest parts of the British Isles, according to his old lodgekeeper, who talked a great deal about wind and rain and damp salt air and nothing but mile upon mile of sand and sand dunes and wild hedgerows.

Poor Katherine. He wondered sometimes if she regretted not marrying him. Sometimes he convinced himself that she probably did.

After three years, when he tried to approach the owner of Tŷ Mawr, he found that the man had gone traveling in Europe and no one seemed to know exactly where he was to be found. A year later the owner was back, but the marquess's uncle had died unexpectedly and there was a great deal of business to be attended to, since he had inherited and there were numerous female relatives to be settled satisfactorily.

And so five years had passed.

She was still there. It seemed that she must have accepted her exile. It surprised him somewhat. She had been a headstrong girl. He would have expected that she would try to make some sort of escape. Of course, Lambton undoubtedly kept her without funds. To what would she escape?

The owner of Tŷ Mawr was only too eager to rent to him. Ashendon leased the house for six months and left for Wales without further delay.

His lodgekeepers had not exaggerated. He traveled close to the coastline of South Wales, passing through the towns of Newport, Cardiff, and Swansea, and coming eventually to the Gower Peninsula—all high plateau, fit for nothing but sheep, and stark cliffs and golden beaches and wooded valleys. And finally the steep descent to the one great sweep of beach that was headed not by cliffs but by sand dunes, and then a sandy road and smaller lanes lined with ferns and wild plants. And the village of Rhos, which hardly seemed to merit the label, so small was it.

It was a blustery day in late February when he arrived, the sky low and heavy with gray clouds, the sea menacing looking and flecked with foam, angry breakers spending themselves against the sand. There seemed nothing here except the elements.

And she had spent five years here? Poor Katherine.

It was a relief to find that the house was at least both warm and well aired. The housekeeper had done a good job of keeping damp and neglect at bay. He had brought his cook and his valet with him—and his most useless but beloved dog.

He awoke early the next morning. Indeed, he had not slept a great deal at all. He was feeling all the madness of having come. She had never liked him. She had ended up hating him. No doubt she blamed him for everything—for ruining her dream of bliss, for ruining her reputation, for having her whipped and exiled. Hatred, he realized suddenly, having spent five years convincing himself of the opposite, was more likely to grow and fester with time than to fade.

He must be the very last man on earth she would want to see.

And having arrived, he realized that his plans had never proceeded farther than this. He had pictured himself leasing Tŷ Mawr and traveling to it. He had pictured her sad and broken, willing now to accept him on any terms. He had pictured himself taking her back to civilization, wooing her love, living happily with her for the rest of a lifetime.

Had this five-year exile broken her spirit? he wondered. And was that what he really wanted? She had been a headstrong girl, very conscious of what she wanted, very determined to get it at all costs. She had been a girl so accustomed to being given her own

way—her father and her brothers had all spoiled her—
that she could not seem to conceive of the idea of not
getting it.

He had often wondered why he had loved her so
passionately and so enduringly. Perhaps it was merely
the lure of what could not be had. During any of the
five years since he had first met her he could have
had almost any woman he had wanted—for years he
had been one of the largest prizes on the marriage
mart. But he had only ever wanted her.

He did not know how he was to approach her.
Leave his card at her aunts' house and then pay a
call? Would she see him? Would she have a choice?
Would she make a scene?

He went walking during the morning. He instinctively sought out the more secluded parts of the park
instead of walking down the sloping lawn to the gates
that would take him out onto the sand dunes and
across them to the beach. He felt almost as if he were
hiding, afraid of being seen by someone who would
carry word to her and send her in her turn into hiding.

Patch was sniffing at his heels and running circles
around him, daring him to break into a run or to play
at catching her. And then the collie ran off, first this
way and then that, exploring her new surroundings,
sniffing noisily at every unfamiliar stone and bush.

He wandered into the woods, which were somehow
sheltered from the sea gales and apparently flour-
ishing, though the trees were still bare after winter.
Spring was coming, though. The ground at his feet was
covered with the fresh green shoots of daffodils, and it
looked as though many of them were about to bloom.

He was glad it was almost spring. Somehow during
spring everything seemed possible.

And then his dog started to bark hysterically and
darted off through the trees.

There was a girl farther down the slope, apparently
in the process of picking the buds, though he could

see that she held none when she jumped back from the approaching dog and then froze in terror.

He had once seen a cat that was being chased with great ferocity by Patch stop in its tracks and turn. And he had then proceeded to watch the indescribably hilarious scene of his fierce dog running in unholy terror with the cat in hot pursuit. If it had been possible for Patch to climb trees, he did not doubt that she would have dashed up one to the topmost branch and cowered there until he went up to rescue her. He found his dog's cowardice utterly endearing.

"She will not touch you," he called to the girl. "She is all bark and no bite."

Patch was ingratiating herself with this new acquaintance in her usual undignified and unladylike manner. He hurried downward through the trees to reassure the girl.

She was dressed in a plain gray cloak, the dress visible beneath it equally plain. She wore no bonnet and had her fair hair dressed smoothly over her head and knotted simply at her neck.

He was quite close to her before he recognized her. She had always reminded him of a sparkling gem. She had always had more curls and more ringlets than any other young lady. She had always dressed more fashionably than anyone else, with more frills and flounces and bows and ribbons. And her face had always held the assurance that she knew herself beautiful and desirable and eligible. One had almost been able to read in her face that she was the daughter of an earl, though strangely there had seemed to be no conscious arrogance in her.

She had changed almost beyond recognition, he thought, feeling at the same time as if a powerful fist had slammed into his stomach and robbed him of breath. In five years she had left behind her girlhood without a trace and had become a woman.

An amazingly beautiful woman.

And so the meeting was being forced upon him before he was in any way prepared for it. He had no idea what had brought her into the park of Tŷ Mawr. But by some strange coincidence they had come to the same place at the same time.

He watched recognition widen her eyes and stain her cheeks with color. When the color faded, her face was unnaturally pale. She stood absolutely still and silent. As did he for several moments.

"Lady Katherine," he said at last. He did not bow. He considered doing so, but it seemed somehow inappropriate.

Her eyes hardened. There was no other expression on her face. "Kate Buchanan," she said. "The lady you named no longer exists."

He could not think of a mortal thing to say to her. After five years of living for this moment, he was mute, his mind a blank.

"I believe," he finally said, "you are trespassing."

Her mind had not even begun to cope with the situation. She could note only trivialities. He was taller than she remembered, broader shouldered. But perhaps it was his greatcoat that gave both impressions. He was still one of the handsomest men she had met. His hair was thick and dark, somewhat disheveled by his hat, his features sharply chiseled. His eyes were even bluer than she remembered—their blueness had always fascinated her. Dark eyes would have suited him better. Dark eyes in a brooding, austere face. But they were blue.

She would not have expected him to have a playful dog. Something sleek and fierce would have been more fitting. The collie was doing dancing steps in front of her and yipping and then jumping up against her master, eager to be moving again. She expected that at any moment he would cuff the dog and send it sprawling. Instead he reached down and tickled the dog beneath the chin—absently, it seemed. He did not remove his eyes from her.

That stillness in him, that brooding quality, that lack of humor had always unnerved her, even during the early days of that Season, when he had danced with her at every ball and occasionally sent her nosegays the mornings after and sometimes had taken her driving in the park during the fashionable hour. Ernest and Algernon, the two of her brothers who had been in town at the time, had started to tease her about him and warn her that he was wooing her. Even then, though she had been attracted and flattered, she had been uneasy in his company. She had never been sure she could like him.

What had he said now? She was trespassing? Oh, yes, it was exactly what she would expect him to say. Exactly! And she *was* trespassing. She was horribly in the wrong. But, dear God, what was he doing here?

Reality was beginning to intrude. He was the gentleman who had leased Tŷ Mawr? But why? Had he known she was here? He must have. It would be just too incredible a coincidence otherwise.

And she was aware suddenly that she was alone with him in the woods. Alone and in the wrong. These woods belonged to him for as long as he had leased the property. And she remembered what had happened on another occasion when she had been alone with him and in the wrong. She had kept the five-year-old memory long suppressed, but it came rushing back now with startling vividness.

She remembered the shock of his kiss, of the fact that his lips had been parted and his tongue had played with her lips until she parted them and opened her mouth. And then the shock of his tongue deep inside her mouth, exploring, stroking, sliding in and out while her temperature soared with his and her half sleep had converted into something else that made her just as helpless.

She remembered the weight and heat of his body, clothed only in shirt and pantaloons, when he had come beneath the bedclothes with her, the feel of his hands, smoothing, searching, pinching, and ... unclothing both her and himself. And then the full weight of his body, his strongly muscled legs pushing hers wide, his hands coming beneath her.

And the feel of him coming inside her, bringing sharp pain for a moment, and then a growing ache, a building madness as he withdrew and thrust repeatedly until everything shattered into a feeling she had never experienced before or since.

She remembered it all now in one vivid, flashing moment, the fact that she and this man had shared that, the ultimate intimacy. And the fact that he had said nothing afterward. She had woken later to find him sleeping on the floor in front of the door again. And the next day, the last of their journey back to London, he had been silent and severe, just as if it had never happened. He had mentioned it again only the following day, when he was making her his offer—before Papa had joined them. She must marry him, he had urged. He had had her virginity. She might be with child.

She had taken the chance that she was not. She was in Wales with her aunts before finding out for sure that she was not, although she had lived through the hell of being four days late.

And now she was alone with him again. She turned sharply away in the direction of the stile. But his hand closed on her upper arm before she could take more than a step or two.

"You do not have to leave," he said.

She jerked her arm from his grasp, alarmed by the sensation created by his touch. "It will not happen again," she said. "I will not trespass again. I beg your pardon."

"Katherine."

His voice was harsh and stayed her again. She turned back to look at him. He was standing with his hands clasped behind him. His dog was sitting beside him, an alert look on her face, ready to resume the walk at the first promising sign.

"Katherine, how are you?" he asked. His eyes were roaming her face. Seeing all her loss of beauty. She was acutely aware of the plainness of the way she dressed her hair and of the equal plainness of her clothes. They must be woefully unfashionable. She had known almost nothing of fashion for five years.

"This is no accident, is it?" she said. "You knew I was here. You came to Tŷ Mawr deliberately because I was here. Why? To ask me how I am?"

He did not answer for a while. He had always been a disconcertingly silent man. One whose expression gave away nothing. "Yes," he said at last.

She almost laughed, except that there was nothing funny about his answer. She had refused him—all of five years ago. She had released him from all obligation for what she had done and for what he had then done. It was ancient history. If she had thought of him during the past five years—and she supposed she must have done so even if she had kept him from her conscious mind—she had imagined that by now he would be married to someone who was worthy of his consequence and that his carefully chosen bride would have dutifully presented him with his heir and another son as insurance. He was the sort of man who would be that tidy about his life. Or so she had thought.

Of course it was possible that he was married, that he did have an heir and maybe other children too.

"I am well," she said. "So you do not have to stay any longer. Did you expect to find me broken in spirit, my health gone? Did you expect to find me miserable and perhaps even suicidal? I have lost my looks, which is only to be expected of a woman who is now three-and-twenty, and doubtless if I were in London even my lowliest maid would not deign to wear the unfashionable clothes I now wear. But I am not any of the things you expected."

"You have not lost your looks," he said quietly, startling her.

"Well, then," she said, "you may go back home reassured. I am well. Was it conscience that brought you here? After all this time? Is your sense of duty so powerful?"

"I thought," he said, "that perhaps by now you would have come to realize that it is preferable to be married to me than to have to spend the rest of your life here."

Her eyes widened in shock. He had come to offer her marriage—again? But why? Why?

"Your obligation to me ended five years ago," she told him, "when I said no."

"It is easy to say no in the heat of the moment," he said. "Then one does not realize that the rest of a lifetime can be a long and tedious business."

"It was not easy," she said. "I knew that it meant giving up everything and everybody I had ever known and loved. I knew that it meant being whipped for the first time in my life—my father had warned me that that would be one of the consequences of my refusing you. It was terrifying in anticipation. In actual fact it was too painful to be terrifying. There was only the pain." She watched him frown briefly, the first change of expression she had seen on his face. "And I knew that after that I would be sent here for the rest of my life. I had never been here, but I imagined what it would be like, and I was a girl who enjoyed crowds and gaiety. No, it was not easy to say no. The only fact that made it possible was that it was even less possible to say yes."

"You still loved him," he said. "That was understandable, I suppose. But even that must have died in five years."

"I did not love him," she said, "even though I had eloped with him less than a week before. Perhaps I never did. Did you ever consider that? Perhaps it was all just a combination of his dashing appearance in his lieutenant's uniform and his charm and the fact that both my father and my brothers had forbidden me to have any dealings with him and the fact that you had had the audacity to warn me against him." There was bitterness, even anger, in her voice. He thought he knew everything. He knew nothing. He had never asked. Perhaps if he had asked—if he had asked the right way—she would have told him the full truth. But no, he had had all the answers.

"He was a fortune hunter," he said. "He almost ruined my sister. I prevented them just in time from running off together."

"Yes, he was a fortune hunter," she said. "I have not forgotten how he faltered when you came after us and pretended that my father had washed his hands of me and cut me off without a penny. And how eagerly he accepted the sum you paid him to leave without me. Why did you come after us? I have never understood that." They had not been good at communicating. She had not asked questions either. She had expected him to supply the answers without having to be asked.

"I could not knowingly see him ruin any innocent," he said.

"And so you did it instead," she said.

"Yes." His dog was prancing again and then made off to explore alone among the trees.

She had not been fair, really. It had not been rape. She had been as eager for it as he had.

"I was able to provide for you," he said. "I would have treated you with respect. I would have been faithful to you."

All of which Lieutenant the Honorable Leonard Hastings would not have done.

"Well," she said, "I refused you, even knowing all the possible consequences. And after five years the consequences still seem to me infinitely more desirable than the alternative would have been. You may return to London with a clear conscience."

He did not move or change expression. This time when she turned away he did not try to stop her. She made her way back to the stile, trying not to hurry, trying not to break into a run. Her back prickled. She had to sit down on top of the stile, her legs were shaking so. She must be out of his sight, unless he had followed her. She did not look back to see.

The full force of it was hitting her as she gazed across the sand dunes to the beach and the sea and inland to the sandy road and the houses beyond, her aunts' house among them. It was he who had leased Tŷ Mawr—the Marquess of Ashendon. He had come there because of her, because of some leftover and quite mistaken sense of obligation to her. It must go hard with a man of his pride and consequence to know that he had debauched a lady of quality and had been thwarted in his attempt to put all right again by marrying her.

She would never have expected it, though. She would have thought he would have left her father's house with the burden of guilt and obligation lifted from his shoulders. She would have expected him to forget her in a matter of days—or weeks, at the longest. She would have expected that he would have relished the thought that she was to be whipped and sent into exile for having led him into such a dangerous situation.

Why had he come after her and Lieutenant Hastings? Why had he ridden hard for all of two days to catch up to them before it was too late? Why had he paid Lieutenant Hastings such an enormous sum from his own pocket to relinquish his claim to her? Why had he endangered his own freedom by taking her back to London when he might have sent for her father and kept himself out of the matter?

She had asked herself the questions before, of course. Many times, though after the first few months she had pushed everything ruthlessly from her mind and her life and forgotten it all. As if something like that could possibly be forgotten. . . .

She had thought at the time that he had come because he cared. But he had been chillier than ice on the return journey and more silent than the grave.

And then on the second night she had struggled free of a nightmare to find him bent over her, shaking her by the shoulder. There had followed that most incredible incident of her life. But it had not seemed wrong, despite the fact that even a kiss granted to a gentleman could compromise her. It had not seemed wrong. She had thought he cared. She had thought he loved her. It was the only explanation for everything that made any sense.

She had loved him during that half hour or so. Not only with her body but with her whole being. She had felt the rightness of it, of finding out this way that he had cared for her all the time. She had felt all the wonder of its happening just after he had rescued her from something that might—that would—have kept him from her forever.

But it had been all lust on his part. Cold, cynical lust. He had known, of course, that he must offer her marriage when they reached London. Then why not have her during the journey? And so he had had her and then resumed the coldness and the silence.

But why had he come after her? She had never answered the question to her own satisfaction.

She got down from the stile and made her way slowly toward the road and her aunts' cottage. He was a strange man. But he had discovered what he had come to discover, and in the process he had been reminded yet again that she detested him, that any fate was preferable to being forced to marry him.

He would go away now. Within a day or two—before the daffodils bloomed—gossip would tell of the new tenant of Tŷ Mawr leaving almost before he had arrived. Everyone would be disappointed. But no one would be really surprised. What, after all, did a place like Rhos have to offer a young and single gentleman of *ton*? An English marquess, no less.

She might have had a chance again for marriage, she thought, coming to a stop at the side of the road, though there was no vehicle approaching in either direction. He had strongly implied that he had come to offer it to her.

She might after all have found her exile at an end after only five years. She might have returned to England and even to London, respectable again as the Marchioness of Ashendon. She might have had a normal life as a wife and mother.

The emptiness might have been filled.

She had been long aware that that one experience with physical love she had had at an inn somewhere north of London had something to do with the loneliness she often felt. For a very brief span of time she had known the illusion of intimate closeness with a man. And she knew that her body and her mind and her emotions all craved such closeness as a regular, daily part of her life. Not just that physical act, but everything that it might symbolize. Everything it had not symbolized on that particular occasion with that particular man.

She had loved him. For half an hour of her twenty-three years of life she had loved him with all her being. And for the five years that had followed that half hour she had hated him as she had not thought it possible to hate anyone.

Why had he come? What was it really that had prompted him to come? She would never know, she supposed. She would never see him again.

The Misses Worsley, Lady Katherine Buchanan's aunts, lived in a cottage of modest size. They kept a few servants and were considered the social leaders of the neighborhood. But they were not wealthy. Their younger sister had made a brilliant marriage to the Earl of Lambton, considering the fact that their father

was a gentleman of no very significant fortune or social standing. They had remained unmarried. On the
death of their father, when a male cousin had inherited his house and property, they had taken their small
inheritance and moved here on the recommendation
of an old friend, who had grown up in Wales.

The Marquess of Ashendon had learned all these
details about them when Lady Katherine had refused
him and had been sent to live out the rest of her life
with them.

He called at the cottage during the afternoon, intending merely to leave his card and return for a visit
the next day. But of course this was the country, not
London with its strict code of etiquette. He found himself being admitted to the front parlor only moments
after being asked to step inside the hall.

There were four ladies present. Three of them were
rising to their feet as he entered and curtsying and
looking very gratified.

"My lord," the eldest lady said graciously, "what a
singular honor you do us."

"Miss Worsley?" He made her an elegant bow.

She presented him to Miss Martha Worsley, her sister, and to Mrs. Morris, the rector's wife, and to Miss
Buchanan, her niece. *Miss* Buchanan. There was no
mention of her title.

He made his bow to each of the ladies in turn and
accepted the chair offered him. Lady Katherine was
the only one who had remained seated, her eyes on
the hands in her lap. She was dressed in a neat but
plain blue dress that fell loosely from a high waistline
but made no other concession to fashion. She wore
her hair as she had worn it in the woods during the
morning.

The contrast with the way she had looked five years
ago startled him even more than it had a few hours
before.

It seemed she had not mentioned the morning's
meeting to her aunts. They appeared unaware that

their niece had already met him. And they appeared not to know who he was. He had wondered if they would, if Lambton had given them any details of the events that had led to his sending his daughter to them. Not that his would have been the name given as of the man who had ruined her, of course. Unless she had told him herself, Lambton did not know that they had lain together during one of the nights they had spent on the road to London.

"It is a wondrously picturesque part of the coast," Mrs. Morris was saying. "It has always amazed me and my husband, the reverend, that Tŷ Mawr has remained empty for so long."

"I suppose, ma'am," he said, "that most Englishmen remain unaware of the beauties of Wales. If they would come here but once, I am sure they would return time and time again." And yet it was a bleak part of the world, he thought. It was a suitably cruel place of exile for a young lady who had sparkled with a love of society and social activities.

Mrs. Morris simpered and the course of the conversation for the next few minutes was set.

Lady Katherine got to her feet. "I will have Mari prepare the tea tray, Aunt Hetty," she said, and she left the room without looking at him.

She returned shortly after, carrying a plate of cakes, while the maid who had taken his card and shown him into the parlor brought a large tea tray. Lady Katherine seated herself behind it and poured the tea. She brought him his and offered him the plate of cakes without once raising her eyes to his or uttering a word. She did not need to talk, of course. The other three ladies kept up a lively conversation, which needed only agreeable and encouraging remarks from him at predictable intervals. It was not the sort of conversation that needed his full attention.

It was hard to believe that he had once made love to her. That he had been inside her body and given her his seed. It would never have happened if he had been fully awake, and if she had been. The discipline of years would have made it impossible, had all his defenses not been down. But she had been wailing in the throes of some nightmare and he had got up from the floor, half-asleep, to shake her by the shoulder and release her from it. And then she had looked up at him with dazed, fearful eyes and reached for him.

He had been deeply ashamed afterward. He had never forgiven himself in all the years since. He had appointed himself her guardian because she was too young and heedless and impulsive and gullible to look after herself. He had gone after her to rescue her from an unscrupulous man. And then, in the process of taking her safely home, he had violated her. The fact that he knew he must marry her as soon as they returned to London—he had not dreamed that she would refuse, even though he had known she hated him—had been no excuse at all. Neither had the fact that he had loved her. Especially not that.

"Yes, indeed," he remarked in answer to Miss Martha Worsley's claim that spring appeared to be well on the way. "I noticed this morning that the wild daffodils are about to bloom in the woods at Tŷ Mawr." He hoped he had the Welsh pronunciation right.

"And the sun is shining at last," Miss Worsley said. "It does a great deal to lift one's spirits when the sun shines."

"I could not agree more, ma'am," he said. It was time for him to take his leave, though Lady Katherine had not once looked at him or spoken to him. He had looked a great deal at her, and he would not be at all surprised to learn that the other ladies had noticed the fact.

"I will take my leave, ma'am," he said to Miss Hetty Worsley, "with thanks for the tea and hospitality."

He got to his feet as she and Miss Martha Worsley did likewise. He bowed to Mrs. Morris and to Lady Katherine.

He should have returned to London without further

ado after his earlier encounter with Katherine, he thought. It had still been morning. He could have been well on his way by now. There was no point in remaining here. She still hated him. *And after five years the consequences still seem to me infinitely more desirable than the alternative would have been.* Her words had knifed into him. She had certainly released him from any lingering obligation he might feel toward her. Not that there was anything lingering about it. He would always have an obligation toward her. Even apart from the exile, which must have made it difficult for her to meet gentlemen of her own class, she could never marry because in a moment of rash irresponsibility he had taken her virginity.

"I believe," he said, when there was really no need to say anything more at all, "I will take a walk before returning to Tŷ Mawr, and enjoy the countryside and the early spring air."

"There is nothing more beneficial to the health, I and my husband, the reverend, always say," Mrs. Morris told him, "than a few good breaths of sea air."

The sea air was far too chill and blustery for his tastes, but he bowed to the rector's wife.

"There are so many lanes and paths," he said, "that I do not know which is the most pleasant to take, or which will give the most pleasing prospect of the surrounding countryside. Perhaps Miss Buchanan would care to take a stroll with me?"

He looked directly at her and raised his eyebrows. He was being grossly unfair, he knew. Miss Hetty Worsley looked surprised but not displeased. Miss Martha Worsley clasped her hands to her bosom and nodded and smiled.

"Kate, dear," Mrs. Morris said, "you must take his grace up the hill. Not by the road, you understand, but by the lane to the Llewellyn farm."

It was not the first time during the conversation that the rector's wife had elevated him to the status of a duke, the marquess thought irrelevantly. He was ashamed of his impulsive suggestion. She had made herself quite clear this morning. But he had been planning this visit for five years, dreaming about it, pinning all his hopes for his future happiness on it. He could not give up so easily.

"I promised to help you sort the linen, Aunt Martha," she said hastily, still not addressing herself directly to him.

"Oh, nonsense, dear," her aunt said, sounding as breathless and eager as Lady Katherine had sounded trapped. "That can wait for another time. Do take a walk with his lordship."

Miss Worsley looked as if she were about to suggest sending a maid along as chaperon. He hoped she would not. But she said nothing. Perhaps she had remembered that her niece was no longer a girl.

"It is very kind of you, my lord," was all she said.

"I shall fetch a cloak." Lady Katherine got to her feet abruptly and hurried from the room.

"Dear Kate does not have many chances to walk out," Miss Martha Worsley said.

"And such a lovely young lady," Mrs. Morris added.

And then she was back again, wearing the same cloak she had worn during the morning, bonnetless, as she also had been earlier. And she was still not looking at him.

"I will not be long," she told her aunts. "Good day to you, Mrs. Morris."

She preceded him from the room and from the house.

She would not take his arm, though he offered it, and it must appear strange to her aunts if they were watching from the house that she did not.

"No," she said. He thought she was about to add the words "thank you," but she changed her mind and closed her mouth.

The wind whipped about them, forcing him to hold his hat on. He removed it before they had gone far.

Did the wind always blow so strongly here? he wondered.

"Will you lead the way toward the Llewellyn farm?" he asked. He did not even try to tackle the Welsh "ll" sound.

"If you wish," she said, swinging to her left, away from the sea toward a narrow track heavily bordered with wild ferns and hardly meriting the name of lane.

He could see that it led quite sharply upward, as did the road by which he had traveled the day before. The whole land swept upward toward the plateau of the peninsula. The only flatness was the wide, curved stretch of the beach, surely five miles long.

She walked with a rather long, swinging stride, he noticed. It was graceful, if not quite ladylike. He did not think she had walked thus five years ago. Then she had walked with small steps, as if she had no particular destination in mind.

He realized that she was not going to initiate any conversation with him.

"It is bleak here," he said. "Miles and miles of nothing. And hills to climb in almost any direction one cares to take. And wind. I suppose it is inevitable so close to the sea. It must be an unappealing place to live."

"There you are wrong," she said. "It is the most beautiful place on earth to live."

He looked at her face in profile beside him. She sounded as if she were disagreeing with him, not simply for the sake of being disagreeable but because she meant what she said. Could anyone find this place beautiful? Tŷ Mawr was pleasantly situated, and there was a certain picturesque quality about the village. There was a stark beauty about the whole area, he supposed. But as a place in which to live out one's life?

"But lonely?" he asked.

"No. Not to me."

Her answer was delivered perhaps a little too

swiftly. A lone seagull flew overhead as she spoke, causing her to look up. Its cry was mournful.

"If you are lonely," she said, "you should go back to London. It is almost the time of the Season. You will find all the company you could want there. You will find no one to your liking here."

"No," he said, "not *all* the company I could want. And there is someone to my liking here."

"I will have none of you," she said. "I made myself clear on that point this morning. You are wasting your time here."

She still had not looked at him, he noticed. She was looking straight ahead and she was walking rather fast, her cloak brushing aside the ferns, although the gradient was steep and she was breathless.

"Perhaps," he said. "But it is mine to waste. I intend to stay for a while."

She had no more to say. And he could think of nothing else either. He had never been good at talking from the heart. With a few close friends—all male— it was possible, but never with a woman. Certainly not with her. Taciturnity, the need to be a man and bear every burden on his own shoulders, was so inbred in him that he now found it impossible to speak his mind. He had been given the impression over the years that that very quality made him attractive to many women. Lady Katherine had never been one of them.

But it was too late for him to change. He thought it was too late.

She stopped when the path bent sharply to the left and he could see the buildings of a farm a short distance away. She turned and looked downward, and he did the same.

Yes! he thought instantly as the full force of the wind whipped his breath away for a moment. Oh, yes. Yes, it was incredibly beautiful. The grass- and gorse-covered hills curved about the beach, the church and the cottages of the village huddled against them as if for shelter. The tide was almost full in, the foam of the breakers stretching in a seemingly unbroken line for five miles. The water sparkled in the sunshine. The freshness of the salt air bit into his face.

He could almost understand why she had called it the most beautiful place on earth to live.

"Yes," he said, "it is lovely."

"But not nearly as lovely as Hyde Park or Vauxhall Gardens," she said, sarcasm in her voice. She had not believed him, he realized. She had thought him being merely polite. Perhaps his tone of voice had lacked conviction.

The wind had torn long strands of her hair free of the pins. It lay over her shoulders, and one long strand blew across her face. She reached up with both hands as he watched and pulled all the pins free before shaking her head. He swallowed, watching her long fair hair, wild and tangled and lovely, stream out behind her.

It was something she would never have done five years ago. Five years ago she would not even have ventured out of doors without a bonnet. Her cloak and dress were flattened against her in front.

"Katherine," he said quietly, "give me a chance."

She turned her head sharply and looked at him for the first time—with wide eyes that brightened with tears. Perhaps it was the wind that brought them there. Certainly her face was without expression.

"A chance for what?" she asked. There was incredulity in her voice.

He shrugged. How could he put it into words? "To persuade you that life with me would not be the horror you seem to think it would be," he said. "To give you the chance of a home of your own and marriage and motherhood."

"I want nothing to do with you," she said. "Can you not see that I have a different life now? That all that happened seems like something that must have happened to another person? That I want no reminders of it?"

"But you must have a woman's needs," he said. "And you must want children, surely?"

If it was the wind, it was causing two tears to spill over and trickle down her cheeks.

"No," she said. "I am happy as I am. And even if I did need those things, it would not be from you."

"But it could not be with anyone else," he said. "I had your virginity."

He remembered suddenly how he had hoped and hoped that his seed had taken root in her. How he had waited for weeks for Lambton to summon him back. How he had sent his old lodgekeeper on his first trip into Wales three months after she had been sent there. He remembered the acuteness of his disappointment when they returned to report that she showed no sign of being with child. And he had despised himself for wanting so desperately to have that unfair hold over her.

"You do not need to blame yourself," she said. "It was not rape. I felt a lust to match your own that night. And it was all my fault. All of it. Do you think I enjoy being reminded of all those sordid details? Do you wonder that I shudder at seeing you again?"

Her words tormented him like a thousand devils. He swallowed.

"I hate you because you were a witness to my shame and stupidity," she said, "and because you had been right all the time. I hate you because I hate myself as I was then. I am different now. At least, I like to believe I am different. And yet my hatred of you is as raw as ever. And worse because I know you do not deserve it."

"Let me put it right, then," he said. "Let me marry you."

She turned her eyes on him again. They were brimming with fresh tears. "You do not understand, do you?" she said. "There is nothing in that past life I can admire. There is nothing I wish to recapture. I have no wish to go back to any of it."

"You were very young and inexperienced," he said. "And he was a practiced charmer. You must learn to forgive yourself."

"I have made peace with myself," she said, looking away from him again and gazing down at the scene spread below them. "Here. This place has been my salvation. I want you to go away. Please. If you feel you owe me anything, though you do not, then please go away. I do not want you in my life."

The words could not be plainer. Yet there was a huge sadness in her voice and in her face as she spoke and during the silence that followed her words. And there was a terrible sadness in him, a final loss of the faint hope that had sustained him through five long years.

He reached out with one hand and cupped it beneath her chin. She closed her eyes and stood very still. He touched the pad of his thumb very lightly to her lips. He was memorizing her, the look of her, the feel of the smooth coolness of her skin, the smell of her hair. He wondered how he would live his life with the illusion of hope finally gone.

And then she jerked her head away from him.

"You were always so totally without feeling," she cried, her control gone, her voice shaking with passion. "All was propriety and duty and obligation with you. Always, from the first time I met you. There was no knowing you, and I came to discover that there was nothing to know. You were always as cold as ice and totally lacking in all emotion. Even in your lust. I woke afterward to find you gone from my bed, and the next day you were as controlled and as passionless as ever. The day after that you were offering me propriety, urging propriety on me. And it has lasted five years? Duty has brought you here even after so long? I needed comfort later that night and the morning after, but you would not be able to understand that. I needed the comfort of your arms even if not of words. But you had nothing to offer me, nothing that

I could possibly have wanted. Why would I want your name when there was nothing else? I would rather be dead." She stopped suddenly and drew a shuddering breath. "I would rather be dead," she repeated hoarsely.

She picked up the front of her dress and began to run back down the path, placing her feet and angling her body in such a way that she would not hurtle downward out of control.

He took a few steps after her but then stopped. He watched her go until she was at the bottom of the hill and turning in the direction of her aunts' cottage. He noticed that her steps slowed to a walk before she arrived there.

He stood where he was for several minutes longer, a faint and painful hope coming alive in him again.

Aunt Hetty and Aunt Martha were both in the parlor. Aunt Hetty opened the door when Kate came into the house, still half panting and horribly disheveled. She had no choice but to go into the parlor herself. She smiled at them both.

"The wind," she said, laughing. "There is never any point in spending time on one's hair, is there?"

"Perhaps you should have worn a bonnet, Kate," Aunt Hetty said. "Especially when stepping out with a gentleman."

"He is a wondrously handsome man, Kate dear," Aunt Martha said, "and a marquess. I can scarce believe a marquess would come here. He had eyes for no one but you during tea. I noticed it and Mrs. Morris remarked on it after you had left."

"It was kind of Mrs. Morris to call," Kate said lamely.

Aunt Martha was smiling and nodding. "Perhaps he has leased Tŷ Mawr for a few months, for the spring and the summer. I am sure it would not be surprising if his admiration for you grows into a *tendre*. It would be a splendid thing. Your dear mama, may God rest her soul—"

"It would not do," Aunt Hetty said firmly but not unkindly. "He is a gentleman of *ton,* Martha. We must remember that Kate's reputation has been ruined with the *ton.*" Aunt Hetty was not one to mince words.

"But it was a very long time ago," Aunt Martha said, smiling reassuringly at her niece. "And I am sure it could not have been so very dreadful. Your papa did not give any details, Kate, my love. But knowing you—"

"If the Marquess of Ashendon does become particular in his attentions," Aunt Hetty said, "you have a choice of two courses, Kate. You can discourage him, or you can tell him the full truth. You must not try to hide it from him."

"But—" Aunt Martha began.

"No," Aunt Hetty said, holding up a staying hand. "It is the only course, Kate. You must see that. There is only heartbreak and humiliation for you in trying to hide the truth, only to have it come out later. It will come out, whatever it is. The *ton* does not forget. Your mama always used to tell us that. They never forgot that your papa married beneath him. They had a way of looking at her, she told us, a way of holding their heads, a way of smiling."

Kate had not known that of her mother.

"Perhaps," she said, "it is time you knew something of what happened."

"We would never pry, Kate," Aunt Hetty said.

"We love you as you are, dear," Aunt Martha said. "It really does not matter to us what you did to cause your papa to send you to us. For our own sakes we are glad he did."

Kate was not usually a watering pot. But for the second time that afternoon she felt tears well into her eyes. "And I bless the day he punished me by sending me to you," she said. "I have a previous acquaintance with the Marquess of Ashendon."

They both looked at her in some surprise.

"I was unwise enough to encourage a half-pay officer whose ambition was to marry a fortune," she said. "I was young and very silly and even more headstrong, and when Papa and Ernest and Algie forbade me to have anything to do with him and when the Marquess of Ashendon warned me against him, I flirted with him all the more. I was exhilarated by a feeling of power over him. Then I . . . I eloped with him." She did not feel inclined to give them anything but the official version of what had happened. The truth was just too shameful. "We were two days on the way to Scotland by the time the Marquess of Ashendon caught up to us. He paid off my faithful officer and then took me back to London. We were two days and two nights together and of course we were seen. He offered for me the day after we returned. I would not have him."

"Oh, my dear." Aunt Martha broke the silence that followed, her hands clasped to her bosom in a characteristic gesture. "Why? He is so very handsome. And he must have loved you dearly."

"No," Kate said. "He has no feelings at all. He merely did what was right, for which I should honor him, I know. I can only hate him."

"Hatred, Kate," Aunt Hetty said, "is a sin."

"But what a strange coincidence," Aunt Martha said, "that he has rented Tŷ Mawr, Kate dear, when you live so close."

"Oh, Aunt Martha," Kate said, "it is no coincidence. He has come here deliberately. He is such a very honorable and dutiful man that he still feels he has an obligation to me. He has come again to persuade me to marry him. I met him this morning in the woods when I was trespassing. And this afternoon he tricked me into walking with him."

"It sounds to me as if he has been constant in his regard for you, Kate," Aunt Hetty said. "It sounds to me as if he is not deserving of your hatred."

"Oh, Kate," Aunt Martha said, "this is more romantic than any book. For five years he has carried a torch for you, and now he has come like a knight in shining armor to sweep you off your feet. Our dear Kate a marchioness. And he is so splendidly handsome. I always did have a soft spot for tall men with dark hair. And blue eyes."

"He has no feelings," Kate said again, "and there is no romance. I told him a short while ago that I would rather be dead than married to him. I will not see him again. If he comes to the house, you must both tell him that I am out or ill or—or anything you like. I have begged him to go away, but I am not certain he will go."

"If he stays after your telling him that, Kate," Aunt Hetty said, "I will be even more confirmed in my opinion of the constancy of his feelings."

"Oh, Kate, dear," Aunt Martha said, "they are such lovely blue eyes. There is not even a suggestion of gray in them as there is so often in eyes that are called blue. They are as blue as the sky on a summer's day."

Aunt Hetty leaned across from her chair and patted Kate's hand. "You look rather as if you had been dragged through a hedge backward, Kate," she said. "You had better go upstairs and comb your hair. And you had better ask yourself if a man without feelings pursues a young lady who behaved so foolishly even five years after her refusal of his offer and across the full width of the country."

"Oh, Kate," Aunt Martha said, "I do believe he must love you. But do go and comb your hair, dear. It looks as if the birds have taken to nesting in it."

Kate fled upstairs to comb her hair.

It soon became known for miles around that Tŷ Mawr had a tenant at last and that he was none other than an English marquess—a young and handsome and single gentleman. But if interest fluttered in a few female bosoms, it quickly died again. It became com-

mon knowledge almost immediately that he had an
eye for Miss Kate Buchanan, niece of the Misses
Worsley of Rhos. It was hardly surprising. She was
young and lovely and she was after all a lady, was she
not? Lady Katherine Buchanan. Her father was an
English earl.

The church at Rhos was fuller than usual for morning service the Sunday after the marquess's arrival.
The rector was gratified. He had rather thought his
sermon the week before had been superior. Word of
it must have spread. And this morning's sermon was
even better.

The Marquess of Ashendon nodded courteously at
the end of the service to the few acquaintances he had
made and shook hands with the rector at the door
and commended him on his sermon. Then he bowed
to the Misses Worsley and their niece as they left the
church and asked if he might walk Miss Buchanan
home.

The congregation, spilling out of the church and
gathering in small groups outside for the obligatory
half hour of gossip before returning home for their
Sunday dinners, nodded significantly at one another.
Some of them smiled indulgently at the couple walking away from them, side by side, though she had not
taken his arm.

Obviously a courtship was in the making. They
made a handsome couple, Mr. Llewellyn remarked to
Miss Martha Worsley.

She knew now that he was not going to go away.
She had made herself clear enough to him. She had
even insulted him and spoken deliberately to hurt him.
But he had not gone away. And just like the last time,
he had trapped her into walking with him by asking
her in the company of others, when it would have
seemed ill-mannered to have refused.

Why was he still pursuing her?

Aunt Martha thought he loved her. Even the less

romantic Aunt Hetty thought that his coming now after five years was evidence of the constancy of his feelings. And yet she herself had accused him of having no feelings. She had always believed he had none.

And yet he had come after her and Lieutenant Hastings. And he had come all the way here. And had stayed here.

It took them only a few minutes to walk the short distance to her aunts' cottage. They said nothing during those minutes.

"Thank you," she said. "I am sorry to have brought you out of your way." She turned to go inside the house, relieved to be leaving him.

"Don't go in yet," he said.

She looked at him in surprise. He had said nothing all the way from the church.

"I am going to invite your aunts and a few other people to dinner tomorrow evening," he said. "You will come too?"

"No," she said.

"Then I will settle them to something after dinner," he said, leaning slightly toward her, "cards perhaps, if they all play, and come to fetch you."

Her eyes widened in amazement. "But why?" she asked him. "Why are you doing this?"

"Because I am not convinced," he said, "that you will not have me."

"How many ways are there of saying no?" she asked him. "Have I missed any?"

"When I mentioned your womanly needs," he said, "and your need for children, there were tears in your eyes."

"It was the wind," she lied, mortified. She had hoped he had not noticed those tears.

"I can satisfy your needs," he said. "You were very well satisfied that once."

"Oh, how dare you." She closed her eyes.

"I can give you children," he said.

She opened her eyes again and looked at him. And

she remembered something she had long forgotten
and had denied to herself even at the time. She remembered that along with the knee-weakening relief
at finding she was not with child by him five years ago
there had been the bizarre, incomprehensible stabbing
of disappointment.

"What would you have done," he asked, almost as
if he could read her mind, "if you had been with
child? Would you have come back to me?"

"No," she said. No, she would not have gone back.
She had made a firm decision on that. But who knew?
If there was to have been a child of her body and the
choice had been between making it a bastard or giving
it his name, perhaps she would have chosen the latter course.

"Has there been anyone?" he asked her. "Any man
who has shown interest in you? Any man you have
been interested in?"

"That is no concern of yours," she said.

"It is." His eyes looked directly back into hers.
Aunt Martha was right, she thought irrelevantly. His
eyes were purely blue. "You would not be able to
marry him, Katherine, without offering a difficult explanation first and perhaps being rejected as a result.
And I would be the one responsible for that."

"You make too much of it," she said. "I have no
wish to marry."

"You say I have no feelings," he said. "The same
cannot be said of you. You have eyes that are more
expressive than you would wish them to be with me,
I do not doubt. Your voice tells me that you are happy
as you are. But in your eyes there is a great sadness."

"Because you have come here and disturbed my
peace," she said. "Because you have brought back
memories that I would prefer never to remember."

"I do not trust what your voice tells me," he said.
"I trust your eyes. Ah, you lower them too late. Until
your eyes can assure me that you want neither me nor
the things that only I can offer you, I will be living at

Tŷ Mawr, Katherine, and meeting you and speaking with you as often as possible. And you cannot go away from here, can you? You are in perpetual exile here—unless you allow me to take you away as my bride."

She kept her eyes lowered. And she suddenly wondered why she did not simply accept him, why she had not accepted him five years ago when her mind had been pulsing with terror at the prospect of being whipped as the first punishment for refusing him. But she knew why she had not accepted him. She had known at the time and she knew now, though she had not rationalized it in her mind for a long time.

"Your aunts are approaching," he said. "You will come to dinner tomorrow evening."

It was not a question. She did not answer.

And then she could feel nothing but shock as he took her right hand in both of his and raised it to his lips, drawing back her leather glove so that his lips touched the bare skin on the back of her hand. It felt as if her stomach performed a complete somersault, though she knew from a single experience of the past that it was not really her stomach that was responding to his touch but her womb.

Her aunts had come up to them, Aunt Martha looking like the proverbial cat that had swallowed the proverbial canary, and even Aunt Hetty looking remarkably pleased with herself. And the marquess was making himself agreeable to them and issuing the invitation to dinner. Her aunts accepted it with alacrity, of course.

And then he was gone. Her aunts contained themselves only until they were all inside the house before expressing their gratification—at the invitation and at the satisfactory progress of the courtship.

"Well, Kate," Aunt Hetty said, "you told him you would rather be dead than married to him, and yet he walked you home this morning and stood talking with you. What do you say now about the constancy of his feelings?"

"And he kissed your hand, dear," Aunt Martha added. "There is no more romantic gesture, I have always thought, than a gentleman's kissing a lady's hand."

Kate could still feel the imprint of his lips against the back of her hand and the desire for him throbbing deep in her womb. She could find no answer for either of them. She fled upstairs instead. She seemed to be doing rather too much fleeing upstairs lately.

He had invited the Reverend and Mrs. Morris to dinner, along with the Llewellyns and the Pritchards, with their grown-up son, and Mr. Jenkins, who had recently retired from his position as choirmaster at one of the Welsh cathedrals—one with an unpronounceable name. And the Misses Worsley were invited too, of course. There would be even numbers, with Katherine. She would come. He did not doubt that she had believed him when he had threatened to go and fetch her if she did not come.

She was wearing a rose-pink gown that he remembered. She would be mortified if she realized that, he thought. It was woefully out of fashion now, but it looked new. He guessed that she had not worn it above once or twice in five years. Or perhaps not at all, before tonight. Her hair had been dressed higher than usual and two strands had been curled and allowed to fall loose over her temples, almost to her shoulders.

It seemed that everyone looked at her appreciatively, including Mr. Dafydd Pritchard, who must be a year or two her junior. The Marquess of Ashendon found himself wanting to punch the unoffending young man in the mouth.

After dinner he organized two tables of cards in the drawing room. Fortunately Miss Martha Worsley and Mr. Jenkins were deep in conversation about the relative merits of trained choirboys and spontaneous congregational singing, and Katherine sat quietly listening. The marquess was not forced to make up a third table.

"I noticed a harpsichord in your aunts' parlor, Miss Buchanan," he said, coming to stand beside her chair and touching his fingertips lightly to her shoulder, careful to keep them on the silk of her dress and not on the bare flesh close to it. "Do you play?"

He knew that she played. She had been an accomplished pianist and she had had a sweet singing voice. He had been careful now to ask in her aunt's hearing so that she would not be able to deny her skill.

"A little," she said, her eyes straying to the pianoforte.

"Rather more than a little, my lord," Miss Martha Worsley said, breaking off her conversation with Mr. Jenkins for a moment. "Kate is very modest."

"Then you will play for us?" He tightened his hand a little on her shoulder.

She rose to her feet without another word and crossed to the instrument. She stood looking down at it for a while and rubbed her forefinger over one key.

"It is a long time since I played a pianoforte," she said, her voice wistful.

He took a pile of music out of the bench and allowed her to make her choice. Then he stood behind her, listening to her play and watching a strand of hair that had pulled loose from her chignon curl invitingly on her neck. He wanted to lift it with one finger and set his mouth on the place where it now lay.

She had not lost her touch or her absorption in her playing. She seemed to forget about him for half an hour and even seemed unaware when he moved closer to turn the pages.

"Sing for me," he said quietly when she had finished.

"I know nothing," she said just as quietly, her eyes on the keyboard.

"Sing for me," he said again. "Please?"

He did not expect that she would, and he would

not raise his voice so that someone else would urge her to grant his request.

She sang something he had never heard before. In a language he had never heard before. Something sweet and haunting and sad—like her eyes.

"Ah," Mr. Jenkins said when she had finished. He had got to his feet and strolled across the room toward them. "There is nothing more designed to reduce one to tears than a Welsh folk song. Your pronunciation is improving, Miss Buchanan."

"Thanks to your tuition, sir," she said, smiling.

Obviously the recital was at an end. Mr. Jenkins strolled across to one of the tables to watch the game in progress, and Katherine got to her feet and folded the music on the stand. He would have to think of something else.

"The owner of Tŷ Mawr has some interesting collections," he said. "Hundreds of seashells, each one apparently different from every other. And spoons. Ornamental wooden spoons."

"Welsh love spoons," Miss Martha Worsley said. "I had heard of the collection, my lord, but I have never seen it."

He had not been looking for a chaperon, but perhaps it was as well.

"Then perhaps you and Miss Buchanan would care to step into the library to see them, ma'am," he said.

This time she could not avoid taking his arm. He offered one to each lady, and her aunt took one without hesitation. Katherine's arm was light on his. And trembling quite noticeably. And it burned into him like a branding iron.

Lord, how he had dreamed of her touch, both waking and sleeping, for five years. He had allowed her to become an obsession with him. His life would have been more comfortable if he could have forgotten her.

They looked dutifully at the shells, Miss Martha Worsley exclaiming at their beauty.

"I have never been fond of the seaside," he said.

"I always thought a seashell was a seashell. I thought they were like peas in a pod, I suppose. These are exquisite and all quite unique."

"Yes," the aunt said. "I have picked up many in my years here, my lord. I have a workbox inlaid with them, and I never tire of looking at them. I do not know how anyone looking at seashells could doubt the existence of God."

It was a statement that ought to have been funny but was not.

"And the spoons," he said, turning to them. "They are all skillfully carved and all, like the shells, unique. You called them Welsh love spoons, ma'am?"

"Oh, yes," she said. "They are quite a tradition in Wales. Hetty and I went to see an exhibition of them in Swansea a few years ago—it was just before you came to us, Kate, dear. I believe the tradition started with young men carving plain spoons to hang about their young ladies' necks. And then gradually the spoons grew in size and were decorated in various ways. Each type of design symbolizes something, but I cannot remember what. An expert would be able to tell you the message each of these love spoons conveys, my lord."

But she did not spend long looking at them. She shuddered rather elaborately after a few minutes.

"I left my shawl in the drawing room," she said, "and it is rather chilly in here. If you will forgive me, my lord, I will go back to join the others. But do not let me rush you."

She smiled and almost hurried from the room in order to make her point. Miss Martha Worsley, he thought, was a matchmaker and was trying to secure the happiness of her niece.

"I will return too," Katherine said, her first words since they had left the drawing room. "It is chilly in here."

"No," he said. "Let us not disappoint your aunt by hurrying back to the drawing room on her heels."

She bit her lip.

"I wanted the chance to tell you how beautiful you look this evening," he said.

She looked unhappily into his eyes.

"You were always very pretty," he said, "when you were all frills and flounces and ringlets. You had the prettiness of a young girl. Now you have the beauty of a woman."

"You do not need to say all this," she said.

"I do," he said. "I would be sorry later tonight when all my guests had left if I had not spoken the words to you."

He lifted one hand and set the backs of his fingers lightly against her cheek. She did not jerk back as he expected her to do. He watched her swallow.

"Let me kiss you," he said softly.

"No." Her eyes slipped to his neckcloth.

He withdrew his hand with the greatest reluctance.

"Marry me," he said.

"No." She looked into his eyes again. "When will you stop asking?"

"When you say yes," he said, "or when your eyes tell me that you want me to go out of your life forever."

"Oh, my eyes, my eyes," she said, annoyed now. "You see in them what you wish to see."

"No," he said. "I see what is there, Katherine."

He hoped he was not deluding himself. He did not believe he was.

"I want to go back to the drawing room," she said.

"Yes," he said. "Any longer alone together would be improper. Come, then."

She had not pulled away from his touch, though she had refused to allow him to kiss her. She had refused his marriage offer, but there was sadness in her eyes.

Almost a look of yearning.

Was he deluding himself? he wondered again. He did not believe so.

*   *   *

For two whole days she dared not venture outside. Perhaps it was as well that the weather was chilly and damp, with occasional squalls of drizzling rain. But even indoors she did not feel safe. She found herself glancing through the windows far more often than she wished, watching for his arrival so that she might escape upstairs in time to avoid him.

Though she was not sure that would be possible. Her aunts were in a flutter, even Aunt Hetty.

"He is showing a remarkable preference for you, Kate," she said.

"He has little choice," Kate said. "This part of the country is not abounding in women of my age."

"But he obviously made his choice before coming here," Aunt Hetty said. "He made it five years ago and has been constant to it ever since. Fidelity in a man is a quality to covet."

"But he did not choose me five years ago," Kate said, wondering why she was allowing herself to be drawn into an argument. "I was forced upon him. He offered out of a sense of honor."

"I do not believe you were forced upon him, dear," Aunt Martha said. "He went after you, did he not? Why would he have done that if he did not love you?"

Kate had no answer beyond the obvious one, that the Marquess of Ashendon was incapable of love.

"And now he has come after you again," Aunt Martha said with a sigh.

"I believe it altogether possible that he will make you a formal offer very soon, Kate," Aunt Hetty said. "You would do well to think seriously about accepting it. This is no life for you. Sometimes I feel your loneliness."

That was unfair. She had never complained, even at the start. She had always tried to be cheerful, until she had no longer had to make the effort. Cheerfulness had become a part of her.

"I refused him in his library the other evening after Aunt Martha left us alone," she said.

"Oh, Kate, dear," Aunt Martha said in mild reproach.

"I hate him," Kate said, realizing that she must sound like a petulant girl.

"But why?" Aunt Hetty set down her knitting in her lap.

How could she explain to them why she hated him? And it had become a strange sort of hatred, all mixed up with attraction. When he had asked if he might kiss her, she had had that feeling in her womb again and a weakness in her legs. She had wanted him to kiss her. She had wanted to feel his mouth on hers. She had wanted to know if he would kiss her open-mouthed again, as he had on the only other occasion when he had kissed her. And she had wanted to feel his body against her own, masculinity against femininity. It had been an erotic and explosive mix that once.

She had been surprised when he had released her as soon as she said no. She had expected him to kiss her anyway. Ever since then, she had tried to suppress the suspicion that she had been disappointed not to be forced. She did not like to think that perhaps no with her did not always mean no. She would have blamed him afterward if he had kissed her and explained righteously that she had said no and she had meant no. All the blame would have been on him. She would have believed that implicitly.

And she hated him yet again for holding up a mirror before her face and forcing her to see herself in a less than flattering light.

"How can you hate him, Kate dear?" Aunt Martha asked when the silence had stretched. "He is such a very amiable man and handsome enough to make me almost wish for youth again."

"I do not want to marry him," Kate said. "I made that clear five years ago and I have made it clear now. But he is persistent. I do not believe he will take no for an answer."

And yet he had a few evenings ago. She had said

no and he had not kissed her. He would not force her to kiss him and he could not force her to marry him. But he would keep asking. She knew he would. But why? She could not understand his persistence.

"Because he loves you, Kate dear," Aunt Martha said with a sigh.

Aunt Hetty picked up her knitting again and said nothing to contradict her more romantically minded sister.

Kate had not gone out for two days. Neither had he come. Perhaps he had gone back to London, she thought, and felt—what? Hope? Disappointment?

What would she feel if she discovered that he had left? She examined the question quite thoroughly in her mind and forced herself to answer it. She realized it was something she was not in the habit of doing. She had stopped being open and honest with herself long ago. Five years ago. Perhaps longer.

How would she feel? If he had gone away, it would be because he had accepted her refusal. He would never come back. She would live out her life here, perhaps single, perhaps married in time to someone whom she could like and respect. But she would never see him again, or even hear of him. Her father never wrote to her. Her brothers wrote very rarely, and when they did they never wrote of people she knew.

She would never know whether he lived or was dead. She would never know when he married or whom he married. She would never know how many children he had.

How would she feel never to see or hear of him again?

She would feel nothing, she told herself, because she would suppress all memory of him and all feeling for him as she had before. She would be happy again as she had been for almost five years. The cost of the happiness she had achieved was a certain deadness within.

But she was not sure she could die that death again.

It was another reason for hating him. She had not realized how very fragile was the peace she had achieved until he had arrived to shatter it, perhaps forever.

After two days, she could stay inside no longer. She always spent hours of every day out of doors. Only a very heavy fall of rain could keep her housebound. But after the two dreary days the sun shone, and even the usual wind dropped to no more than a delightful breeze.

Kate pinned up her hair securely, donned her cloak, and went outside. She was very tempted to slip over the stile into the woods to see what progress the daffodils had made in the week since she had last seen them. But she dared not. She did not want to encounter him at all. To do so when she was again trespassing would be just too mortifying.

She avoided the roads and lanes too. She had not heard of his leaving. She did not want to meet him by accident if he was out walking or riding after two days of inclement weather.

She would go down onto the beach, she decided. He would hardly go there. A gentleman of such immaculate elegance would not wish to damage his Hessians with sand or risk spotting his clothes with salt spray. And the beach was what she needed today. She needed to be away from the land, close to the sea, close to the source of her peace for the past five years.

Fortunately the sea was at almost full ebb. She walked for almost a mile over the dunes and across the soft sand beyond them, and then across the hard, flat sand that was covered by water at high tide. She walked almost to the edge of the water and felt cut off from the world. All that was left was empty beach, stretching for miles to either side of her, and the sea, vast and perpetually in motion and roaring in such an elemental manner that she was unaware of sound.

She strolled parallel to the sea, just beyond the wet

sand, keeping her thoughts blank, opening herself to the healing power of nature.

It appeared to be working until peace deserted her again, abruptly and far too soon. The dog had not barked this time to warn her of its approach. She became aware of it only when it came within the line of her peripheral vision, streaking eagerly toward her. And then it came right up to her and pranced eagerly in front of her and jumped up with its sandy paws to stain her cloak.

"Oh," she said, "you startled me. But I would far prefer that you not bowl me over." She rubbed her hand hard over the collie's tossing head and laughed at its lolling tongue and eagerly cocked ears.

And then she looked beyond the dog. Any hope she might have had that it had escaped and come for a lone run on the beach was dashed. He was still some distance away, but he was coming toward her—or toward his dog. She did consider pushing the dog aside and striding on, hoping that he would take the hint that she did not want to speak with him. Dogs were not so easily shrugged off, she knew, and she did not believe the master was either.

She stood still, and the collie sat at her feet, panting, like a friendly guard.

He had wandered into the woods, hoping that perhaps she would be there again after a few days of unpleasant weather. But he was not surprised to find the woods empty. He could remember telling her that she was trespassing. It was hardly likely that she would come back while he was in residence.

He considered walking on and crossing the stile, over which she must have made her entrance to the woods, and calling at her aunts' cottage. But it was morning. The afternoon would be the more courteous time to call.

Could she be persuaded to walk out with him again? he wondered. If he asked in the presence of her aunts?

They were on his side, he knew, especially the younger one, who had deliberately left them in the library alone together on Monday evening.

But was there any point in walking out with her yet again? To try to persuade her once more that life with him was preferable to the life she could expect here? To ask her again to marry him? She would say no again and would keep on saying no as many times as he asked.

What he should do was go back to the house, have his things packed, and set out on his return journey to London. There was no point in staying longer. He was wasting his time, deluding himself with false hope. He was harassing her and behaving dishonorably toward her.

And yet there were her eyes. They told him every time they looked into his that she was unhappy. She was unhappy to see him, she told him. She had been happy before he came. She would be happy again after he left. He did not believe it. He could not believe it. Because it was a look of something more than just unhappiness. He could only describe it to himself as a look of yearning.

She looked at him with unhappiness and yearning. Yearning for what? For him to go away and leave her in peace? But that would be a look of anger, not of yearning.

No, he could not give up. Not yet. He would stay for a week longer, anyway. Perhaps two.

He left the woods and wandered down the sloping lawn to the wrought-iron gates that led to nothing except the sand dunes beyond. He had never been through the gates. The dunes and the beach and the sea did not invite him. He had always been inexplicably afraid of the sea, even though he was a strong swimmer and enjoyed boating on rivers. There was something too vast, too far beyond human understanding about the sea.

But this morning he opened the gates and followed

his eager collie through them and up onto the grass-strewn dunes to gaze out over the beach. It was vast this morning. The tide was out. He shuddered at the same time as he felt an unwilling pull to the power and majesty of it all. Wales, he decided, or the little he had seen of it, was a wild and empty land, and yet there was something about it—something that tugged at the emotions. He was reminded for no apparent reason of the Welsh folk song Katherine had sung in his drawing room.

The Welsh were an emotional and a passionate people, he had heard. Perhaps those feelings had come from the country itself, from the rugged landscape and from the sea, which seemed to dominate everything. The country was surrounded by it on three sides.

Patch had run back and forth across the sand dunes for a while and then ran down onto the beach and turned to look up at him with an eager, intelligent face and cocked ears and wagging tail.

"Well," he said, "just for a short while, I suppose. I dread to think of the massacre I am about to commit against my boots, but I will have you to blame." He chuckled.

But before he could reach the bottom of the dune, the collie had turned, become even more alert, and gone streaking off toward the distant line of water. He set his fingers to his mouth to whistle her back, and then spotted the distant dot of a human figure.

It was impossible to know with his eyes that it was she. But he knew it with his heart. He felt no doubt at all. He stood still for a moment longer. He was not sure he could face another meeting with her just yet—and in such bleak surroundings. And she must have come here herself to be sure of being quite alone. He would, of course, be the person she most wanted to avoid.

But he must see her again. He must speak with her again. He must try to find the words with which to persuade her. Perhaps if he failed now he would cut short his visit after all. Perhaps he would set out for London tomorrow morning. Or perhaps even this afternoon.

He finished his descent and strode across the beach in pursuit of his dog, and in pursuit of his own dream.

She did not say anything when he drew close and stopped, a few feet away from her. She looked at him, but she would not break the silence. He was not wearing a hat this morning, she noticed. He had learned some wisdom at least during his week in this part of the world.

He said nothing either for a while. Perhaps they would stand and stare at each other all morning, she thought.

"Shall we walk?" he asked eventually, gesturing along the beach in the direction she had been taking. His collie bounded to its feet, alerted by the word *walk,* and made off ahead of them.

She fell into step beside him. There was no point in arguing this point, at least. They walked for a while in silence. His Hessians were flecked with sand, she noted with some satisfaction.

"Tell me why you hate me," he said eventually.

She looked away, toward the sea.

"Is it because of Hastings?" he asked. "Do you blame me for spoiling your life? Did you know that he finally married an heiress four years ago, squandered all she had, and then abandoned her to run off to Italy with someone else?"

"No," she said without looking at him, "I did not know."

"But you still blame me?" he said. "You think it might have turned out differently if you had married him?"

"No," she said, "I am sure it would not have."

"But you hate me anyway," he said, "for stopping your flight, for exposing his avarice to you and causing him to leave you?"

"I have not thought of Lieutenant Hastings since coming here," she said. "I have no interest in thinking of him now."

"Why, then?" he asked her. "Why do you hate me so implacably? Is it because I so lost control that one night? I should have begged your pardon immediately afterward, or at the very latest the next morning. But somehow it seemed woefully inadequate to say I was sorry. And so I said nothing."

"Were you?" she said. "Sorry, I mean?"

"More sorry than I can say," he said. "Although I did not realize at the time that you would have the folly to refuse me when we had returned to London, it was still unpardonable of me to do what I did. What happened between us should have happened for the first time in our marriage bed."

She turned her head more sharply away from him and watched one weak breaker gradually whiten into foam as it fought the ebb tide. The tide must be just about on the turn.

"A few days ago," he said quietly, "you said that you had needed to be held."

"I lost my temper," she said. "It would have been better if I had said nothing."

"Why did you not ask me?" he said. "To hold you. You must have known that I would have. You must have known that I came after you to be of service to you."

She looked back at him suddenly, feeling the unwise anger building again. "Is that what you were doing when you lay with me?" she said. "Servicing me? Consoling me for the loss of Lieutenant Hastings? You would have serviced me further by holding me, had I asked? I am very glad I did not."

She saw the answering flash of anger in his eyes. "You must have a strangely inaccurate memory of that night if you can believe that," he said. "You insult me with your sarcasm."

"You need not listen to my insults," she cried. "You

can go back to your own life any time you wish—with my blessing and with a clear conscience. I do not want you here. I do not want you in my life. I hate you. You can ask me a thousand times to marry you and I will say no a thousand times. You are wasting your time here."

"I can see that I am," he said.

She had never seen him angry before, though he was in perfect, icy control of himself. They had stopped walking and were standing face-to-face, glaring at each other. His dog, which had run on ahead, was loping back toward them.

"I will take my leave of you," he said, bowing stiffly to her. "You may rest easy. I will be gone within the next couple of hours."

But he hesitated as he was about to turn away and reached into his pocket to jerk something out. He held it out to her, his fingers closed over it, but before she could either take it from him or refuse it, he stepped forward and slipped something hurriedly over her head.

Then he turned and strode away from her. The collie raced ahead up the beach.

She watched him go. She had won. There would be no more such encounters. She could regain her equilibrium and her peace of mind.

I will be gone within the next couple of hours.

Gone forever. She was looking at him for the last time. For the last time ever. She would never see him again. She would never hear his voice again.

Her eyes strayed downward. Hanging from the thin black ribbon he had thrown over her head was a small, inexpertly carved wooden spoon. Her hand closed tightly about it.

"No!" she shrieked, furious with him. "You cannot do this to me."

He stopped abruptly and turned toward her. She would have thought he was out of earshot. She stared mutely at him, and after a few moments he took a few steps back toward her.

"Cannot do what?" he asked. His voice carried to her, though apparently he had not raised it.

"You cannot do this to me," she called again. She did not know herself what she meant. She was caught in a terrible panic.

He strode toward her and came to stand in front of her once more. His eyes looked directly into hers. "Do what?" he asked again.

She launched herself at him suddenly, the sides of her fists pounding harmlessly against the capes of his greatcoat. "I hate you!" she cried. "I hate you, I hate you."

"Katherine." His hand was hard against the back of her head and her face was being pressed against the capes she was still pummeling. "Katherine."

"I hate you." Her voice was muffled and she was crying noisily against him, all dignity gone.

"I know." His arms were about her like iron bands. His cheek was against the top of her head. "I know."

"I hate you," she said one last time, without any conviction at all.

He would have cried with her if he had known how to cry. But he could not remember a time, even back to his infancy, when it had not been instilled in him by his parents, his nurses, his tutors, his schoolmasters that it was unmanly to cry, to show any strong emotion, to reveal any weakness whatsoever.

But he would have cried now if he could have. He had been striding away out of her life, away from the hope and the dream that had sustained him through five lonely years. He had been walking into a frightening emptiness. And then her call had stopped him, an outpouring of hatred. Except that it had not sounded like hatred, and her sobs did not sound like hatred. And he was holding her in his arms for the first time since that night, and he was still here with her.

With renewed hope, like a sharp pain in his heart. Hope despite her words.

"Why?" He whispered the word against her ear when she had finally stopped crying and had relaxed her weight against him. "What have I done to you, Katherine?" And then finally the inspiration came. "What have I *not* done?"

But the weeping and the weakness were at an end. She pushed herself away from him without looking up at him, fumbled in a pocket for a handkerchief, wiped her eyes and her cheeks with it, turned away from him and blew her nose, and then took a few steps away.

"You will want as much daylight as possible for your journey," she said. "You must be on your way. I shall walk here for a while longer. Good-bye."

"I have always found talking—talking from inside myself, from my heart—more difficult to do than anything else in this life," he said. "I was taught that I must keep all emotions and all that is personal locked away from anyone else's eyes, that it is unmanly to wear one's heart on one's sleeve, so to speak. I was a good pupil. Perhaps that was because my father died when I was fifteen and I became head of a large family, with responsibilities for huge properties and innumerable dependents. I was taught to be strong. But I have realized lately that there was a flaw in my education."

He paused, but she said nothing. She stood facing away from him, her head bowed.

"I will go away," he said, "if you still wish it after we have finished what has been started here this morning. But I know that I will forever blame myself if I do not talk to you first, if I do not do what I was taught never to do and what I find almost impossible to do."

"I have forgotten how to talk," she said quietly. "I knew how once. I talked too much. I revealed too much of myself. But everything of importance about myself was pushed deep inside, even beyond my awareness, so long ago that I am not sure I can ever talk again."

"I wanted you from the moment I first saw you," he said. "You were like the sunshine. You were everything I was not. I followed all the rules. I courted you as a man is supposed to court a woman. I expected that after a suitable time I would offer for you and be accepted and live happily ever after with you. Until Hastings came along with his charm and his seductive wiles and I saw all the sunshine and all the smiles and all the encouragement that I had expected for myself going to him instead. I suppose I was conceited. Or perhaps just woefully ignorant. I had never courted any woman before."

Her head dipped lower.

"And then you ran away with him," he said, "despite the fact that I had been presumptuous enough to warn you against him and despite the fact that I knew your father and brothers to be wise to his game. You went away with him."

"I did not." Her hands had come up to cover her face. She spoke very low. "No, I did not."

He waited for her to continue.

"I was very foolish," she said. "I encouraged him despite Papa and Ernest and Algie—and despite your warning. I encouraged him because you were cold and silent and I wanted to make you jealous, to goad you into doing or saying something, though I did not think it was possible. You seemed a man totally without feelings. But I had played with fire. He was angry when I refused to elope with him and when I started shunning his company. I became a little frightened of him, I believe. And then there was that evening at Vauxhall." She paused for a moment. "A lady, a woman, came and whispered to me when everyone else in the box was distracted by something else. She told me that you were waiting beyond the dancing floor and wished to solicit my hand for a dance. I was so foolishly naive. It was something you never would have done. But I so wanted it to be you that I did not hesitate. I went."

His eyes had widened. He stood rooted to the spot. Patch was chasing her tail somewhere to his right, he noted irrelevantly without turning his head.

"It was Lieutenant Hastings, of course," she said. "He tried to pretend for two whole days that it was not abduction, but it was. I told him I would not marry him even when we reached Scotland, and I told him I would screech the roof down if he touched me on either of the two nights I spent in company with him. But he would not take me back. And then you came."

He found that he had been holding his breath.

"But why did you not tell me?" he asked, breaking a long silence. "When I came up to you, why did you let me think the worst of you? My God, I would have killed him."

"How could I tell you?" Her voice was higher-pitched than usual. "How could I admit to you that I had gone running to you when I thought you had merely sent a messenger for me in a most improper manner? You had never expressed any real interest in me. You were always very correct and very proper and very cold."

"Katherine . . ." he began. He thought he might cry after all. "You should have told me. But why did you refuse me when we arrived back in London? Why? It makes no sense to me."

"I was so happy when you came for me," she said. "I thought that it must mean you cared. I thought you would say so. And then there were the first day and the first night. I had thought you cold before. Now you were pure ice. And then the second night. In my naivete I thought it was love. I was not really aware that that could be done without love. I thought that finally the nightmare was all over, that finally . . . But the next day you were colder and more silent than ever. You cared not one jot for me when I had made a fool of myself for you. The whipping Papa had promised me and this—" she gestured about her "—were preferable to marrying you when you felt nothing for me except perhaps contempt."

"Katherine." He had taken a step toward her. He was whispering. "It *was* love. What happened that night was love. But I was so ashamed ... And I was so uncomfortable and so unhappy with the knowledge that you had preferred him but that you were going to be forced to marry me. If I had only known. Oh, God, if I had only known."

Her hands were still over her face. He set his hands on her shoulders, passing one of them in front of her, and turned her. But she did not take her hands away or lift her head.

"It is what happens when one person sends no messages at all and the other sends all the wrong messages," he said. "No communication takes place."

She said nothing.

"I decided to wait three years," he said. "I thought that perhaps in that time your love for him would have cooled and it would seem the reasonable thing to do to marry me. I was not going to try to force your feelings. I thought that perhaps you would grow to care for me if I treated you kindly. Circumstances kept me away the year before last and last year. This year I came."

She nodded.

"I have loved you every moment of every day for five years," he said. "I have lived for this visit. I have lived on hope. I do not know what I will do if that hope is finally killed. I will not know how to live without it."

"You were so cold," she said. "Always so very cold. I never understood why I loved you."

He clasped her wrists and drew her hands away from her face. She lifted it to look into his, and now that look in her eyes was naked and unmistakable yearning.

"Not always," he said. "You must remember that

night, Katherine. You cannot have forgotten. That was the real me. I had burst past the barriers of my training. And this is the real me. I have never talked like this. It is incredibly difficult. Perhaps that is why I spent all of yesterday carving spoons, until I finally produced that sorry specimen. It still seemed easier to do than talking." He laughed suddenly, more with nervousness than happiness.

"Oh," she said, her eyes widening, "I have never seen you smile before."

But he could not hold the smile. "I must ask it once again," he said. "The last time I will ask, Katherine, I promise. Will you marry me? Please will you marry me? Not because it is the sensible thing to do. Not because it will be an escape from this place—this place is actually rather lovely. And not because you have needs or because you want children. But because I am offering my heart? Will you?"

"Yes," she whispered. "Oh, yes. Yes, my lord."

"John," he said.

"John."

And then he smiled at her again.

He noticed that one of her hands crept up to the spoon and clasped it very tightly. Then she smiled back, slowly at first, and finally with all the sunshine that had caused him to love her five years before.

She felt delirious. She hardly dared believe that this was all happening.

"Are you not going to ask the other question?" she asked.

"The other question?" He bent his head closer and looked at her inquiringly.

"The other question you asked me in the library," she said.

He looked blank for a moment, and then the smile—the startlingly attractive smile—returned to his eyes. "May I kiss you?" he asked.

"Yes." She nodded and laughed. "Yes, that question. And yes, you may." She was glad suddenly of the breeze that must have whipped color into her cheeks and would mask her blushes.

He kissed her.

And then she believed. It was far too unfamiliar and far too wonderful an experience to be imagined. And far too carnal. His arms came tightly about her waist and hers about his neck and his mouth opened as it met hers. Her own opened in response and they kissed deeply, warmly, and lingeringly, unheeding of the collie who pranced about them, barking.

"Mm." His blue eyes were gazing into hers, heavy with what she could only interpret as desire. "Better even than I remembered."

She smiled and reached up to smooth back a lock of his hair, which had fallen over his forehead.

"Will we go and tell Aunt Hetty and Aunt Martha?" she asked.

"And the rector," he said. "I have a special license in my room at the house. I hoped I would need it. Or would you prefer to wait until we can return to your family?"

She shook her head. "My family is here," she said.

He nodded and kissed the end of her nose. "The owner of Tŷ Mawr was very eager to sell to me," he said. "Shall I buy it? Shall we make it our occasional home?"

She laughed. "Shall we plan the whole rest of our lives while we stand here?" she asked.

"I do not see why not," he said, kissing her mouth again and then joining in her laughter.

"John," she said and closed her eyes. "John. It suits you."

"The tide is going to be murdering my boots soon," he said, turning his head. "Shall we walk back? I have something to show you before we go to your aunts'."

"What?" She smiled at him.

But he would not tell her. He took her hand and

laced their fingers together and they walked briskly back toward the sand dunes, talking a little, lapsing into easy, happy silences occasionally. With her free hand she held tightly to her spoon—her love spoon. He took her over the dunes to the gates into the park of Tŷ Mawr and up across the lawn and into the woods

"There," he said, stopping at last and gesturing with one arm. "These are what you came trespassing for, are they not?"

"Oh." She looked about her, her breath catching in her throat, tears threatening her vision. Everywhere, all about them, the daffodils were blooming. Bright yellow trumpets of bold hope and joy. "Oh, yes, I have always come here to see them. Every spring. There is no lovelier flower than the daffodil."

"As bright and cheerful as the sun," he said. "Just like you."

She laid her head impulsively against his shoulder. "Thank you for bringing me here," she said. "How perfect this sight has made the morning."

"We must always be here for the blooming of the daffodils," he said. "We will come each spring. Perhaps next year we can bring our first child, Katherine, and show them to him."

She smiled, her cheek against his shoulder. "Yes, John," she said. "Or to her."

"Just one more question," he said, looking down at her. "And then no more for today, I promise."

She smiled up at him once more, eyebrows raised.

"May I kiss you again?" he asked. "Here, among the daffodils?"

"I think I have always yearned more at daffodil blooming time than any other to be kissed," she said. "To be loved. By you." She turned and set her arms about his waist and lifted her face to him. "Yes."

He smiled at her and lowered his mouth to hers,

while Patch, sensing another lengthy delay in her morning's walk, stretched out among the daffodils at their feet, set her head down on her forepaws, and gazed up at them, waiting patiently for the resumption of something interesting.

A Golden Crocus

by Patricia Rice

Illinois, 1885

My dearest sister,
 In only a matter of days I will be able to see your loving face again. You do not know how I long to hear your sweet voice. You are the home I no longer have, and I long for your company. Are these words too strong for the affection I feel has grown between us this past year? Your letters have given me the strength to excel and succeed as I have never done in the past, and I am about to reap the rewards of my endeavors. I hope you will share in my happiness.

 Do you have any idea how strong an influence you have become on my behavior? Whenever I think to stray, I need to only ask myself, "What would my angel think of me should she discover my failings?" and my feet are turned to the paths of righteousness once more. You are all that is good and modest. Your letters remind me of my duties with such quiet rectitude that I cannot fail to heed them. I cannot wish to think what would have happened to me in this year past had I not your memory to keep me strong.

"Sister?" Lorna exclaimed in disgust, throwing the letter to the bed without reading more of it. "He calls you sister? I have never seen such self-serving, fatuous idiocy in all my born days. No wonder he is a lawyer."

Elizabeth looked at her flamboyant cousin, then carefully refolded the letter, smoothed the wrinkles, and pressed it back into the box containing several more packets of similar missives. "We cannot all be as you are, Lorna. I am not good at revealing myself to others, but I had hopes ..." She looked troubled as she closed the box and tucked it away in her lingerie drawer. "We have exchanged such intimate thoughts with each other. That is why he calls me sister. It is as if we have known each other all our lives. No one knows more of me than Richard."

Lorna looked amused. "I don't suppose he has so much as held your hand, if all you have done is exchange letters?"

Elizabeth fidgeted with the cameo brooch pinned to the high collar of her gown. "Of course not. We had only just met when he had to return to Chicago. He promised to write and tell me how he fared in his new position. We have so very much in common, our understanding was spontaneous. Surely that must count for something?"

Lorna gathered up the sheafs of paper she had been working on earlier. "You refine too much on a meeting of the minds. I number countless men among my correspondents, but I do not think of them in terms of undying affection merely because we are agreed on many subjects."

Looking vaguely rebellious, Elizabeth straightened the various bottles adorning her dressing table. "But we are not like you. I am not in the least worldly, and Richard admires that. He believes a woman's place is in the home, that women are the moral guardians of men, and simply because of their greater strengths, men are meant to go out into the world to protect and defend us. And I feel he is right. What you do is unfeminine and dangerous. I am terribly afraid for you, Lorna."

Lorna shoved her sheafs of paper into a leather carrying case and shook her head. "You are changing the subject, Elizabeth. We have discussed my 'dangerous' occupation on too many occasions for there to be any point in rehashing it now. The subject here is your reading something into this man's letters that is not there. He calls you 'sister,' not 'sweetheart.' Do not pin your hopes on his proposing to you when he arrives. Personally, I would fly in the other direction if any man spouting such nonsense came toward me, but that is your affair. I just do not wish you to get hurt by hoping for what does not exist."

"You did not read the letter carefully." Clearly mutinous now, Elizabeth slammed a perfume bottle into place. "One does not use words like 'loving' and 'sweet' with a sister. It is just difficult to express another level of affection when we have barely been in each other's company. By calling me 'sister,' he acknowledges that we have gone beyond being just friends."

Lorna shrugged, checked the draping of material over her bustle in the mirror, and reached for her hat. "For your sake, I hope you are right." She gave her usually serene cousin's mulish expression a look of concern. "But I wish that you had kept your heart out of this until you know your affections are returned."

The rebelliousness disappeared, replaced by a pleasant smile as Elizabeth stood and hugged her stylish cousin. "You play the part of hard-hearted lady journalist very well, but I know you love me as I do you. I do not mind that in your search to imitate men, you must hide your feelings as they do."

Lorna gave her cousin a quick hug. "We all have different ways of expressing affection, I suppose. Mine is by forgiving you your misunderstanding. Do not let your parents wait up for me this evening. I am likely to be quite late."

Elizabeth stepped back and shook her head with concern. "I hope you will have someone trustworthy with you. You may consider Illinois a bastion of rural safety, but you are stirring up a lot of trouble with your city thinking."

Lorna adjusted her hat and picked up her carrying

case. "Terence will be with me, but I don't fear your angry farmers, dear. It is their wives for whom you need feel concern. They are going to have a hard time of it when they try to rise above their years of oppression."

She sailed out of the room, leaving Elizabeth to shake her head in dismay. She did not share Lorna's views on the rights of women, but she felt more sorry for her cousin than angry with her. Women were not equipped to deal with the harsh realities of the world. They were too frail physically and emotionally to go out and do battle every day. The strain of doing so was beginning to tell on Lorna. The laughing cousin she remembered from years past was rapidly turning into a brittle woman, too caught up in her crusade to ever know the kinder pleasures of love and home. Elizabeth wouldn't exchange places with her for the world.

Richard nervously fiddled with the knot in his tie, ran afoul of his tie pin, gave it up and reached for his top hat. His long wool overcoat fell open to reveal his double-breasted waistcoat beneath, but he gave his image in the mirror only a casual glance. He already knew he dressed with a level of sophistication unknown in this small, rural town. He hoped it would impress and not repel the woman he had come to court. The intelligence of her letters led him to believe that she would be open-minded in her opinions.

Still, he was nervous, and he wasn't fond of the feeling. He could face a courtroom full of hostile faces and not quail at the task of turning their opinions around, but the idea of facing one lone woman had him shaking in his shoes. He wasn't certain why this was so, and that unnerved him even more.

He had said nothing to express his hopes in his letters. It had been a year since he had seen Elizabeth. He could very well have idealized her image. But her letters had kept her refreshing innocence and captivat-

ing intelligence in his mind ever since. She was all that
was modest and pure, while still exciting his heart and
soul. He was eager to know her better, to learn if she
could possibly share his need for companionship.

As he stepped out into the windy streets outside
his boardinghouse, Richard recognized he was setting
himself up for disappointment. Even if Elizabeth returned some small portion of his affection, it still
might lead to nothing. He had accepted a job in California, a million miles away in terms of all that was
familiar to her. It would take something much greater
than affection to make her willing to leave the com-
forts of the home and family she had known all her
life to go away with a relative stranger.

He had only a few short weeks in which to convince
her that he would be enough to replace what she had
now. The task seemed insurmountable, but the alternative was worse. He hadn't known a true home in so
long that he couldn't count the years. He longed for
one now. He had worked his way through the university and his apprenticeship and the long, lonely years
of hardship with the single goal of finding a good
woman and starting his own family when he had the
income to support them. He had that income now. He
sincerely hoped that Elizabeth was the woman. He
didn't relish the prospect of going to California alone.

When he reached the house, a maid answered the
door, giving him a brief reprieve before he would meet
again the woman on whom he had pinned so many
hopes. He was escorted into a comfortably appointed
parlor, where he was left to admire the collection of
material wealth displayed upon every shelf and spare
inch of wall. Richard knew Elizabeth's family was
more comfortable than wealthy, but to one who had
known starvation, the extravagance of these decora-
tions was reassuring. He wanted a wife who knew how
to feather his nest appropriately.

While he waited, he admired an upright piano, the
back of which was decorated in a wine-red portiere

with gold tassels. The top of the piano sported a collection of ornate frames bearing photographs and daguerreotypes of various family members looking stiff and uncomfortable. He picked up one showing Elizabeth and tried to remember this unsmiling woman as the young girl he had laughed with last summer. It made him even more nervous.

Putting down the frame, he examined the dragon-headed brass candlesticks, an assortment of vases, and a collection of fans that spilled from the piano onto the wall and the table beside it. Exotic peacock feathers mixed with elegant ivory, but he could only think of how long it must take to dust them.

The lounge behind him was covered with embroidered cushions and protected with lovingly crocheted doilies. He took a seat on the edge, afraid he would disturb the arrangement of cushions and covers. This position left him staring at the painted Chinese pugs on the hearth. Fortunately for the porcelain, the house had steam heat and there was no fire in the fireplace. He listened to the constant tick of the clock on the mantel and waited for the sound of footsteps.

He breathed a sigh of relief and stood up as he heard the patter of feminine feet on the hall carpet. In a swish of silk, she was standing there, and Richard gazed his fill.

She was more lovely than he remembered. Her golden hair was parted in two loops over a wide, clear forehead and hung down in dangling curls to frame a heart-shaped face of translucent loveliness. A smile swept swiftly over pink lips before disappearing behind a mask of shyness, and he felt his heart register a pleasant thump. She was everything he remembered and more.

"Elizabeth?" He held out his hand for her to take and realized it was shaking slightly. This was the woman he meant to marry and share the rest of his life with. A decision of that magnitude justified a slight case of nerves.

Her small hand rested easily in his. "Richard. It is so good to see you again."

She spoke softly, so softly he barely heard her. He squeezed her fingers and released them, fearful he would make her as nervous as he. The long train of her skirt brushed his legs as she entered the room, and he almost sighed with pleasure at this physical contact. He caught the slight scent of violets as she passed, and he breathed it in eagerly. Letters could never replace the reality of touch and scent.

"Do I dare tell you how much more beautiful you are than I remember?" he murmured as she took a seat on the lounge. Daringly, he took the place beside her.

Her lashes swept upward briefly so she might meet his gaze, then she turned her eyes modestly to the floor. "You will make me blush if you say such things. Pray, let us talk of more important topics. How was your journey?"

Richard didn't consider his journey in the least important, but he couldn't leap into the conversation with his hopes and desires. He had no wish to terrify the angel of modesty beside him. The devil of it was, he couldn't see his way around to ever telling her how he felt. She was too virginal, too unworldly to understand his base nature. Their philosophical discussions had touched on many topics, including love and friendship, but they had certainly never veered anywhere near the physical demands of love and marriage.

It was up to him to lead the way. That thought alone was enough to unman him. He couldn't possibly risk even holding her hand when her family could walk in on them at any moment. He played with the brim of his hat like a nervous schoolboy while he sought some safe topic of conversation.

"The railroads are improving significantly," he managed. "Despite the rain and cold outside, I made the journey in the greatest of comfort, sitting beside a stove and reading a book. Can you imagine how it must have been for our ancestors?''

He wanted to kick himself for the immense insipidness of his remarks, but his brain seemed to disconnect as the scent of violets filled his nostrils. He could barely steer his gaze away from the bows on her gown, which rose and fell with her breathing. He imagined unfastening those tiny ivory buttons at her throat, and a shiver went down his spine. How was he going to teach carnal knowledge to a woman undoubtedly wearing three petticoats, two chemises, and a corset?

One step at a time, he admonished himself. He had to win her trust first. With that thought firmly in place, he set about listening and conversing with some semblance of intelligence.

By the time an hour had passed, Richard was a physical and nervous wreck. They had struggled from talk of his journey and railroads through the weather and on to the political situation, but the task of conversing on these topics was in no way similar to spilling out everything he thought on a piece of paper. He had to watch every word so as not to offend, and he had to do it while wondering if he might catch a glimpse of her ankles.

It came almost as a relief when the front door flew open with a gusty March wind and in swept a laughing woman, carrying what could only be a briefcase. Richard heard her laughter floating from the foyer and rose from his seat at the feminine sound. Elizabeth jumped up too, hurrying to call to this unexpected interloper.

"Lorna! You are home early. Richard is here. Come meet him. I will send Sally for some hot tea for you."

Led by an eager Elizabeth, the woman entered the parlor. Amusement still danced in her eyes as she held out her hand for Richard to take.

Feeling very much as if he were the source of her amusement, he took her extended hand and wondered if she wished him to shake it or bow over it. There was rather an element of command in her presence that made either seem quite feasible. She solved his dilemma by giving his hand a quick shake and removing her fingers from his grasp.

"So, you are the Richard I have heard so much about. You do not look a paragon, but as I have never yet met one, I suppose I wouldn't know."

She swept through the room, disposing of her gloves and hat with careless gestures as she located the radiator and warmed her hands over it. Richard tried to keep from staring. Her hat now off, he could see that her hair was red. Not auburn. Not strawberry blond. Red. And thick. She wore it piled high, but windswept strands came loose at all angles. She didn't seem aware of it.

A redhead's freckles sprinkled her nose, making her look more a mischievous child than the full-grown woman she so obviously was. The severe cut of her tailored jacket emphasized not only the full swell of the ruffled bodice beneath, but the narrowness of her waist and the long line of her hips. Richard had difficulty diverting his gaze as she turned to warm her backside against the heat.

"I doubt that I am a paragon, Miss . . ." He stumbled. They were not yet formally introduced, and he did not know her full name.

"Sanderson. Lorna Sanderson. Richard Dillon. I'm so sorry. I've made a muff of it already, haven't I?" Elizabeth hurried to his side. "Lorna is my favorite cousin. She's come to stay a few weeks. I hope you will come to know and like her as well as I do."

Richard nodded politely. "Miss Sanderson." Then the name finally registered somewhere in the dim recesses of his mind, and his eyes narrowed as he gazed at her. "Lorna Sanderson? The journalist and lecturer?"

This time, the amusement dancing in her eyes was very definitely at his expense. "Go ahead and say it, sir: the battle-ax who preaches women's rights. I'm not ashamed of what I do."

He was making a real muck of it now. He turned an anxious gaze to Elizabeth, who was watching him with equal anxiety. With an inner sigh of relief, Richard smiled reassuringly at her before turning back to the woman who so blatantly wished to defy him. "You have no need to be ashamed. You have made yourself well heard at a time when many could not. I will admit to being pleasantly surprised that you are also young and beautiful." This last he said with a hint of amusement, in reference to her charge of being a battle-ax.

She had full pink lips that pursed slightly when she was thinking, he noticed as she turned a contemplative gaze on him. There was nothing shy or demure about Lorna Sanderson. She was as direct and straightforward as the wind that had blown her through the door. It made dealing with her considerably easier. A man would know exactly where he stood in this woman's eyes.

"From Elizabeth's praises, I had not thought you a flirt, sir. You are excused this once. Do not let it happen again." Having delivered this salvo, Lorna turned to her cousin. "Am I in time for dinner? If so, I will run upstairs and make myself presentable. Tell Sally to bring me my tea there."

Having been pointedly reminded of the lateness of the hour, Richard soon made his excuses and departed, with Elizabeth's invitation to return on the morrow. He felt almost relieved when struck with the cold wind as the door closed behind him. Dealing with the vagaries of nature was so much easier than coping with women.

Lorna arranged her papers on the podium and looked out over the crowd spilling through the doors. She didn't bill her lectures as speeches on women's rights. She had too much finesse for that. They were advertised as "Educational Treatises on the Betterment of Living," and she made excellent suggestions throughout the series on how women could live healthier, more active, more fulfilling lives. She made no apology for the fact that many of these suggestions required a woman to step outside her usual role, and that she frequently referred to the good that could be done if women were allowed a voice in political decision making. By the time she was done speaking, it was more than obvious that if women were the moral guardians of the world, they would be much better able to guard if they were in positions of power.

Her message riled the men, no doubt, but they had been relatively quiet in this small town where visiting lecturers were treated with respect. It was taking a little while for her message to completely sink in. By now, the little ladies ought to be asking their husbands why they could not take over the task of paying the bills as well as keeping the household accounts. And once they had a good grasp of how much money was available outside those household accounts, they would begin questioning where the excess went. When they began asking why their husbands should have boxes of Cuban cigars when little Johnny ought to have new shoes, or why the tab at the local tavern should more than equal their grocery budget, then the trouble would begin.

Lorna relished her role of troublemaker. Looking out over the rows of feminine faces bright and eager and ready to learn, she felt her spirits soar. Her own mother had bowed to her husband's every wish until the day he died, and then she had been nearly suffocated under the burden of trying to support a home and family while having absolutely no knowledge of how to do so. Lorna wouldn't wish that fate on anyone, and she was here to see that as many women as possible could escape from it. The scowls and frowns on the few male faces in the back of the room told her she was making progress.

Terence ushered in the last of the late arrivals,

found them seats, and closed the auditorium doors. Terence was her indispensable ally. They had grown up together in the same neighborhood, under much the same set of circumstances, only his father had been an abusive alcoholic. He could readily see the advantage his mother would have had if she had been able to leave the home and support herself. He was enthusiastic in his support of her lectures, and he made life generally easier for Lorna by arranging everything for her. He had made it his business to develop contacts on every major newspaper in the Midwest. He was almost single-handedly responsible for her popularity.

Lorna almost wished she was capable of being like other women in desiring a husband and home. Terence would be her ideal mate, and in fact he had pointed this out to her more than once. One of these days, when she was ready to settle down, perhaps she would take him up on his offer. Right now, she just couldn't imagine herself tied to hearth and children, no matter how fine a man Terence might be.

As she spoke, Lorna was aware of heads nodding in agreement with her words, of faces brightening with sudden discovery, and of a few frowns and negative shakes. She focused on the timid, the women who hung on every word with a dazed expression of fear and hope. These were the women she wanted to reach most. These were the women who needed to hear that they did not have to suffer for the rest of their lives for a mistake made when they were young.

To her amusement, Lorna recognized Elizabeth's beau slipping into a back seat. The fatuous Richard had come to see if she was a bad influence on her cousin. A little fire and brimstone ought to singe his ears. Self-satisfied men like that raised her hackles.

Murmurs of approval and excitement rippled through the room as Lorna launched into a full-scale tirade that on some occasions brought her audience bounding to its feet in applause. This audience was a little more subdued, but she felt their response, and she increased her vigor. In the back of the room, more men spilled through the doors.

She didn't like seeing those men standing back there like that. The seats were full. The doors had been closed. They should have been denied entrance. Lorna hastily scanned the crowd for a glimpse of Terence. He was unobtrusively moving to the back of the room, but she didn't feel relief. Having grown up on the streets, Terence was tough and wiry and strong, but he wasn't a six-foot farmer with shoulders like an ox. She toned down her voice a trifle to give him time to persuade the intruders to leave.

The faces of several of the women had turned from attentive to frightened as they glanced nervously over their shoulders. A woman on the far side of the audience quietly got up and slipped to a side exit. Lorna's lips tightened at this evidence of the fear those bullies had wrought within their own families. She would like to hand out whips to every woman in the audience tonight—let those men know what it felt like to be physically helpless. She wanted to see those men on their knees.

Instead, one of them came forward, yelling obscenities as he located his wife among the crowd and went after her. Terence shouldered his way in front of him so the woman had time to make good her escape, but other men began to follow the lead of the first. Lorna was reminded of a herd of sheep as they barrelled mindlessly across the room, searching for their ewes. What she needed was a good collie.

A shrill scream split the air as one of the men found his target and slapped her. The crowd began to shift nervously, then panic with the onslaught of irate husbands and fathers. Chairs tipped over as their occupants hurried toward the exit to avoid husbands, trouble, or their own fears. Those few who stayed behind were trapped in the crush. Feet caught and tripped over fallen chairs, long skirts tangled in wooden rails, and soon feminine voices were as loud and obstreperous as the males'. Lorna silently cheered on the women wielding umbrellas and parasols and applying them roundly to masculine ears, but she decided it was time to depart when she noted a particularly irate contingent of men heading in her direction.

The room had erupted in utter chaos and Lorna couldn't find Terence. There was no one to notice as she scooped up her skirts and stepped down from the speaker's platform—no one except those bullies with their eyes fixed on her, that is.

Trying not to panic, Lorna skirted around two women beating ineffectively on a stoic farmer who was attempting to pull his wife from the melee. She would have stopped to cheer them on if it weren't for the fact that she caught a glimpse of one of the massive farmers coming up from that side. The nearest exit seemed a million miles away.

A bulky man a head taller than she stepped in front of her, and Lorna hastily stepped backward, nearly bouncing into a rotund stomach behind her. Caught, she looked quickly to either side to see several more men closing in around her. She despised feeling helpless. From now on, she would carry a whip.

"Reckon you ain't got a man to teach you a lesson, so we agreed to do it for you," the one in front drawled without inflection. "Women out here are likely to get hurt without a man. You'd best get yourself back where you belong."

He didn't seem entirely unreasonable. He wasn't foaming at the mouth. He wasn't even drunk. He looked to be a respectable farmer in his checked shirt and galluses. But he was wide and tall and he was reaching for her, and Lorna was quite certain she didn't want to hear his lesson.

The gray arm of an alpaca suit intruded abruptly, coming down hard on the man's arm as it reached for her. While the farmer turned slowly in surprise, a second gray arm went around Lorna's waist and dragged her out of the circle of men.

In seconds, she found herself chest to chest with Elizabeth's beau. At his urging, she dazedly slipped behind him and watched as Richard confronted the monsters of injustice who had threatened her.

"If any lessons are to be taught here tonight, they'll be lessons in manners," he admonished. "Gentlemen do not physically maul ladies. There is no honor in harming someone smaller than you. If that's understood, I suggest you gentlemen take your—"

Lorna gasped as one of the men swung wildly in Richard's direction. He couldn't sidestep the blow without exposing her. Instead, he blocked it with one neatly cuffed wrist and swung swiftly and with great effect with his other fist. His attacker crumpled into the crowd behind him.

As two more men entered the fray, Lorna gave a scream of outrage and reached for a chair. Obviously, these men also needed to be taught that it was unfair to fight five against one. While Richard sank a blow into the stomach of the one grabbing his tie, Lorna swung a wooden folding chair over the head of the one coming up from behind.

They had nearly settled the fracas by the time Terence shoved his way through the dissipating crowd to their side. One man lay groaning on the floor, two others had been carried off, and a couple of angry wives had begun applying fists and purses to their husbands' arms to steer them away. With the simple expedient of stepping in front of Lorna and applying his fist to a jaw, Richard halted the obscenities coming from the last offender.

"You should have let me have him," Terence muttered furiously as he caught Lorna's arm and pulled her toward him. "He needed his head parted down the middle, like his hair."

Lorna shook herself free. "Let's just get out of here. Are you all right, Mr. Dillon?"

Richard was brushing off his suit and examining a torn cuff, but he looked up quickly at her inquiry. His gaze took in the other man's possessive stance, and he shrugged, mentally removing himself from the scene. "I've been worse."

"Come on, Lorna. Let's get out of here." Terence took her arm a second time, attempting to steer her toward the nearest door.

Irritated, Lorna brushed off his hand, reached for her handkerchief, and applied it to the slight trickle of blood on her defender's mouth. "I'll be fine, Terence. Mr. Dillon will see me home, after I see that he's all right. I've got to get back before my uncle hears about this and comes looking for me. See what you can do to settle the rest of this mob."

Angry voices still echoed through the auditorium. Some women wept, others talked furiously, still others seemed to be in fits of the vapors, while angry or worried men milled about, anxious to get their womenfolk home. If anything, the crowd seemed to be growing as word of the fracas spread outside the hall. Terence glared at Richard, transferred his ill humor to Lorna, then stomped off to do as directed.

"I'm quite fine, Miss Sanderson. We had better get you out of here before this melee erupts all over again." Richard took her handkerchief and blotted the trickle of blood himself.

"I thought you'd never ask." With relief, Lorna took his arm and allowed him to lead her around the fallen chairs and angry clumps of people toward the far doors. She'd dealt with mobs before, but never quite so close at hand. She hadn't expected this quiet crowd to explode. Obviously, neither had Terence. He was usually right at her side when there was any danger.

"I'm grateful for your defense, Mr. Dillon. I don't know what would have become of me if you hadn't come to my rescue." Lorna couldn't believe what she heard herself saying—she sounded like a simpering ninny. But she spoke the truth. She was more than grateful for his aid. Next time, she would be better prepared.

"You would no doubt have received a rather crude lesson in the reasons women do not make nuisances of themselves in public." Richard guided her from the hall into the still darkness of an early spring evening. Apparently the door they had chosen led to a back alley and not the front, where people still milled about.

"Women!" she exclaimed. "It wasn't women making nuisances of themselves back there. We were very quietly minding our own business when that rampaging ox stormed through the room. Do not blame that fracas on women, sir." Oddly, Lorna still continued to cling to his arm. Her nerves were a trifle shattered, she admitted. It was good to have a strong arm to lean on while she maneuvered around wet puddles on the walk.

"Of course, how foolish of me. I should have realized a roomful of women plotting rebellion would be perfectly harmless. The problem certainly lies with the poor maligned husbands who have watched their pleasant homes turn into battlegrounds for viragoes."

She ought to be furiously angry, but the image he set before her caused Lorna's voice to be laced with amusement. "Well, I'm certain all the ladies will go straight home and brew the poor dears cups of coffee to settle their hurt prides, and from now on, they will never lift another word in protest. I'm quite sure they have all learned their lessons tonight."

He sent her a darting glance. "You know you have only whetted their appetites for more. You enjoy wreaking havoc, don't you?"

Lorna caught his arm tighter as she nearly slipped on a wet patch and tried to right herself. He held her firmly until she was steady again. She lifted her skirt more carefully now as she fell into pace with him.

"I enjoy showing women that they have alternatives. They do not have to endure life being beaten and walked over. They do not have to watch their husbands drink up the money needed to feed their children. They do not need men if they can get a little education, stand up for themselves, find jobs, and grasp some of the power that men have wielded alone for far too long."

Richard snorted inelegantly. "Is that what you thought you were preaching back there?"

"That's what I *know* I was preaching back there. You don't think a man is going to get up and tell them all that, do you? Men are far too fond of having everything their way. It's time women stood up and took what was rightfully theirs."

Her voice soared with the same righteousness that had lifted it earlier. Richard grinned and glanced down at her fiery red hair.

"Well, you tell me what is rightfully yours and I'll keep my hands off of it, all right?"

They had come to her uncle's front porch and stood facing each other. Lorna had the urge to smack him, feeling somehow that his words had a more intimate meaning than was obvious. As a matter of fact, he seemed to be looking at her in a way that he should only be looking at Elizabeth. It made her insides tingle, made her more aware of him as a man and not just a casual rescuer.

With a cry of exasperation, she flung open the door, rushed through it, and slammed it in his face.

Terence ignored a squabbling couple, helped a lady to her feet and into the hands of her anxious companions, sent somebody's father in search of his daughter along the far wall, and wished the whole place to the devil. He was still smarting from the brush-off Lorna had given him. The fancy man in the pretty suit wasn't her kind. He had disapproval written all over his face. They were probably having a rip-roaring argument right now. That was probably why Lorna had gone with him. She wanted someone to fight with after a night like this.

Well, he'd give her something to think about when he saw her tomorrow. This traveling life had to stop sometime, and now was as good a time as any. Maybe tonight's fracas had shaken some sense into her. She should stick to writing magazine articles and stay out of crowds. She ought to know by now that he wouldn't be anything like her father. He would never object to her writing. He supposed it would be all right if she did an occasional lecture or two in respectable surroundings. He just wanted her to stay home where she was safe and out of trouble and let him take care of her for a change.

That didn't seem too much to ask, but for a woman like Lorna, it sounded like a death sentence. Terence knew that. They'd talked about it often enough. He wanted marriage, but marriage of necessity entailed children. Lorna didn't want children—not yet, anyway. Or so she said. He was beginning to doubt if she knew the truth herself. She liked his kisses well enough, but she was quick to avoid anything else. He was beginning to think that despite everything they meant to each other, maybe the problem was more than just Lorna's reluctance to marry. Maybe her reluctance was to marrying him.

His eye caught on a bewildered female wringing her gloved hands and straining to see through the crowd. She wore her hat straight and neat over her blond tresses. Her prim gown with its tight bodice and bustled skirt only served to accentuate her exceedingly feminine curves. He had met her only once, but he remembered her. She didn't belong here.

Terence strode over fallen chairs and abandoned parasols to get at Elizabeth, and even then, he was almost too late. A drunken rowdy he had noticed earlier stumbled into her path and grabbed her fragile shoulder. She gasped and tried to step away, but the drunk only grinned and held tighter. Terence watched her face turn pale before he could get to her. He didn't even want to imagine what the wretch must smell like, much less consider his drunken hands on her. He kicked aside the last chair and grabbed the drunk's coattails.

"Be on your way, sir. A gentleman doesn't go about molesting young ladies." He jerked, and the drunk went staggering backward. Releasing Elizabeth, he fell, but Terence had already grabbed the lady's waist and pulled her from further harm.

Lorna's cousin was light and fragile in his arms, a bundle of terrified helplessness as she watched the drunk fall to his face and stay there. She was actually clinging to Terence's lapels, for heaven's sake. She was irresistible.

He leaned over and kissed her pretty pink lips.

She jerked with shock, pulled back, and smacked him soundly on the cheek.

Terence grinned. "I deserved that, but I'd do it again. It was worth the pain."

Elizabeth glared at him, a vision of outraged innocence. Her cheeks were flushed as pretty a pink as her lips now, he noticed while waiting for her to recover her tongue. He had to get her out of here or Lorna would have his head on a platter, but he didn't dare make another move toward her until she had leashed her temper. He'd learned that much in these years of dealing with her cousin.

"You are a scoundrel, sir. Just tell me where I may find my cousin and I shall leave you alone to find some other woman to molest."

"Lorna is fine. Your beau is taking her home as we speak, and that's where I'm going to escort you. You have no business being in this place." Terence grabbed her elbow and steered her firmly toward the door.

Elizabeth resisted. "I found my own way here, I can find my own way back. I do not need your assistance."

He kept moving, half dragging her forward with his momentum. "In case you haven't noticed, we had a near riot here tonight, Miss Sanderson. The streets aren't safe. Whatever made you come here tonight, of all nights?"

Given little other choice, Elizabeth hurried to keep up with him. Outside in the crisp air, she managed to free her elbow and stride briskly down the street so that he was forced to follow. "I heard there was trouble and I came to help. I am perfectly safe out here, sir. This is my hometown, after all. You would do better to go back and help clean up."

"You are beginning to sound like your cousin. I will see you home, and there's the end of it."

She responded with stony silence, refusing to utter a single word despite his attempts at cheerful banter. The challenge was too good to resist. Terence racked his brain for a topic that would rouse some comment.

According to Lorna, her cousin was a thoroughly domesticated little lady who believed a woman's goal in life was to marry and have children. In his experience, ladies like that had only one subject for conversation. Eyes gleaming, he pounced upon it.

"I'm trying to persuade Lorna to marry me. How should I go about it?"

Startled, Elizabeth turned wide eyes in his direction to see if he jested. Apparently deciding he did not, she forgot her intention to freeze him out. "Get a job," she responded seriously.

This time, it was Terence's turn to look startled. He had expected romantic suggestions like candy and flowers. Her practical advice shattered his complacent notion of this woman's character. She was much more like her cousin than he had imagined.

"A job?" He knew he sounded like an ass, but he couldn't immediately summon any other response.

Elizabeth nodded firmly. "A job. Lorna adored her father. She should have been his son instead of his daughter. Even after he died and she realized how he had left her mother helpless, she couldn't help trying to take his place. What she needs is a man who can support her so she doesn't have to worry about supporting herself any longer, a man who is just like her father but doesn't expect her to behave like her mother. Does that make sense?"

"No," he stated flatly as they reached their destination. "And yes, in some odd way. But she knows I can find employment anywhere. I have contacts all across the country. I'm not only a good journalist, but I also know the newspaper business inside and out. I've been asking her to settle down for months."

"Then you will have to settle down on your own and hope Lorna realizes she can't live without you." Elizabeth lifted her skirt and started up the porch steps.

"She'll hate me for deserting her." Terence stayed where he was, not following her up the stairs. His mind was too busy whirling around this new notion.

"Give her plenty of warning." With that, Elizabeth swept inside the house, leaving him no further opportunity to question her.

Terence was left to walk back to town through the icy night, wondering if it was just the cold air seeping around his heart or if it was something else. The idea of walking away from Lorna and making his way through life alone sent shivers down his spine.

"Your beau has considerably more sense than I thought," Lorna admitted reluctantly, checking her hair in the mirror and making a face at the reflection. "We had a long talk after last night's lecture. Did you know he will be taking a partnership in an established practice out in California?"

Elizabeth worried at the fingers of her gloves. "I know. California is such a long way away. I don't know why he chose there."

Lorna lifted her eyebrows slightly as she turned to look at her cousin. "Because there are more opportunities for young men out West. He would have to work years to gain such a position here."

Elizabeth lifted her shoulders slightly and strolled to the window overlooking the front yard. "He is very ambitious. That worries me. Our sentiments correspond so exactly in everything else, I cannot understand why he does not agree with me in this. A man whose only interest is his business does not make a good father or husband."

Spoken from the heart. Considering the number of hours Elizabeth's father spent at his office, Lorna nodded sagely. She ought to warn poor Richard about this cloud on his horizon. His eagerness to sweep Elizabeth off to California had been quite apparent last night. "I would think a young and eager man would be as interested in his family as in his work, if he chooses the proper mate," she answered thoughtfully.

"Who in the world could that be?"

Lorna jerked her head up, surprised at this response until she realized Elizabeth was not asking about Richard's mate but someone she saw outside. She joined her at the window and frowned at the sight of the woman coming up the walk.

She looked vaguely familiar, but she didn't appear to be one of the well-dressed ladies of the neighborhood. The feathers and roses on her hat were sadly bedraggled, and the velvet trim on her jacket was worn shiny in places. The outfit might have been striking some years ago, but it had long been ready for the dust bin. The haggard face beneath the roses had the same well-worn appearance of the woman's clothes.

"Uh-oh." Lorna suddenly placed the face. Sweeping up her skirts, she hastened from the room, Elizabeth close on her heels.

They arrived at the front door at the same time as the maid. Shooing Sally away, Lorna opened the door herself. The woman on the other side smiled with relief.

"I do have the right address. Thank heavens." She

seemed so relieved to find Lorna that she didn't know how to go on from there.

"I remember you from the lectures, Mrs. . . .?" Lorna raised her voice inquiringly.

"Slovoski. Mrs. Stanley Slovoski." That was a question she was prepared to answer. Obviously gathering her courage, she knitted her fingers together and continued, "Could you spare a moment of your time?"

Despite her appearance, the woman had a cultured voice, and Lorna stepped aside to allow her in. "Come in, Mrs. Slovoski."

Elizabeth watched anxiously as Lorna escorted their unexpected guest into the family parlor. She wondered why her cousin hadn't taken her to the guest parlor, but their visitor's expression as she gazed around at the clutter of magazines and books and sewing baskets and other accoutrements of family life answered her question. To Elizabeth, the well-worn furniture and carpet in this room were something to hide, but to their guest, they appeared to be every material comfort she could dream of. She touched an old velvet cloth across a lamp table with the reverence of one who possessed little. To have shown her into the rich guest parlor would have been cruel.

"Please have a seat, Mrs. Slovoski. Would you like some tea or coffee?" Lorna indicated the horsehair sofa before the fireplace.

Elizabeth had never seen her cousin quite so solicitous. She lingered in the background, waiting for instructions.

Their guest shook her head negatively. "No, thank you. I don't wish to be any trouble. I just . . . You seem to be such a sensible lady. . . ." She fluttered her hands helplessly in her lap.

Lorna glanced over her shoulder to Elizabeth. "I would like some coffee. Would you . . .?"

Elizabeth disappeared down the hall, understanding exactly. The woman looked as if she had not eaten in a week. The tray would carry more than coffee.

Beneath the bedraggled feather dangling from the woman's hat, Lorna could discern more than a shadow on the sallow skin. She tried to keep from frowning. Mrs. Slovoski was one of those women who appeared all too frequently at her lectures: the ones with the bruised faces and looks of despair in their eyes. They seldom attended more than one or two of the sessions, but their images remained imprinted on Lorna's memory long after that. Now here was one she could reach out to personally, and she was terrified of the responsibility. She had no idea what to say.

She pulled up a chair across from her and asked briskly, "Now, Mrs. Slovoski, what can I do for you?"

The woman averted her eyes to the empty fireplace, then reluctantly returned her gaze to Lorna. The words spilled out of her as if they had been dammed up too long. "I am married, but we have no children. My husband blames me because I am glad there are no children. We barely have enough money for ourselves. He is a hard worker, but no one will pay him what he is worth because he is not educated and he does not speak English well. He is very unhappy. I thought ... if I could just find work ... But I don't know how to do anything." This last came out as a wail of despair.

Lorna wondered what had possessed this woman, who obviously came of good family and education, to marry an immigrant who could not even support himself, but she couldn't ask. People did odd things. Perhaps she had fancied herself in love with him. Perhaps she had needed to rebel against her family. Perhaps she had found herself alone in the world and without resources and had taken the first offer to come her way. Any and all of the above could be true. What mattered now was the present, and she had no easy answers.

"Women are often told that they do not know how to do anything, but we can do many things. If you can take care of a home, you can cook, you can bake, you can clean, you can sew. These are all services that are in demand somewhere. The problem usually is that we do not know where to go to market those skills. And then the next obstacle, after we succeed in finding a position, is the men in our lives. They do not like to feel like failures when their women go out to work."

Mrs. Slovoski was nodding her head eagerly. "Exactly. I offered to take in laundry, but Stanley went into a rage. He is very proud. I want to make him happy, not to upset him, but we cannot go on living like this."

Elizabeth carried in the coffee tray. Lorna was given a reprieve while cups were passed around and a selection of small sandwiches and muffins was presented. She scarcely tasted anything while she contemplated what she must say to this woman. Had she not seen the bruise on Mrs. Slovoski's face, her answer might have been different, but she had seen the effect of those bruises on Terence's mother and countless other women since then. She firmly set her resolve and waited for an opening.

When the coffee had been sipped and the sandwiches tasted, Lorna found her opportunity. "Mrs. Slovoski, you will not like what I have to say. I know you have come a long way, hoping to hear some easy way out of your situation, but as you already know, there is no easy way. I could help you find a job, but that will do you no good if your husband will not let you keep it. This is what my lectures are all about. You are going to have to decide who is more important, your husband or yourself. Is his life and what he wants more important than your life and what you want? Women have been trained for generations to believe the man's wishes come first, but what he wants is not necessarily what is right. It may not even be right for him. Men are not infallible."

Mrs. Slovoski stared down at the coffee cup in her lap. "I cannot live without him. I must do as he says."

Lorna made a rude noise. "It is more likely that he

cannot live without you. Men are quite helpless on their own. They don't know how to cook and feed themselves, but we do. You only need the courage to believe that you can find a job and support yourself, if necessary. What would you do if something were to happen to your husband? How would you live then? You would find a way, wouldn't you?"

The woman looked up with a light of hope dawning in her eyes. "Yes, yes, I would. I bake very well. There is a restaurant ... I baked for them several times, until Stanley discovered what I was doing." The light dimmed. "But he will not let me go back." Her fingers went to the bruise hidden beneath her feather.

Elizabeth dared to intrude. "Could you not stay home and bake and then sell your goods?"

The woman shook her head. "It takes much flour and sugar and other things that I do not have. Stanley would never give me money for those things."

They had ignored the knocking at the door, letting Sally answer it, but they could not ignore the sudden intrusion of Sally and the new arrival. Elizabeth looked up and squealed, then leapt to her feet to run to Richard.

"We forgot! I am so sorry. Please, come in. We are all ready, but ..."

Mrs. Slovoski was already on her feet. "I did not mean to keep you. Thank you so much for your kind words. I must be going now."

Lorna hurriedly rose and caught her arm. "Not yet. There is still one other solution. If you will not leave Stanley, then you must find someone to invest in your bakery. The investment would be very small. Flour and sugar are not that expensive. You could price your goods so that you may repay the investment quickly, with a little interest. After that, the profits would be yours. Do you think you know how to price your goods?"

The woman nodded uncertainly. "I was very good

at mathematics. I think so. But who would invest in me?"

Lorna whirled to confront Richard. "Mr. Dillon, I think a small investment of ten dollars would be sufficient. You can afford that, can you not?"

He looked startled and wary, but he reached in his pocket. "Do I get a bill of sale or a note or anything in return?"

Lorna snorted. "Lawyers. You are all alike." But she took a piece of stationery from the small desk in the corner.

Too overwhelmed to understand anything that was happening, Mrs. Slovoski found herself signing a note and going out the door with ten dollars more than she had arrived with. Elizabeth and Lorna waved her away, then turned back to their other guest, who looked as if he had been run over by a very fast wagon.

"Do I get some explanation?" he asked skeptically as Elizabeth smiled at him with delight and took his arm.

Since both women launched into explanations at once, his look of bewilderment did not ease for quite some time; but when he finally grasped the import of what they were saying, he frowned.

"You may kiss my money good-bye, but that is of little account. You have no idea what you may have brought down upon that poor woman's head, or your own. When her husband finds out that she has been sneaking around behind his back selling pies, he will want vengeance. I hope she will be wise enough to keep your names out of it."

"You are being stuffy, Mr. Dillon. Personally, I would have preferred it if I could have persuaded her to leave the monster, but women have been taught all their lives that they are frail and helpless and need men to protect them. It is difficult to persuade them otherwise. It is rather frightening to think of taking care of one's own self without the support of any other. Oh—that must be Terence now. Let us go." Lorna swept out of the room to fetch her coat and muff, not giving even a second glance to her cousin's beau.

Richard turned his gaze to Elizabeth, who was picking nervously at her gloves. "She is very set in her opinions, is she not?"

Elizabeth nodded hesitantly. "But she is so often very right."

There was nothing he could say to that. The prospect of going off to California on his own was one of the reasons he was here now. He didn't want to do it alone. Women weren't the only ones frightened of loneliness, but men weren't allowed to say such things. As the sound of Lorna greeting Terence in the hall drifted in to them, Richard offered his arm to escort Elizabeth out to join the others. This business of communicating feelings was very tricky, he decided. A man couldn't admit any weakness, so how did he go about telling Elizabeth how he felt? And if he didn't tell her how he felt, would she think that he was cold? Her letters indicated that she wanted warmth from a man.

Richard let the matter slide as they set out in the carriage he'd hired to take them to the pond where Elizabeth wanted to have a picnic. The March weather was alternately warm and chilly and it was altogether too early for a picnic, in his opinion. But the sky *was* a brilliant blue, and he wouldn't dream of denying Elizabeth her wish.

The women laughed and chattered and responded gaily to Terence's lighthearted teasing as the carriage jolted over the rutted road. Richard had never been one to speak his thoughts lightly, and he couldn't contribute to the frivolity with any degree of success. By the time he stopped the carriage, he was completely silent, and Terence was the one handing the women out.

Richard watched in quiet dismay as Elizabeth

laughed over some inconsequential jest that Terence made. Her laughter chimed like bells, and he wanted to be the one setting the bells to ringing. When Terence was the first to take Elizabeth's arm and lead her toward a redbud showing its first shades of pink, Richard felt even more incompetent than ever.

A gloved hand tugged at his elbow, and he bent to hear Lorna whisper, "I do believe Terence is trying to make me jealous. He's been acting very odd of late. Let us show him we are above such games."

With a feeling of gratitude, Richard took Lorna's arm and started down the trail leading alongside the pond. Elizabeth was already skipping among the trees as if she were a caged bird suddenly freed to the elements. Terence was staying right with her. Richard extended his arm to Lorna, and they walked more sedately toward a curve in the trail where the edge of the pond disappeared from sight behind a wooded outcropping of land.

"She is so beautiful and lighthearted that she makes me feel an old man at times," Richard said thoughtfully as combined laughter rang out behind them.

"Elizabeth? I never thought of her as lighthearted. She is ploddingly prim at most times, until I would like to shake her. But she is such an amiable, goodhearted creature that I cannot stay angry with her for long."

Richard studied this assessment for a minute. The woman holding his arm and walking serenely beside him was taller than her cousin. Lorna's head came past his shoulder, and he could sense the strength in her. She did not need his arm for support but took it for her pleasure. She did not expect anything of him, and it was easy to be silent in her company. He could reflect on his situation with Elizabeth without feeling nervous for his lack of conversation.

"When I met her last summer, and from the letters we have exchanged, I felt that she was a serious-minded young woman, one who had a mind of her own but believed in the traditional role of women. I thought I knew her well, but we are not the same people we seemed to be on paper, I fear."

Lorna smiled. "I think you have come very close to what Elizabeth expects everyone to think of her. She is a dutiful daughter and will someday be a dutiful wife. On the outside, she is what everyone wishes her to be. The inside, I fear, is a different matter. Women are taught certain roles and learn to play them well. That does not mean those roles portray who they really are."

Richard turned on her a look of surprise. Lorna met his gaze bravely, and he noticed her eyes were a dark green with golden flecks. She was rather attractive in a bold way, with her untamable red curls and brash mouth that smiled when it shouldn't and spoke what usually went unsaid. Her words now gave him fodder for thought, but he wasn't thinking very well.

"Do you play a role?" he asked daringly.

Lorna shrugged lightly, her mouth turned slightly upward as she looked away. "I play many roles. What about you?"

Talking with this woman could be dangerous. Richard attempted a truthful answer. "I don't think I play any roles. I have always known what I wanted and gone after it in a straightforward manner. I would not know how to act differently."

"That is because what you want and how you wish to go about getting it correspond with what the world expects of you. You are very fortunate."

Richard heard laughter some distance behind them, and he didn't turn to see what Terence and Elizabeth were doing now. He refused to play the part of jealous lover. His eyebrows went up a notch at that thought, and he turned his attention more carefully to Lorna.

"I should think the world would expect both of us to act the parts of jealous lovers right now. I don't know about you, but that does not correspond with what I wish. Does that mean we are playing parts rather than acting as ourselves?"

Lorna laughed. "That will take some thought. I do not play the part of jealous lover because I am not. I think it may be Terence who wishes me to play that part, but I am not cooperating. Your case is a little different. I don't think Elizabeth expects you to be anything but who you are. Therefore, there is none to think you must play the part of jealous lover if that is not what you are. But if you are jealous, you are playing a part by not behaving so."

Richard shook his head. "That is too much introspection for me. Let us do something more entertaining, like see what's on the other side of that old tree over there. If it's not too muddy for you?"

Without a word of ladylike protest, Lorna was off and running toward his goal before he could set one foot in front of the other. She ran as competently as she did everything else, and Richard gave a shout of laughter as he accepted her unspoken challenge. It would take some concentration to keep up with her.

He only caught up with her just before the dead tree hanging over the pond's edge. He passed her at the last minute, grabbing an overhanging branch and swinging around to catch Lorna. She slid solidly into his arms, and they both teetered precariously on the edge of falling, their laughter spilling over from the excitement of the race.

What he did then was completely irresponsible, but so very natural that he could not stop himself. She was happy and content in his arms as they struggled for balance, not shying away with maidenly protests, and Richard couldn't find the will to release her immediately. Instead, he bent to brush his mouth against hers.

It was meant to be a tribute, a small salute to her gallant race. Or perhaps it was a forfeit he meant to claim as winner. He didn't pause to think about it. He merely bent his head slightly to capture her mouth and found himself captured by a bolt of electricity instead.

She didn't fight her way free. She remained where she was, her hands pressed to his overcoat, her lips responding tentatively to his. Richard knew he should halt there, but he didn't seem capable of behaving rationally at the moment. The warmth of her in his arms enveloped him. The sweetness of her mouth tempted him. Electricity held them bound. He tightened his embrace and deepened the kiss.

Her fingers closed on the cloth of his coat while her head turned to fit more comfortably against him, giving him better access to her mouth. When she parted her lips at his demand, Richard felt that the patch of snow under his feet ought to melt beneath them.

He had never held a lady in a passionate embrace before. He could smell the light fragrance of her skin, feel the silky brush of her hair. For all her strength, Lorna was a slender woman, and his arms closed around her and lifted her upward effortlessly. She trusted his support, and his body responded so strongly that Richard was forced to gasp for breath.

It was then that she looked up at him, her eyes wide and round and filled with the same surprise and wonder as must surely be in his own. And then she was gone, slipping easily from his hold and fleeing across the field, and all he could do was follow.

She was right, of course. What had happened between them was nothing more than a physical response to their exercise. He would have to apologize later, when they were alone. Oddly enough, his mind rebelled at that idea. An apology meant that he was ashamed of what they had done. He wasn't ashamed. It felt like the most honest moment of his life.

Terence watched Lorna approach the bend some distance in advance of her escort. That was typical Lorna. She'd probably outraged the dignified lawyer with some defiant remark and was now victoriously escaping the field of battle. The chip on Lorna's shoulder was a trifle big for most men to deal with.

He continued with his self-appointed task of carrying the lunch baskets from the carriage. "Do you promise that there are apple tarts in here?" He lowered his eyes to Elizabeth's laughing ones and grinned down at her. Elizabeth was a great deal easier to please than Lorna.

"I promise there are, but I don't promise you'll get one," she teased. "You must treat me with great respect and not laugh at me anymore or you'll not see a one of them."

"You were the one who spun herself in circles until you were so dizzy you fell down. I cannot help that. Must I be all grim and solemn and reprimand you for your silliness to gain an apple tart?"

"No, you must be very solicitous and concerned and say, 'My dear Miss Sanderson, are you hurt? Shall I carry you to the cabin?' And then I shall be very grateful and give you apple tarts."

Terence laughed as she lowered her voice to imitate his and then employed a syrupy tone for her own. "You ought to be on stage, Miss Sanderson. You are every bit as naughty as any actress I have ever known."

"And I suppose you know a great many?" she replied in the ringing tones of mock censor.

"And suppose I do?" He threw open the door to the cabin that had been their destination and offered his hand to help her inside.

They were still laughing when Lorna and Richard joined them. The party settled with great gaiety in this one-room fishing cabin where the men made a fire in the fireplace while the women spread out the hamper of food on a blanket on the wooden floor. If there were undercurrents between the couples, they went undetected while large quantities of cold chicken and apple tarts were consumed between outbursts of laughter and chatter.

At Lorna's suggestion that they tour the woods after lunch, Elizabeth declared herself quite content to sit beside the fire and sip warm cider while her cousin worked off her unladylike exuberance. Terence agreed wholeheartedly, helping himself to the last tart. Lorna glanced wistfully at the bright sunshine outside, then resigning herself to inactivity, began piling dishes into the hamper.

"I need to work off some of that chicken, Miss Sanderson. Would you do me the honor of accompanying me for one last walk?" Richard reached for the overcoat he had discarded in the cabin's warmth.

Elizabeth gave him a smile of approval when Lorna's expression brightened. "You are a good person, Richard. Not everyone is so considerate."

Terence gave Lorna a look that a brother reserves for a pestilent nuisance of a sister. "Consideration is a two-way street. If Lorna wants to walk, she is quite capable of doing so on her own. You needn't freeze your feet off to oblige her, Dillon."

"I owe her a rematch on our earlier race. Besides, hiking while there are still patches of snow on the ground is an opportunity I might not have again anytime in the near future."

That remark echoed in the silence of the cabin after Lorna and Richard had left. Elizabeth gazed thoughtfully at the fire while sipping from her mug of cider.

"I take it he means because California does not have snow," Terence said idly, just to fill the silence.

"I wouldn't know. I know abysmally little about California," Elizabeth stated simply.

"Finding a life's mate is a difficult process, isn't it?" he asked. "The books make it seem so very easy. One simply fixes their fancy on another, follows the form of courtship, and it leads to happy-ever-after. But how does one know that fancying one person over another results in greater happiness if other factors go against one's desires?"

Elizabeth laughed softly. "Only you could have put

it so. I suppose the books would have it that love will overcome all obstacles. If you truly love Lorna, you will not mind if she continues traveling and lecturing while you settle down to what you want to do, because you will want what makes her happiest."

"But that would mean that if she returned my affection, she should want what makes me happiest." He raised an expectant eyebrow at her.

He didn't receive the expected smile. She sadly returned her gaze to the fire. "I suppose that in every marriage there must be one person who loves the other more. I cannot see how else it is done."

Terence frowned at that thought, removed himself from his reclining position, and went to gaze out the window at the pair walking toward the woods. He wasn't at all certain that love entered into it. Lorna was the only woman he knew intimately enough to consider settling down with. They had been through a lot together, and those shared emotions had led to physical responses often enough. They were comfortable with each other. That had seemed more than enough reason to make her his wife. But he was quite certain that Lorna didn't love him. He was less certain of his own feelings. He supposed that meant he would be the one to do the compromising.

He looked down at the peaceful young lady gazing at the fire's dying embers and felt a moment's unease. She belonged to another. He had no right to use her in his war to win Lorna's heart. Picking up the basket, he held his hand out. "I've changed my mind. We need to walk off lunch. Let us join the others."

Elizabeth raised her eyebrows slightly but hastened to fasten her coat and return her hands to her gloves. She sent him a look of curiosity. "You haven't been very attentive to Lorna today. Don't you think she's noticed by now?"

He didn't answer but hurried to douse the fire so they could leave the cabin. The thoughts he was having now didn't correspond to the innocence with which he had originally offered to stay behind.

Richard and Lorna hadn't wandered far. They stood at the base of a rocky knoll that protected a patch of daffodil buds from the wind. The flowers were not yet open, but the afternoon sunshine warmed this place. Elizabeth swung around and admired the sheltered cove as she joined them.

"There must have been a house near here once. See, there is a forsythia almost in bloom. And I think that's a lilac." She pointed out several bushes lining a path to the pond. Then she turned and examined the face of the rocky crag above them. "And up there! Look, the crocuses are blooming! Aren't they lovely?"

The broad patch of bright gold glittered in the afternoon sun like a sparkling treasure just out of their reach. Seeing something at last that he could do to appear the gallant, Richard reached for a rock above his head and started to swing himself up to the patch. He was reaching to pick one of the tiny blossoms when Elizabeth called out to him.

"Oh, don't! You can't pick them. They fade and die when you pluck them from their roots."

Richard looked down at the sturdy blossom his fingers had already plucked. The deep gold of the crocus burned as warm as the sun despite its bed near a patch of ice and snow. Surely a flower as strong as this one ought to make a lovely bouquet, like the violets that would appear a little later. But he didn't wish to ravage the glory of the blooms if they couldn't be preserved. Heeding Elizabeth's warning, he climbed back down, carrying the one tiny flower.

"I'm sorry, I'd already picked this one."

Elizabeth took it from his hand and tucked it carefully into the lapel of his coat. "Then we might as well make use of it while we can."

She serenely accepted Richard's hand as they returned to the carriage, and the other couple followed them in relative silence. The gay laughter of earlier had become something quieter, more thoughtful, as the party returned home.

"I talked to Mr. Harris at church on Sunday. He said he was looking for a good young journalist. He started talking about wishing he could spend more time fishing. I think he's looking for someone he can groom to take his place."

Elizabeth spoke so excitedly that she touched her hand to Terence's arm without thinking. She didn't withdraw it in time. He covered it with his own hand as he stared down into her dancing eyes. For a demure miss, she had the most delightfully lively eyes.

"You think I ought to apply for a position here?" A startlingly large question was beginning to form in Terence's mind, a question he didn't dare to dwell on. This was Lorna's cousin. The two women must be more alike than he recognized. That was the reason he found himself so drawn to her.

"Oh, yes!" Elizabeth was practically dancing with excitement as she tugged on his arm, pulling him down the street toward the newspaper office. "Wouldn't it be lovely? Lorna could live here, where her family is. I'm sure she'll agree that's for the best once she thinks about it."

Gently, Terence tucked her hand more properly around his arm and slowed their pace. "You're forgetting," he reminded her, "your beau wishes to move to California."

The excitement faded from her eyes, and she slowed her pace to a more sedate one. "Yes, of course. But Lorna will have Father and Mother to turn to. One ought to have family to rely on."

Terence didn't think Lorna cared a whit about having her aunt and uncle nearby. She spoke of them politely but thought them quaint and old-fashioned. He rather admired them himself. He'd never known a stable family, but he couldn't explain any of that to Elizabeth.

If he were going to get on with his life as he planned it, he had to begin somewhere. Patting Elizabeth's hand, he started more firmly in the direction she led him. "Well, let us meet the man, then. It can't hurt to just talk."

Elizabeth wasn't smiling any longer, but she followed without protest.

"He's doing what?" Lorna stared at her cousin with disbelief.

Elizabeth was wearing one of her new spring gowns with rows of ruffles over her bustled overskirt. She looked very feminine, very petite, and very proper, everything that Lorna was not. She tried not to glance down at her own stiff wool traveling dress. She barely had the proper number of petticoats. She certainly wasn't wearing a bustle or ruffles. What she was wearing was practical, she told herself, but a small twinge of something feminine inside wished she were something else. She forced her attention back to her cousin's reply.

"Terence is taking a position at the newspaper. Mr. Harris really likes him. I think he's going to groom him to take his position someday. Wouldn't that be excellent? He could be editor of the town paper. You must be very proud of him."

Lorna wanted to scream, "What about me?" but that was scarcely an appropriate attitude for an independent feminist. Terence was free to do as he pleased. She had just always thought what pleased him was to be with her.

Shaken, she scarcely noticed the maid answering the door until Sally intruded by introducing the guest to the parlor.

"Good evening, ladies. I trust I'm not too early." Richard stood there, hat in hand, looking questioningly from one serious face to the other.

He didn't get an immediate reply. Elizabeth's father and mother appeared from the family parlor to greet him, and all parties took seats. As it became apparent that her aunt and uncle meant to interrogate this suitor for their daughter's hand, Lorna managed to excuse herself and escape. She gave Richard a fleeting smile of sympathy, but she couldn't bear to remain in the stuffy room any longer. She needed an outlet for the emotions rioting through her.

Terence was deserting her. He was going to settle into this dismal town and become a staid and proper citizen like her uncle. She couldn't believe it of him. She'd thought they'd shared the same beliefs, the same ideas. She'd been planning a grand tour of the West. He obviously had been planning something else entirely.

What was she going to do without him? She would have to hire someone. Where would she get that kind of money? Perhaps she could find someone else sympathetic to the cause. A woman this time. She wasn't going to invest any more time and energy in men. With growing fury at Terence's defection, Lorna stalked off in the direction of the boardinghouse where he stayed.

Before she had marshalled all her arguments, she saw him walking toward her. They had grown up together, but she almost didn't recognize him as he approached. He was wearing a hat! He looked rather distinguished in the tall-crowned felt, but he didn't look like the rabble-rouser she knew. His hair was freshly barbered and looked polished and smooth in the light of the street lamp. The unusually warm air of the day was cooling, but he didn't wear an overcoat. She could see the glimmer of the gold chain of his pocket watch stretched across his vest. If she didn't know better, she'd think he was going courting.

He looked surprised to see her, but not as surprised as when she set into him.

"How could you?" Lorna stopped in front of him, not caring how it looked to see a plainly dressed woman accosting a gentleman. "I thought we were partners. I thought you believed in our cause as much as I do. Why are you doing this? Why here? What can you possibly hope to achieve by staying here in the middle of nowhere?"

Terence caught her arm and gently steered her back in the direction from which she had come. "I do believe in the cause, but I believe I can serve it better from here. I'm old enough now to realize I can't change the world, but I might be able to change some small part of it. I'll have the newspaper as a forum. Mr. Harris isn't entirely opposed to our view. We can print articles on the western states allowing women to vote, make it seem an acceptable thing. We can follow the trials of women who seek relief from their husbands' ill treatment. We can stop hiding the truth, promote women's rights, support the temperance committee. It will take time, but I believe I can make a difference."

"One small town isn't enough! We must spread the word nationwide. There are women and children dying out there! Terence, how could you desert them like this?" Lorna swung around to confront him.

He had no choice. He couldn't make her see when she was angry. He needed to calm her down, redirect her energies, show her how he felt. He caught her arms and lowered his head to hers.

Lorna didn't allow him to do more than press his mouth lightly against her lips. She shoved away and glared at him. "I'm not a silly little girl who will fall for your persuasive kisses, Terence. I thought we understood each other. I thought we might share something together. Obviously, I was wrong."

She stalked away, her outdated brown skirt trailing over the green spring grass that only days before had been dotted with dirty snow. Terence watched her go with an aching emptiness that he had never succeeded in filling. The tempestuous hustle and bustle of touring with Lorna had kept the hollow forgotten much of the time, but it had never gone away. He had hoped . . .

But the last of his hopes was walking away.

"Well, it's late. We'll bid you a good evening, Mr. Dillon. I'm sure we can trust Elizabeth to see you out." Smiling politely, Elizabeth's parents made their excuses and departed, leaving the courting couple momentarily alone.

Standing to see them go, Richard caught Elizabeth's hands as soon as her parents were out of sight. She was quite beautiful in the lamplight. The serene glow of her face was like that of a Madonna from an old work of art. She made no protest at his presumptuous move but merely waited for him to reveal his thoughts.

Nervously, he clasped their hands together. "Your parents are quite civil to me. I feared they would take umbrage at a stranger courting their daughter."

"They have confidence in my ability to make my own choices in friends."

She was somehow so distant from him that Richard did not know how to respond. It had been so easy to communicate with pen and paper, but now that he was here, holding her hands, he couldn't feel the same familiarity. There was nothing but this politeness between them. He knew she felt the same as he on many subjects, but intellectual discussions weren't sufficient basis for the kind of marriage he had in mind. He needed to draw them closer together, to feel the kindred spirit burning in her, the spirit that would make her agree to cross the country for him.

Helpless to know how to go on, Richard carefully bent to place a soft kiss on her lips. Elizabeth turned her head to his, allowing the liberty, and his heart soared. He pressed a little further, but she did not seem to know how to respond. With a small feeling of disappointment, he lifted his head again.

"Thank you for the lovely evening, Elizabeth. It is good to feel at home with someone as I do with you.

It has been a long time since I've known a proper home."

A smile flickered briefly across her face as she walked with him toward the door. "Everyone needs a home," she murmured. "Perhaps we are like plants and need to sink roots somewhere."

His thoughts instantly went to the golden crocus that had wilted into transparency almost immediately after plucking. He wished she had not conjured up that image. Not daring to do more in full view of the neighborhood, Richard touched his hand to Elizabeth's cheek as he stood in the doorway.

"We just need to find the proper soil, I suppose," he admitted. He tried to satisfy himself with the smile she bestowed upon him as he turned away, but it wasn't enough. He could feel the lack grinding somewhere deep inside. He wanted this woman to be his bride. He needed her quiet serenity to form the basis for the home he wished to have. He needed her companionship in the distant land he would soon call home. But he had the uneasy feeling that something wasn't right—something was missing, and he didn't know how to find it. He must be doing something wrong, but he didn't know what.

Pondering the matter, Richard nearly ran into Lorna on the next street. Or rather, she nearly ran into him. He caught her arms to steady her and didn't let them go as he looked down into her face. He could see tears shimmering in her eyes, and they disturbed him. He didn't think a woman as strong as Lorna cried.

"Why are men so stupid?" she cried before he had time to say anything. "Why are they so blind? Can we really be so different that we don't even speak the same language? Do we use the same words but have different meanings?"

Since his thoughts were traveling along much the same path, her words struck him forcefully. He kept his hold on her while he tried to find the proper response. "I think perhaps we do," he answered carefully. His legal training made him think an argument through step-by-step, but she wasn't giving him time to work his way clearly to a conclusion. "I think men are more of the world and think in wider meanings. Women are of the home, and their words are centered on what they know around them. 'Home' to a man could mean the city or state. To a woman, it means the house she lives in."

"Balderdash!" Lorna threw off his hands and glared at him. "I don't have a house to live in. I live in hotels and other people's houses. 'Home' has many meanings for me, just as it must for you. I just think men are deliberately obtuse when they speak to women."

Richard had the oddest urge to hug her and to laugh. She was so angry that he could almost see steam coming from her ears. Her red hair was definitely a fiery signal of her temperament. But instead of angering him, her temper made him feel more alive than he thought possible.

"And men think that women speak in riddles. How is it that we ever get along, do you think?"

"We don't!"

To Richard's dismay, her eyes puddled with tears again. Helpless, he reached out a hand to her, but she smacked it away.

"Just look around you." She swung her hand in a grandiose gesture. "Men keep their women locked up behind closed doors as if they were possessions, like their pianos and cookstoves. Do you think women like to be thought of as some kind of inanimate object to be smacked and pushed around at a man's whim? We have thoughts and feelings too, but do men ever question them? Of course not. Their only concerns are for themselves."

"You speak in generalizations. That's not always true. Much of the time we are prevented from talking with women as we would like. Like now. If you were a man, I could ask you to come with me and have a cup of coffee and talk. But you and I know that if we walked into a café at this hour, the whole town would talk and your reputation would be ruined. When would I be allowed the intimacy of having a private conversation with a woman? Not until we are married and stuck with each other. What happens if a man marries, only to find he and his wife have no common interests about which they could converse?"

Lorna stared at him. "A modern woman could go with you during the day. It is only this hour that makes it unseemly. Surely you and Elizabeth have much to discuss."

His smile was wry. "You and I have just said more in these few minutes than Elizabeth and I have discussed in days. Why is it I find it so much easier to speak with you than with the woman I wish to marry?"

Lorna opened her mouth and shut it again. Richard admired the way her face glowed with intelligence. She wasn't beautiful like Elizabeth, but the red of her hair and the simpleness of her gown spoke of a strong character, and the character appealed to him. She was tall enough to reach past his shoulder, but her waist was incredibly slender. He wanted to test it with his hands. The thought of his hands on her waist made him think of moving his hands even higher, and he found his gaze focusing on the proud swell of her breasts beneath the brown cloth. He gulped and forced his eyes back to her face.

Her cheeks were slightly pink, as if she knew what he was thinking. She didn't step away as she ought. She was a bold woman. Richard lifted one hand to her waist, as if to guide her somewhere.

She spoke hastily. "Terence is taking a job at the newspaper here. He wants to settle down. He asked me to marry him once. How could he ask to marry me and then leave me like this?"

"Did you tell him you would marry him?" he heard himself asking. But he was more interested in the way the gaslight flickered across the red of her hair and the way her supple waist felt beneath his hand. He wouldn't dare touch Elizabeth like this. That in itself gave him an odd sensation.

"I didn't tell him no," she whispered, looking away. "I think I'd better go."

She made no effort to leave. They were both too aware of the spring night. From somewhere, a warm breeze rippled their hair, and the sweet scent of a honeysuckle hedge was all around them. It seemed natural to be standing here like this. Richard wrapped his arm around her and led her to a bench nearly hidden by winter-bare shrubbery.

"Not yet. Perhaps we can help each other. If I can help you understand Terence, maybe you can help me understand Elizabeth. I'm afraid to even touch her as I'm touching you now."

He was brushing a straying strand of hair back from her face. Lorna turned to meet his gaze directly, without timidity. He liked that. She made it so easy for him. He felt none of the nervousness he did with Elizabeth. He didn't understand why. He just knew it was so. He bent and pressed a kiss to her mouth to see if she would respond as Elizabeth had.

It was nothing the same. She had wide, full lips that melted easily beneath his. Richard put his arms around her and pulled her closer, and she made no protest. She even brought her hands to his shoulders so they were better balanced as he bent her slightly into his embrace. He felt her slight gasp as he deepened their kiss, but she was warm and pliant and willing in his hands. This was what he had wanted. This was what he had expected.

This wasn't the woman he had expected it from. Slowly, reluctantly, Richard forced himself away from her. He stared down into startled eyes, guessing she was as amazed as he. He could almost feel their hearts beating in tandem. It was an impossible feeling. He scarcely knew this woman. She was nothing like what he wanted in a wife. This was just a momentary aberration, albeit an aberration that had already happened twice.

"Terence is a fool if he lets you go," he muttered furiously, not certain at whom the fury was directed. "I will tell him so if you like."

Lorna brushed her hands lightly against his shoulders, as if to steady herself, then pulled them back to her lap. She looked more thoughtful than shy after what had happened. "He wants what I cannot give him," she answered pensively. "I will never be the domestic wife he imagines. I think he would like to have the home and family he never had as a child; I should have seen that. Perhaps I'm the one who has been blind."

Richard held her hand in his. "What will you do now? You cannot go gallivanting about the countryside alone."

She attempted a small smile. "I will find some woman to travel with me, I suppose. It will be much more proper." She darted a look up to him. "If you kiss Elizabeth as you have kissed me, I don't think you'll have any trouble persuading her to do as you like."

Her words struck Richard like a blow in the stomach. She rose from the bench and he followed her, but she held out a hand to stay him.

"I can find my own way home. I need some time to myself, if you don't mind. Thank you for taking your time with me. Perhaps not all men are hopeless, after all."

She left him feeling bereft. It was as if he'd found something valuable, only to have it torn from his hands before he could appreciate what he'd found. She was an extraordinary woman. He had kissed her like a man possessed, and she'd not played the part of coy maiden afterward. Perhaps she had been kissed many times. But he'd seen the surprise in her eyes, and he didn't think so. She'd felt what he had, what he shouldn't have felt. And she was releasing him from obligation by walking away now. He wasn't at all certain that he wanted to be released.

Shaken to the core by the realization that all his careful plans could be coming asunder so easily, Richard slowly turned and walked back toward his boardinghouse. He needed time to straighten out his muddled thoughts.

"I have only the one more lecture, then I must make arrangements to leave. I've been interviewing several women for the position of travel companion, since Terence will be staying here." As they walked, Lorna trailed her gloved fingers along the frail greenery of a privet hedge coming to life. The fact that this childish gesture wasn't at all ladylike did not seem to concern her.

Elizabeth was more occupied with her cousin's words than her actions. "Surely you do not mean to leave so soon? I hoped, I thought ... Richard will be here only another month. I'd hoped you'd stay until we ..."

Lorna lifted auburn eyebrows as she glanced at her usually imperturbable cousin. "Until you married? Has he asked you yet?"

Elizabeth hesitated. The sky blazed a bright blue and a robin was singing somewhere close by. Spring was almost here. She had always thought to be married in the spring. "He hasn't asked, but he is very cautious. We have an understanding. It is just ... Well, there is so little time. If only we could be engaged for a little while, and then he could come back here and we could be married. But to marry, and then to move ... I'm not certain I'm strong enough."

"Perhaps you should marry and then he should go off to find a home for you. That would give you a little time to adjust, and he would know that he had a wife waiting for him."

"Perhaps that is it." She didn't sound very certain.

"I wish you would stay. I find it so easy to talk to you."

Lorna's better feelings battled with her lesser ones. For the moment, the better ones won. "You could write. I will send you my new address as soon as I have it. I won't travel very far, so that when you announce your wedding date, I can come here to see you married."

Elizabeth sent her a worried look. "What about Terence? I thought maybe you and he ..."

Lorna shrugged. "It would never work; I see that now. He is my very best friend, and I wish him happiness, but I could never live here. I need travel and excitement and adventure. I need people who think like I do. I need new places and new ideas. Even if I settled down and did nothing but write, can you imagine how the ladies here would think of me? Terence needs a wife who will fit in, who will attend teas and report to him so he knows all the news. He needs a helpmate, not a rebel."

It was a brilliant day, with all the prospects of the future before them, but neither appeared happy with their plans. Elizabeth played wistfully with a pussy willow branch she had plucked, and Lorna stared morosely at the road ahead.

Their wandering thoughts were interrupted by a woman who rushed from a side street to greet them. It took them a moment to recognize the drooping feather and worn velvet, but the woman's words told them who she was without introduction.

"I have come to pay back the first dollar on my loan," she said eagerly, pressing a crushed and folded bill into Lorna's hand. "You will see that it goes to the gentleman, won't you? I can't thank you enough for what you did for me. I have more orders now than I have time to fill. I actually raised my prices and the orders still come in! If only I had a bigger stove and someone to help, I could do twice as much business. I'm setting aside a little every day so I can put a down payment on a new stove, and to pay back the loan, and I still have enough left to buy little extras."

Lorna shook the woman's hands. "That's marvelous! And how is your husband doing? Is he working again? Does he mind your working now?"

Some of the happiness drained from the woman's face, but she managed a brave smile. "He's found a job out of town. He comes home on Sundays." She bit her lip and looked down at her feet. "I haven't told him what I'm doing." She looked up again at the silence greeting her statement. "But I will, I promise. I just wanted to be certain that I could do it all on my own. It's not as if I'm working for someone else, now, is it? I'm my own boss, and I work at home. Now that he's working again, I think he'll understand. I mean to buy him one of those cigars he likes so much, and surprise him with it when he comes home. Then I'll tell him how I earned the money."

The woman hurried away shortly after that. Lorna and Elizabeth exchanged looks.

Lorna was the first to speak. "I refuse to marry if I must ask my husband's permission to do something I enjoy. Women aren't children who must be guided by a man's supposed wisdom."

"I thought when people married, it meant they loved each other and wanted each other to be happy. Why can it not be that way?"

Lorna gave her a sharp look. "Do you love Richard? Has he said he loves you?"

Elizabeth picked at one of the fuzzy buds on the branch. "Mama says these things come with marriage. If you trust and respect a man when you marry, you will come to love him afterward."

"You just saw an example of the fallacy of that," Lorna pointed out. "Women may marry because they must, but that does not mean they will ever come to love their spouses. I trust and respect Terence, but I'll never love him as more than a brother. Once I thought that might be enough, but I realize it's not now."

Elizabeth gave her cousin a swift, terrified look, then returned to demolishing her branch. "How will you know if you love a man?"

Lorna turned around and began a brisk stride back toward the house. "When I'm insane enough to want to carry a man's baby, then I'll know I'm either ready to be locked up, or I must be in love."

Elizabeth laughed, but it was a weak imitation of her usual laughter.

"Do you usually attend church on Sunday, sir?" Elizabeth twirled her parasol and looked up at the man walking by her side. He looked very distinguished in his new outfit, and she wondered if she had worn it to impress Lorna. She was sorry if that was so. Lorna hadn't attended services.

"You must call me Terence as your cousin does, and no, I do not usually attend because we are so often on the road. I thought the time had come to change my ways."

Elizabeth brightened. "Then you really do mean to stay! That is wonderful."

He gave her a look of curiosity. "I told you I meant to take the position at the newspaper. Did you think I would change my mind?"

She turned her head to glance up the road and away from him. "Lorna was so adamant ... I thought perhaps she might change your mind."

Terence tucked her arm firmly in the crook of his. "Lorna and I grew up together, but we've grown apart these last few years. We can always hope she will consider this her home and come back to visit, but I don't expect more."

Elizabeth gave him a fleeting look of alarm at his tone and his touch, but then the sight ahead of them distracted her. "Look, there is Lorna with Richard. They must have come to meet us."

The two were in deep discussion but looked up and waved at Elizabeth's call. They hurried forward, and

Richard properly took Elizabeth's arm, relieving Terence of his duty. She was left somewhat uneasy by this change of position, perhaps knowing that Terence and Lorna no longer wished to remain together as a couple. But though they did not touch, they did not seem awkward with the situation as they fell into step.

"Lorna tells me you wished to go bicycling if the weather was fair, but I haven't found enough bicycles to rent. I thought perhaps we could just stroll through the park, then stop at the drugstore for sodas later. Will that be a sufficient substitute?"

Elizabeth smiled obligingly. "We will ruin our dinners. Mother expects us all to come eat with them. Perhaps we can save the sodas for afterward."

The conversation suddenly seemed stilted and polite, but she couldn't understand why. These people were all her friends. They had much in common and there should be plenty of topics to converse on. But there seemed to be a strain between them that she could not identify. Richard didn't seem to be quite listening to her, and Terence and Lorna had nothing to say to each other. She sought for some common topic.

"Did Lorna tell you that Mrs. Slovoski has become very successful in her baking business? Your generous loan has been well utilized."

Richard frowned slightly. "I am still not comfortable with interfering in the lives of others. What if her husband objects? It looked to me as if she had been beaten before."

Lorna turned around to look back at him. "But now she has the confidence to leave him if she must. That is the whole point!" Her eyes widened at the sight of something over their shoulders.

Before more than a gasp could escape her, Richard was looking behind him to see what she saw. The sight of a man carrying a shotgun on this lovely spring day was a trifle jarring, but he saw no immediate reason for alarm. He tugged slightly on Elizabeth's arm to

keep her walking away from the man. There as no
point in taking chances.

"Hold up there!" The shout echoed from behind
them as they entered the iron gates of the park.

This time, Terence turned to look also. Without hesitation, he grabbed the arms of both women and
shoved them behind him as he stepped forward to
stand beside Richard.

"Hold it there!" the man screamed, approaching
rapidly and removing his gun from his shoulder. His
words were slurred with drink and a heavy accent, but
the shotgun spoke for him.

"Run," Richard whispered to the women. "We'll
handle this."

"I will not," Lorna responded angrily from behind
him. "There are four of us. What can he do?" She
bent to pick up a rock lining the walk.

"I come to get my wife back." The man lurched as
he stepped up to the walk from the street. His heavy
work clothes were stained and tattered, and his eyes
showed the red of heavy drinking, but he was a large
man and a formidable adversary. The shotgun he held
aimed at them made him doubly dangerous. He glared
blearily, trying to aim at the women. "Tell me where
she is," he demanded.

He swayed, and the shotgun nearly dropped from
his hands. Elizabeth gave a scream of fright, and cursing, Terence turned around and shoved them behind
a brick column of the park fence. Richard bravely held
his place.

"We don't know you or your wife," he said calmly.
"We've just come from church. Would she have
been there?"

"She's gone! That troublemakin' woman gave her
big ideas. Who's goin' to fix my dinner now? I'm goin'
to kill her!" He waved the shotgun wildly, trying to
fix his aim on the women, who seemed to have disappeared into a brick wall.

"You can't leave Richard out there all alone,"

Lorna whispered hysterically, pushing at Terence. "It's me he's looking for. Let me out there!"

"You stay put or I'll tan your hide," Terence informed her impolitely. "I'm going over the wall to get behind him. You do anything to distract him, and I'll go after you with a shotgun too."

Elizabeth grabbed her cousin's arm as they cowered behind the column. "Listen to him, or you might risk their lives."

Terence gave her a brief nod of gratitude, then pulled himself onto the wall. He disappeared over the other side, leaving the women to watch the scene unfolding with anxiety. The park was deserted at this hour on a Sunday. Elizabeth was torn between the wish for someone to arrive and save them and the fear that an innocent bystander would stumble upon them and be killed. Her greater fear was for the two men bravely trying to hold off the drunken husband until he could be calmed down.

"Get out of my way!" the man was screaming in guttural tones. "If I can't have a wife, you won't either!"

Elizabeth gulped as she saw Terence move silently behind the man. Richard must see him too, but she couldn't imagine what either man could do. The shotgun was aimed directly at Richard's heart. Her own heart pounded furiously in fear.

"I can't let them do this," Lorna whispered behind her.

Before Elizabeth could stop her, Lorna stepped out of the bushes and from behind the column. "You want me, come and get me, Mr. Slovoski," she called.

The sudden distraction brought the shotgun swinging upward. Richard ducked and dived at the man's legs at the same time as Terence leapt on him from behind. The combination assault threw the man backward, and the shotgun exploded into the air.

Elizabeth screamed and grabbed a fallen branch from the ground. While fists flailed and the men strug-

gled to hold their attacker before he could fire another
barrel, she came at him with the heavy branch. Lorna
approached from the other side, wielding her stone.

As the big man roared in drunken rage, stumbling
to his feet to throw off his assailants, Lorna smacked
his head with the rock and Elizabeth hit his arm with
her stick. He roared again, but with less power. Richard grabbed the gun and jerked it away, giving Terence the chance to drive his fist into the man's chin.
Slovoski swayed and hit the ground.

The street suddenly seemed to fill with people
drawn by the shotgun blast. As men hurried to surround the fallen drunk, Richard turned and caught a
white-faced Lorna before she could follow the rock
she'd dropped to the ground.

"My word, that was brilliant!" he cried, hugging her
to him. "You distracted him at just the right moment."

She murmured something less than comprehensible,
clung to his coat, and stared as a policeman came to
slap handcuffs on their assailant.

Terence quickly stepped over the prone figure to gently remove the stick from Elizabeth's frozen fingers. She
looked up at him helplessly as the stick fell away.

"Are you all right? I'm going to have to kill that
blasted redhead for nearly getting you killed, but let
me see you home first. You shouldn't be exposed to
this kind of thing." Terence caught Elizabeth's hands
in one of his and used his other arm to guide her
around the growing crowd.

She cast a quick look over her shoulder to where
Richard was comforting a terrified Lorna, and nodding
carefully, she allowed herself to be led away. She
didn't know herself right now. She certainly couldn't
claim to know what was going on in anyone else's
head. She just knew she wanted to go home, and this
man was taking her there.

"It's all going to be all right," Richard said soothingly, taking Lorna in his arms in the dark shadows

of the porch that evening. "I've talked to the police. Mr. Slovoski will be behind bars for some time to come, certainly enough to dry him out a little. His wife was with neighbors. He tried to beat her, but this time she had the sense to run. I've advised her on what steps she can take against her husband if she wishes. I can't do more than that. At least now she has the means to support herself. That should give her enough confidence to think clearly."

Lorna stood in the circle of his arms and rested her head on his shoulder. "Having a lawyer around could become very comforting, I think. But you frightened me to death out there today. I thought he would shoot you to get at me."

"Terence is still ready to skin you alive for jumping out like that. He cares a great deal for you, you know." There was a question in his voice that could not be expressed in words.

"I know, and I care for him, but it's not the same, is it?" Lorna asked wistfully, pulling slightly away from him. "I had better let you go up to Elizabeth. Aunt Jane insisted that she go to bed, but she's rested now and waiting for you."

Richard skimmed his hand across her cheek. "There are things I want to say, but I don't feel free to do so. But today reminded me very forcefully that we have only one life to live. We ought to live it as fully as we can. I don't think I've been doing that. I never expected to have much in my life, but now I want everything, and I'll not give up until I have what I want. Will you wait for me here while I go up to see Elizabeth?"

Lorna didn't know what to say. She thought she understood him, but she didn't trust her own judgment any longer. And she couldn't bear to hurt Elizabeth— not gentle, trusting Elizabeth. Yet ... She looked up into this man's eyes and wished she could read the future. He was a strong man, one who would want his way in everything. He would go to California because that was where his future lay. He harbored an affection for Elizabeth, but was affection enough to comfort her cousin when she was so far from home?

Lorna prayed Richard knew what he was doing. She nodded her head. "I'll wait. If I know him, Terence will be here shortly. I'd rather he not yell at me inside."

He brushed a kiss across her cheek, then lightly across her lips. She shivered at the touch, then watched him stride determinedly inside. She wouldn't allow the yearning she felt to cause her to do anything foolish. She could stand on her own. She didn't need anyone.

Terence came striding up the walk some minutes later. His figure was so familiar to her that she could recognize him in the dark, and she smiled. She could even recognize his mood from the way he walked. He had made up his mind about something and was about to lay down the law. She really ought to let him go inside and make a fool of himself, but Richard and Elizabeth deserved this time together. She whistled softly to catch his attention.

He immediately diverted his path and found her in the shadows. "What are you doing out here? You'll freeze. It's scarcely spring and you act like it's summer."

"You always did treat me as if I were a little girl without any sense, Terence. I'm quite warm, thank you. I wanted to tell you how proud I was of you today before you started yelling at me."

He caught her hands and found them wrapped warmly in heavy gloves. "You could have got us all killed, you realize."

"You could have got yourself and Richard killed. I didn't think that any better. Let us not argue tonight. I want to remember you as my good friend. I'm going to have to leave shortly, and I want to ask you a favor."

He searched her face in the darkness, catching some glimmer of the seriousness of her expression from the lights behind the curtained windows. "You know you can ask anything of me."

She smiled. "You're my best friend, Terence, and Elizabeth is my dearest cousin. If things don't work out between her and Richard, will you look after her? She is meant to be someone's wife, but I don't think she's meant to be the adventuring sort. I very much fear that she will be like that flower she told us about. If he tries to uproot her, she will wither and die."

Terence grew still. He clasped her hands tightly and threw a glance upward to the light in an upper-story window. Then he returned his gaze to Lorna. "He's with her now? Will he ask for her hand?"

"If he does, I think she will put him off. She's not ready to leave home yet. It will be very difficult for them."

He breathed a sigh of relief and released her. "No, it won't. I'll settle the matter now. He's too strong-minded for a gentle soul like Elizabeth. She'll listen to me."

He seemed so sure of himself as he strode toward the door that Lorna had to laugh and call after him, "What about Richard? If he's so strong-minded, don't you fear he will carry her off with him? He really does want to marry, you know."

"Then he can marry you, damn it," he answered as he pounded on the door knocker. "The two of you deserve each other."

That was as much of a blessing as he was likely to give her, Lorna mused as someone answered the door and let him in. But it was enough. She only hoped she had not mistaken Elizabeth's feelings. Her very proper, very demure cousin had been hanging on to Terence for dear life today. Terence, not Richard. Surely she would not have done that if there wasn't already something between them. Please, don't let it be wishful thinking, she prayed.

Restless, unable to stand still, Lorna wandered out into the yard. Glancing upward, she saw the silhouette of a couple outlined in the sitting room window. Her heart fell to her feet as the couple embraced. She had so hoped . . .

She turned away, unable to bear the surge of pain. She had not thought it would have mattered so much. She had known him only a few weeks. It had been foolish to think a man like that would want a red-headed hellion for a wife. He would never have a moment's peace. He was much better off with Elizabeth. She would be a good wife for him. She felt sorry for Terence, but he would find someone else. He was a good man. He would find a good woman.

She heard the clatter of shoes on the porch steps, and she swung around, startled. A glance told her the couple was still in the upstairs window. She didn't know if she could bear to feel Terence's disappointment along with her own. She didn't call out to him but stood motionless, waiting.

"Lorna!" The voice was anxious, frantic. "Lorna? Are you out here?"

She glanced back to the window, then to the man striding across the lawn. It couldn't be. Her heart pounded helplessly. "Richard?" she called in disbelief.

His strong arms wrapped around her and lifted her recklessly from the ground. "You know what I want to do with you, don't you?"

"With me?" she squealed as he swung her around in a mad circle.

"With you." He lowered her until their mouths met.

Her head was spinning from more than his whirling around. She clung to his shoulders and parted her lips and felt the power of his kiss all the way to her toes.

Richard brought her down against him and wrapped her tightly in his arms, pulling his coat around her so she felt nothing but the warmth of his body. Never had she felt so sheltered and secure as she did now.

"I want to marry you, then I want to kiss you until you're putty in my hands, and then I'm going to take you to my bed and make wild love to you. Am I scorching your delicate ears yet?" he whispered into one of the aforementioned items.

"More than my ears." Her cheeks flamed and her body ached and she was certain she was already melting.

"Good. Now tell me you'll be my wife and go to California with me to convert the sinners and raise the flag for women's suffrage. We'll be good together, I promise. I'll bail you out of jail and defend your ladies and you'll keep me from becoming a boring, pompous old fool."

"Really? You'll really do all that? You won't mind if I'm called names and half of society thinks I'm a rabid madwoman? You don't mind that I'm not pretty like Elizabeth? You can't have thought this through. Put me down, Richard. You need time. Elizabeth hurt you." She struggled to pull away.

He raised a hand to find her breast. She wasn't wearing a corset. Sighing with unmitigated delight, Richard caressed the full curves his hand discovered until she quivered in his arms and forgot to pull away.

"Elizabeth is a lovely woman, and I wouldn't hurt her for the world, but we both know she'll be happier here. You and I are different. We need new horizons. Elizabeth didn't hurt me, but you can. I never thought I'd have the nerve to say this to any woman, Lorna, but I love you. You're the only woman I could ever love. You're the only woman I could ever talk to. And you're the only woman I want to make love to for the rest of my life." This last he whispered in her ear as he bent his head to kiss her into acquiescence.

"Thornbushes transplant easier than crocuses, I guess," she murmured moments later.

"I think I've found a rose among the thorns. Was that a yes?" He ran his hand deep into the upsweep of her hair and held her tight.

"That's a yes, my love. Just don't ever write me a letter that begins 'dearest sister.' "

He laughed, and the embracing couple on the lawn complemented the one silhouetted in the window above, while the spring breeze sent the yellow heads of a patch of crocuses to nodding sleepily in their beds.

Hyacinths for Victoria

🍎

by Patricia Oliver

1. April Showers

The pale April sun, which had accompanied Lady Victoria Lovelace over the forty-odd miles of country roads that separated Tunbridge Wells from Ashford, faltered in its brave battle with the encroaching clouds. As the deep maroon traveling chaise passed beneath the imposing stone archway leading into Ashford Grange, the sun gave up the fight, and the two occupants of the coach heard the first drops of the impending shower splatter on the highly varnished roof.

The elderly prune-faced female, who sat with her back towards the horses, sniffed audibly. "I warned you how it would be, milady," she remarked in tones that implied she was inured to having her advice consistently disregarded. "April is a most unreliable month and cannot be depended upon to provide the mild weather one naturally associates with springtime."

"You are quite right, Peckham," Victoria said absentmindedly. "As I recall, you did warn me that we were in for another shower."

In point of fact, she had not been thinking of her abigail's weather prognosis at all. No sooner had the intimidating stone entrance to Ashford Grange loomed over the carriage than Victoria's thoughts had flown back to quite another April afternoon seven years ago, the last time she had passed between these same imposing pillars bearing the family crest of the dukes of Ashford. Back then it had been a joyous occasion, she remembered. On April the fifteenth she would celebrate her eighteenth birthday, which was also to be her wedding day. And she had been accompanied by her dearest papa, who waxed eloquent on the matrimonial coup of the Season he had achieved for his youngest daughter.

Victoria had to smile as she remembered Lord Bradley's delighted amazement—almost as great as her own, for that matter—when he discovered that his little Victoria had bagged the catch of that year's Marriage Mart. Though how either of them could claim any credit for bringing the affair to such a gratifying conclusion, Victoria was hard put to imagine. Although accustomed to a certain amount of attention at the local assemblies held in the neighborhood of her father's estate near Cranbrook, Victoria had not for a moment expected that her ethereal fairness and small figure—far too small for real elegance, her mother had often enough repeated—would make more than a faint ripple in the modish circles of London's *haute monde*. Had she not been a notable heiress, Victoria had often thought with no hint of rancor, she might have faded gracefully into the ranks of the less fortunate young ladies who were making their come-out that Season.

The very fact that she had come to London at all that spring was the result of pure chance, Victoria remembered. The widowed Earl of Bradley had little patience for the exhausting round of social activity associated with London, and was in no hurry to lose his youngest daughter, whom he considered far too tender for the trials of matrimony. Had it not been for her cousin Alexandra Howard, who had, at the advanced age of nineteen, firmly refused to venture

into the maelstrom of a London Season without the
support of her cousin Victoria, the latter might have
spent her eighteenth birthday at Ashford Grange as
she had so many others, and the debacle of that particular April afternoon seven years ago would never
have occurred.

But Alexandra had prevailed, and Victoria's father
had yielded to the inevitable. A taste of the *ton* might
give his darling daughter a little Town bronze, he had
agreed, Victoria recalled. And so she had gone to
London, possessed of an alarming array of gowns and
feminine fripperies for every conceivable occasion.
Her doting papa had insisted upon doing the pretty for
his favorite daughter, she remembered, her expression
softening at the memory of that gentle man who had
supported her unhesitatingly in the hour of her greatest distress.

Victoria sighed, her thoughts full of heartbreak and
betrayal again, despite her resolution to dwell firmly
on the present rather than on the past. Unfortunately,
the past would not be entirely banished and, if truth
be told, that harrowing Season contained some of her
most treasured memories. It was in London, of course,
that she had first seen Derek Seymour, then Viscount
Hardwicke, and the answer to every young girl's
dreams.

Derek. The mere recollection of his name brought
a shudder of mixed emotions to her small frame. Victoria pulled the scarlet velvet cloak trimmed with bea-
ver closer around her shoulders.

"Are you cold, milady?" Peckham inquired solici-
tously, her wrinkled countenance becoming even more
creased as worry lines appeared on her forehead. For
all her abigail's starchy demeanor, Victoria knew from
long experience that the aging Peckham was devoted
to her mistress's well-being. It had been Peckham who
had contrived to get her packed and out of the Grange
in the early hours of the dawn following the crumbling
of all Victoria's dreams of happiness and love.

She smiled. "Not really. I am rather looking forward to seeing everyone again," she remarked. "It's been so long. . . ." She let her words trail off into silence.

"Far too long, if you ask me, milady," the abigail grumbled. " 'Tain't right to cut you off from your family. I said so then, and I'll say it again, milady."

"I cut myself off," Victoria reminded her gently. They had this argument every year when the annual celebration for her great-aunt, Lady Letitia Richardson, came up, as it always did of course, since Lady Letitia shared the same day of birth as her great-niece, Victoria Letitia Lovelace, who also happened to be her favorite godchild. For the first time in seven years, Victoria thought with relief, she had not been obliged to dredge up some plausible excuse for not attending the traditional birthday party for her dear Aunt Letty. Not that Lady Letitia had believed a single one of them, of course, and so she had informed her godchild every year, chiding Victoria—in her none too subtle way—for being a silly peagoose to ostracize herself from her friends and family merely because some irresponsible and undoubtedly totty-headed journalistic hack had publicly labeled her a jilt. Victoria had to smile at her godmother's staunch support, but there could be no obscuring the unsavory truth: Lady Victoria Lovelace was indeed a jilt.

"Well," the abigail muttered testily, "it should never have happened, I always said. But this year things will be different. Mark my words, milady. Things will be back to normal again."

Normal? Victoria repeated bitterly to herself. How could anything ever be normal again? Derek had changed everything in her life, right from the moment she laid eyes on his broad shoulders and thatch of unruly dark hair, which curled so romantically about his elegant cravat. She remembered as though it had been yesterday. It had happened at Lady Littlefield's opening ball of the Season, Victoria's first real London ball. And although the Metropolis had been a little thin of company, there had been enough of London's *haute monde* in attendance to dazzle the country-bred young lady she had been then. Lord Bradley had been her escort, and Victoria had felt very grown-up and wonderfully *à la mode* in her slim white satin gown with its over-gown of silver-spangled ivory net. She had danced with her papa and suddenly noticed that several of the exquisitely gowned matrons in scandalously low décolletages were casting inviting glances his way. She had teased him about it but secretly yearned to scratch their eyes out for daring to look at her papa that way.

And then her eyes had settled on Viscount Hardwicke, and her papa had been forgotten. The viscount had been dancing with the Pentergast chit, she recalled, a vision of auburn-haired loveliness in a gown of shimmering amber satin that was far too mature for her, Victoria had thought at the time. And he was smiling lazily down at Miss Pentergast, who looked as though she were ready to swoon with pure ecstasy. Victoria's heart had done a swift somersault, and she had gazed her fill for several long minutes, hoarding the sight of him away in her memory to incorporate into her romantical dreams when she returned to Kent. Not for a moment had she entertained the slightest illusion that such a spectacular specimen of masculine beauty would waste a second glance on *her*. So she had memorized every muscular line of his lithe body, every plane of his lean face, and tucked it away in her mind for future enjoyment in private, then proceeded to dance with several eager young men Lady Littlefield had introduced to her. When it came time for the supper dance, which she had promised to her papa, they had been interrupted by a deep voice from behind her, which she knew—although she had never heard it before—to be *his*.

"Lord Bradley," he said politely, "dare I hope that you might permit me to dance with your lovely daughter?"

It all sounded so innocuous—a dozen other gentlemen had pronounced almost identical words—but Victoria had known instantly that it was no such thing, for her papa had paused for a long moment to stare intently at the viscount before he replied. "Hardwicke! How are you, my boy? I trust your parents are well? I had hoped to meet them here in Town."

"My mother has been plagued by a lingering cold, my lord," the deep voice responded pleasantly. "So my father and I have only yesterday escorted her up from Hampshire. I am sure she will be pleased to hear that you have finally come to enjoy the London Season, my lord." He had looked down at Victoria then, and her papa had introduced her and relinquished his dance to the younger man.

After that things had happened with lightning suddenness, and so unexpectedly that Victoria had been thrown into a romantical haze of bliss. She had found herself caught up in a frantic whirlwind of balls, routs, venetian breakfasts, theater engagements; always with Derek at her side, gazing down at her with his lazy smile, catching up her fingers for furtive kisses, his warm hand on her elbow, her waist, her blushing cheek. And then that first stolen kiss in the wooded copse at Mrs. Stanton's *fête champêtre*.

Victoria had strayed into the small grove, looking for wild hyacinths, her favorite spring flower. And Derek had followed her there, twitting her on the color of her eyes, which rivaled the blue of the hyacinths. Or so he said. She had smiled at him, she remembered, mesmerized by the warm glow of love in his amber eyes. She had told him about the hundreds of hyacinths growing on her papa's estate, great drifts of them on the slopes around the lake, and even mentioned their Latin name of *scilla,* hoping in her childish way to impress him with her erudition. But the viscount had only laughed at her—hearing not a word of what she said, she could have sworn—and put his arms around her. She had blushed furiously, Victoria re-

membered, but made no protest when he brushed her
lips with his. He had spoken with her father that very
morning, he said, and everything was agreed upon.
It wanted only her consent—would she please, *please*
consent, he begged—to make him the happiest man
alive. He had slipped his ring on her unresisting finger,
a blue topaz ringed with diamonds—hyacinth-blue to
match her eyes, he had said. How could she resist the
net of magic he had woven about her? It was a fairy
tale come true, a seductive dream from which she had
not emerged until that dreadful day when . . .

But no, she thought crossly. She was not about to
spoil her first birthday at the Grange in seven years
with memories of that rogue's perfidy. Much better to
remember the incident as a lesson in the consequences
of a young girl's naive infatuation. Although Victoria
knew in her heart of hearts that it had been no mere
infatuation. She had fallen in love with the Viscount
Hardwicke—with Derek, as he had insisted she call
him—and the intensity of that emotion had illumi-
nated her life with its purity and brilliance. It had been
the kind of love she had dreamed of, and Derek had
been the ideal Prince Charming. She had worshipped
him with the pure, single-minded devotion that only
an innocent such as she could have imagined for a
moment would appeal to a man of the viscount's
worldliness. Doubtless he had tired of her innocent
adulation, she thought with the clarity of hindsight.
Perhaps if she had been less innocent, she might not
have been so frightened. Perhaps if he . . . Perhaps if
she . . .

But it was no use repining, Victoria told herself impatiently for the umpteenth time. All that might have
been was now in the past. She must concentrate on
the future. Such as it was.

The Countess of Kennaway gazed up at the ominous gray sky as she descended the front steps of the
Kennaway town house on Berkeley Square shortly be-

fore ten o'clock that April morning, and shook her blond head in dismay. Lord Kennaway, who stood beside the open door of the elegant traveling chaise, waiting to settle his mother into the highly polished vehicle, noted her anxious glance at the sky and smiled at the maternal arguments he knew he would have to fob off, as he did every year at this time when the April weather did not live up to her ladyship's expectations.

"One would think we were still in the middle of winter," Lady Fanny exclaimed crossly as she placed her small gloved hand in his and prepared to take her seat in the carriage. She paused, as the earl had known she would, and gazed up at him with a coaxing smile on her lovely face. "You really would be far more comfortable in the carriage with me, my dear, than driving with cousin Robert in that silly curricle of his."

"Would you have poor Monroyal drive all the way down to Ashford by himself, my lady?" he chided gently, raising his mother's gloved fingers to his lips and gazing at her with a wicked gleam in his eyes. "What a heartless wench you are, my love. Shame on you."

"That is no way to address your mother, Derek," the countess reprimanded him. "And naturally my invitation was intended to include the marquess as well. There is plenty of room for all of us."

Kennaway raised a dark eyebrow and grinned down at his mother. "And you would have your abigail sit on his lordship's lap, I suppose," he teased. "I can guarantee that Robert would enjoy that immensely."

The countess jerked her hand away and slapped at his sleeve. "Can you never be serious about anything, Derek?" she said with a moue of annoyance. "You know how I worry about you taking a chill. Remember what happened to your father. . . ." Her words trailed off, and the earl knew that his mother still missed his father, who had indeed succumbed two years ago to a lung congestion brought on by a chill contracted while out shooting grouse in the rain.

He looked up at the lowering sky. "It is not yet raining, Mama," he remarked cheerfully. "And perhaps it will not do so. April is notoriously fickle, as you well know. If it does indeed shower, I promise to stop at the nearest inn and drink a hot toddy. Does that not sound eminently sensible?"

Fickle indeed, he thought disgustedly. How well he knew the fickleness of April. It was a month he detested. And even more than that, he detested the obligatory pilgrimage down to Ashford Grange every year to celebrate Lady Richardson's birthday on April the fifteenth. The devil fly away with all such family traditions anyway. If the old dragon had not been his mother's favorite aunt, he would have stopped attending years ago. Seven years ago, to be more precise. He suddenly realized that the countess was staring at him strangely and forced himself to smile.

"You are a sad trial to me, Derek," she said, and he saw her lovely blue eyes cloud with sadness. The earl knew that his mother was not referring to the weather, or to their imminent journey into Kent, or even to the state of his health. This argument, too, they had had many times before.

"Let us not discuss that now, Mama," he said rather brusquely. "When the time comes, I will do my duty to the family, never fear."

The countess sighed. "You say that every year, Derek. And every year I grow older and have nothing to show for it. I swear to you, my dear, if you do not give me a grandchild soon, I shall accept old Noddy's offer and go off to live with him in Scotland, and wash my hands of you."

This piece of news caused the earl to stare at his mother rather intently. "Are you telling me that Noddleton finally came up to scratch, Mama?" he demanded, startled at the unpleasant prospect of losing his mother to Lord Noddleton, an unfaltering admirer of hers even before her marriage to his father over thirty years ago. "Surely you are bamming me, love?"

"Nothing of the sort," Lady Fanny answered shortly. "Dear Noddy has made me four offers over the past year, and the next time he does so, I have a fancy to accept. I am tired of rattling around in that huge house of yours all by myself. At least Noddy will not abandon me to go jauntering off to Spain at the drop of a hat."

"I went on government business, Mama, as you well know," Kennaway pointed out patiently. "I thought you would be glad that I managed to get home in time to escort you down to Ashford. I hadn't expected to be back for another month, you know."

"I know, dear," the countess said with some asperity. "No doubt you had hoped to be detained in Madrid for a full month." She threw him a roguish glance from under her long lashes. "And don't try to deny it, Derek. I know you too well. Even Robert didn't expect to see you back so soon, and the dear boy had already offered to escort me, you know."

"What had I offered to do, my lady?" A tall gentleman dressed in a voluminous driving coat embellished by at least twelve capes, impeccably fitted cream cord breeches, and Hessians polished to a radiance that spoke volumes for the industry of his valet, alighted from the bright yellow curricle, which had appeared out of nowhere and drawn up with a flourish behind the traveling chaise. "Am I late, my dear Lady Fanny?" he inquired, bowing gracefully over the countess's hand.

"As always, Robert," her ladyship replied with a laugh. "I was just telling my wastrel son here that he need not have left all those Spanish beauties languishing in Madrid just to rush back to England to escort his poor old mother down to Kent this year."

Derek met his cousin's eyes over his mother's elegantly coiffed head and grinned. "Her ladyship has just delivered her yearly lecture on the duties and obli-

gations of the heads of noble houses, namely mine. I
have assured her that I intend to comply when I reach
a stable and responsible age, probably forty-five or
-six—another ten years at least, I should imagine.''

The Marquess of Monroyal let out a gasp of mock
horror. "Oh, no! Never say you will succumb to parson's mousetrap so early in your promising career,
Derek. For myself, I intend to follow old Ridgeway's
example and wait until I am fifty or more.''

"Pshaw!" exclaimed Lady Kennaway disgustedly.
"You are a worse rake than my son, Robert. And if
you want some chit like Honoria Littleton to make a
complete fool of you as she did to the Duke of
Ridgeway, then I'm glad I won't be around to witness
your decline into senility. And that goes for you, too,
Derek. I shall insist that dear Alexandra invite Noddy
down to Ashford immediately to comfort me.'' With
this dire warning, the countess stepped into the chaise
with an angry flounce, leaving the earl to shrug his
shoulders and swing himself up into the yellow curricle
beside Lord Monroyal.

"What set off that explosion?'' the marquess inquired as soon as his team of flashy bays had crossed
Westminster Bridge and turned south towards Rochester. "Not still harping on that unfortunate affair with
the Lovelace chit, is she?''

When Kennaway made no answer, the marquess
glanced at his cousin and shrugged. "Must have been
all of six years ago, if I remember correctly,'' he added
encouragingly.

"Seven,'' came the curt reply.

No sooner had he spoken that Derek cursed himself
for revealing just how closely he had counted the years
since that other birthday celebration at the country
seat of the dukes of Ashford. He had been eager—
impatient, actually—to get down to Kent, and had
fumed at his parents for dawdling at the King's Head
Inn in Rochester for refreshments. His mother had
teased him, he remembered, until he had finally flung

out of the inn and ridden *vent-à-terre* down to Ashford, almost foundering his horse in the process.

The April sun had shone brilliantly that year, and he had taken it for a good omen. What a blind fool he had been. All his closest friends, Monroyal and Simon Weatherby—the present Duke of Ashford—among them, had done their best to dissuade him, but Derek had listened to no one. How he wished now that he had! But he had thrown advice and caution to the winds that night of Lady Littlefield's ball when he had first laid eyes on that diminutive, ethereal chit with huge hyacinth eyes and hair of spun silver. She had reminded him vividly of a fairy princess from one of those children's books he had more than once been called upon to read aloud to his nieces at bedtime.

He had found out that she was Bradley's youngest daughter, and that her name—Derek grimaced as he recalled it—was Victoria Leticia, and that she was that old dragon Lady Richardson's grand-niece. He had lost no time in approaching her, and her father, the earl, had given him a long, level look before relinquishing his daughter into Derek's care. In that calculating look Derek had seen the Earl of Bradley weighing Viscount Hardwicke's—as he had been then—somewhat notorious reputation as a confirmed rake against the indubitable benefits of the viscount's title and wealth as his father's heir. What had tipped the scales in his favor, Derek was later convinced, was Lord Bradley's long-standing friendship with the Earl of Kennaway, Derek's father. And so he had danced the supper dance with her, and later led her in to supper, and claimed a second dance immediately, a waltz, he thought, remembering the delicate grace of her and the smell of hyacinths that clung to his memory long after her father had carried her off home.

And three weeks later she was his affianced bride.

"You are mighty quiet today, old man," Monroyal remarked as he swung his team into the yard of the King's Head and tossed the ribbons to a stable-lad. "I don't know about you, but I've worked up quite a thirst. Join me for a tankard of ale?''

Glancing about him at the familiar thatched roof and cobblestone yard of the posting-inn, Derek stepped down and followed Monroyal into the low-ceilinged taproom, where old Mr. Hudson, the inn-keeper, welcomed the two gentlemen effusively. They took their ale into the private parlor, where they were joined sometime later by Lady Kennaway, who insisted on trying some of Hudson's famous roast duck and braised pigeon pie, followed by the flaky lemon tarts for which the inn was renowned in that part of Kent.

Lady Kennaway glanced at her son several times during the meal, of which he partook only sparingly. And when he handed her back into the chaise, he was not surprised that she demanded to know what had happened to his appetite.

"You are not coming down with something, are you, Derek?'' she inquired, an anxious frown creasing her lovely forehead.

Overcome with sudden tenderness, he kissed her cheek and grinned reassuringly. "You worry too much, love,'' he chided her. "If you are not careful, you will get wrinkles and old Noddy will have none of you. And I assure you, I am not coming down with anything fatal.''

No, he thought ruefully as the carriages resumed their journey towards Ashford, he had come down with fatal foolishness seven years ago and mercifully survived the ordeal—although at the time he remembered wishing that the devil would come to claim him. His life was a living hell anyway. Yet all the time he had imagined himself in heaven, poor fool that he was.

Derek had never been quite certain how he had managed to convince Lord Bradley to take his suit seriously. Nor how he had convinced that shy, delightful, fairylike creature to accept him. But accept him she had, smiling up at him with those trusting blue eyes that effectively dampened his growing ardor and defused any lecherous thoughts that happened to stray into his overheated mind. And stray there they certainly had, Derek thought cynically. And why not? Her obvious innocence had paralyzed and inflamed him simultaneously. He could hardly wait for the fifteenth of April to make her truly his.

And then, the day of the wedding. . . . He was never to discover exactly what happened, but suddenly she was gone, slipping off secretly into the cool April dawn. He had never seen her again. All he had left was her topaz ring, returned to him without a word by her white-faced father. His own father had been hardly less forthcoming, merely stating in his dry, clipped voice that if his son must disgrace the family name, he would much prefer not to hear about it in future.

His mother had not spoken to him for three months. If she knew anything—and if anyone did, it had to be Lady Kennaway—she never mentioned the affair again. At least not in his hearing.

Derek was still lost in a brown study as they passed through the village of Charing. Four miles beyond that, the huge stone archway marking the entrance to Ashford Grange loomed into sight.

The shadow cast by that centuries-old stone monument to the Ashford line felt strangely ominous in the gathering dusk. Quite suddenly, Derek felt tempted to turn right about and drive back to London. But of course this was utterly ridiculous.

As the curricle swept under the arch, Derek felt a spatter of raindrops on his face.

2. Hearts Asunder

No sooner had the rain-spattered maroon traveling chaise drawn up under the elegant porte cochère of Ashford Grange than the heavy oaken door swung open, and the butler descended the shallow steps, followed by a phalanx of liveried footmen. He stood back while one of the lower minions threw open the lacquered door of the coach and adjusted the steps, then stepped regally forward to assist the honored guest to descend.

"Welcome back to the Grange, Lady Victoria," he murmured stiffly, although beneath his shaggy brows his eyes betrayed a kindly twinkle. "Very pleased we are to see you again, milady," he added. "Very pleased, indeed."

Victoria smiled delightedly, the years dropping away as though they had never been. "Thank you, Higgins. Thank you. I am happy to be back again. How is Mrs. Higgins these days? I heard that she was laid up last winter with a touch of influenza."

The butler assisted Peckham to alight and turned back to Victoria. "She is much recovered, thank you, milady. And mighty glad to see you again she will be, and that's a fact." He led the way up the steps, his shoulders bowed. With a sudden pang Victoria realized that the Ashford butler—whom she had known all her life and had always considered immortal—was finally beginning to show signs of age.

Seven years was a sizable period out of anyone's life, she thought ruefully. And those seven years must have left their mark on her as well as on old Higgins. Misery was not exactly recommended to maintain one's youthful illusions and *joie de vivre*. And although Victoria could not honestly say that she had been miserable for the entire period since she left the

Grange that fateful April morning, a fair amount of her time—particularly her nights during those first terrible months—had been spent agonizing over the perversity of Fate, which had filled her cup to the brim with bliss only to shatter it irrevocably with an utterly unexpected and diabolical twist.

"Victoria!" The shriek of unadulterated delight was followed immediately by a blur of green and the sound of running feet, as the Duchess of Ashford ran across the front hall to fling her arms unceremoniously about the new arrival in clear violation of all social rules governing the acceptable comportment of high-ranking ladies.

"Oh, Victoria," the glowing duchess said in no less exuberant tones, "I'm *so* glad you came early. We don't expect the rest of the family before tomorrow afternoon at the earliest, so you and I can have a wonderful coze, my dear." She placed another affectionate kiss on Victoria's cheek and gave a very unduchesslike giggle. "I have been so looking forward to this, love. You have no idea."

"I suggest that you restrain yourself, my love, at least until Lady Victoria has had time to settle in," an amused masculine voice drawled from the stairway above them.

Victoria raised her eyes and sustained a slight shock. The man who came sauntering down the wide pink marble stairs was everything her cousin Alexandra had described in her frequent letters. The Duke of Ashford was an imposing figure of a man, tall and dark, with lean, angular features that were too harsh to be deemed classic. His gray eyes under heavy brows were presently filled with a tender glow and fixed on her cousin with a warmth that made Victoria blush. The duke's ill-concealed feelings for his wife were echoed in the slow curl of his sensuous mouth as he grinned at her.

The aura of rakish sensuality that Alex's husband exuded, almost like animal magnetism, reminded Vic-

toria all too vividly of another gentleman who had
suddenly changed into a similar predatory brute seven
years ago and terrified her out of her wits. How the
diminutive, gentle Alexandria had found the courage
to put herself into the hands of such an obviously
dangerous creature, Victoria could not imagine. The
very notion of intimacy with a man of Simon Weatherby's decadent appetites—all rakes had decadent appetites, did they not?—appalled her. Of course,
Victoria knew very little about intimacies of any kind
and nothing about the conjugal bliss her cousin occasionally mentioned in her letters, but she found it well-
nigh impossible to reconcile her idea of bliss with any
man, and definitely not with one who looked like the
Duke of Ashford. Or like Derek Seymour, for that
matter, a little voice inside her whispered. Victoria
shuddered.

"Don't tell me you have caught a chill, Victoria,"
her cousin exclaimed. "I shall never forgive you if
you do anything so missish. Come, Simon," she added,
reaching a hand out to the duke, which he took in
both of his and kissed with obvious pleasure. "You
remember my little cousin Victoria, don't you?"

Victoria felt the full force of the duke's gaze upon
her and quailed. "How do you do, your grace," she
murmured, feeling dreadfully stiff and pompous, but
quite unable to think of anything else to say.

"You must call him Simon," Alex insisted. "After
all, you are real cousins now, don't you agree? And I
want to take you up immediately to meet Venetia, my
dear," she continued without waiting for an answer.
"She is nearly two already, and—"

"I think you should allow Victoria to remove her
cloak and enjoy a cup of tea before you make her
walk all the way up to the nursery, my love," the duke
put in gently, an amused smile on his lips.

Victoria marveled at the tenderness she detected in
Ashford's voice as he addressed his wife. It sounded
suspiciously like a caress and suggested a whole world

of shared intimacies, an exciting yet comfortable emotional plateau gradually achieved, she felt sure, over the ebb and flow of their days together. And during their nights, too. Victoria did not for a moment doubt that her cousin's nights had evolved into warm, enviable oases of love and passion. Alexandra had hinted as much, of course, but even if her cousin had been less indiscreet about the source and center of her delirious happiness, Victoria was not such an innocent that she could not see for herself the emotional bond Alexandra had established with her new husband.

Enviable? Yes, Victoria admitted with sudden clarity. Alex had captured this man's heart and given herself to him without reserve. And Victoria envied her. Yes indeed, she thought with a flare of resentment, here she was about to celebrate her twenty-fifth year, and she had never experienced the natural joy and fulfillment of a man's intimate love. Of Derek's love, that same voice in her heart added softly. On that frightening evening seven years ago, Victoria had been given a glimpse of such intimacy, but to her it had seemed like a terrifying, almost disgusting ordeal. Clearly the duke did not inspire any disgust in Alexandra. Ashford must be a tender lover, Victoria reasoned, uneasy at the improper direction of her thoughts. How else could her cousin gaze at him with such obvious adoration? She slanted a speculative glance at the duke, only to find his gray eyes regarding her quizzically, almost as though he had read her thoughts.

She blushed and turned to her cousin. "How is your father, Alex? I look forward to meeting his new lady."

"They arrived two days ago, my dear. Papa is quite unable to stay away from Venetia for any length of time. He dotes on her almost as much as Simon does. Lady Margaret is Simon's aunt, as you know, but she is much sweeter-tempered and infinitely better looking." Since these words were accompanied by a melting look at the duke, Victoria had to assume that her

cousin was funning. She quickly repressed another
stab of envy.

What might have been her destiny had Derek not
been foxed beyond all recognition that moonlit evening? she wondered. Might she not have been, at this
very moment, the Countess of Kennaway? Perhaps
even the happy mother of Derek's children? Yes, she
thought wryly, most definitely a mother. Victoria felt
her throat grow taut and her eyes prick with unshed
tears. Being a mother had been an essential part of
the dream she had cherished; it came immediately
after that hoped-for meeting with Prince Charming.
Unfortunately her innocent dream had contained no
hint of what might happen if her Prince Charming
turned out to be—as indeed he had—anything but
charming.

Victoria sighed and closed her eyes. Derek had
spoiled it all, and she would never forgive him for
destroying her illusions of how *real* gentlemen should
behave. Looking back over those seven dreary years,
of course, Victoria had to admit that the illusions of
a seventeen-year-old were highly unrealistic at best,
foolishly naive at worst. And unless she could bring
herself to accept the suit of Mr. John Rowling, the
son and heir to Sir Joshua Rowling of Charing, Kent,
and the only one of her suitors who still regularly
offered for her hand, she would definitely become an
ape-leader like poor Aunt Sally. Poor John! So kind,
so loyal, so attentive, so solidly respectable. So dull.
Victoria sighed again and wondered, for the third or
fourth time since embarking on this return to her past,
what Derek would be like after all these years. She
would not see him, naturally. Heaven forbid! Alexandra had assured her, barely a month ago, that the Earl
of Kennaway had left for the Continent on a special
government mission. He would be away for several
months, Alex had assured her cousin, so wouldn't Victoria please, *please* break her stubborn vow never to
come near the Grange again and join them when all

the family would be gathered to celebrate Aunt Letitia's birthday?

The bedroom door burst open and Alexandra swept in. "I really am delighted that you came, Victoria," she repeated for the fourth time since Victoria's arrival, her heart-shaped face wreathed in smiles. "Here, let me bathe your poor forehead." She took the damp cloth from Peckham, and shooed the abigail out of the room.

"I was thinking the very same thing, Alex," Victoria murmured. "I'm glad to be back. Of course, I've kept in touch with everyone—almost everyone—" she corrected herself hastily, "but it is not the same as being here at the Grange literally awash with Richardsons, and Weatherbys, and Howards, and all the others." She paused infinitesimally. "Is the countess coming?" Victoria did not have to specify which countess she meant, of course. Her cousin *knew*.

"Yes, of course," Alex replied with another smile. "Lady Kennaway wrote me only last week to confirm that the Marquess of Monroyal had offered to escort her, since her dearest Derek"—here she slanted her eyes mischievously at her cousin—"had been called away on government duties in Spain. No doubt her dearest Derek is even now up to his elegant knees in love-stricken senoritas throwing out lures and fluttering their dark eyelashes at him." When Victoria made no reply, the duchess added the rider, "Derek was always one for the ladies, as you know, dear."

"I do not know anything of the sort," Victoria retorted sharply. "And I would much prefer to talk of something else, if you don't mind."

After a slight, pregnant pause, the duchess complied. "Have you ever met the marquess? A most dashing and dangerous fellow, if I can believe half of what Simon tells me. They are good friends, of course. Did I ever tell you that he dangled after me for a short time before Simon abducted and seduced me?

At least I think Monroyal was dangling. One never knows with a man like that, so proficient in flirting and so *terribly* tempting."

Victoria stared at her cousin in consternation. "How can you talk of another man in those terms, Alex?" she demanded. "Are you so lost to all sense of decorum that you can think of other men like . . . like *that*? What if Simon hears you, you shameless hussy?"

"Oh, Simon knows very well how seductive Robert can be." She giggled and blushed becomingly. "He is—or *was*—a rake, too, you know, before he came into the title. So he knows all there is to know about seducing women." She paused for a fraction of a second and then lowered her lashes to hide her hazel eyes. "I confess I am glad he does, my dear Victoria, for I don't think I could abide a cold fish for a husband." She glanced up then, and Victoria saw her cousin's expression take on a decidedly saucy cast.

"Speaking of cold fish, my dear," she continued with a bubble of infectious laughter, "Mr. John Rowland is coming this year. He always writes to ask if you will be attending," she added when Victoria widened her eyes in amazement. "The poor fellow was overjoyed when I actually invited him to stay at the Grange for Aunt Letitia's festivities. Positively incoherent with gratitude, I should say."

Victoria raised herself on one elbow and looked her cousin in the eye. "Why at the Grange?" she demanded. "Mr. Rowland has an aunt in Ashford, as you must remember. He could easily have stayed there." For some obscure reason, the idea of having to confront John Rowland at every turn during her stay at the Grange did not appeal to Victoria at all. She did not wish to receive another offer from that gentleman. At least not quite yet. Perhaps this summer she might make up her mind, once and for all, if life at Rowland Hall with John would be preferable to spending the rest of her days as a spinster aunt to other women's children. But she had not wanted to face that dismal alternative at this precise moment, so her cousin's news was unexpectedly disturbing.

"I thought it might cheer you up, dearest," Alexandra said soothingly. "I merely wanted to be helpful. Living in such close quarters—although it is rather difficult to imagine the Grange as crowded—might give you the opportunity to see if Mr. Rowland is the man for you, my love. Perhaps you will discover that his table manners are unacceptable, or that he is bad-tempered at the breakfast table, or that he does not look well in evening attire, or any number of appalling flaws that would cause you to strike him from the list of eligibles immediately. Don't you agree, dear?"

"No, I don't," Victoria interrupted firmly. "And if you do not let me rest, Alex, I will look like an old Tabby when Mr. Rowland arrives. You would not want that, would you, dear?" she added dryly.

The duchess grinned and agreed that such a thing would not do at all, but Victoria hardly paid attention. Her mind was busy with Alexandra's artless comments on the seductive powers of a man as darkly dangerous as Simon Weatherby.

What would she have done in her cousin's place? she wondered, alarmed that the idea had even crossed her mind.

Late the following afternoon, after a delightful morning spent playing with baby Venetia up in the nursery and assisting the Duchess of Ashford in welcoming the numerous family members who began arriving shortly after nuncheon, Victoria escaped to her room for a well-deserved hour's rest. Seeing so many of her relatives, both distant and closely connected, had been an exhilarating if exhausting experience, and she had gladly acquiesced to Peckham's suggestion that she lie down for an hour before tea.

Victoria was glad she did, for when she descended the staircase shortly after four o'clock that afternoon, she felt rested and ready to assist her cousin in pour-

ing tea for the throng of guests who would even now
be congregating in the large drawing room to sample
Mrs. Higgins's famous lemon tarts. She sighed. Contrary to all her expectations, Victoria had begun to
enjoy herself. She had always loved children, and the
delight of having her numerous young cousins all together for once gave her particular pleasure. She had
requested the duty of overseeing the nursery during
the children's dinner hour that evening, for although
most of them had arrived accompanied by their nurses,
a voice of authority was necessary to keep the re-
sulting chaos reasonably under control.

Her mind busy with such details, Victoria had at
first lent a deaf ear to the voices from the hall below,
undoubtedly late arrivals from one branch of the family or another. Then a familiar silvery laugh wafted up
to her on the landing, and she gave a start. Lady
Fanny! A wave of joy swept through her and she ran
lightly to the head of the pink marble stairs leading
down to the entrance hall. Yes, there she was! Victoria
felt a sudden rush of affection. Although she had not
seen the Countess of Kennaway for seven years, they
had—not surprisingly, given the circumstances—devel-
oped a geniune friendship and were constant
correspondents.

It had been to the countess that the distraught Victoria had fled for comfort after she had run back to
the Grange from the fateful summer house encounter,
and Lady Fanny—as she liked to be called—had
opened her arms to the young motherless girl, who
had no one else to go to. Victoria had trembled at the
thought of her father's fury had he been apprised of
the full extent of the viscount's perfidy. Lady Fanny
had counseled against it, and had undertaken the unpleasant task of informing her husband, Lord Kennaway, that the match the earl had so fully approved of
for his son and heir had been broken. She had also
volunteered to tell Lord Bradley of his daughter's sudden decision to return home immediately. Victoria

never knew exactly what part of the sad story Lady Fanny had told her father—and her ladyship knew the whole of it, for every sordid little detail had poured out unchecked as Victoria huddled, her face swollen with tears, in the countess's private sitting room that night.

Lady Fanny had stood her friend throughout the entire ugly affair, Victoria recalled, even when it became apparent that she was adamant in her decision to end the engagement to Lord Hardwicke. Her ladyship had been at her side during that uncomfortable interview with Lord Bradley, and Victoria was convinced the countess had saved her from the full force of her father's wrath and enabled her to depart the Grange before the house was astir. For this, and for remaining her friend and correspondent over the years, Victoria would be eternally grateful to the woman who, by all accounts, should have been outraged at the humiliation she had inflicted upon her son.

And now Lady Kennaway was here! Overcome by the urge to embrace this compassionate woman who was both a friend and confidante to her, Victoria swept quickly down the stairs, her eyes never leaving the countess's smiling countenance. Lady Kennaway opened her arms and Victoria stepped joyfully into them, her happiness bubbling to the surface as the countess returned her warm embrace.

"Lady Fanny!" she exclaimed. "What a delight to see you again. I have missed you," she added softly, drawing back and searching the older woman's face anxiously.

"And I have missed you, too, my dearest Victoria," Lady Kennaway replied, her voice husky with emotion. "It was very naughty of you not to come to me for Christmas last year. I am very cross with you, love."

Her tone denied the severity of her words, and Victoria blushed. "I was already promised to friends in Devon, my lady," she began.

"Fiddlesticks!" her ladyship retorted quickly. "I don't believe a word of it, dear. And I do not intend to let you get away so easily next time, I assure you. As it was, you condemned me to three weeks at Lady Babbington's boring house party."

Victoria laughed, unable to believe that anyone of Lady Fanny's congenial nature would find any social gathering boring. "Lord Noddleton was not with you?" she inquired archly.

"Oh, yes," the countess said offhandedly. "Noddy was there, of course. And he kept me tolerably entertained, for which I am eternally in his debt."

Victoria smiled at Lady Fanny's casual mention of her elderly suitor, Lord Noddleton, whom she happened to know her ladyship was seriously considering as her next husband. A murmur of voices behind them distracted her, and Victoria turned her eyes from the countess's glowing face to the two gentlemen who were being divested of their greatcoats by a solicitous Higgins. One of the gentlemen was unknown to her. The other ... Victoria felt her smile congeal as she met the hostile amber eyes fixed implacably upon her. The other gentleman was very well known to her indeed.

3. *The Past Remembered*

For a moment frozen in time, the Earl of Kennaway stared into a pair of startled blue eyes. In that heart-stopping glance, the past came rushing back to him in all its bittersweet dimensions. She was still small, and delicate, and ethereally fair, he saw in that first flash of recognition. Her eyes were still as blue as the wild hyacinths in the wood where they had first kissed. The memory of that idyllic moment caused a painful tight-ening in his chest. Lord knows, he had fought against these memories for years and had thought himself im-mune to this kind of foolishness. But before he shut his mind to the insidious pull of her fairylike beauty, Derek was forced to acknowledge that Lady Victoria Lovelace was even more beautiful than the shy fairy princess who had charmed his heart away.

As he watched her slender form sweep gracefully down the staircase, a radiant smile of welcome on her beautiful face, a knife twisted inside him. That smile, that loving embrace had been for his mother, he told himself grimly. She had not seen him, not even glanced his way. He experienced—for perhaps the first time since their betrothal had ended—the sharp pang of despair at being excluded from this woman's life.

He heard an intake of breath and turned in time to catch his cousin's admiring stare. Derek scowled as he glimpsed the saturnine smile that flickered on Lord Monroyal's face. Then his mother's voice broke into the sudden silence and Victoria looked away.

"Let me present this handsome rogue to you, my dear," she said. "Robert Stilton, Marquess of Mon-royal. My lord, this is Lady Victoria Lovelace, a very, *very* dear friend." The countess smiled gently as the marquess raised Victoria's fingers to his lips in an ex-aggerated, lingering salute that made Derek's blood boil. Victoria herself seemed merely bemused at the intensity of Lord Monroyal's captivating smile, Derek noticed, suppressing the urge to pound his rakish cousin into the ground. "And you remember my son, Lord Kennaway, of course, my love," the countess continued lightly, quite as if they were casual strang-ers. Derek bowed coldly, unwilling or unable to con-tribute a single word above his muttered greeting.

After that first anguished glance, Victoria did not meet his eyes again, but instantly turned to his mother and offered to escort the countess upstairs to her room before joining the other guests in the drawing room.

Derek watched the two ladies resume their friendly chatter as they climbed the stairs together, caught up in a conspiracy of intimacy that effectively left him out in the cold. He felt again the stab of nostalgia for what might have been, for the happiness he had held briefly in the palm of his hand, and which had—quite inexplicably and irrevocably—slipped out of his grasp, leaving him with a brittle, corroding anger, and oddly lonely in spite of the many ladybirds and restless society matrons who had crossed his path in the past seven years. None of them had left a trace of their passing, he realized with a flash of intuition. Whereas Lady Victoria—his very own fairy princess—had left a scar as deep and painful as it was enduring.

"So *that* is the fair Victoria," the marquess drawled, a touch of cynical amusement in his gray eyes. "My condolences, old chap. You should never have let that one get away. She is quite exquisite." He regarded Derek speculatively for a moment, then added, "I don't suppose you would care to tell me why she did— escape, I mean."

"No, I wouldn't," Derek said curtly.

"Ah, well, I suppose not," the marquess continued with an easy laugh. "But you can at least tell me if you have any further ... ahem ... any further interest in that direction, coz," he added delicately.

Derek's scowl became more pronounced. "I have no further interest in the lady, if that is what you mean," he said coldly. He would have said more, but at that moment he heard a flutter of satin and their hostess came quickly into the hall to greet them. When the duchess saw him, Derek thought she looked almost as startled as Victoria had, and he smiled grimly.

"I returned from Spain more speedily than I expected, my dear Alexandra," he explained in answer to the duchess's oddly flustered expression. "I trust I am not *de trop*," he added dryly, watching the play of emotions on her heart-shaped face.

"What a ridiculous notion," she replied promptly.

"I am more than delighted to welcome two extra gentlemen, as you well know."

"You are supposed to say two *charming and attractive* gentlemen, my dear," drawled the marquess, raising the duchess's fingers to his lips. "You are blooming, my love. Marriage agrees with you."

"Unhand my lady, Robert," came a deep voice from the doorway. "Unless you wish to meet at dawn down behind the stables, of course." The duke sauntered up and shook hands with both gentlemen and then tucked his wife's hand into the crook of his arm and stared down at her possessively. "Haven't I warned you not to have anything to do with rogues like these, my love?" he teased.

Alexandra dimpled up at him and Derek felt the knife twist again in his heart. Victoria had looked at him with just such sweetness, he remembered, quite as if she had thought him the only man in the world. He had grown addicted to her shy adoration and had outdone himself to please her, to bring that soft smile to her lips. She had smiled at him when he kissed her in the woods, he recalled, a smile full of innocence and trust. She had not smiled for him today, of course, only for his mother, and perhaps a glimmer for Robert, blast his soul.

"My lord?"

He jerked his thoughts back to the present and realized that they were all regarding him oddly. "I beg your pardon, Alexandra," he murmured.

"I was just telling Simon that I think we should warn you—"

"About Victoria?" he interrupted brusquely. "I have already seen her, my dear. She is upstairs with my mother." He heard the harshness in his voice and forced himself to smile, but the duchess must have seen the anguish in his eyes, for she turned to her husband.

"I believe these gentlemen could use something rather stronger than tea, Simon," she said. "Will you

take them into the library for a glass of sherry before
you bring them into the drawing room to face Aunt
Letitia?"

The duchess smiled at him, and Derek felt himself
relax. Yes, he thought as he followed Ashford and
Monroyal down the hall, he would need something a
good deal stronger than tea if he were to survive a
week of watching Victoria's eyes fill with an emotion
verging on terror every time she looked at him. What
had he done to inspire fear in the woman he had loved
so ompletely, he wondered? A woman who still had
the power to take his breath away.

The Earl of Kennaway had no answer to this unthinkable question, but he vowed to find out. His future sanity depended upon it.

The following morning, Victoria succumbed to cowardice. Instead of descending to the breakfast room,
as she had firmly intended—mainly to convince everyone, including herself, that she did not give a fig for
the Earl of Kennaway—she slipped up to the nursery
to have her toast and tea with the children. Even so,
the toast stuck in her throat, and the weak tea tasted
like day-old chicken broth. But at least the pandemo-
nium created by a dozen small children vying for her
attention—when they were not stealing one another's
toys—distracted her thoughts from the gentleman who
had invaded her life again so unexpectedly.

It was precisely the unexpectedness of his arrival
that had disconcerted her, she reasoned, retying the
bright-red bib around little Susanah's fat chin for the
fourth time.

"No, Bertie," she said sternly to her cousin Cecilia's
youngest son. "Porridge is to eat, dear, not to throw
on the floor."

Bertie shoveled another large spoonful out of his
bowl.

"I said *no,* Bertie," she repeated more vigorously.

"Do you want me to tell your mama that you have been a bad boy?"

The child regarded her speculatively, his expressive eyes full of devilment, and so like his father's, the jovial Lord Weston, whom Cecilia had accepted shortly after Victoria's betrothal was announced. Victoria returned the boy's stare until he gave up the tussle and returned to his porridge.

She had never been particularly close to her cousin, but had envied her when she married her good-natured lord, who obviously doted on her. She had felt again the pangs of frustration when Cecilia gave birth to their first son, Christopher. And now her cousin had Bertie, too, a chubby child, full of mischief, and so huggable it made Victoria's throat ache. It just wasn't fair, she thought, that none of her own dreams had come true.

Victoria was thankful when these dreary reminiscences were interrupted by an under-footman, who came to announce that Lady Victoria's presence was requested downstairs. The servant, whom Victoria did not recognize, must be new, for he could not tell her which of the many gentlemen guests had asked for her company.

"All I can say, milady," the lad stammered nervously, "is that the gentleman is awaiting your ladyship in the library."

Her first thought, of course, was that this arrogant summons could only have come from Lord Kennaway. And as she stopped in her own room to wash the porridge off her fingers and tidy her hair, her second thought was that she would do well to leave his lordship kicking his heels for half an hour before putting in an appearance. Her third thought was perhaps the most disturbing: What would Derek possibly want with her? The idea of being alone with him still terrified her, even after all these years; but curiosity won the day. After all, the austere Ashford library was not the deserted summer house, so what harm could befall

her? Besides, she would definitely leave the door ajar.
Just in case.

Victoria pushed open the library door and noted
that a brisk fire was burning in the big hearth. She
glanced around nervously, then let out a sigh of relief.
Or was it disappointment? a little voice within her
murmured wryly.

"Good morning, Mr. Rowland," she said politely,
treading across the deep burgundy carpet towards the
slender man who had been standing at the window.
"You wished to speak with me?"

John Rowland was hardly a man to stand out in a
crowd, Victoria thought ruefully, as that gentleman
bowed stiffly and a little awkwardly over her hand. His
stature was slight rather than muscular, his regular,
somewhat sharp features would never be called handsome, his manner of speech was ponderous, and his
learning, though certainly extensive, was orthodox in
the extreme. Yet to those in his immediate circle of
family and friends, John was kind, generous, and entirely loyal, as Victoria had every reason to know. So
what if his own father, the old and crusty Sir Joshua
Rowland, called his only son a dashed dull dog? she
thought. And so what if Victoria herself occasionally
agreed with that old reprobate?

"I do wish you could bring yourself to call me John,
my dear," Rowland said with gentle reproof, his
brown eyes searching her face. "It is not as though
we are exactly strangers," he added, in what Victoria
recognized as his jesting tone. "I have known you
since you were in the nursery."

"Yes, that is quite true, Mr. Rowland," she replied
carefully, wondering if he were about to make her
another offer. His sixth? Victoria sincerely hoped not.
She felt strangely unsettled this morning. "But neither
are we family," she added succinctly.

She wished she had not been quite so blunt, when
she saw the flash of pain in his eyes.

"If we are not," he said steadily, "it can hardly be

laid at my door, my lady. I believe I have made my wishes in that respect abundantly clear. Regardless of what my father may say, I am entirely devoted to you, Lady Victoria. And always shall be." He paused for a moment, as if waiting for a signal from her to renew his suit. When none as forthcoming, he sighed. "That is not the topic about which I wished to speak, however," he continued. "Although it directly concerns our future together, I must admit."

Suppressing the urge to point out any future they might have together was of a strictly nebulous nature, Victoria smiled. "And what might that be, Mr. Rowland?"

The gentleman cleared his throat and looked uncomfortable. "I was given to understand by her grace that a certain gentleman would not be among the guests this year. Yet when I arrived from Charing this morning, what do I find but his lordship's crested chaise in the stable yard." He paused and regarded her accusingly, a circumstance which only served to stir Victoria's ire. "Can you deny that he is here?" he demanded, showing the first signs of agitation.

"Why should I deny anything?" Victoria retorted, her temper rising dangerously. "If you are referring to Lord Kennaway, sir, you are correct. His lordship arrived yesterday. Although why his comings and goings are any concern of mine—or *yours,* for that matter!" she added sharply, "I cannot imagine." She stared at him mulishly. "Perhaps you would care to enlighten me, sir."

Mr. Rowland cleared his throat again. "I can see that the villain has already upset you, my dear," he began, taking both her hands in his and drawing her closer.

"It is not his lordship who has upset me, Mr. Rowland," Victoria lied, attempting to extricate herself from his grasp without appearing to do so. "It is you, sir, who are upsetting me with all this farradiddle. Now, release me, if you please. And I will thank you

to remember that I am *not* your "dear," sir," she
added peevishly.

"I should hope not," a harsh voice echoed from the
doorway, which neither of them had heard open.
"And release the lady, Rowland. You are making a
cake of yourself."

The earl had not slept well, a fact he attributed to
having suffered through an interminable evening in
the company of fully three-quarters of his living relatives. His ill humor had started at the dinner table,
where he had been seated—in what he could only consider a deliberate maneuver on the part of his hostess—beside Lady Victoria. The duchess's ruse had not
borne fruit, since Derek had been quite unable to exchange a single word with the lady, who had not so
much as glanced his way during the entire meal. Instead, he had been obliged to listen to Lord Monroyal,
seated on Victoria's left, regale her with all the latest
on dits from Town and flirt quite outrageously with
her. Occasionally Monroyal would—out of sheer perversity, Derek was convinced—attempt to draw him
into the easy banter that flowed from his golden
tongue. Since Lady Victoria studiously ignored every
such attempt—much to the secret amusement of the
marquess, the earl did not doubt it for a minute—
Derek reciprocated with stony silence, a state of affairs that did not lend itself to a congenial interlude.

In the drawing room after dinner, the situation had
grown insufferably worse. He had dawdled as long as
possible over his claret, and extended the discussion
about the recent activities of the British Army on the
Continent as long as he dared, but eventually Ashford
had indicated that it was high time the gentlemen
joined the ladies.

As he entered the drawing room with Lord Monroyal, the first sight that met his jaundiced eye was
the charming picture of his mother and the woman
who had jilted him years ago sitting in complete har-

mony at the pianoforte, playing a duet. He was overcome by a murderous urge to strangle them both.
Particularly his lady mother, who had signaled to him
with a quite reprehensible insouciance, he thought,
and then turned to whisper something to Victoria. It
must have been perfectly outrageous, because Victoria
had blushed prettily and shaken her silvery curls.

"I think your mother is signaling you, coz," the marquess remarked laconically.

"I know," Derek replied shortly, refusing to acknowledge the maternal command.

"Perhaps she plans to lure you into singing a duet
with the ravishing Lady Victoria," Robert drawled,
amusement in his voice. "Now that would be something to make all the Tabbies sit up and take notice."

He had refused to answer his friend's provocative
remarks and retired to the billiard room, where he
had spent the rest of the evening missing shots like a
rank amateur.

In addition, he had drunk rather too liberally of the
duke's excellent brandy, and as a result his temper
was somewhat unpredictable when he descended to
the breakfast room that morning. The sound of an
argument in the library distracted him from his somber thoughts, and when he recognized Victoria's angry
voice insisting that she was not anyone's "dear," he
pushed open the door. The sight of Lady Victoria
struggling in Mr. Rowland's embrace did little to improve the earl's disposition.

He routed a chagrined Rowland with a few choice
insults and then turned to scowl at Victoria, who was
rubbing her wrists and avoiding his eyes.

"Did he hurt you?" Derek asked after a considerable silence had elapsed. His voice sounded harsh to
his own ears, and he wished he did not feel quite so
murderous again. He did not consider himself a violent man, and although he enjoyed his weekly bouts
in Jackson's Saloon on Bond Street with other gentlemen of sporting proclivities, he had never been ad-

dicted to boxing the watch or other dangerous pranks much indulged in by the rowdier members of his set.

Victoria shook her head.

"You are quite determined not to speak to me, I see," he remarked, unable to keep the bitterness from his voice. When she did not reply, he added in a softer tone, "Do you hate me so much, Victoria?"

She looked at him then, her eyes huge and luminous, reminding him once again of the wild hyacinths he had picked for her seven years ago when they were in love. Presumably she had loved him then, he thought. At least she must have cared a little, for why else had she accepted his offer? Why else had she allowed him to kiss her out there in the sunlit glade? True, that first kiss had been but a chaste touching of lips, for though he ached to crush her to him and plunder her mouth of its sweetness, he had not dared to break that wall of innocence that seemed to surround her, keeping her safe from sensual libertines like himself. He would wait, he had decided. Wait until she was truly his, until she would not ... could not deny him. So he had kept his fires banked, even though desire for his Victoria had gnawed at him constantly, until he had thought he could not resist another day, another hour, without tasting the sweet pleasure of her. He had become so restless that finally he had resorted to another woman, but the restlessness had persisted until he realized that only Victoria could bring him peace. Only Victoria would satisfy him.

Yes, he remembered that restlessness well. It had turned his life into a purgatory after she had left. He still felt it, he realized with a sudden start. Could it be that he still lusted after his illusive fairy princess? he wondered, knowing, even as he asked himself the question, what the answer was. He shrank from it, refusing to acknowledge that he was still love's fool.

Suddenly he had to know the answer to that other

question. What had come between them? He stepped
closer to her and was startled to see her flinch.

"What happened, Victoria?" he demanded softly,
the whisper of her name on his lips sounding almost
erotic in the silence of the room. "Why did you run
away from me without a word? Without even a note?"
Without caring that you broke my heart, he wanted
to add, but pride stopped him.

Victoria looked at him full in the face then, and he
was taken aback by the fury in her blue eyes. "What
happened?" she choked. "How *dare* you stand there
and ask me what happened?" She paused and drew a
deep breath. "You are utterly despicable," she said,
her voice quavering slightly. "And I presume you find
it amusing to mock me, sir. Well, let me tell you that
I refuse to stay here to be insulted. I shall leave immediately, and I trust I never have to speak to you
again." She turned towards the door, but Derek was
there before her, closing it firmly and leaning against
it.

"Open that door instantly," she commanded, eyes
wild in the paleness of her face.

"Victoria, listen to me." He was growing angry himself now. "Believe me, I am not mocking you. I truly
do not know what happened to turn you against me."

She tossed her head and her lips curled sarcastically.
"So, you are a liar now, too, as well as a ..." She
stopped abruptly, and he saw pain in her eyes. Pain
and the memory of terror. "I cannot believe that you
do not know," she continued hoarsely. "Do not take
me for a fool, my lord. I was taken in once, but it will
not happen twice, I can assure you. Now let me go.
You cannot keep me locked up in here."

"Why are you frightened of me, Victoria?" he
asked abruptly.

She quailed visibly, and the sight of her fear
wrenched at his heart. "Frightened of you?" she repeated scornfully. "You do not *frighten* me, my lord.
You *terrify* me. You are a monster, the very monster

they warned me against. Yes, my lord, I was warned of your . . . your aberrations. But I wouldn't listen. I thought . . . I thought you loved me." Her voice died away in a sob, but the terrible words reverberated in the quiet room until Derek thought he would go mad.

The uncomfortable silence was interrupted by a knock, and Higgins opened the door to inform Lady Victoria that the Countess of Kennaway was desirous of her company on a drive into the village.

Derek could not mistake the relief on Victoria's face as she smiled woodenly at the butler. "Thank you, Higgins. I will go up to her at once."

Short of slamming the door in the butler's face, there was no choice but to let her go. And a moment later, Derek found himself staring at the closed door, a multitude of questions unanswered, and a mystery uncovered which he vowed to solve, even if he had to corner a reluctant lady to do so.

Victoria had to force herself to appear at the nuncheon table when she returned from her drive to the little hamlet of Wye, situated in a picturesque valley on the river Stour. The countess had conceived a sudden desire to examine the ruined Norman tower that sat like a weathered gray sentinel on a hill overlooking the hamlet. Several of the younger guests had accompanied the countess's phaeton on horseback, and required little encouragement to agree to her suggestion that a stroll among the battered fortifications and scattered stones long since fallen from the crumbling walls was in order. They soon dispersed among the ruins, and Victoria could hear their excited exclamations and laughter as she strolled around the outskirts of the old tower arm-in-arm with the countess.

After failing to elicit more than absentminded responses from her companion, Victoria turned to Lady Fanny and noticed an unusually serious expression on the countess's lovely face.

"Is something troubling you, my lady?" she murmured. "It is not like you to be so distracted."

Lady Fanny gave a small chuckle. "Am I rated such a featherhead and sad rattle, my dear, that I am not allowed to entertain a serious thought?" she quipped. "But if you must know, I am worried about Derek."

Victoria gave a start of surprise. Whatever was bothering the countess regarding her son must be a weighty matter indeed, for by unspoken agreement between the two ladies, Lord Kennaway's name rarely entered their conversation. "His lordship is not ill, I trust," she inquired tentatively.

"Oh, no!" Lady Fanny exclaimed. "To be truthful, sometimes I wish he were; then at least I would be able to do something about it. I know that is a dreadful thing to say, my dear, but my disobliging and feckless son is bent on making my life a complete misery."

Victoria stared at her in astonishment. "Forgive me, my lady, but Lord Kennaway appears to be as attached to you as ever. What has he done to distress you so?"

The countess wrung her hands and Victoria's heart went out to her. "I am being excessively mopish this morning, my love, but I cannot help it. Seeing the two of you together again after all these years brings it all back. You know how I looked forward to having you as a daughter, my dear Victoria. Yes, yes," she interpolated hastily, when Victoria's face went stiff. "I know, I should not be talking to you like this—you of all people." The countess scrambled in her reticule and produced a wisp of lace with which she blew her small nose vigorously. "Forgive me, love. I am being very gauche to speak of such things, but I cannot help wishing that . . . that . . . ." Her voice trailed off weakly.

"Wishing that I had succumbed to your son's nefarious designs, my lady?" she said stiffly, her tone one of incredulous disbelief.

"Oh, no, of course that is not what I meant at all, dear," the countess cut in, her lovely eyes wide with shock. "Please don't think that I condone Derek's improper advances in the least. He behaved like a beast, but then gentlemen often do, my love, especially when their passions overcome their common sense."

"His lordship was foxed to the gills," Victoria remarked coldly, thoroughly discomposed at the direction their conversation had taken.

"It can be quite exciting, actually," the countess continued, with astonishing frankness. "I remember a time or two when Derek's father—" She stopped abruptly and stared at Victoria in horror. "I cannot believe that I said that, child. I am obviously more blue-deviled than I thought. But I do so wish for grandchildren, and Derek refuses point-blank to select a mother for them. You are the only female he has ever—"

"I find this discussion distressing in the extreme, my lady," Victoria interrupted brusquely. "Your son had the unmitigated gall to pretend ignorance of the entire debacle," she added, her voice shaking. "Can you believe such perversity?"

"You did beg me not to betray your confidences on the matter, my love," the countess reminded her. "And I have kept my promise, dear."

"But he claims not to *remember*!" Victoria said through gritted teeth. "How could he not *remember*? Can you tell me that?"

"Very easily, my dear." The countess glanced at her speculatively and Victoria wondered what new indelicacy her ladyship was about to utter. "So Derek has spoken to you about that night?"

"Yes," Victoria said curtly. "I have asked him not to do so again."

Lady Fanny smiled, rather wistfully Victoria thought. "I wish you would reconsider, my dear child," she murmured. "I know I should not ask it of you, but after all these years I think he should be told. I believe he still has a *tendre* for you, Victoria."

Victoria blushed furiously, and she hoped the countess could not hear the wild hammering of her heart.

"You are mistaken," she said bluntly. "He does nothing but scowl at me."

"So I noticed," Lady Fanny murmured, seemingly restored to her natural good spirits. "And I wonder why."

4. Hide and Seek

That afternoon the April sun grew more inviting, and Victoria had the happy notion of shepherding a group of her little relatives out into the sheltered woodlands of the park to play. The elder members of the party gathered on the sunlit terrace for innumerable cups of tea and the latest gossip, but when one of the more daring young ladies suggested that it was time for the traditional game of hide-and-seek, a considerable number of the unmarried guests came down to join the fun. Victoria was startled to see both Kennaway and the marquess among them.

"I had thought you above such childish games as this, my lord," Victoria chided the marquess when he strolled up to stand beside her.

"I am drawn by the sweet prize, my dear lady," he responded smoothly, regarding her through hooded eyes. "I had hoped that I might persuade you to tell me where to find you," he added with his seductive smile.

Victoria blushed and laughed. "Then you will be sadly disappointed, my lord. For I do not intend anyone to find me."

"You cannot be serious. Have you no desire for a clandestine kiss, my dear? And all perfectly within the bounds of respectability, too. Sanctioned by our venerable Lady Letitia, no less." He grinned, and Victoria had to admit that he was an attractive devil. But from what she had heard, Lord Monroyal was even more depraved in his appetites than Derek had been. She had no intention of repeating that terrifying experience, no matter how charmingly the gentleman smiled at her.

"Did you hear that, coz?" the marquess remarked lazily, and Victoria started nervously when she saw that Derek had joined them. "Lady Victoria refuses to tell me where she plans to hide. Perhaps you will have better luck, old man." The marquess spoke with his habitual mocking tone, but Victoria sensed that the careless banter concealed a barb of irony.

"I already know where the lady will hide," the earl said unexpectedly, drawing a crack of laughter from his cousin.

"Unfair of you, Derek," he drawled. "Did you not hear Lady Victoria say she does not intend to forfeit a kiss?"

"You cannot know anything of the sort, my lord," Victoria blurted out without thinking. This morning's frank discussion with Lady Kennaway had left her shaken and unsure of herself. Her grievance against his lordship—firmly sustained over seven long years of self-imposed exile from Ashford Grange—had been challenged in ways she had never imagined. "It is not where you think, of that you may be sure," she added tartly, and instantly regretted her wayward tongue when the earl's amber eyes lit up with cynical amusement.

"How do you know what I think, Victoria?"

She had been thinking of the summer house, as he must have known. The memory of what had happened there brought a flush to her cheeks, and she turned away to the group of eager players clustering around her. "It is time to begin," she announced. "You all know the rules by now. The ladies will have fifteen minutes to hide. The gentlemen will hunt for them, and the first gentleman to find a lady may claim the prize."

"A kiss!" a young voice called out from the crowd.

This was greeted by hoots and whistles, and a good many giggles from the young ladies.

The particular version of the game played every year at the Grange—reportedly invented by the enterprising Lady Letitia herself, many years ago when she had three marriageable daughters to settle—was the highlight of the birthday celebration week and much anticipated by the younger set. No lady was supposed to reveal her hiding place, of course, but interested gentlemen had been known to wheedle the secret from certain young ladies. Victoria had been so coerced himself—most willingly, she remembered now—by the man she had later repudiated. It was unthinkable that another gentleman might steal a kiss that was rightfully his, Derek had argued. So she had told him, and he had found her almost immediately in the old summer house down by the stream.

He remembered, too. She saw the memory in his amber eyes before she turned away. She had not been reluctant to forfeit the prize he had demanded then, and he had kissed her for the second time, a warm caress that had left her lips tingling with delightful sensations. How could she have known that the following evening, after the birthday ball, he would take her down to the summer house again to break her heart and shatter her dreams forever?

Forever. What a long, lonely life lay ahead of her, Victoria thought. She ventured a glance in the earl's direction and caught him watching her, a quizzical smile on his lips. Could Lady Fanny be correct in her assessment of her son? she wondered. In so many ways—like that caressing smile and the gleam of passion in his eyes—the earl was still the man she had loved to distraction long ago. There was a suggestion of gray at his temples, and the lines on his face had deepened with the passing of time. But in too many heartrending ways he was still the Prince Charming who had invaded her childish imagination and promised ... Oh, how she wished things had been different

between them, for in spite of herself, the memory of
his tender kisses tugged at the edges of her consciousness. And he knew just where to find her, a perfidious
voice whispered inside her. He knew then; he knew
now.

But of course she could no longer hide in the summer house, could she? That would seem like an open
invitation to the rake in him, she told herself disgustedly. She could never sink to such depths of depravity
as to invite another kiss from the Earl of Kennaway.
Yet when Lady Letitia, ensconced in her comfortable
stuffed chair on the terrace, rang the starting bell vigorously with her frail hand, Victoria found her steps
leading her down the path towards the stream. Girlish
giggles could be heard all through the woods, as young
ladies ran here and there looking for the perfect hiding place. Of course, it should not be *too* perfect, for
no one wanted to remain with her kiss unclaimed,
and the chance of being kissed by one of the dashing
gentlemen down from London lent a special piquancy
to the game.

Dressed as she was in a green wool gown with long
sleeves, Victoria knew she would soon be invisible
from the house. The gentlemen were not supposed to
peek, but all the ladies knew they did, and Victoria
wondered if a pair of amber eyes had noted the direction she took. Of course, he did not need to peek,
that little voice reminded her. He knew where she
was going.

Or imagined he did, Victoria thought uncertainly,
as she reached the banks of the little stream and stood
looking down into the shallow, rippling water, her
mind in a turmoil. If she turned left, she could cross
at the footbridge and climb up into the hayloft on the
Home Farm. That hiding place might well be already
taken, though, and if that were the case, she might
continue on to old Mrs. Dawson's cottage and hide in
her small potting shed. No one would find her there;

it was a long walk from the Grange. If she turned right ...

She wasted two or three precious minutes dithering by the stream. Then she turned right and ran lightly along the bank, pushing through clumps of rhododendrons, climbing over a recently fallen branch, skirting a rambling riot of newly leafed blackberry vines, until she came to the bend in the stream beyond which, nestled behind the overgrown honeysuckle vines, lay the old, semiabandoned summer house.

Carefully, Victoria pushed aside the curtain of vines that half obscured the entrance and moved up the three shallow steps into the shaded interior. It was far more overgrown than she remembered, but that was to be expected after seven years. She stood still in the cool green bower, listening to the wrens twitter in the eves, the rustle, probably of a field mouse, in the darkest corner of the stone floor, and the hum of an anonymous insect in the thick growth of greenery that almost hid the small structure from view.

Victoria took a deep breath, filling her lungs with the remembered smells of the place. So much had remained the same, she thought. The roof above perhaps harbored more spiders than before, and one could hardly glimpse the stream through the crowding vines on the latticed walls. But the floors were still covered with fallen leaves, the two old wicker armchairs still boasted red velvet cushions—more frayed, perhaps, and spilling their stuffing onto the floor. Victoria finally steeled herself to examine the last piece of furniture, a monstrously overstuffed sofa, crouching, squad and complacent, against the farthest wall.

A shudder shook her as memories flooded back. Unpleasant memories this time. Memories of betrayal, of lost innocence, of terror. Driven by a wild urge to blot out the disenchantment, to render the past less corrosive, Victoria reached out and ran her hand along the cracked leather back of the sofa. It was hard and rough to the touch, and suddenly she felt tears gather in her eyes.

"Oh, Derek," she murmured, the whisper of her voice startling in the dim shadows around her.

"Sorry to disappoint you, my dear," a lazy voice drawled from the doorway behind her. "I may not be Derek, but I must insist upon claiming my prize."

The earl was peripherally conscious of the young ladies scattering through the wooded park like a frenzied cloud of colored butterflies, but his eyes were fixed on the slim figure in green disappearing among the trees. She was going towards the stream, he thought with a flicker of excitement. Yet she had made a point of warning him that her chosen hiding place was not the one he imagined, hadn't she? Or did she have another, quite different motive for mentioning the summer house?

It had been the scene of their last meeting, Derek remembered, but he retained little but a blurred image of what had transpired that night of the birthday ball. He must have been more castaway than he had expected to be, considering all the toasts he had drunk. Toasts to Lady Letitia, whose birthday celebration would be extra special that year because it would be marked by another wedding in the family. Toasts to Lady Victoria, who would be eighteen years old on the morrow, a milestone her father had insisted she cross before setting foot on the uncertain path of matrimony. Toasts to the happy couple, whose union would be blessed by a distant cousin in the clergy and attended by more than the usual number of relatives gathered for the occasion. And finally, innumerable toasts from his closest friends, who had congregated in the library at midnight for their own symbolic farewell to one of London's most elusive bachelors. Those toasts—to Victoria, naturally, but also to each and every one of his flirts and ladybirds over the past five or six years—must have pushed him over the edge of dubious sobriety into the realm of riotous irresponsibility.

He had felt the need for fresh air and had convinced Victoria to steal away into the woods with him. She had come willingly, even gladly, her face pale in the moonlight, her timid smile as glowing as ever, and her eyes shining for him. And he had taken her to the old summer house. What happened there still lay hidden in the foggy depths of his memory, but an occasional disturbing flash would rise to the surface and leave him strangely uneasy. Images of a quarrel. A quarrel? That was impossible, he had told himself many times in the painful days that followed. Why would they quarrel? In a few hours they would be married, and his waiting would be over. Victoria—his own sweet Victoria—would be his forever. Forever? The earl gave a cynical grimace and turned to observe the other participants in this yearly charade.

"I don't suppose you would care to tell, coz?" the marquess remarked with deceptive nonchalance.

Derek eyed his friend coldly. "Tell what?" he queried, although he knew only too well what was on Robert's mind.

The marquess grinned wolfishly. "Where the delectable Victoria is hiding. What else?"

"Stay out of this, Robert," the earl said flatly.

"I distinctly understood you to say that you had no further interest in the wench, coz," the marquess responded with mock surprise.

"Just stay away from her, Robert," Derek repeated, his voice hardening.

"What a dog-in-the-manger you are, old chap," the other drawled, his thin lips curling cynically.

Derek ignored this deliberate barb, and when the sound of Lady Letitia's starting bell rang out, he turned on his heel and went into the house. He would go out through the side door and cut across the rose garden, behind the shrine to Aphrodite—an aberration attributed to the second Duke of Ashford, past the sunken gardens, and into the woods at the far side of the park. It was not the most direct way, of course, but Derek wished to avoid any chance of being followed by his rakish cousin, who had seemingly set his sights on Lady Victoria. Out of pure perversity, the earl was convinced. Nevertheless, he did not need the handsome marquess around when he confronted his erstwhile betrothed in the summer house.

As he approached the hidden structure from the far side, the earl thought he heard voices and quickened his pace. The notion that some other man had found her first, and was perhaps, even then, kissing his Victoria—why was he still thinking of her as *his*? he wondered—made him grit his teeth with rage. The summer house was so well hidden that it took him a moment to discover the entrance and push aside the tangle of honeysuckle vines clogging it. He heard the voices more clearly now, and one of them was definitely Victoria's. It broke off abruptly and he heard Lord Monroyal's startled exclamation. Derek ran up the three shallow steps and stood in the doorway. At first the shadows confused him, then the figure of a man turned to face the entrance, and the earl saw that the marquess held the limp form of Lady Victoria cradled in his arms.

For a split second the two men stood staring at each other, then the earl stepped forward. "What in Hades do you think you're doing, Monroyal?" he growled, his brows lowered in a thunderous scowl. "I thought I told you to keep out of this."

"You should have known better than to throw that kind of a challenge my way." The marquess's voice was devoid of its habitual drawl.

"If you have harmed her in any way, I shall murder you."

The marquess became very still, his slate-gray eyes suddenly expressionless. "What makes you think I wish to harm her at all?" he said softly, his eyes never leaving his cousin's threatening face. He broke the

tension with a thin smile. "Rumors seem to lay that
distinction at *your* door, coz. Not all of us are in the
habit of mauling innocents, you know," he continued,
the taunt in his voice unmistakable.

Derek clenched his fists until his knuckles turned
white. "You will pay dearly for that insult," he
growled. "Give her to me and get your scurvy hide
out of here before I commit mayhem." He held out
his arms, and after a moment's hesitation, Monroyal
placed the unconscious Lady Victoria into them and
stepped back.

"You are quite *de trop*," the earl said in a flat voice.

The marquess regarded him keenly for a moment
and then said with quiet deliberation, "And if *you*
harm the lady in any way, my friend, you will answer
to me." Without another word, he turned and disappeared into the curtain of greenery, leaving Derek
more than a little disturbed at the specters raised by
the marquess's warning.

After a slight pause, the earl carried Victoria to the
ungainly black sofa and gently laid her down. He sat
beside her and chafed her cold hands, but it was several minutes before her eyelids fluttered and she
opened her eyes. Derek marveled, as he always did,
at the startling hyacinth-blue of her eyes, and restrained the sudden urge to wrap his arms about her.
Abruptly, the blue irises darkened with recognition,
and he saw a flicker of panic in them. She attempted
to sit up, and when he gently pushed her back, he saw
the fear explode into terror.

"Please, Derek, don't . . ." she moaned softly, and
then, in a sudden burst of energy, thrust his hands
away and scrambled to her feet. She swayed uncertainly, and the earl put a steadying arm about her
waist. He felt her sag against him for a brief moment,
then she went rigid and pulled away.

"Did Monroyal hurt you, Victoria?" he demanded
brusquely, fear knotting his stomach.

Victoria shook her head, looking tense and miserable. He wanted to comfort her, but when he touched her face, she flinched visibly. The earl gazed at her for several moments, disconcerted by this obvious rejection. A sudden unpleasant thought struck him.

"Did you come here to meet Monroyal?"

She shook her head again. "No, of course not."

Derek took a deep breath. The next question came unbidden to his lips. "Then why are you here, Victoria?"

"Why are *you* here?" she countered, ignoring his question.

Before he could stop himself, he had spoken a truth he had refused to acknowledge until that moment. "I wanted to kiss you again, Victoria."

The words hung in the shadows between them for a long moment. He might as well have said he intended to murder her, he thought bitterly, watching her startled eyes meet his briefly before flitting towards the curtained entrance.

"Yes," he said, his voice tinged with self-loathing. "Even after you jilted me in front of the whole family and made me the laughingstock of London; after you ran off on our wedding day without a word, even a note of explanation; after you refused to answer my letters or receive me when I called. Even after all of this mistreatment at your hands, my dear Victoria, I still want to kiss you. I must be every kind of fool imaginable, of course, and I despise myself for it. But I also came to find out why, after all these years, you are still afraid of me." He paused, surprised at his own intensity. "You *are* still afraid of me, aren't you, Victoria?"

There was a long silence, and Derek began to wonder if she would answer at all.

"Yes." When it came, the answer was so soft he barely heard it.

"Tell me why."

Another pause. "You really do not know?" Her

eyes were fixed on him now, as if willing him to tell her the truth.

"No. I am beginning to suspect it must have been something terrible.

"Oh, it *was*." The words were no more than a sigh, but they chilled his bones.

"I know you find this hard to believe, Victoria," he began, hardly knowing how to bridge this gaping chasm between them, but determined to try. "But I really cannot recall."

"No, I find it impossible to understand how you could not ... but Lady Fanny told me this morning that you might be telling the truth."

"My *mother*?" he exclaimed in alarm. "Are you telling me that my mother knows what happened?" Somehow the notion of Lady Fanny being privy to his disgraceful behavior—for he could no longer deceive himself that it was anything less—made the earl intensely uncomfortable.

Victoria glanced at him in surprise. "Yes, of course. Who else could I go to? Lady Fanny has always treated me like a daughter, you see, and I had no mother of my own. I could hardly appear before my father in that state, he ... he would have killed you." She turned her face away. "All I could think of was getting away. I didn't know what else to do."

Her last words sounded so forlorn and hopeless that Derek wished he could take this woman in his arms and wipe those terrible memories away. He knew this to be impossible, of course. The past—and particularly that last evening together in the summer house—had left its indelible mark on both of them and blighted their lives forever. Forever? No, perhaps not forever, he thought with a sudden surge of hope. He could do nothing to change the past, of course, but he could—and *would*, if only Victoria still cared—change the future.

"I am surprised my mother did not insist that you stay," he said gently. "Marriage to me would have

banished those maidenly fears soon enough, my dear."
The solution was so obvious that he could not imagine
why Lady Fanny had not insisted upon it.

Victoria swung around to face him, and the earl was
startled to see the contempt in her eyes. "I might have
known you would say that," she said with barely suppressed fury. "Marriage covers a multitude of sins,
doesn't it? How convenient for you, my lord." The
bitterness in her voice was tangible. "Society would
have turned a blind eye to your disgusting behavior if
you had married me. But what about me?" she cried
with such distress that the earl was stunned. "Do you
really imagine I wished to be treated like your ...
y–your *doxy* for the rest of my life? And after that
enlightening display of your true colors, my lord, I
could not ... I really c–could not bear it." She turned
wildly towards the doorway. "I must go," she
whispered.

The movement jolted Derek out of the frozen paral-
ysis this revelation had produced in him and he
grasped her arm. He felt the blood drain from his face
as he gazed down into her frightened eyes.

"What did I do to you, Victoria?" he demanded
harshly. "I have a right to know what crime I committed to set you against me in this way."

"Ask Lady Kennaway, my lord," Victoria said in a
stiff little voice. "She knows exactly what you did."

"I'm asking *you,* my love. I wish to hear it from
your own lips."

Victoria felt herself tremble as the earl loomed over
her, and she was very aware of his hand firmly grip-
ping her arm. He still had the power to frighten her,
she thought disjointedly, noting that his amber eyes
were dark with anger. Or was it passion again? she
wondered, remembering that other night when they
had come to the summer house. His eyes had been
full of passion then, that she did know. Uncontrollable

passion. Yet he could still thrill her, too, she realized, watching his eyes drop to her lips.

"From your very own lips," he repeated, every hint of harshness gone from his voice.

Victoria shuddered. She had not counted on the dangerous attraction this man could still exercise over her. She wondered if he felt it, too. He had wanted to kiss her again, he had said, and quite unexpectedly Victoria wanted him to. She veiled her eyes, hoping he had not read her immodest thoughts.

"Very well," she said, pulling away from him with a certain reluctance. "If you must know, my lord, I shall tell you. You destroyed all my dreams." She sighed. "Foolish and naive as they undoubtedly were—I can see that now—but they were my dreams; they represented what I was then, young and foolish if you will, but full of illusions about love." She paused and looked up at him again. If she did not know the truth, she might have once more been duped into believing him the Prince Charming of long ago. "Illusions about *you*, Derek," she added, and was dismayed when he raised her hand to his lips and kissed it lingeringly.

"You destroyed my trust," she added, ignoring the tremor of excitement she experienced at his touch. "And deprived me of all the things I most wished for in life. I wanted what Lady Margaret has found with Alex's father; I wanted what Alex has with the duke. I dreamed of being a wife and mother," she whispered in a choked voice. "I was an innocent, my lord, and my poor father knew what he was about when he said I was too young for marriage."

She pulled at her hand, still held firmly between his, but she was caught fast. "Please release me, my lord," she said stiffly. If she did not get away from him very soon, she thought, she would break down and cry.

"You still have not told me the whole of it, Victoria," he said.

"But I just did—"

"No, love," he said, smiling at her with such warmth that Victoria felt her cheeks flare with color. "I realize now that I must have been disgustingly foxed, a crime for which it is far too late to apologize, I am afraid. But I cannot believe I would . . ." He stopped abruptly and his face became very still. "Surely I did not—" He tried again. "I vaguely remember a quarrel. Did we quarrel, Victoria?"

She smiled tightly. "You might call it that," she said, feeling the panic and desolation of that frightening encounter enveloping her again. Suddenly she wanted to get it all out. Make him hear the echoes of a seventeen-year-old girl's terror, force him to face his own monstrous actions. She straightened her shoulders. "Actually, you kissed me, my lord," she said in a dead voice. At his look of surprise, she laughed shortly. "But instead of making me feel safe and cherished, I felt . . . invaded, powerless. But that was only the beginning. You behaved like a m–madman. Your hands . . ." At the memory of his hands roving all over her shrinking body, Victoria shuddered anew. "You t–touched me . . ." She could not say it, but her own hands fluttered up to her breasts and then down the length of her body. "I begged you not to hurt me, but you paid no heed." She took a deep breath and closed her eyes. It was easier if she did not have to look at the arrested expression on his face, his eyes suddenly cold and bleak. "Then you tore my dress down to here." She indicated her waist with a helpless gesture. "And kissed me. All over. I struggled, but you l–laughed at me." She turned her back on him so that he would not see the pain on her face. Where, oh where, she thought desperately, was she to get the courage to tell the end of that dreadful tale?

"Then you picked me up and laid me on the sofa," she whispered, steeling her mind for the worst part. "I closed my eyes, then, for I dreaded to see the intentions reflected in yours. I couldn't bear to see that look in your eyes. I felt your hand on my ankle, and

I was petrified with terror." Victoria wrapped her arms about herself tightly and shivered. "Then it was on my knee, and I felt I must surely be living a nightmare. That man could not be *you;* I didn't want to believe it. But it was." She paused again, her heart thudding, her limbs trembling as though the nightmare were happening all over again.

"Suddenly you stood up, and I scrambled away. I don't know how, but the next thing I knew, I was running through the wood, holding my ruined gown about me. Then I was in Lady Fanny's room, in her arms. I told her everything. . . ." Victoria felt a renewed explosion of anger at this man who had betrayed her innocence, and she swung round to face him. "So now you know the whole, my lord," she choked, careless of the tears streaming down her face. "Can you blame me for not wanting to see you ever again?"

5. The Summer House

Lord Kennaway stood perfectly still, conscious of the invisible pulse of life around him in the shadowy world of the summer house. Even after the sound of running feet had faded into the silence of the wood, he remained as Victoria had left him, staring at the empty doorway. After what seemed like an eternity, he rubbed one hand across his face as though anxious to wipe away memories newly awakened from the past. He had encountered a Victoria here in the woods today whom he had never known before. She was still the delicate fairylike creature he had lost his heart to seven years ago, but there was an emotional depth to her now that he had not suspected. Her revelations had shocked him, that was undeniable, but they had also shown him what he needed to do to win her back.

And that the earl definitely intended to do. Victoria had been far more innocent than even her father—who had at first flatly refused to give his little girl into the dubious hands of a London rake—could have guessed. And Lord Bradley had been right: Victoria at seventeen had been unprepared for passion. But a surfeit of brandy had betrayed him into disregarding that very innocence that had so bewitched him, the earl acknowledged painfully, and his kisses—instead of awakening his fairy princess to the delights of passion, had given her such a disgust for him that she had fled back into the safety of her childhood home.

He was in a pensive mood as he walked back across the park, where the hiders and seekers had long since disappeared, and the predinner pall of silence lay over the house.

Much to the annoyance of her abigail, Victoria dawdled longer than usual at her toilette that evening. She toyed with the notion of pleading a megrim and sending for a supper tray in her room, but Peckham's instant scowl when her mistress tentatively suggested this cowardly tactic cast a definite damper on the notion. In the end, Victoria allowed herself to be cajoled and bullied into a vastly becoming gown of green satin, overlaid with glittering gold netting, and clasped beneath her small breasts with a band of sequined gold velvet. As Peckham fastened the delicate emerald necklace and slipped the matching bracelet onto her slim wrist, Victoria reflected that the abigail was right—she did indeed look very elegant in the new gown.

Unfortunately, the color reminded Victoria of the soft new leaves of the chestnut trees in the park, and trees always reminded her of Derek. Thoughts of the earl brought a flutter of apprehension to her already battered heart. The scene in the summer house that afternoon had left her feeling drained and strangely vulnerable. Restless, too, she thought with a quirk of a smile at the pale-faced woman in the mirror. Her intimate encounter with Derek had awoken all her carefully buried dreams from their seven-year slumber. What troubled her was that these long-suppressed dreams were no longer those pristine illusions of a seventeen-year-old chit besotted by love. They had undergone a subtle change, and Victoria was not quite comfortable with her altered state of mind—and of heart, she admitted ruefully.

"Shall we add a ring this evening, milady?" Peckham inquired, breaking into Victoria's uneasy musings.

"No," Victoria answered automatically. Her dear papa had given her numerous beautiful rings, including a large emerald belonging to the set she had on, but Victoria never wore any of them. Even tonight, the thought of seeing any ring on her fingers but the one she had sent back to the earl was unendurable. What had happened to it? she wondered. Had he given it to one of his many *amourettes*? The memory of that precious moment when Derek had placed the hyacinth-blue topaz on her finger had been one of the most difficult to suppress, and even now, when she was feeling particularly ill-used by Fate, she could almost feel the weight of it on her bare finger.

Finally, when she could delay no longer, Victoria left her room and trod reluctantly down the stairs.

Later that night, as the house lay in silence around her, Victoria's heart engaged in a bitter dispute with her mind. At the conclusion of this exhausting exercise, she had been forced into the painful admission that her heart was correct—she was still wildly in love with the Earl of Kennaway. She also had to conclude that, given this situation, there was absolutely no chance of finding the least degree of happiness with Mr. John Rowland. Having thus deferred to her heart in matters so closely concerning it, Victoria knew exactly what she must do about Mr. Rowland's suit.

That decision to eliminate at least one of her quandaries came as a relief, but the question of the earl was a different matter entirely. He had wanted to kiss her again, that much she knew. He had said so, hadn't he? But after she poured out her tale of his iniquities, Derek had made no move to do so. And tonight he had been strangely remote, watching her sardonically as she laughed at Lord Monroyal's banter. More than likely he did not care anymore. How could she expect him to after seven years? And the thought of enduring his indifference at the birthday ball tomorrow was more than Victoria could bear.

There seemed to be only one solution, she realized eventually, after hearing footsteps pass her door as the gentlemen came up to retire. She would leave in the morning, at first light. Just as she had before. She would run away from pain and disappointment, her mind reasoned.

But she would also run away from love, murmured her heart.

The next morning nothing turned out as Victoria had planned, for no sooner had she set foot outside her door than she was accosted by her cousin Alexandra, who hugged her effusively and begged her to devise outdoor entertainment for the children.

"The darlings are driving the servants out of their wits, my love," the duchess complained, her normally serene temperament showing signs of stress. "And M. Gautier has just informed me that the oysters have not yet arrived. He is in a rare taking, believe me, and threatens to tender his notice if something is not done immediately. As if I could conjure up oysters out of thin air," she added ruefully.

Victoria also learned that Mr. Rowland, whom she had determined to confront with her newly formed decision, had gone out riding. After entrusting Higgins with an urgent message for her erstwhile suitor, Victoria herded the children out into the park, where she spent an exhausting morning organizing various games with them, all of which seemed to require an inordinate amount of energy.

By the time the bell called them in for nuncheon, Lady Letitia had come downstairs and was deriving no small pleasure in trying to override most of the instructions the duchess had given concerning the arrangements for the grand birthday ball that evening. Noting the increasingly rigid smile on Alexandra's face, Victoria came to her cousin's rescue by proposing a game of hazard, a pastime to which their factious great-aunt was extraordinarily partial. It was not until teatime that she learned that the earl and Lord Monroyal had taken themselves off that morning early with the intention, Higgins informed her, of driving up to Canterbury in the marquess's curricle.

"Dashed odd thing to do, if you asked me," Lady Weston remarked pettishly when the ladies gathered in the drawing room for tea. "But just the sort of thing one might expect of London gentlemen," she added, glancing maliciously at Victoria. "There can be nothing here in the country to hold their interest, don't you agree, cousin?"

"You are probably right, Cecilia," Victoria replied absentmindedly; although to tell the truth, she was more than a little glad to be free of both gentlemen. Her interview with Mr. Rowland immediately following nuncheon had not gone as well as she had hoped. She had been subjected to a long recitation of that gentleman's sterling qualities, which she might have borne with fortitude and patience had not Rowland launched into a point-by-point comparison of such qualities with those of a certain nobleman of dubious reputation. At that point, Victoria had terminated the interview by announcing her reluctance to marry anyone, and exited the library with the feeling that one weight at least had been lifted from her shoulders.

Victoria's disinclination to participate in that evening's festivities increased as the afternoon wore on, and when it came time to dress for the formal dinner, she fervently wished she had made her escape that morning, as she had intended. But it was too late now for retreat, she thought, or for hiding in her room. No, she would go down with a smile on her face and play the role Aunt Letitia had decreed for her. After all, the birthday ball was as much for her as for Lady Letitia, was it not? And perhaps in another fifty years, when she was Aunt Letitia's age, if she lived that long, and was Aunt Victoria to dozens of young Richardsons, Howards, Weatherbys, and as yet unplanned young cousins, she would be able to be as cantankerous as her great-aunt was today.

The notion was infinitely depressing, and Victoria shook it off impatiently as she entered her bedchamber. She had ceased to celebrate her birthdays since the disastrous events of her eighteenth anniversary, and it seemed rather ironic that she should play such an important part in this one, now that she was practically an ape-leader. Lady Letitia had insisted that Victoria open the ball tonight with a gentleman of her aunt's choosing, and short of protesting that she would much rather not make a spectacle of herself, Victoria had been unable to dissuade her. The lucky gentleman would undoubtedly be the Duke of Ashford, she imagined, as was his right by reason of rank.

Peckham had already laid out her ball gown and prepared her bath, but the abigail's face appeared more prunelike than usual, Victoria noticed. With a sigh, she turned to sit at the dressing table, and it was then that she saw the posy and paused, her heart suddenly galloping wildly. A single perfect white rosebud amid a cluster of blue hyacinths. Like the ones that grew in such profusion in the woods, a perverse voice whispered in her heart. The same hyacinths she and Derek had gathered together so long ago. A surge of dizziness swept over her, and she closed her eyes.

"Who sent the flowers?" she asked finally, gesturing towards the blue-and-white bouquet.

Peckham snorted. "Higgins wouldn't say, milady," she replied, her lips pursed in distaste. "Gets above himself, that man, if you want my opinion. Too grand by half for the likes of me," the abigail added peevishly.

"No doubt you said something disagreeable, Peckham," Victoria remarked, well aware that her temperamental dresser was not much liked by the Grange domestics for her sharp tongue and haughty airs.

Peckham gave another snort of disapproval. "Like as not it's that rascally marquess, milady. If you take my advice, you had best keep away from the likes of him. Up to no good." She glowered, taking out the pins from Victoria's hair and letting it fall in pale gold waves around her shoulders.

No, Victoria thought with a tremor of excitement. It was not the marquess who had sent the posy. Derek had sent her hyacinths the night of her last birthday ball; she remembered them vividly. Her gown had been white then, and the blue flowers had shown to advantage against the pristine satin. Tonight her gown was blue—hyacinth-blue, with silver spangles on the tiny bodice and around the low neckline. Victoria had ordered it from the modiste in Canterbury when she decided to come to the Grange this year. Perhaps an unfortunate choice of color, she realized later, since it reminded her so painfully of Derek, but it became her as no other color did. With diamonds at her throat and ears and scattered throughout her pale hair, which Peckham had gathered in a fashionably high knot, Victoria knew she looked her best. Impulsively she fastened the posy between her breasts with a diamond broach, tinglingly aware of the cool petals against her skin.

Victoria smiled at her shimmering reflection in the cheval glass and marveled that she could still appear so blooming after seven years of isolation from the glitter and gaiety of the *haute monde*. Suddenly, she was overwhelmingly glad that she had not run away this morning. If the earl chose to ignore her—and he might well do so after her revelations of the previous afternoon—then she would flirt with all the single gentlemen present tonight, including the dangerous marquess. Most particularly including the marquess, she thought, a wicked smile tugging at her lips.

She felt gay and a little reckless as she went along the hall to her great-aunt's rooms. The two birthday ladies would descend together, Lady Letitia had decided, and Victoria had acquiesced. As she trod down the grand stairway of pink Italian marble, she found herself reliving the joy of that previous birthday ball, when she had also descended beside Aunt Letitia to dance with the man of her dreams.

That same man was still the man of her dreams, Victoria mused, but whether he would dance with her tonight or ignore her completely must be left to the Fates to decide.

6. *The Charade*

Lord Kennaway could not recall afterwards who had been seated beside him at the formal dinner in the Grand Hall that evening. He supposed that conventional politeness must have led him to address an occasional comment to those mysterious females, but he could not have said what they talked about to save his life. His eyes seemed incapable of seeing anyone but Victoria, and his ears were attuned to none but her low, musical voice.

She had quite taken his breath away as she entered the drawing room beside Lady Letitia. A cloud of hyacinth-blue satin, sparkling with silver sequins on the bodice and a silvery net overskirt, reminded him vividly of the fairy princess he had once hoped to make his own. The glint of diamonds in her pale halo of hair made him think—in a flight of poetic fancy quite unlike himself—of dewdrops in the moonlight. He must be losing his wits, as the poets were always blathering on about, he thought fleetingly. Although he had to admit that even that disreputable fellow Byron seemed to have a rare insight into the matter when he wrote "She walks in beauty . . ." Derek could not remember the rest of the line, but the words reflected exactly what he saw in Victoria.

Careless of the breach of etiquette he was committing, the earl stared, entranced at the vision of beauty walking beside his great-aunt. He glanced at the old lady and met her eye. She must have read his thoughts, for she raised an expressive eyebrow and smiled enigmatically. He acknowledged her glance with a slight inclination of his head and wondered whether the temperamental old Tabby was in the mood to be generous tonight. Rather reluctantly, the earl had approached his great-aunt with his unusual request upon his return from Canterbury, where he had set his plan in motion. He was neither the host nor the ranking nobleman present, but he needed to set the tone of the evening by opening the ball with Victoria. Lady Letitia had smelled intrigue, as she always could, and had insisted upon hearing the whole.

"As I recall, my dear boy," she had remarked with a knowing smile that made Derek squirm like a lad again, "you opened the birthday ball seven years ago with Victoria, and where did that get you, can you tell me? Mad as fire over the scandal, your father was; I remember it well. Nobody would tell me exactly what occurred, of course. As if I hadn't eyes to see!" she snorted. "Plain as a pikestaff, it was. Rushed your fences with the chit, didn't you?" She paused to glare knowingly at him, a malicious twinkle in her faded blue eyes. "I don't know what your rig is, my lad, but I won't countenance anything that is likely to hurt Victoria again. Do you hear me?"

Yes, he had heard her, all right, the earl recalled,

his temper flaring briefly at the memory of the old
lady's blistering criticism. And he had wanted to put
his hands around her delicate neck and shake her, he
recalled. But tantrums had never worked with Aunt
Letitia; she merely threw a more violent one. So he
had schooled his features into a smile and revealed
part of his secret, inviting the old harridan to play a
role at which she rather fancied herself a dab. But
he had not been able to pry the answer he wanted
from her.

"And what was *that* all about?" a voice drawled at
his elbow.

The earl turned to grin at his cousin, their previous
altercation forgotten. "I begged—yes, Robert, actually
begged—the old vixen to let me open the ball with
Victoria."

"And she refused?"

"No. But she wouldn't agree, either. Bent my ear
with a scathing recantation of all my sins, of course.
In the end, she will do just as she pleases, as she
always does. She might take it into her head to select
you, old man. Merely to spite me."

"Don't let that overset you, my lad," the marquess
replied with his soft, deceptive smile. "I shall plead
senility, naturally."

Derek smiled reluctantly. "That would be a sight to
see, but I trust it won't come to that. More than likely
she will select Ashford."

He had not even been able to lead her in to dinner
when Higgins appeared at the drawing room door to
announce that the festivities were about to begin. He
had escorted an old marchioness, hard of hearing and
with a passion for hunting, which, for all he remembered she may have expounded upon all through the
meal, while Derek gazed at Victoria, seated in the
second place of honor at the duke's left.

The gentlemen were not allowed to sit around with
their port this evening, but rather accompanied the
ladies up to the immense ballroom on the first floor,

where the musicians, imported from London for the occasion, were tuning their instruments.

The earl divested himself of his marchioness as expeditiously as possible and made his way to the end of the room where a dais had been set up with comfortable chairs for Lady Letitia and her retinue. From that elevated position, the old lady could survey the proceedings with ease. It was from here that she announced the lucky couple chosen to open the ball. Everyone knew that Lady Victoria had already been chosen, as she had been on her eighteenth birthday celebration. Derek could see her now, standing beside her aunt, waiting to be handed over to the man who would lead her out onto the floor.

Derek found himself holding his breath. He had stationed himself where Aunt Letitia could not fail to see him, but the faint, condescending smile she threw at him was not exactly comforting. He felt a light hand on his sleeve and heard his mother's voice.

"Don't look so downcast, dear," the countess whispered as she made her way towards the dais. "I have asked Aunt Letitia, as a special favor to me, to be kind to lovers tonight. I thought that might appeal to the old reprobate's sense of the romantic."

But we are not yet lovers, he wanted to remind her, but Lady Kennaway had already passed on into the crowd around the dais. *Not yet.* Would they ever be? he wondered, his eyes seeking out Victoria again, fresh and radiant as a flower among the older women. She had not looked his way. Perhaps deliberately? Suddenly, the thought of seeing her handed over to another man—even a happily married one like Simon Weatherby—made his stomach knot, and he turned towards the door. At least he did not need to stand around to see it, he told himself.

"Running away, coz?" a familiar voice drawled beside him.

Derek stopped dead in his tracks. "I do not care to stand around tamely to be snubbed by that old bitch," he growled in a furious undertone. "She is quite capable of doing so, you know."

"Have you ever stopped to think how the Tabbies will react if—by one of those perversities of Fate—the old gal chooses you?" the marquess asked innocently. "Or the entire *haute monde,* for that matter?"

"I don't care," Derek responded tautly. But Robert's words raised the old specter of his broken betrothal seven years earlier, and the voracity with which the *beau monde* had chewed over the scandal for many weeks after he had returned to London, a jilted man. So it was that the earl was standing with his back to the dais when he heard his name called. At first he thought he had imagined it, but when Lady Letitia repeated it with her customary impatience, he saw the truth in Robert's amused gaze. The old Tough had chosen him after all.

He turned and met Victoria's eyes briefly before making his way, through the strangely silent throng of relatives, towards the dais. They were unreadable, but he thought she looked pale, her expression caught somewhere between dismay and surprise.

"Don't dawdle, lad," Lady Letitia said in her strident voice. "We all want to dance before midnight strikes and turns us into pumpkins." She gestured to the orchestra, which struck up a waltz. With a merciful lack of fanfare, she placed Victoria's hand in the earl's and then turned to the duke. "You may lead me out, Simon," she announced, quite as if she were bestowing a regal favor.

Derek heard nothing but the music, the soft, sensuous rhythm of the waltz, and saw nothing but the faint apprehension in Victoria's eyes as he placed a hand gently on her waist and guided her onto the floor. He was vaguely conscious of the hushed silence, followed immediately by a flurry of voices, but all he listened for was Victoria's voice. When she lowered her eyes to stare at his cravat, he racked his brains for the *mot juste* to break the awkward silence, but his years of practiced repartee seemed to have deserted him.

"Smile for me, Victoria," he murmured at length, "or people will think you are still angry with me, love."

She raised her eyes at this, and he felt captivated anew by their blue brilliance. "I should imagine it more likely they think you are angry with me, my lord," she replied rather stiffly. "I can only suppose this is another of Aunt Letitia's Cheltenham games, and I beg you will hold me innocent of having any hand in it."

He was momentarily confused by her words. "What game are you referring to, my dear?"

"Forcing you to dance with me, of course," she replied ruefully, dropping her eyes again.

The earl laughed then, feeling a surge of relief. If the chit thought he had been forced into dancing with her, he had more fence-mending to do than he imagined. Then an unpleasant thought occurred to him. "I am sorry if Aunt Letitia's choice has embarrassed you, Victoria," he began. "But I was not forced. Actually, I begged the old harridan to select me—although I did not really expect her to do so. She shares your opinion of me, I am afraid." He paused and looked down into her eyes, filled now with doubts and questions for which he had no answers.

"I am glad you wore my flowers," he said, abruptly changing the subject. His gaze lingered on the posy pinned to her low bodice, and then was drawn to the tops of her breasts, mounding delightfully from the blue satin. He allowed his eyes to travel up her slender throat and rest briefly on her lips before meeting her eyes. She had blushed faintly under his deliberate scrutiny, and her eyes were wary. He smiled. "You are the most beautiful woman in the room, my love," he murmured, entranced at the hint of a smile that twitched at her lips.

"You said that before," she said. "At that other ball. Do you remember?"

He didn't remember at all, of course, but it sounded like the kind of thing he might have said. "Yes," he lied, watching her smile broaden and feeling justified in this small deceit. "You have always been the most beautiful woman to me."

"The flowers are lovely," she said softly. "But why the white rose?"

"It reminded me of you, Victoria," he confessed, a little embarrassed at revealing this somewhat maudlin streak he had so recently discovered in himself. "And the hyacinths will always remind me of our secret place, the summer house."

What Lady Victoria might have replied he was not to know, for the music stopped and other gentlemen crowded around to solicit dances from the birthday girl. Derek retired to the sidelines, where he propped up the wall for an hour before his mother demanded he stand up with her for a country dance. After that he danced with the Duchess of Ashford, his hostess, but studiously avoided Lady Weston, who tried in vain to catch his eye. He had no interest in dancing with anyone but Victoria, and waited impatiently for Lady Letitia to retire for the evening.

At midnight, he glanced at his watch and caught Lord Monroyal's eye as the marquess joined the set of a cotillion with an awestruck young cousin in sprigged muslin, who appeared quite dazzled at her good fortune.

Robert closed one eye lazily, and the earl felt a glimmer of excitement at the game he was about to set in motion. A game he had staked his future happiness on winning . . .

At twenty minutes past midnight, Lady Richardson retired to her rooms amid a chorus of good wishes an an occasional kiss on her still-youthful cheek from those in special favor with the old lady. Victoria was one of these privileged souls, and as she deposited her salute on the softly rouged cheek, she was hardly surprised to hear a last word of advice from one who considered her understanding of human nature only a shade less omniscient than the Almighty's.

"That young man of yours seems to have reformed his ways, my dear," Lady Letitia stated with the full weight of her authority clearly in evidence. "I would give him another chance if I were you, girl. You aren't getting any younger, you know."

Before Victoria could protest that the gentleman in question was no longer her young man, Lady Letitia had swept away on the arm of her hostess, and the marquess had appeared at her side to claim his second dance.

"What did that old dragon say to put you in such a pensive mood, my dear?" Monroyal asked, a lazy smile crinkling his gray eyes at the corners.

Victoria returned his smile. "Oh, I believe she was trying to justify—as nearly as my aunt ever justifies her actions—her selection of Lord Kennaway to open the ball with me. She seems to think that Derek has reformed in some way. I cannot imagine what she meant, that's all."

"Can you not?" The skepticism in his voice made Victoria look up and she saw that he was laughing at her. "If anyone would know, my dear, that person must be you, Victoria." He paused, and then continued in a more serious tone. "Come, my dear," he said abruptly, taking her elbow firmly. "Let us walk on the terrace for a few minutes." And before Victoria could recover from her surprise at this request, she found herself standing at the stone balustrade on the terrace, looking down the sweeping lawns to the beginning of the woods, which stretched out into the night, glittering eerily—almost magically—in the moonlight.

Lord Monroyal lounged against the stone wall, his back to the moonlit scene. "You hurt him more deeply than you appear to realize, Victoria," he began with-

out preamble, his voice devoid of its usual bantering
tone. When she opened her mouth to protest, he
raised a hand to forestall her.

"And, of course, he hurt you too. Why else would
you have thrown everything away and run back
home?" He smiled gently at her to take the sting out
of his words. "I am not asking what happened, my
dear, because I can guess, being a man myself, and
one not much given to restraint of any kind. But whatever Derek did to you all those years ago—and I am
not suggesting that it was not a shock to a chit of your
tender years—I would like you to remember that it
was probably no better and no worse than what men
have been doing to the women they love—and to
many they do not, of course—ever since the world
began. You probably understand that better now that
you are somewhat less naive." He smiled again, rather
a sad smile, Victoria thought, and her heart was
touched.

"I have known Derek a long time," the marquess
continued. "And you are the only woman he has
loved, Victoria."

Victoria felt a perverse urge to find fault with this
rogue's smooth argument. "Did Lord Kennaway send
you to state his case for him?" she demanded.

Monroyal let out a crack of laughter. "Lord, no!"
he exclaimed. "Derek would have my liver for breakfast if he knew I had presumed to talk to you about
him at all." He took her hand and raised it to his lips,
almost absentmindedly, she thought. "You ask if he
has reformed," he continued. "I suppose that age has
brought him some wisdom; but it is you, Victoria, who
have changed the most."

"I cannot imagine what you mean, sir," she responded coolly, although her emotions were in turmoil
at what Monroyal was suggesting.

The marquess only laughed again. "You know very
well what I mean, my dear. You cannot hoax me, you
know. For one thing, you are no longer the innocent

chit you were seven years ago, frightened of her own shadow. For another, unless I am very much mistaken, you would not want to be treated like an innocent. Oh, yes, my dear. Do not shake your head and look affronted. I have seen the way you look at Derek, and it is not the way a silly chit would do so, with stars in her eyes. You look at him as a woman looks at the man she loves, Victoria, and you see him as a man, not as the Prince Charming you thought you were to marry seven years ago."

"You are making all this up, rogue that you are," Victoria tried to say, but her voice sounded unconvincing even to herself.

The marquess raised her fingers again for a prolonged caress, and then he smiled his old teasing smile. "Anything you say, my dear. And that is enough of this serious talk. Let us flirt for a while before Derek finds us. All I ask is that you think well before you send him packing a second time, Victoria."

"He has not given me that option," she blurted out before stopping to think.

The familiar amusement made the gray eyes glitter in the moonlight. "Ah, but he will, Victoria. Believe me, he will." He gazed over her shoulder and a broad smile lit his handsome face. "And speaking of the devil," he murmured gently, "here he comes. Derek, old man, how very inconsiderate of you," he continued, raising his voice. "You might at least give a chap the chance to steal a kiss before you come barging out like that."

Victoria sensed the earl's presence as he came to a halt close behind her, but she did not turn. She wondered fleetingly if these two men could be playing some private masculine game with her. She was still reeling at Aunt Letitia's startling choice of Lord Kennaway as her first partner. And then there was that cryptic advice from her aunt to give Derek a second chance. And now here she was on the terrace alone with Derek; at least Victoria was fairly certain that

she would shortly be alone with him. His first words
confirmed her suspicions of a conspiracy.

"You are *de trop* again, Robert. A most annoying
habit."

The earl spoke rather sharply, but Victoria was still
observing Lord Monroyal's face, and she caught the
hint of complicity in his lazy smile. And then he
bowed and was gone before she could be sure.

7. Hyacinths for Victoria

Victoria turned around slowly and lifted her eyes to
the earl's face, its angular planes starkly etched by the
moonlight. It was a handsome face, she thought. Not
darkly mysterious and seductive like the marquess's
classical features, of course, but certainly handsome.
And although she had denied it, both to herself and
to the marquess, Monroyal had been right about her.
She *had* changed. The silly chit she had once been
would never have dared to let her eyes wander over
a gentleman's face, across the wide forehead, down
the muscled length of his cheek, to rest—with a surge
of almost shameful longing—on his generous mouth.
But this was the face of the man she loved, and she
gazed upon it now with the eyes of a woman in love.
A woman who longed to be loved, who suddenly
craved it with the pent-up urges unconsciously building inside her for seven years.

He had wanted to kiss her yesterday, she mused,
her eyes fascinated by the curve of his bottom lip,
which seemed to pout slightly, as though inviting a
kiss. Did he still wish to do so? What would he do if
she kissed him first? she wondered, feeling the unfamiliar pull of desire. She wished she dared, but there
was still enough of the innocent in her to render her
incapable of such overt shamelessness.

And then the lips curved into a smile, a knowing smile that made Victoria's pulse dance wildly. Surely the rogue had not read her thoughts? Her eye flew up to meet his, and she saw in the amused amber glitter that he had indeed done so. Or at least guessed her immodest intentions.

"You have interrupted Lord Monroyal's dance, my lord," she said quickly, trying to regain a grip on her sanity.

"Dance?" His voice was full of laughter, and she realized that his former sternness had been feigned. "I do not recall that you were dancing with the scoundrel, Victoria. In fact, I distinctly heard him mention a stolen kiss."

"Nonsense!" Victoria exclaimed, strangely anxious to rule out such a possibility. "There was no time, anyway."

"More fool he, then," he retorted. "How much time does a chap need to kiss a beautiful girl in the moonlight?"

"I am not a girl any longer, Derek," she felt obliged to point out. "I shall be . . . that is, I turned twenty-five less than an hour ago."

"I know, love. And I want to be the first to give you a birthday kiss." Before she could protest, his hands gripped her shoulders and his mouth was on hers. Warm and moist and gentle. Just as she had known it would be, although the gentleness disconcerted her. His last birthday kiss had been much rougher, more possessive, acknowledging no resistance. It had frightened her then, but tonight she found herself yearning for a tangible sign that he still felt strongly about her. Strongly enough to forget her innocence in the heat of his passion, and to kiss her as a man kisses a woman, not a nervous chit just out of the classroom as she had been then.

"Happy birthday, Victoria." He drew back and stared down at her, a gleam of amusement—and something else she could not put a name to—in his moonlit eyes.

To cover her disappointment, she mocked him. "Ah, but you are not the first, my lord," she said primly.

"Monroyal?" The sternness was serious this time.

"Of course not. I mean Aunt Letitia. We exchanged birthday greetings before she retired."

"Oh, that old harridan does not count, my dear. Although I suppose I owe her thanks for her support tonight."

"Support?" Victoria repeated, puzzled.

"She chose me to dance with you, Victoria. The old girl still has a streak of romance in her old bones."

Victoria was startled and strangely elated. Her aunt's words of advice as she retired from the ballroom rang again in Victoria's head. A second chance? Could Lady Letitia be the instigator of this odd charade they seemed to be playing out?

"Whatever are you talking about?" Victoria asked, her voice oddly breathless.

"After you revealed the unpalatable truth about my behavior that night in the summer house, my love, I realized that the only way I can acquit myself in your eyes is to reconstruct what *should* have happened that night. In some small measure, I hope to erase the ugly memories we both have carried around with us all these years."

Victoria stared at him incredulously. "That is impossible," she said abruptly. "What is done cannot be undone."

"That is true, of course. But I had hoped that if you will humor me, my love, we might get it right the second time around."

Victoria laughed uneasily. "Your wits have gone begging, my lord," she protested. "So much has changed since then."

"But so much remains the same," he persisted gently. "The summer house is still here, rather more dilapidated than ever, I fear, but still standing. And you and I are still here, Victoria. And we are here together tonight. We have opened the ball together; you are wearing my flowers. Even old Aunt Letitia entered into the spirit of this re-creation of the past. And what harm can there be in a little make-believe if it will dispel some of those unpleasant memories?"

Indeed, Victoria thought, intrigued by the idea of exorcising—for curative purposes only, of course—that terrible scene from her past that had caused her so much grief. She glanced down at her bare finger and a sigh escaped her. "We shall have to pretend that I wear your ring, my lord," she murmured, conscious of a sharp pang of nostalgia. She had not meant to say that. It sounded as though she regretted giving it up, which was not the case at all. How could she have kept a memento of such betrayal? Victoria turned away and gazed out onto the moonlit park towards the trees, which seemed to beckon her into their shadowy recesses.

Suddenly his arms reached around her and he lifted her left hand. "Oh, yes, you do, my sweet," he said, slipping the diamond and topaz ring on her finger. "Does that help you to remember the role, Victoria?"

Oh, did it! She gazed down at the diamonds twinkling in the moonlight and at the deep-blue topaz—so like her eyes, he had said—and the wonderful memories came flooding back, swelling her heart and bringing her close to tears.

"So like your eyes, my love," he murmured again, the warmth of his breath moving her hair, his arms still around her. Without conscious thought, Victoria relaxed against him, seven years of her life dropping away.

"Yes, I remember it well," she admitted. "Today was to have been our wedding day." Standing here within the shelter of his arms brought everything back as sharply as if she had been transported into the past. They had stood at this very spot, arms intertwined, and Derek had carefully patted the pocket of his coat and chuckled.

"But you have forgotten the license, haven't you?" she said suddenly, hating herself for trying to break the charade she wanted to go on forever. "So it cannot be our wedding day after all."

The earl patted his coat pocket and pulled a folded paper halfway out. "Wrong, my love. How could I forget the license? There is nothing to stop us. Except a change of heart, that is."

Change of heart, she thought. Yes, she had certainly had a change of heart. But that heart had belonged—as the marquess had astutely pointed out—to a silly chit scared of her own shadow. For the first time since that night, Victoria allowed herself to wonder what might have happened had she listened to the countess. Would the miscreant, informed of his disgusting behavior, have come, penitent and remorseful, to beg her forgiveness, as Lady Fanny had promised he would? And dispensing forgiveness to the abject sinner could be so sweet, the countess had hinted ever so delicately, a knowing smile on her lips.

But that silly chit—horrified at the perceived baseness of it all—had refused to grant a reprieve. Victoria was suddenly quite sure that if the earl took such liberties with her person now—always supposing they were betrothed and a step from the altar, she reminded herself quickly, and not playing this sweet charade—she would be rather more lenient to the culprit.

"You seem to have thought of everything, my lord," she said wryly, glancing up at him to find his eyes full of a gleam that made her heart skip a beat. "What do we do now?"

He smiled and released her. "I believe we took a romantic stroll in the woods, my lady," he said, offering his arm. Caught up in the spell of the charade, Victoria returned the smile and followed his lead.

She should never had gone, Victoria thought. Perhaps she should not go now, although for the life of her she could not find a reasonable excuse for not allowing him to lead her down the shallow steps and across the freshly mown grass to the edge of the wood. There she stopped abruptly. "It is darker than I remember," she murmured, suddenly very much aware of what was to happen next.

"No. If anything, it is lighter, my dear. The moon is truly full tonight. Just about here, under this old oak, you complained that your slippers were getting damp. I picked you up and carried you, do you remember?"

Without warning Victoria felt herself swung up into the earl's arms, and she did indeed remember it vividly. The warmth of his body and the distinctly masculine smell of him came back with a rush of nostalgia. She had felt so safe, she thought. So deceptively safe in his arms.

Tonight she felt safe, too, but tonight she knew what was coming, and the knowledge made her tremble, not with fear but rather with anticipation. A delicious tingling sensation at the pit of her stomach.

Only when they reached the summer house, and the earl pushed in past the thick curtain of vines, did Victoria feel her first tremor of apprehension. The dry leaves from last summer crackled under his feet, and the bands of shadow from the lattice roof crisscrossed the stone floor with mottled stripes of moonlight. She must have windmills in her head, she thought uneasily, to come here in the middle of the night, alone, with a gentleman to whom she was definitely not betrothed, one who might even now be harboring thoughts of revenge for what she had made him suffer long ago.

Lord Kennaway put her down but retained her lightly in the circle of his arm. In the dusky interior of the summer house the darker shapes of the furniture loomed menacingly, and Victoria resisted the impulse to shrink against his chest. An involuntary shudder shook her.

"Cold, my love?" His voice caressed her out of the dimness and her brief alarm subsided.

"No," she whispered, acutely conscious of his hand resting warmly on her hip.

"You missed your cue there, my dear," he replied with a low chuckle. "You complained of the cold that night, and I folded you in my arms, thus, to keep you warm." He suited action to words, and Victoria felt his arms imprison her against his chest.

"I do not remember any mention of cold," she protested, possessed by a sudden, irrational surge of panic. "In fact—"

"Perhaps you remember this," he murmured, stopping her lips with a lingering kiss.

The sweetness of it undid all Victoria's defenses, and she felt herself melt against him, as his hand came up to cradle her head. She lost herself for several moments in this highly gratifying embrace, before she pulled back and stared up at him. If they were to exorcise the demons of the past, shouldn't they be honest about what had really happened between them?

"No," she said firmly. "It did not happen that way at all."

Derek raised his head and Victoria detected a sudden bleakness in his expression. "You are right, of course. It didn't." He paused to search her face. "Tell me what you remember."

Victoria took a deep breath. For some inexplicable reason she was having difficulty associating this man, whose kiss left her yearning for more, with that other man of seven years ago, whose embrace had filled her with terror. Yet they were one and the same, were they not?

"You . . . you frightened me then. You were so different from the man I had imagined. I didn't know you were castaway, of course; all I saw was that you didn't seem to know who I was. You became a stranger."

"How did you imagine me?"

Victoria lowered her eyes and laughed self-consciously.

"I was very naive; I can see that now," she began, surprised that she had never actually confronted this truth about herself before. "I thought . . ." She paused, seeing for the first time that what she had demanded of this man seven years ago had been unrealistic and unfair. "I thought you were perfect," she said simply. "To me, you *were* perfect." She paused again, her eyes seeking his in the dimness. He still was perfect, she thought, watching the band of moonlight play over the strong line of his jaw. He was still everything she wanted in a man, except that now what she wanted was quite different from what she had imagined she wanted at seventeen.

"And when you discovered that I was very imperfect indeed, you had a change of heart?" The words were spoken softly, but they seemed to fill the old summer house with a deafening noise. Had her actions really appeared so callous and selfish as he made them sound? she wondered, appalled at the thought. *You hurt him more deeply than you appear to realize,* the marquess had said. And he was right; the idea was new to her. Hadn't she always imagined herself the only victim of Lord Kennaway's improper behavior that night? Yet the marquess had clearly suggested that Derek had suffered, too.

He was still holding her loosely against him with both arms, and Victoria could feel the rough texture of his coat under her palms, laid flat against his chest. So close, Victoria thought. They were so close together, yet still so far apart. The chasm of misunderstandings yawned between them; she felt it like a physical presence separating them. With sudden clarity, she saw that the man she loved, the man she had loved in spite of everything for seven long years, would not cross that chasm unless she made the first move. Gingerly, she ran her palm up his coat until her fingers slipped under the lapel. It was warm there. She felt safe. She was so close to happiness again, her heart felt ready to burst.

"I fear that *I* was the imperfect one," she said quickly and urgently, before she lost her nerve. "Very imperfect. Very naive. Very foolish indeed." Why else should she have thrown everything away and run back home? the marquess had asked. And again, he had been right.

Victoria felt the earl's sudden stillness and took a deep breath. There was more that he had to know. More than she needed to tell him. What he might do with that truth was out of her hands, of course, and Victoria could not allow herself to hope for miracles.

"And there was no change of heart, Derek," she murmured, feeling the blood rush to her cheeks at the implications of this confession. "There never was a change of heart."

She lowered her hot forehead against his chest, closed her eyes, and waited for lightning to strike. If he had brought her out here to pay her back for jilting him, now would be the time to do it, she thought miserably. She was more vulnerable now than she had ever been. No longer could she hide behind outraged innocence or frightened immaturity. And she had exposed her heart to the one man who had the most reason to hate her. Would he drop this game of make-believe they were playing and reveal his true intentions in bringing her to the woods?

The silence in the summer house was absolute. Even the rustling insects in the eaves seemed to be holding their collective breaths. Then the earl's hands were on her shoulders, holding her at arm's length, his eyes blazing down at her with a strange, almost savage gleam in their amber depths. Victoria heard him let out a shuddering breath, and then he laughed, his fingers squeezing her painfully.

"Are you trying to tell me, my sweet peagoose, that we have wasted seven years of our lives avoiding each other, when we could have been . . ." He paused, and his eyes dropped deliberately to her lips. Victoria felt a wave of dizziness threaten to overcome her, and was glad of the fierce grasp of his hands digging into her

shoulders. "When we might have been far more plea-
surably entertained?" he finished, his voice dropping
to a throaty whisper that triggered ripples of sensations along Victoria's nerves.

She trembled, and instantly his hands gentled on
her skin.

"Cold?" he murmured, his eyes daring her to miss
her cue a second time.

"F–freezing," she replied with unexpected shyness,
after the merest hint of hesitation.

He chuckled deep in his throat, and Victoria thought
she had never heard a more welcome sound. The
chuckle came to her out of the past, conjuring up the
Derek she had loved and lost, fusing him with the man
who held her in his arms tonight in the old summer
house. It was a distinctively male expression of satisfaction, anticipation, arousal—all those emotions that had
so frightened her then, but which now washed over her
and gave her the sensation of opening a door into a
warm room. A room she had imagined closed forever.

And then the earl pulled her roughly into his arms,
and the Derek of long ago was back, his hands moving
sensuously over her back, her waist, curling round her
hips to bring her closer into the hard curve of his
body. And his mouth on hers, exploring, tasting, de-
manding her surrender, inviting her to make her own
demands, showing her the way to ecstasy. When his
lips started to trace her neck and came to rest on the
curve of her breast, Victoria felt the old panic rise in
her throat. He must have sensed her fear, for she
heard the chuckle again and felt his mouth tremble
with laughter in the hollow of her breasts.

"Relax, love," he murmured warmly against her
skin. "Tonight it is not wine but the smell, the touch,
the taste of you, Victoria, that has intoxicated me."
Abruptly he raised his head and gazed intently at her.
"Does that frighten you, sweetheart?"

The cool April night brushed the damp places
where his lips had burned her skin, and Victoria shiv-

ered. Yes, she thought to herself, the cold terrors of
the past had momentarily sought to freeze her heart
shut again, but she could feel that fleeting hint of panic
dissipating in the glow of his amber eyes and the warm
intimacy of his voice.

"N–no," she murmured, willing herself to believe.
"Not any more. At least not yet," she amended, the
specter of her ripped gown suddenly rising in the shadows to taunt her. She moved restlessly in his embrace,
turning to look out through the trellis to where the
moonlight twinkled on the surface of the stream.

As if the earl read her mind, his hands slid smoothly
up her body to cup her breasts, pulling her gently
against him. Victoria held her breath, the memory of
the sound of ripping silk loud in her ears.

"Your gown is in no danger tonight, love," he whispered close to her ear, his warm breath fanning her
neck. "When we get to that part, I will take it off, not
rip it. And you will help me, Victoria."

His words gripped her heart with cold hands. So
there was to be revenge after all, she thought, the
familiar freezing sensation of fear once more invading
her, crowding out the brief joy. For the first time,
Victoria sensed the squat presence of the old-fashioned
sofa sitting patiently in the background, waiting for
the next scene of this charade from the past.

But she was *not* in the past, she reminded herself
sharply, forcing all her newly formed dreams into the
deepest recesses of her mind. She was seven years
older and very little wiser. She had allowed this man
to seduce her once more into believing in magic, in
moonlight, in love. But nothing had really changed at
all, had it?

Determined to undo as calmly as possible all the
damage done anew to her poor heart, Victoria reached
for his hands to free herself from their deceptive
warmth. They would not budge. She pulled at them,
her panic heavy and cold in her stomach.

"Release me, my lord," she said, her voice cool and

crisp with fear. "This make-believe has gone on quite long enough. The charade has been amusing for you, no doubt, and possibly for Aunt Letitia as well. But I am no longer amused. The past is over with and cannot be recaptured or re-created or relived." She drew a deep breath. Oh, but how she wished that it might be. "So, you may escort me back to the house, before I freeze to death out here," she added tonelessly.

She felt herself turned roughly to face him, but she refused to meet his gaze. She was not quite ready to see the cynical amusement of betrayal in his eyes again.

"Make-believe?" He repeated, an odd note in his voice. "Charade?" And then he chuckled again, and the amusement held no hint of cynicism. "You silly, adorable wigeon," he said with unexpected tenderness. And then she was crushed up against his chest and the smell and feel of him invaded her senses until she wished that she could stay there forever, caught in the warm comfort of his embrace.

"What makes you think this is make-believe, my love?" he whispered in her ear.

But Victoria was hardly listening. She could think of nothing but escaping a painful repetition of the past. "You have made a fool of me, my lord," she choked. "I see it all now. With your make-believe ring, and your make-believe flowers, the make-believe waltz, even the make-believe license." She paused to pull frantically at the topaz ring on her finger. "Take back the ring, my lord. I want no part of your make-believe." Her grief was so intense that Victoria felt the tears gathering in her eyes.

"Listen to me, Victoria," the earl said gently, holding her firmly by the shoulders and looking down at her, alarm mixed with the tenderness in his gaze. "*Listen* to me. There *is* no make-believe, sweetheart. And if anyone is a fool here it is certainly I. Perhaps this whole idea was foolish beyond price. Perhaps I should have told you up there on the terrace instead of bringing you down to the summer house. Perhaps the ghosts here are too ugly to be exorcised. Perhaps—"

"Whatever are you talking about?" Victoria felt her panic slowly subside, replaced by a tentative—very tentative—ray of hope. If there was no make-believe, did that mean that . . . ? She shied away from the thought of what it might mean.

Lord Kennaway looked down at her, a mixture of amusement, confusion, and exasperation in his eyes. "I can see that I should have gone about this quite differently, my love. But did you really imagine I carry our ring about in my pocket all the time on the off chance I can put it on your finger again?"

Victoria stared at him, a secret surge of joy curling slowly up inside her. "Are you saying that you . . . ?" She dared not finish the thought.

"Yes, love." He grinned then, and her fears dropped away in a rush, leaving her limp with relief. And with renewed joy. "What do you think I was doing in Canterbury yesterday?" He pulled her back into his arms and nuzzled her ear.

"Then the license in your pocket . . . ?" she whispered, willing this miracle to be true at last.

"Is quite real, my love," the earl whispered back, and Victoria felt his lips smile against the curve of her neck. "And if you say yes to me a second time, my sweet, today really will be our wedding day. I will never let you get away again, Victoria." His lips moved from her cheek to rest lightly against her mouth. "And tonight . . ." Victoria trembled at the sensuous undertone in his voice. "Tonight will be our wedding night, Victoria. Aunt Letitia has promised to arrange everything."

"Oh! She has, has she?" Victoria felt the last clinging traces of the past dissipate in the waning moonlight. "In that case," she murmured, slipping her arms around the earl's neck and leaning into him with a wantonness she could not have conceived of seven years ago, "we should not disappoint her, should we, my love?"

The Apple Blossom Bower

❦

by Margaret Evans Porter

1

As Sir Edwin Page guided his horse along the rutted road leading out of Painsford village, he was conscious of a lingering depression. To be sure, the weather should have put him in a cheerful frame of mind, for the sun shone brightly and the mild breeze so common to Devonshire carried with it the scent of young grass and delicate spring flowers. The winding Harbourne River and the vista of low hills to the south were especially picturesque.

The baronet's chief regret on this glorious morning was that he was so alone in the world. He felt he was breaking some immutable law of nature by remaining a bachelor, for the songbirds had already paired up to build their nests, and the young otters dwelling along the riverbank had selected their mates. Moreover, 1794 was nearly four months gone, which meant he would soon turn thirty. In all likelihood he would celebrate his birthday alone, hardly a pleasant prospect.

And yet, he reminded himself, his present state of single wretchedness was not beyond remedy.

A curve in the hedge-bound track brought him to a straighter stretch where he generally guided his mount from a trot into an easy canter to make up time. Two other riders had halted just ahead of him, blocking the way, and he was forced to rein in.

A man in mud-spattered breeches, whom Edwin recognized as a local exciseman, stood in the road, arguing with a young female seated upon a sturdy Dartmoor pony. The animal's broad back carried another burden: a pair of small wooden kegs that had evidently aroused the officer's suspicions.

"If you refuse to let me inspect those casks," he was saying sternly, "I'll have to seize them."

"But I've told you," the girl replied, "they contain naught but cider. My mother is sending them to my uncle as an Easter gift."

"If that's so, why won't you let me open them?"

Immediately deciding to intervene, Edwin called out, "Good day, Miss Kelland,' "And my respects to you, Captain Harper."

Both antagonists, heretofore obvious of his presence, swiftly turned their heads.

"Sir Edwin," the exciseman said in relief, "you're a justice of the peace, are you not? Please be so good as to inform this young woman that I have the authority to inspect any and all goods being transported in this district."

"True," he said agreeably. "On the other hand, Captain, you needn't be concerned that Miss Kelland might be carrying contraband." He studied the girl's impassive face and was disappointed to find that she was so unmoved by his presence. His own mood had substantially improved at the sight of her, and he deemed it fortunate that he'd been obliged to ride to Dartmouth. If fate were truly kind, that was also Annis Kelland's destination.

"I've no cause for concern?" Harper echoed. "I know who she is—the daughter of a villainous smuggler, who was tried and committed to Exeter Gaol for his crimes."

"As my father died more than a decade ago," said

Annis, her pointed chin jutting upward, "I can hardly be considered guilty by association."

Edwin could only guess what her feelings must be at having her parent's unlawful trade and subsequent imprisonment held against her. Seeking to spare her further embarrassment, he said firmly, "Captain Harper, you have made a grievous error, and the possible consequences will not reflect well upon you. Squire Dundridge is a mild-mannered gentleman, but I hardly think he'll be pleased to learn that you detained his stepdaughter on the high road and accused her of being a free trader."

The officer was clearly affronted. "I was only doing my duty, sir. The gentry may choose to close their eyes to what goes on hereabouts, but I must keep vigilant."

"And I'm sure you will," Edwin said soothingly.

"If all smugglers had pretty faces," the exciseman grumbled, climbing into his saddle, "I'd have no luck catching any of 'em." He rode off at a brisk trot.

A blushing Annis turned to the baronet. "I thank you for rescuing me from that land shark, Sir Edwin."

Her use of smuggling cant amused him. Grinning, he asked, "It *is* really cider you've got in those casks?"

She failed to dignify his teasing question with a reply. Flicking her pony with the peeled willow switch that served as her whip, she rode on.

He wasted no time catching up with her, for he'd not had an opportunity to speak privately with her since last autumn's apple harvest. And this time, he thought with satisfaction, she could not escape so easily.

Her pony eyed the taller horse when it came abreast and tossed his head in agitation. His mistress regarded Edwin with a similar wariness.

Her light brown hair was woven into a long braid that hung down her back—much to his regret. Edwin preferred it loose and unconfined, as it had been on the night nearly six months ago when he'd raked his fingers through the curling mass to learn its texture.

Her loveliness was far from conventional, yet Edwin had been enchanted by it for the past two years. He especially liked her hazel eyes, so large and clear, and her pink mouth with its lusciously plump lower lip. The bones of her oval face were delicate, more refined than could be expected in one of such common stock. Her complexion was lightly and unfashionable tanned, and the freckles scattered across the straight nose and along her cheekbones bore testimony to her aversion to hats. A snowy white kerchief was crossed over her full breasts, and the rest of her figure was flattered by a flowered bodice worn over a serviceable skirt of russet cloth.

The young woman's charming countenance and superbly endowed figure had first captured his attention, but lately he'd been even more impressed by her quiet dignity. Annis Kelland made no apology for what her father had been, but neither did she boast of her mother's success in making an unusually advantageous second marriage. She kept her thoughts and feelings to herself, and that detached quality was damnably frustrating to Edwin, increasingly desperate to achieve a greater intimacy with her.

"Where are you bound this sunny morning?" he asked her.

"To Dartmouth."

"So am I."

"But I shan't be riding all the way," she added quickly. "Pippin must be shod, so I'll leave him with the blacksmith at Tuckenhay and continue to the town by boat."

He was terribly sorry to hear it but managed to conceal his feelings. "It's certainly a fine day to be out on the river," he commented. "I wouldn't mind taking the ferry myself."

She reacted with such obvious consternation that he knew his suggestion found no favor with her. Nettled by her apparent indifference, he wondered if he would ever be able to please this elusive, country-bred charmer. All these months he'd been thinking about her, wondering if she was also thinking of him. If so, it obviously hadn't been with the sort of affection he craved.

"At this season your stepfather's orchards must be a splendid sight," he said, another attempt to draw her out.

"So they are. Old William, the furze cutter, says it's the loveliest spring he can recall."

"I imagine he's seen a goodly number of them. Dartmouth is rather far to go by yourself," Edwin ventured, insinuating that she really should let him accompany her the rest of the way.

"I don't mind," she said blithely. "My stepfather was against my coming—he disapproves of my riding about the countryside unescorted, but it's what I prefer."

They came to a spot with an unobstructed view of the river, higher and broader than usual due to recent rains. The large wooden wheel that powered Bow Mill spun steadily, churning up the waters.

Breaking the rather awkward silence that had fallen, Edwin said, "I trust Squire Dundridge is well."

He noticed that her mobile mouth drooped slightly before she answered. "He enjoys his customary excellent health. My mother also."

"I shall call upon them one day soon. You may tell them that. And," Edwin added with a meaningful glance, "I hope I'll find you at home. Next time I won't send a note beforehand—perhaps by catching you unawares I can save you the trouble of hiding yourself, as you did when I last visited Orchard Place."

A blush transformed her face from sun-kissed gold to mortified pink. "There were certain duties I needed to take care of. The lambing had just begun, and Shepherd Martin required my assistance."

Edwin doubted her assertion, being perfectly aware that Squire Dundridge's flock was not a large one and that his shepherd was the most skilled in the neighborhood, but he let it go unchallenged.

Nothing more was said while they rode through the village of Bow, several houses clustered near a stone bridge over the river.

Edwin silently and heartily damned Garth Corston to hell. If his friend hadn't chosen this inopportune time to visit him, he could have offered to take Annis to Totnes Fair on Easter Tuesday. As his mount preceded the marmalade pony over the narrow bridge, he consoled himself with the reflection that his inability to raise the subject was sparing him another deflating rejection. There would be another fair in May, but now that he'd seen her again he wasn't sure he could wait the three weeks until then.

This impromptu meeting was proving what he had suspected for several months: that his obsession with Annis Kelland had intensified rather than lessened over time. Where it would lead he couldn't be sure— so much depended upon whether or not his tender feelings for her were reciprocated. He'd certainly thought so last autumn, while holding her in his arms beneath her stepfather's heavily laden apple trees. On that starry October night, lust and an excess of the squire's heady cider had prompted a passionate overture, and Annis had done nothing to discourage it. When he'd kissed her she'd been anything but aloof and her eager response had confirmed that she did care for him, if only during that brief, heated moment.

All too soon they arrived at Tuckenhay. Edwin, not yet ready to part from Annis, escorted her to the blacksmith's shop. He was helping her to dismount when a trio of children darted out of the adjoining cottage.

"Miss Annis, Miss Annis!" a red-cheeked little boy cried ecstatically. "Come inside, do, and see the new kittens!"

"Our mum has baked fresh buns," the little girl

volunteered shyly. "We're selling them to the travelers for a penny apiece, but you can have one for nothing."

"I'll gladly pay," Annis assured her with a fond smile. "And of course I must have a look at your kits. How many are there, Tim?"

"Four," was the boy's prompt reply. "I'm to have one of the toms for my very own."

Turning to the oldest of the group, a gangly youth, Annis explained that she wanted to leave her horse to be shod. "Is there room in your stable to keep him overnight, Ned? I may not be able to collect him till tomorrow."

So she expected to spend the night in town, Edwin surmised, and instantly altered his own plans to coincide with hers.

" 'Twill be no trouble, miss," the lad declared, untying the cords that secured the casks to the sidesaddle. "We can always find a stall for old Pippin." He asked if Sir Edwin also wanted to have his horse shod, and after receiving a negative reply he led Annis's pony away to the forge.

Edwin waited patiently while Annis went inside to speak to the blacksmith's wife and to inspect the new kittens. She returned within a few minutes, the little boy and girl tagging along beside her. By this time he'd transferred her kegs to his own horse.

"You can't carry them to the boat yourself," he told her.

"Ned could take them. There's no need to delay your journey, Sir Edwin."

"That's for me to decide, Miss Kelland."

She bade her young friends farewell, promising to bring each of them a present when she returned on the morrow. Then she and Edwin set out down the narrow, winding street that led down to the quay, their progress hampered by carts, livestock, and dogs.

"I can get Sue a new ribbon, but I've no idea what I should buy for Tim," she admitted. "What *do* little boys like? Last time I bought him a whistle carved from a reed, and his parents have yet to forgive me for it."

"He might be glad to have a spinning top," Edwin opined as he led his horse around the village pump. "That was my favorite toy when I was his age. They are very engaging children, but why do you give them presents?"

"Because I remember how much I enjoyed receiving trifles from customers at the Castle Inn, back in the days when my mother worked there."

Edwin, familiar with her history, knew she alluded to the period during her father's confinement in Exeter Gaol, when her mother had served tables at the principal inn at Dartmouth. It was there that Nancy Kelland had become acquainted with Squire Dundridge, who made her his wife within a year of the smuggler's demise, much to the amazement of the Devonshire gentry.

That Annis Kelland had sprung from a class lower than Edwin's was a fact that never ceased to gall him. Gazing upon her now, he couldn't help but appreciate that she was the image of an unsophisticated farm girl in her close-fitting bodice and the simple russet petticoat. He was a baronet, possessor of a vast property and a stately mansion. And yet despite these essential differences, he sensed that they would be well-matched.

Now she wanted nothing to do with him, and he could only assume it was because his advances to her at the harvest home had given her a false impression. He didn't know what he could do to make things right between them. Rescuing her from Captain Harper and delivering her cider kegs to the ferry were not enough, he feared, to repair the damage done by his eager mouth and greedy hands, or to erase the residual mortification she must feel whenever she remembered what they had done together on that memorable night.

*   *   *

The spacious kitchen of the Castle bore testimony to its being Dartmouth's busiest and most popular inn. It was unchanged from the days when Annis had either carefully kept out of the way or else joined in labor, depending upon the whims and commands of the cook. The smells wafting from the bread oven and the range and the turnspit were as mouthwatering as they had been in her youth.

She'd pulled a stool over to an out-of-the-way corner, from which she observed the hectic activity of the cook's minions as they began to prepare meals for the inn's guests and regular customers. Her uncle, whose duties as a waiter had taken him away, poked his head into the room and told her breathlessly that he hoped to resume their conversation once the taproom quieted down.

The landlady, having heard that Annis was on the premises, swept into the kitchen. The cook and the maids suddenly ceased their quarrelsome chatter, and Mrs. Russell broke their respectful silence by advising them to attend to the roasting goose.

"What are you about, my dear, hiding away back here?" she chided Annis gently. "Come into my own parlor."

"I will later," Annis replied, "after I've finished chatting with Sam."

"I'll arrange for one of the other men to take over his post for a little while. A reliable worker, your uncle, and I'd be sorry to lose him."

"I don't think he has any notion of leaving you," said Annis.

The landlady shook her head and the ruffles of her mobcap fluttered. "I hope he won't, but my best people always seem to move on. Your mother did, and I've never ceased to miss her. How is she?"

"Quite well, thank you."

"But why wouldn't she be, living as she does? A squire's lady now, and no one ever deserved good fortune more. No sooner did the news get round that

her man had died in the goal than Squire Dundridge
started coming into town twice a week instead of once
a month. I guessed how 'twould end."

"I certainly didn't," Annis murmured.

"No, I suppose not, for you were no more than
twelve. Well, I must get back to my ledgers," Mrs.
Russell said regretfully. "Pray give Madam Dundridge
my greeting. *Madame,*" she repeated reverently. "She
was plain Nan Kelland when she came to me all those
years ago seeking work. And whatever your poor papa
may've been, your mother was an honest and reliable
worker." With a sharp glance at the aproned females
clustered about the fireplace spit, she added, "You'd
all do well to conduct yourselves as she did, and then
I'd have less cause for complaint."

After delivering this shot, she moved past them, but
before exiting she turned back to tell Annis, "I'll have
a chambermaid make up the same room you and your
mother had when you lived here, the one at the very
top of the stairs. The squire wouldn't want you riding
back to Orchard Place at night, which it will be before
long. Besides, if you stay at the Castle you'll have
more time to visit with your uncle."

Ever since she'd gone to live on her stepfather's
farm so many years ago, Annis had felt cut off from
her Kelland relations. She had always been particularly close to Sam, her father's younger brother, whose
age was near enough hers that he seemed more like
a cousin or brother.

Within minutes he reappeared, saying, "I've been
given half an hour to eat my dinner, and you're to
share it—Mrs. Russell's orders. Polly, bring us something tasty, and be quick about it." He removed his
green baize apron and hung it upon a peg before sitting down at the kitchen table.

Annis joined him, and soon each was provided with
a bowl of soup and a meat pie.

"You should've et with Mrs. Russell instead of me,"
Sam said when they were done.

Annis blotted the corners of her mouth with her napkin. "It's you I came to see. Now tell me, how are all the Brixham Kellands? Does Grandfather's rheumatism still trouble him?"

"No more'n usual, so far as I know," Sam answered. "He'll be glad for any news of you. Since Mum died, he's been gloomy-minded. My sisters have families of their own and live so far off that they'll go a twelvemonth or more without setting foot in Brixham. Papa used to say you should come to live with him, but he gave up hoping for that when Nan wed her squire."

"I'd like to visit him, though," Annis said wistfully. "I could so easily travel to Brixham from here—it isn't that far. We could both go, if Mrs. Russell gave you leave."

"Do you think you should?" Sam asked gravely. "Old Dundridge mightn't like it."

"He's not here to object," she countered. "Nor would he have any reason to do so. I'm a Kelland, and I hope I can call upon my own grandfather without having to justify it."

Sam bowed his head, saying gloomily, "You hardly know what being a Kelland signifies."

"Oh, don't I?" she retorted. "This morning, on my way to Dartmouth, I was stopped by an exciseman. He wanted to know what was in those kegs I brought you."

"Is that all?"

"It was most annoying," she said, her eyes kindling at the memory.

" 'Twas but an inconvenience, nothing more. I've been treated far worse, you may be sure." Turning his hazel eyes upon her, he said, "I want to work on a ship more than anything—always have done. Kelland men have been seafarers for as long as anyone can remember."

Annis knew exactly what was coming, and she placed a consoling hand upon his arm.

"But no ship's master or captain in any Devonshire port is going to take on Jem Kelland's little brother," he grieved. "The customs officers would scour whatever vessel I was assigned to for contraband every time it sailed or returned. They'd be sure to question me about the smugglers who run goods into Dartmouth and Brixham and everywhere else Jem had his contacts. And who could blame them? He was notorious. You wouldn't remember, you were no more than a child, but—" Sam hesitated momentarily, then said, "Ah, never mind. Poor Jem. He never killed that land shark himself, and no one who truly knew him believes he did. Or *could*."

Annis, knowing so little about her father, would have encouraged her relative to continue what to her was an illuminating discussion, but at that moment the headwaiter charged into the kitchen.

"Hurry along, Sam—you're needed in the taproom! I've got a party of ship's officers shouting for their grog, the dining room is full, and just now two fine gents came in wanting to sup in the private parlor. You, girl," he said sharply to one of the cookmaids, "put on a fresh apron and go see what they want."

Annis bounded up from her stool. "She's busy. I'll go to them."

Her uncle's harassed colleague stared at her. "You, miss?"

"Why not, if you're shorthanded?"

Sam put a restraining hand upon her shoulder. "Nay, Annis. B'aint what Squire Dundridge would want."

But for Annis, that was the appeal of it. And although she was rather ashamed of her eagerness to go against the wishes of a man who was consistently kind and generous toward her, she said airily, "He'll never find out. It's the least I can do for Mrs. Russell."

She'd lived at the inn for many years and therefore knew her way to the private parlor, which was commonly assigned to the most distinguished of customers. It was there that her own mother had often waited upon the squire.

After hastily straightening her fichu and smoothing her borrowed apron, she stepped into the room. One of the two gentlemen seated there was Sir Edwin Page, and the shock of his presence nearly sent her scurrying back into the hall before she was seen.

But it was too late. Squaring her shoulders, she advanced to the circular table and handed the baronet a bill of fare.

"What a pleasant surprise to see you again so soon, Miss Kelland," he intoned blandly. "I told Mr. Corston that the service at the Castle is as reliable as the food, and I daresay you will prove that I was right."

A serving maid would probably have bobbed a curtsy. Momentarily at a loss, Annis wasn't sure how best to respond. Smiling tentatively at his companion, a stranger with blond hair and a sunburned nose, she said, "The soup is very good today, sir."

Looking up from the paper she'd given him, the man asked, "And how are the wines? Does your master have something special hidden away in his cellar— a bottle or two that slipped past the excise officers?"

A fiery blush consumed her face, and she couldn't bear to look at Sir Edwin. Twice in one day he'd been reminded of her connection, however distant, to the smuggling trade.

"It would be far too risky for the Russells to keep any untaxed spirits, Garth. We'll begin with a bottle of the best claret. And, Miss Kelland, I should very much like to try the soup."

So began one of the most embarrassing and aggravating evenings of her life, and it was made worse by the fact that she had only herself to blame. As she served the two men their dinner, she had to admit that her ordeal was a fitting punishment for her uncharitable urge to slight the squire. Worse, by impetuously taking on the role of serving wench, she'd disgraced herself before the man she most wanted to please.

Her heart bursting with inexpressible emotion, she

noted how the light of the sconces played across Sir Edwin's chestnut hair, tied behind with a dark velvet ribbon.

For two years she had loved him. They'd met when he called upon her stepfather shortly after inheriting his great-uncle's title and house. Of his life before he'd come to live in Devonshire she knew almost nothing. Now she doubted her curiosity would ever be satisfied. Tonight she had surely lost whatever had been left of his respect, although there probably hadn't been much to lose after the harvest home. There was no longer any need to maintain the frigid civility she had assumed ever since then, which was supposed to communicate that her dignity was unimpaired by what they had done together that night.

She should have known better than to go off into the apple orchard with him, but when he'd taken her hand and led her out of the crowd she hadn't offered a single protest. His hot, desperate kisses had been a revelation. His fingers, which had first moved tenderly across her face and then down her neck, eventually settling on her breasts, had evoked new and incredible sensations. For as long as he'd held her in his arms, it hadn't mattered who he was or what her own father had been or done.

While removing the empty plates from the last course from the table to the sideboard, she listened closely to his discourse with his friend, who had consumed more wine than food and was beginning to dominate their conversation.

"Where did you leave your yacht?" she heard him ask.

"Torquay. I made excellent time from Lyme Regis, considering that the direction of the wind was against me. The pater and mater were after me to stay close by—they wanted me to attend some damned local assembly, the sort of thing I abominate. But I sailed off as soon as I could, and the closer I got to Devonshire, the more I was tempted to make good my threat to pay you a visit. So I interrupted my cruise and wrote to warn you of my imminent arrival."

"I'm glad you did."

Annis, alert to every inflection in that low, pleasant voice, detected the faintest note of sarcasm.

"Ever since I received your letter boasting about that string of horses you've got at Harbourne Court, I've been eager to see 'em."

"You shall ride them as well, if you like. When do your parents expect you back in Lyme?"

Annis returned to the table with the wine bottle in time to witness Mr. Corston's careless shrug. "It makes no difference. They've got Lizzie. She's better company than me, and they're having a grand time showing her off to all the provincials."

"I wouldn't be surprised to learn that the incomparable Miss Corston has more admirers than she can count."

The difference in the baronet's tone was immediately apparent to Annis, and she couldn't help but recall certain vague but persistent rumors of a distant ladylove. To her dismay, her hand trembled as she refilled his empty glass. Had he noticed?

Mr. Corston nodded eagerly when she moved to his side of the table, so she poured more wine for him as well. "How late do the coaches run in this district?" he asked.

"I've no intention of returning to Harbourne Court tonight," Sir Edwin replied. "The roads are in a dreadful state after the recent rains, and the journey is just long enough that I would prefer not to attempt it. Miss Kelland, do you happen to know if any bed-chambers are available?"

To avoid returning his gaze, she stacked the plates onto her serving tray. "I can ask Mrs. Russell."

"I'd be most grateful if you would."

She hoped the landlady's answer would be a negative one, for the prospect of sleeping under the same roof as Sir Edwin Page was singularly unnerving. But her mother's former employer, elated by the prospect of filling all the beds that night, said she did indeed have a room left—the very one she'd offered to Annis.

Knowing how reluctant Mrs. Russell would be to lose paying customers, Annis said, "One of the gentlemen can have the bed that was Mother's and the other can have the trundle I used to sleep on. I shan't mind sharing with Polly, or one of the other girls."

"But it's far from being my best room, as you well know. Not nearly worthy of Sir Edwin Page and his friend."

"You did say the sheets and blankets are clean," Annis reminded her.

"And the rug was beaten just this morning. Very well, they may take the room—better that than letting them seek one elsewhere."

Annis delivered the substance of this message to the gentlemen in the parlor, leaving out the part about the rug.

"I've no doubt we'll be perfectly comfortable," Sir Edwin said with a satisfied nod.

She circled the table once more, taking up the few remaining utensils and Mr. Corston's bowl of soup, which he'd scarcely touched.

Tugging the long braid that hung down her back, he leered up at her and said, "I wonder, is the serving maid at the Castle as accommodating as the landlady?"

"Mind your manners, Garth," Sir Edwin said reprovingly.

"Don't be such a prude, Eddie. She ain't offended—are you, m'dear?"

"Let this be your answer," Annis shot back, tipping the contents of the bowl into his lap.

Mr. Corston leaped to his feet. "You little slut—I'll have you sacked for that, I will!"

"You can't," she told him triumphantly. "I don't work here."

Before storming out of the room, she dared to look

toward the baronet. His eyes met hers for an instant, and she wondered if that could be amusement she read in their glittering depths, or if it was only a trick of the light that made her fancy it.

Now she had really and truly brought shame down upon her head, she told herself as she wandered back to the kitchen. And it made no difference—not really. Sir Edwin Page had probably made up his mind about her long ago. He thought she was only good enough for bussing and groping—and for a tumble in the grass, no doubt—but nothing more.

For days after the harvest dinner she'd held onto a foolish hope that his intentions were more honorable than not, until her mother had set her straight. After scolding her for letting the baronet steal a few kisses, Mrs. Dundridge had warned that titled gentlemen were after but one thing, and as soon as they got it from one lass they sought it from another. If Annis had set her heart on becoming a ladyship, she was destined to be sadly, tragically disappointed.

Much later, the weary young woman reflected upon her mother's doleful prophecy as she climbed the long and crooked stairway to the garret occupied by the inn's female servants. The moment she reached the last step, the door opposite the upper landing swung open and Sir Edwin Page emerged.

"Might I have a word with you?" he asked, his frown an indication that the words would not be the ones she most wanted to hear.

Nodding, she indicated her willingness to tarry.

"I've tried to set Mr. Corston straight about who you are—not that I'm quite certain of it myself. But I was unable to explain precisely *why* you were waiting on tables tonight."

"Not all tables—just yours. The staff was short-handed, and I wanted to help in the only way I could." Essentially that was accurate, but of course she'd had another reason that she dared not admit. If she mentioned her stepfather, whose authority she'd so recklessly defied, Sir Edwin might tell tales against her. "Do you disapprove?" she asked, her voice as frosty as she could make it.

"I do," he said curtly, almost angrily. "And so would Squire Dundridge."

Although she'd already lowered herself in his estimation, she still had too much pride to plead for mercy. "My mother was doing exactly what I did tonight when she met her husband."

He folded his arms across his broad chest and regarded her through narrowed eyes. "Exactly what sort of husband are you seeking, Miss Kelland?"

A wave of anguish crashed over her, leaving her speechless. She wanted *him,* more than she had wanted anything in all her life. No other man was as handsome and clever and strong and passionate as the one who stood before her, but she was not good enough for him.

When it became apparent that she had no answer to his question, he said, "I suspect Mrs. Russell intended you to have this room. Where will you sleep?"

"I'll be sharing the cookmaid's bed."

"I wish you might share mine."

So he did consider her a wanton. In a tone more sorrowful than saucy, she said, "You are very bold, Sir Edwin."

"I wasn't inviting you to do it," he defended himself. "I only said I wished it. Lest you have any doubts, that's a compliment to you, not an insult. There's no cause to treat me as you did my drunken friend."

Half-afraid he might say something still more shocking—and gratifying—Annis wished him good night and sped along the dimly lit passage. And when she glanced back to see if he was still there watching her, his sensuous smile caused her heart to pound so violently that she actually covered it with her hand as if to keep it safely in place.

2

A shot rang out, shattering the perfect stillness of the morning. There was an explosion of breaking glass as the bullet struck one of several wine bottles lined up on a low stone wall.

Looking down at the old-fashioned dueling pistol cradled in his hand, Edwin wondered to himself what his gruff great-uncle would have thought of his skill. The old gentleman had been a superior marksman.

"Well done," Garth Corston commented, not without envy. He had yet to hit any of the objects they had lined up on the low stone wall. Raising his arm, he studied his target. His finger tugged at the trigger. There was a blast of fire and smoke, but the row of bottles remained undisturbed.

"Damn," he muttered.

They had been shooting for nearly an hour now, competing to see which of them could fire, reload, and fire again with speed and accuracy. Both were unshaven and carelessly dressed.

Garth was turning out to be a terrible influence, Edwin thought as he lifted his pistol again. Not once during the past fortnight had they gone riding together—they hadn't done much of anything except drink and dine and play cards, and waste lead shot and powder. Ironically, he'd felt lonelier than ever despite having company at Harbourne Court. It was female society he craved—that of a particular female. But his recent encounter with Annis Kelland had been far from satisfactory, and his chances of winning her seemed depressingly remote.

He'd met Garth Corston at Eton, but their paths had diverged after leaving school, only to cross again in London some years later at the height of the social season. Upon discovering that the easy camaraderie of their boyhood had survived, they'd sampled the delights and tested the dangers of the metropolis together. Edwin, a regular visitor to the Corston house, became acquainted with the family and had even embarked upon an intense but short-lived flirtation with Garth's sister Elizabeth. Upon realizing almost immediately that her parents had certain expectations he was reluctant to fulfill, and that in fact he had no strong desire to marry her, his only option had been to decamp from London with all possible haste.

He'd returned to Somersetshire and the kindly and unpretentious relatives who had raised him, but soon afterwards he was summoned to Harbourne Court by his ailing great-uncle. With the death of the crotchety bachelor, both the baronetcy and the estate had become Edwin's.

The imposing Elizabethan manor and its outbuildings were surrounded by a spacious but overgrown park containing a poorly stocked fishpond and a neglected rose arbor. Despite the fact that the house had gone without a mistress for decades, its furnishings and appointments were fairly well preserved. In the library Edwin had found an antique housekeeping book written by an ancestress at the close of the previous century, and reading it he'd ascertained how very many tasks had been dispensed with by his late uncle's staff, all of whom remained in his employ. The decrepit housekeeper's eyesight had all but failed, and her subordinates resented being told how to do their work by anyone else. The time was coming when he'd have to pension the old woman off.

Garth interrupted his reflections by saying, "I think that boy wants to speak to you."

Edwin looked around and saw one of his grooms coming towards them.

"A message has come from the squire, Sir Edwin," the young man announced. "He asks that you call upon him at—at—" He wrinkled his brow in an effort to recall what he'd been told to say.

"At my earliest convenience," Edwin supplied, handing his pistol to Garth. "Take this—perhaps it will prove luckier than the other one. Only please, do not slay any of my sheep."

"Shall I go along with you?"

"No, no," he responded quickly, preferring to keep Garth at a distance from Annis Kelland. "I'd best have a quick wash and change my clothes." Running his hand across the two-day growth of beard, he added, "And I desperately need a shave."

Within an hour he had completed all of these improvements, and by the time he descended upon the stables he was the model of a respectable country gentleman. The young man who had delivered the squire's summons had just finished saddling Edwin's favorite mount, while the head groom watched from a nearby bench, a piece of hay dangling from his hips. At his master's approach he bounded to his feet.

"Have you and Bart finished mucking out the stalls, Jenkins?"

"Aye, sir," he said, clearly affronted by the implication that he might in any way be derelict in his duty. "There's something I've been meaning to say, Sir Edwin."

"Well, what is it?"

"The horses badly want exercising, and have these two days past. Bart and me can't take more'n two out at a time, and there's a full half-dozen of 'em in need of a good gallop every day. I was thinking p'raps you might want to hire another groom, or else go back to riding 'em yourself."

"I meant to do exactly that. Mr. Corston claims to be an excellent rider, so I can enlist his help. In fact, it was to try my horses that he came to Devonshire." Or so he'd said. Edwin wasn't altogether certain whether or not it was a credible explanation. "We'll discuss the matter upon my return from Orchard Place."

"Aye, sir."

Edwin took his horse's reins from Bart, who gazed up at him expectantly, his Adam's apple rising and falling as he gulped. "What is it, lad?"

"Could—could I ride with you to Squire Dundridge's, sir?"

He regarded the youth shrewdly. "Have you a sweetheart in his employ?"

Jenkins chortled, letting the straw fall out of his mouth. "He fancies Miss Annis Kelland, silly ass that he is. Everyone knows the squire will marry her to a gentleman, not some spotty-faced stableboy."

When Bart whirled upon his senior, fury blazing in his eyes, Edwin gripped him firmly by the shoulder. "Go back to the meadow and ask Mr. Corston if he'd like to ride this morning. Run along, now," he prompted.

"He b'aint serious 'bout the squire's lass," Jenkins commented when the reluctant Bart obeyed their master's order. "He's at that age where he can't help but have a care 'bout the one he can't have. I'll tease him out of it, sir, you'll see."

"Don't be too harsh with him," Edwin cautioned before climbing into the saddle.

"Oh, I'm fonder of him than I let on. He's a good boy, that one, but even the best of 'em wants scolding to keep 'em in line."

The road to the squire's farm carried Edwin southward, past meadows swarming with sheep and their new lambs. The sky was overcast, rather like his mood, for he was concerned that he might be about to receive a scold—or worse—from Squire Dundridge. If Annis had revealed some of the things he'd said to her at the Castle Inn, particularly the part about wanting her to share his bed, he'd have difficulty explaining it to her guardian.

But the squire received him so cordially that these fears were quickly laid to rest. Edwin found him flinging corn to the geese waddling about the barton, a large yard enclosed by ricks and outbuildings, and his greeting was reassuringly warm.

"I didn't expect you so promptly," Dundridge said, dusting off his hands as they strolled to the house, a handsome stone structure with chimneys at either end, a new slate roof, and ivy-covered walls. "My wife is paying a call, and I left Annis in the orchard to supervise the workers there, so we can converse in private—I'm in need of your advice, Sir Edwin."

Squire Dundridge's income, reportedly an ample one, was based upon his extensive apple orchards. He brewed hundreds of hogsheads of cider annually, some of them going to the Plymouth and the navy ships, and the remainder sold to taverns too small to produce their own. Although the squire's social presence had been limited during the eight years since his astonishing marriage to the smuggler's widow, there was no cause to suspect that he regretted what so many of his acquaintance regarded as a misalliance. In Edwin's view, Mrs. Dundridge was a pleasant hostess and an admirable housekeeper and certainly did not disgrace the position to which she had been raised.

The squire led the way to a tidy parlor and after pouring out two glasses of amber liquor, he presented one to his guest. "I should be honored if you would favor me with your opinion of my last attempt at producing calvados. I've tried to get it right, with varying success, since I visited France, and what began as a hobby has become my obsession."

Edwin sampled the contents of his glass, savoring the rich taste of apples mingled with the fiery heat of brandy. "Nectar of the gods," he declared, barely repressing an urge to lick the residue coating his lips. "I wasn't aware that you'd traveled abroad, sir."

" 'Twas decades ago, between wars. My father sent me to the Channel Islands to pick up a few cider-brewing secrets, and from there it was but a short sail to Normandy. I drank calvados night and day—and would still, if Mrs. Dundridge didn't demand that I restrain myself." Setting down his glass, he said on a pensive note, "I'd like for our Annis to see France someday, but I doubt she ever shall."

Edwin lifted his head. "This war won't last forever."

"I hope not, for it's already wrecking our foreign trade. But even if 'twere peacetime, both the girl and her mother would resist any suggestion that she should travel. A great pity."

Edwin was seized by a powerful and inexplicable desire to take the squire's stepdaughter on an extended foreign tour. But not until he'd shown her the part of Somersetshire where he'd grown up, and only after she'd seen London and its many splendors.

"In fact," Dundridge continued, "Annis is the subject I wished to discuss with you. For some time now I've been thinking of buying a horse for her. Oh, she's got her pony Pippin, good enough for hacking about the farm, but to my mind she deserves a mount more worthy of a young lady. And no other man in this district has finer bloodstock than you."

"I'm honored that you should think so, and hope I can provide one that will be to Miss Kelland's liking. What are her requirements?"

"I cannot say. I haven't even broached the subject of a new horse to her, lest she object to my plan. She's too polite to refuse a gift, particularly if it's a surprise. And even if it comes from me," he added, his voice tinged with regret.

Edwin, struck by his sorrowful demeanor, surmised that relations between the squire and his stepdaughter were not as comfortable as he'd always supposed.

"I'd prefer that Annis try out your horses without knowing she's to have one of them. If you put the question to her, she'd tell you which she likes best, and then you can let me know. Does that seem a reasonable course of action to you?"

"Indeed," Edwin said, quick to approve anything that would broaden his association with the girl whose affection he desperately desired. "Just this morning my head groom said my horses aren't getting enough exercise. I'll be sure to mention that to Miss Kelland, and beg her help."

"Perfect!" the squire said enthusiastically. "An appeal to her charitable instincts is certain to be successful. But don't tell her that this is my idea, or even that I gave my consent—women can be so contrary. If she asks if I stated my opinion, simply say that I didn't *altogether* disapprove."

When Edwin joined Annis in the orchard, he found her perched high atop a ladder, dangling among the branches of an old and venerable apple tree. Her hair was unbound, streaming down her back in thick brown waves, and she had pinned up her long skirt and protective apron so they wouldn't hamper her.

"Your trees will soon be in full flower," he observed, craning his neck.

"Yes," she agreed, "within another week or so." Her thumb and forefinger closed around an unfurled pink bud and she pinched it off, letting it drop to the ground. "It's quite painful doing this," she admitted to Edwin over her shoulder, "but it does improve the fruit-bearing. I can only go so high, though, so I must depend upon the bullfinches to strip the blossoms at the very top."

Edwin held the ladder during her descent. As she climbed down, he studied her slender, well-turned ankles and found them very much to his liking.

"I attend to this tree myself because it's my favorite. The men are better and faster than I; they've been doing orchard work so much longer." As she hopped down to the grass, her slippered feet crushed the discarded buds.

"I was sorry not to see you again in Dartmouth, Miss Kelland." He could tell by her sudden silence and the way she was avoiding his glance that she remembered the highly personal nature of their last conversation. "The next morning, when I asked Mrs.

Russell where you were, she told me that you and your uncle had gone off to Brixham together."

"Sam borrowed a friend's gig and took me to visit my grandfather Kelland."

"I didn't know you had a grandparent living."

She nodded. "He's three-score and five years old, and apart from his rheumatism is a hardy old gentleman. He still reads a great deal, and likes to talk of his favorite books—he used to be a schoolmaster."

"Has he any children besides your uncle?"

"No other sons, but I've got two aunts living near Exeter. They married brothers, both farmers. One is very prosperous, I believe, and the other less so. I don't know my cousins well at all," she said with a trace of sadness. "After my father died, Mother had no cause to visit that part of the shire. And in the eight years since she remarried, she's had even less." Abruptly she asked, "What brings you to Orchard Place today, Sir Edwin?"

Prudently keeping to himself the fact that he was there at the squire's request, he replied, "I seek your assistance. I've acquired so many horses recently that Bart and Jenkins haven't enough time to exercise them all as often or as thoroughly as I prefer. Knowing how fond you are of riding, I thought you might come to my aid until I'm able to enlarge my staff. We've got at least three well-tempered horses capable of carrying a lady's sidesaddle, and they'll give you an easier ride than your Pippin."

Annis pressed her hands together, saying fervently, "I would like to ride them, truly, but I doubt my mother would let me go to Harbourne Court. Or my stepfather," she added on a grimmer note.

"Trust me to make everything right with them."

She sighed. "How I wish you could."

He studied her downcast face, then said, "You're troubled by more than gaining their permission to ride my horses, aren't you?"

Annis moved to a broad but crooked lower limb

and perched upon it. "This is the oldest and most famous apple tree on the farm, the original source of the variety known as Dundridge's Glory. Plantsmen used to travel all the way from London to take grafts. I was glad when they stopped—this place has been my refuge since I first came to live at Orchard Place."

They were surrounded and shielded—almost embraced—by the lavishly budded branches. He wanted to make the most of their seclusion, to seize that slender waist and pull her close and kiss her until she was powerless to rebuff him. But he knew that if he did, she would never accept his invitation to Harbourne Court.

"A private and most fragrant bower," he commented, leaning his back against the sturdy trunk. "From what exactly are you escaping when you come here?"

"The squire, more often than not." She ripped away a tiny new leaf shaped like an arrow point and began shredding it into tiny pieces.

"Won't you tell me why?"

"You wouldn't understand. You couldn't."

Her lack of faith hit him like a blow, but her bleak tone was far more disturbing and raised a concern that he hardly dared voice. "Your stepfather doesn't do unseemly things—touch you in any way he shouldn't? Or strike you?" The questions sounded preposterous, but Edwin had already guessed that the appearance of family harmony was deceiving.

Shaking her head, she answered, "He has never even raised his voice to me, much less his hand. He's *never* angry with me." She made it sound like a grievous fault. "Or if he is, he keeps it to himself. But still I know I'm a severe disappointment to him, Sir Edwin."

"I've seen no sign of that."

"Oh, he is excessively generous, and also affectionate. I'm the one at fault, for being too common to ever please him completely. You see, he won't accept me as I am. He wants to turn me into a proper lady."

Grasping the branch above her head for support, she elaborated, "When his cousin Myra in Totnes offered to take me in and teach me to be more genteel, I refused to go, and that displeased him. I was only twelve at the time, but even then I knew it would be a hopeless effort."

"You were right."

She looked over at him, her face reflecting her dismay at his brutal candor.

"True ladies are born, not made," he explained rather more gently. "And you are one, as I recognized within a few minutes of becoming acquainted with you. I'm surprised someone as astute as your stepfather could think otherwise."

Her voice was flat as she said, "He wants greater things for me than I do for myself. That's why he dislikes my riding about the countryside alone on Pippin and discourages my visits to my Kelland relations. I daresay he imagines they are tainted by the smuggling trade, but they're not, no more than anyone else in the district. My father was the only one directly involved in free trading."

Edwin interjected, "And I suppose the squire also objects when you wait tables in a public inn."

"He doesn't know about that," she said quickly, "and I hope he never finds out. It felt wrong at the time, and I should've known better. But the landlady kept telling me how lucky Mother was to marry a squire, and then my uncle said I shouldn't go to Brixham to visit Grandfather Kelland without my stepfather's leave, and that goaded me into behaving stupidly. I wanted to prove that I could do whatever I wished, and in the process came to grief. I shall never cease to regret it."

"There's no shame in being human," he consoled her. "Mind you, I was tempted to give you a good scold myself that night, even though I had no real right to do so. But then, if you'd behaved more wisely I would have missed the great pleasure of watching you give Garth Corston his comeuppance. He deserved much worse than having a bowl of cold soup poured over him."

"I didn't want him ... touching me," she declared, her voice dropping as he moved a step closer.

"Just him, or any man?"

Annis, uncomfortably aware of how close he was, resisted the urge to shy away. His hand moved toward her, and a moment later she felt his fingers graze her head. He plucked something from her hair and held it up on the tip of his forefinger—not a creepy-crawly, as she'd expected, but a tiny petal of palest pink. She studied it in silence, waiting for him to speak and wondering what he would say next.

"This is where we came during the harvest home, isn't it?" he asked softly, his voice a caress. "I kissed you under this very tree. And did some other things as well," he added, a wicked glint in his eyes.

With an assumption of hauteur, she frowned and said, "If you truly think I'm a lady, why must you always remind me of what happened that night? It isn't gentlemanly of you."

"I would be far less gentlemanly to let you think I'd forgot what happened here."

She had no answer to that. To cover her confusion she leaped down to the ground, telling him shakily, "I cannot linger, Sir Edwin. Mother will be home soon, if she's not already, and—" She was silenced by his hand closing upon her arm.

"You'll come to Harbourne Court?"

"Perhaps. If my stepfather doesn't refuse his consent, and my mother can spare me."

His handsome face wore the expression she always watched for, the tender, yearning one that made her feel so wishful and yet so hopeless. Sir Edwin Page might flirt with her from time to time and even kiss her when the opportunity presented itself, but it was almost inconceivable that he would pay court to a humbly born, freckle-faced creature like herself.

His smile broadened, as if he'd guessed her thoughts and was pleased by them. "Every hour that passes until we meet again will seem longer than the one before. Farewell, Annis Kelland."

Watching him stride across the orchard and toward the barton, she no longer felt despondent. His voice, his eyes, his every glance had been proof that he cared for her. If he had tried to kiss her again, then she would have continued to doubt his motives, but he hadn't. Was his new restraint merely a seducer's ploy, intended to deceive her into a false sense of security while he plotted his next advance? Or did it mean that he had honorable intentions after all and was therefore treating her as he would a girl of his own social class?

Her eyes fell upon the bright yellow cowslips blooming abundantly in the grassy patches between the apple trees. The flowers, she knew, could be used to make an ointment that not only improved the complexion but was also supposed to lighten freckles. Thinking that she might do well to take such measures, she collected several handfuls in her apron and carried them to the stillroom at the rear of the house.

While she was spreading the flowers across the worktable, her mother, a matronly woman of middle age with a pleasant but infrequent smile, walked in and began taking inventory of the bunches of dried herbs hanging near the window. "What have you there?" Mrs. Dundridge asked. "Cowslips?"

"I want to get rid of these." Annis touched the bridge of her nose to illustrate.

Wagging her head, the squire's wife said, "Your father, rest his soul, was as freckled as a turkey's egg. I s'pose it came from being out in the sun so much, and on the water."

"I mean to make a lotion," Annis informed her. "Is your receipt book at hand?"

Mrs. Dundridge removed the well-worn volume from its drawer and passed it to her daughter. "You'll want the oil of almonds—it's behind you, on the topmost shelf. What's made you so concerned about your complexion so sudden?" she asked suspiciously. "B'aint for my benefit, much less the squire's. I suppose Sir Edwin Page has been here today. He rode past me a while ago, when I was coming home, and proper cordial he was."

"He came to see me." Annis couldn't quite keep the triumph out of her voice.

Mrs. Dundridge sank down upon a Windsor chair, resting her tightly clenched hands in her lap. "Oh, Annis, do have a care. More likely than not he'll give you a heartache; I've said it before. If you set your hopes upon having him as a husband, you're bound to be hurt."

"I used to fear that, too, but I must have been wrong. He isn't trifling with me—perhaps he was at the apple harvest, but not now."

"His intentions might be pure as springwater, but they can't change what he is. A respectable farmer would do better for you than a baronet."

In the face of this familiar warning, Annis fought to hold onto her optimism. Fetching the mortar and pestle from their compartment, she asked, "Don't you like him?"

"So far as I know there's naught to dislike, apart from his chasing after you last harvest supper and bussing you because he'd drunk too much of your stepfather's cider. But in my experience, marrying above yourself is more of a trial than a blessing. And if your stepfather has encouraged you to hope for something that—"

"He hasn't," Annis said firmly. She turned the pages of the receipt book until she found the entry she wanted. "I'll need your help, Mother. I don't yet have your skill for concoctions."

Her parent heaved a deep sigh. "Very well. And I'll even show you my way of distilling elderflower water so you can wash your face in it at night. But don't think that means I want you marrying Sir Edwin and going off to live at Harbourne Court. Not that it wouldn't 'maze everybody hereabouts if you could become Lady Page," she added with a shake of her head. "Jem Kelland's daughter mixing with the gentry-folk. It'd be a greater scandal than his widow wedding a squire."

Edwin stared down the dining table at his companion's flushed and bloated face. Garth had been drinking steadily all night long, and his mood was extremely variable, jovial and surly by turns. Just now he was scowling as he examined the stem of his empty wine-glass.

His fingers lost their hold and he just missed dropping the delicate piece. "Sorry," he mumbled, setting it down. "Though I daresay if it broke you could easily afford another. Couldn't you?" His bloodshot eyes sought Edwin's stern face.

"Yes. But a replacement might not match the other glasses."

"Lucky man. Rich uncle dies, leave you all this." Garth's broad, sweeping gesture sent the wine bottle crashing to the floor.

The fact that it was empty was scant consolation to Edwin, who fervently wished he could order his oafish visitor off the premises. It was his misfortune that there was no way to do so without offending, and the fact that he had been the recipient of the Corstons' hospitality in London worsened his predicament.

Rising, he surveyed the dark-green shards scattered across the oak floorboards. "The servant will clean it up. Shall we retire?"

"Not yet," Garth said stubbornly, without moving. "Not till you've satisfied my curiosity about exactly how much this estate is worth."

Fighting back the retort that it was none of his business, Edwin said, "I can't boast that my farming income is in any way remarkable, but in time I expect a fair profit from the stud I'm developing. My great-uncle was something of a miser, so he left behind a substantial amount of capital. Not a great fortune by London standards, but quite respectable for Devonshire." He was surprised to see that his friend was hanging upon his every word.

"I wish I had a wealthy relative," was Garth's envious response. And then his eyes grew feverishly bright. "But I'll soon get the money I need. I learned something useful today—about that saucy slip of a girl who waited on us at the Castle Inn. After you left this morning, I fell into conversation with one of your grooms. He told me the whole history of the Kelland lass. *And* her father—her real one, not the squire. He was a smuggler, but I suppose you know that."

"As does everyone else in this district," said Edwin diffidently.

"But are you aware that Kelland saved up a fortune in gold before he was captured and thrown into prison? He hid it away, and his daughter is the only one who knows where."

"For years that tale has been a feature of local gossip, repeated and embellished by idle youths like Bart. I hardly expected you would be gullible enough to believe in a buried treasure. I certainly don't."

"What a dull, stodgy fellow you've turned into." Garth climbed unsteadily to his feet. "You're not at all like you used to be at school."

Unable to stop himself, Edwin retorted. "Neither are you."

3

Of the two horses Annis had ridden that morning, the soft-mouthed bay was her favorite. As they passed through an open gate leading to a grassy meadow, she marveled anew at the way the mare responded to her slightest touch, following her wishes almost by intuition. It was a welcome change from tugging and sawing on the reins, as she had to do with the plodding Pippin.

The stableboy Bart stood upon the drystone wall talking to Mr. Corston, who was exercising Sir Edwin's chestnut hack. Initially, Annis had been troubled by that gentleman's presence, for she still resented his behavior at the Castle Inn. But thus far he'd treated her in a mannerly fashion, helping her to mount and dismount whenever she'd changed horses.

"You may go back to the stable now; I'll ride on with Miss Kelland," she heard him tell Bart.

Reluctant to be alone with him, her spirits fell further. She had already been disappointed by Sir Edwin's failure to join them. She had dressed to please him, in a riding dress of apple-green cloth that even her critical mother said was vastly becoming. Before leaving home she'd gathered a cluster of blossoms from the orchard and pinned them to her flat-crowned straw hat, chosen for the wide brim that shaded and protected her face. But the one she wanted to impress with her improved appearance had been called away by one of his laborers soon after her arrival, much to her sorrow, and she worried that he might not return to see how superbly she was handling his pretty mare.

"I'm glad to have this opportunity for privacy," Mr. Corston said when he caught up to her. "For some days now I've been regretting the way I treated you at our first meeting. Naturally, if I'd known you were a member of a squire's family I wouldn't have been so rude."

Annis focused on the space between the mare's pointed ears. "Don't give it another thought, sir. I had far rather forget our encounter at the inn."

"You should've heard Eddie afterwards—he gave me quite a dressing down, as well as making it clear that you've no need to wait tables for your keep. Besides being supported by the squire, who must have a comfortable income, you are also Jem Kelland's daughter—his only heiress. Or so I have been informed."

"Me, an heiress?" Annis had to laugh at that unlikely description. "Whoever told you so was greatly mistaken. My father left me nothing." Apart from the dubious legacy of his reputation, she reminded herself.

"Come now, ma'am, I am not so easily dissuaded. Kelland reportedly made a fortune through his unlawful trading. How many chests full of gold did he manage to conceal before the revenue officers captured him?"

"None," she stated emphatically.

"That's not what I've heard."

"People in the shire have built up a legend about the money," Annis explained with long-suffering patience. "But anyone from Brixham could refute what you've heard. The only chest I ever knew of was seized by the excisemen, and it contained contraband tea, not gold. The buried ones exist only in the imagination of the person who told you about them, Mr. Corston." Had it been Sir Edwin? She was distressed to think that he might have spread the false tale of her dead father's hidden treasure, for that would mean he believed it.

"If you're hoarding your inheritance in the hope that it will tempt Eddie to marry you," the young gentleman continued, "you might be interested to know that he has been courting my sister. And my parents expect that he'll offer for her in time for a summer wedding."

This was her greatest fear, and his matter-of-fact corroboration hit her like a blow. Wearing her pretty green habit and pinning flowers to her hat and improving her complexion with the cowslip lotion couldn't alter fate if the baronet intended to wed another.

"I'm hoping Lizzie will soon pay us a visit," said Mr. Corston. "Eddie is eager to see her." Slyly he added, "I'm not saying he wouldn't tumble you if he gets the chance, but you mustn't be thinking he has marriage in mind. He wants a true lady for his wife."

"If that is so," she retorted, "I wonder that he has such a boor for his friend." Pulling sharply at the reins, she turned her mount and rode away swiftly in the direction of the stables. Tears of shame and disappointment misted her eyes as the obedient mare bounded across the turf.

Her mother had tried to warn her about the unlikelihood that Sir Edwin had serious intentions toward her, but she hadn't wanted to listen. Henceforth, Annis vowed, she would be on her guard against him, and unresponsive to any future attempts to engage in flirtation. As for Mr. Corston—she had never disliked anyone so much in her life, and she hoped that she'd seen the last of him.

Fully convinced that all men were fiends, Annis brought her horse to a halt and slid to the ground, then led the bay into the stables. Sir Edwin was there, conversing with his head groom, and he came forward to meet her.

"Forgive me for deserting you earlier," he said in low, intimate tones, "but I'm afraid it was unavoidable. What happened to Garth?"

"He wasn't ready to come back yet," she answered.

Cocking one russet eyebrow, he regarded her thoughtfully. "Has he done something else to offend you?"

Unwilling to reveal her latest contretemps with his detested visitor—and future brother-in-law—she answered coolly, "Mr. Corston and I have been furthering our acquaintance."

"Are you ready to try the gray now?"

She shook her head. "It's past time to be going home."

"So soon? But we've had no time to talk, much less ride together. Bart," he called out, "transfer Miss Kelland's sidesaddle from the mare to the gray."

"Truly, Sir Edwin, I must not stay."

"Why ever not?"

"You're so busy."

"Nonsense," he said firmly. "I've completed my most pressing tasks and can now devote myself to pleasure."

His insistence that she select a third horse couldn't alter her determination to depart, but he was adamant about escorting her back to Orchard Place. He lifted her onto Pippin's back, then threw his own saddle across the lean, long-legged gray.

The sound of thundering hooves distracted him from the buckling of his girth, and Annis from her unhappy thoughts. And when a riderless horse—the chestnut that had recently carried Garth Corston—galloped into the stableyard, both her pony and his Thoroughbred twitched their tails nervously and tossed their heads about.

While Jenkins, with Bart's assistance, tried to capture the runaway, Edwin looked to Annis. "My guest has apparently come to grief—there must have been some mishap. Where did you last see him?"

"In the meadow."

"Show me."

They covered the distance at a rapid pace, Pippin struggling valiantly to match the gray's longer, swifter stride. When Annis and Edwin reached the low stone wall that divided the park from the grazing lands, they found Garth lying sprawled facedown in the grass. His riding whip had fallen nearby, among the yellow cowslips.

"He must have tumbled off taking the jump," said Edwin. "I pray he didn't break his neck."

Annis, the first to reach the fallen rider, knelt down beside him to loosen his cravat and press her fingers against his throat. "He's still breathing," she reported.

Edwin gently rolled Garth onto his back. A dirty scratch marred one pale cheek and a small cut near his temple had begun to bleed, but these were the only outward signs of injury.

Gazing down at the man she regarded as her enemy, Annis felt the faintest tug of pity. "If he doesn't come around, he'll have to be carried to the house on a hurdle. I'd best fetch Bart and Jenkins from the stable."

Edwin gave her a grateful look, impressed by her composure and her quick thinking. "Yes, of course, they'll know what to do."

Watching her ride away, he realized that for her this was no uncommon occurrence. Country people, most notably those who lived on farms, were accustomed to accidents. To her credit, Annis had responded not by weeping or fainting, as a more gently reared young woman might, but with decisive action.

An examination of Garth's arms and legs removed his concern about a broken limb. He left his friend's side just long enough to dampen his handkerchief in a nearby stream, and by the time he returned he was relieved to hear a low moan.

"You're going to be all right," Edwin said, placing the cloth upon Garth's forehead. "You've had a fall."

Opening his eyes, Garth muttered, "It was the damned horse's fault. I lost my stirrup, and when he took the wall at an angle I came off."

"Don't try to move yet," Edwin advised him. "Your head struck the ground hard enough to knock you out, and I suspect you'll be dizzy for a while."

The stablehands arrived on foot. Garth, impatient with lying still and quiet, insisted upon getting up without assistance. After stubbornly refusing to be carried to the house, he discovered that in order to walk he needed to lean heavily upon both Jenkins and Edwin. Bart, leading the gray horse and carrying his master's riding whip, brought up the rear.

The housekeeper was prepared to receive the injured gentleman, for Annis had warned her to ready his bed and gather some materials for bandages. Edwin was relieved to find the young woman in green waiting in the hall when he and the others brought Garth inside.

"I'll stop at the doctor's on my way home," Annis told him, drawing on her riding gloves. "I pass right by his house. I don't think Mr. Corston's cut wants stitching, but a bump on the head can have dangerous consequences."

"As he seems more annoyed than anything, I don't believe there's much cause for alarm," Edwin said.

The day hadn't turned out as well as he'd expected. Estate business and now Garth's accident had prevented him from spending time with Annis—as a result she was probably better acquainted with Garth, and the horses, than with himself. He wanted to tell her how much it pleased him to see her in his house and of his fierce longing to keep her there, but doubted the wisdom of expressing either sentiment. Something had gone wrong between them, and until he knew exactly what, he was afraid to speak or act precipitously.

Turning a deaf ear to Garth's curses—he was climbing the stairs, evidently a painful process—Edwin followed Annis outside. The sight of Pippin patiently cropping the grass in the forecourt reminded him of the purpose of her visit.

"Which of the horses did you prefer?" he inquired.

"The bay mare. That black one was a touch too temperamental for my liking, and I could tell at a glance that the gray was too tall."

"They'll need exercising again," he said. "Will you come tomorrow?"

"I can't," she said with crushing finality. "My mother wouldn't like it, and in future I shall be guided by her wishes."

Her unwillingness to return his gaze confirmed that he had lost her favor altogether, though he couldn't imagine how. Frustrated by his inability to take her in his arms and kiss her into liking him again, he watched Pippin carry her down the long, tree-lined drive.

He spent what was left of the afternoon trying to amuse his friend, who was condemned by the local doctor to an invalid's existence. Fretful and out of sorts, Garth was only interested in talking about his sister, and expressed a strong inclination to send for her. Edwin would have much preferred to send Garth back to Elizabeth instead, but knew that was impossible. Two or three days of bed rest, the doctor had said, before he could be up and about again.

Eventually the unwilling patient's eyelids grew heavy, and as soon as he drifted off into sleep Edwin crept out of the room.

Still deeply concerned about the uncertain state of Annis Kelland's mind and heart, he was thinking of riding over to Orchard Place when his housekeeper sought him out and announced that Squire Dundridge had arrived and wished to speak with him.

"I hope I find you at leisure," the older man said when Edwin stepped into the parlor.

"So much so that I had decided to call upon you," he answered. His neighbor's grave expression warned him of trouble, and instinctively he knew it concerned Annis.

"Throughout my ride over here I wondered if I did right by coming," the squire began. "Now that I've done it, I confess I'm reluctant to raise the question that brought me. But for Annis's sake I will, however awkward it may be for all concerned. Sir Edwin, my wife spoke very frankly about you this morning, and from her I learned something I wish I'd known before I gave my stepdaughter leave to spend the day at Harbourne Court."

Edwin regarded him stoically. "Exactly what did Mrs. Dundridge say to arouse your concern?"

"She told me you kissed Annis during our harvest home. Now, I know perfectly well that a young fellow can kiss a pretty lass at a party and not mean anything by it, especially when he's been quaffing strong cider. I haven't come to berate you."

"I'm relieved to hear it."

"But," continued the squire, "I expect you to be man enough to own up if 'twas merely a bit of sport, as my wife believes."

"Sport?" Edwin repeated. "Hardly that. At the time, however, I wasn't completely sure about my specific intentions."

"And now?"

After drawing a deep breath, he admitted, "I'm entirely certain that I want Annis for my wife. I only wish I could be as sure that she'll have me for her husband. From the night I first kissed her, she has resolutely spurned my attentions."

The squire's forbidding expression had softened considerably. "That was done on her mother's advice."

"Perhaps I ought to present myself to Mrs. Dundridge to account for my past conduct, and also to admit the depth of my feelings for her daughter."

"Never fear, I'll make everything right with Nancy." Now beaming at the younger man, the squire declared, "Sir Edwin, the match has my approval, and I grant you permission to do anything in your power to persuade our Annis that she should marry you."

"I'll give it my best effort, sir."

"Kisses are all very well and good," the older man said sagely, "but a few sweet words wouldn't go amiss. If up to now your actions encouraged Annis to suspect you've dalliance in mind and nothing more, you're the one who must convince her otherwise. Her mother's influence has ever been stronger than mine. And always will be," he concluded in the regretful tone of voice he often employed when speaking of his stepdaughter.

Changing the subject to that of his horses, Edwin informed the squire that Annis had ridden two of them earlier that day. "She fancies my bay mare, a gentle and well-mannered creature, and very reliable." Rather like Annis herself, he acknowledged to himself. "Do you wish to have the horse conveyed to Orchard Place immediately?"

Shaking his head, Squire Dundridge replied, "Nay, and not for a few days yet. Because it's to be a surprise gift, the arrangements will have to be made without her learning of them. I'll inform you as soon as I've made up my mind how to proceed."

The squire extended his hand, and Edwin stepped forward to grip it with his own. "Thank you, sir."

"For buying your mare?" the older man asked roguishly.

"For giving your consent. But my happiness can't be complete until I've spoken with Annis and overcome the doubts her mother may have put into her head."

In Edwin's imagination, asking for a young lady's hand in marriage had seemed a terrifying ordeal, and to his surprise and relief it had actually turned out to be a simple and unalarming business. Yet now that his future seemed settled, he couldn't quite dispel his fear that something or someone besides the overly cautious Mrs. Dundridge had turned Annis against him.

During the seemingly endless hour that Annis had listened to her stepfather read aloud, she'd tortured herself with thoughts of Sir Edwin Page's perfidy in making her love him when he had an understanding with Mr. Corston's sister. She was trying very hard to hate him for it, but was fair enough to acknowledge that he'd never once hinted that his feelings for her were deep or lasting. She had deceived herself; it was that simple.

Mrs. Dundridge gathered up her needlework and blew out the candle on her worktable. "Time for bed," she announced to her daughter and husband.

Making no move to go yet, the squire said, "I'll join you upstairs soon, but I need to speak with Annis."

Never having heard that portentous note in his

voice before, Annis gazed at him in trepidation. What could he possibly want to say to her, and why did he look so dissatisfied? She could only assume that he'd heard what had happened at the Castle Inn and was displeased with her for serving the baronet his dinner.

As soon as they were alone together, he said, "I saw Sir Edwin Page today."

"Oh?" she responded lamely, mentally preparing herself for the scold she knew she deserved.

"I've long prided myself on never questioning your behavior, Annis, or meddling in your affairs. But in this instance I am curious to know why our neighbor has received the impression that you don't much care for him."

"He said that? I can't think why he would." Her cheeks began to feel feverish.

As if oblivious to her discomfiture, the squire went on, "From the day he came to live at Harbourne Court, I've considered him the most agreeable of gentlemen, and I should have thought that a young lady would be still more susceptible to his charm."

Annis realized that her stepfather had somehow guessed her great secret. What was the point in pretending indifference, she asked herself wearily, when her pride was already so damaged?

"I care for him," she confessed. "Too much for my own comfort. That's what makes me so afraid of him." Realizing that she'd said too much, she fell silent.

"You do more harm than good by keeping your troubles to yourself, Annis." With an encouraging smile, he said, "Maybe I can help, if you'd only let me try."

She didn't believe that to be possible, but nevertheless she opened her heart to him for the first time during their uneasy eight-year relationship. As she recited the brief history of her unhappy love affair, the squire listened to her intently, his brow slightly creased. He smiled, though not unkindly, when she frankly admitted to having been kissed beneath the old apple tree last autumn. And then she described all that had occurred in Dartmouth last month, including her abbreviated stint as a serving maid.

"It was a foolish thing to do," she said miserably. "Sir Edwin was a perfect gentleman about it, the complete opposite of Mr. Corston, but I could tell he didn't approve. I thought he would keep his distance after that, only he hasn't, so I hoped that he was beginning to feel as I do. Until today," she concluded. "I found out that he *has* been trifling with me, just as mother warned."

Unburdening herself further, she related all that Garth Corston had said to her. "I've never been so hurt—and angry—in my life," she declared, her eyes filling. "That Sir Edwin could believe the gossip about my father and his nonexistent cache of gold is bad enough, but to spread it is worse still. But nothing is as bad as learning about his other lady. That was more than I could bear!"

"What lady?" the squire inquired.

"Mr. Corston's sister. He implied that Sir Edwin is going to marry her."

"It isn't true."

His conviction was unmistakable, but her doubts were not so easily vanquished. "I'd like to believe that, but—"

"I have it from Sir Edwin's lips that indeed there is a lady he would gladly wed, but her name is definitely not Corston."

She clasped her hands in her lap to conceal the fact that they were shaking. "Oh, sir, you must have misunderstood him. His intentions toward me aren't so honorable—he could never marry Jem Kelland's daughter."

The squire rose to his feet. "My dear, your mother is an excellent woman, but you mustn't be swayed by her false notions about Sir Edwin. He isn't deterred by who your father was, and my standing in the community matters even less. I've no cause to question his honor, nor have you—there, that brings the smile back to your face," he observed with pleasure. "Would that your suitor could see you now! He's a splendid fellow, Annis, and very nearly worthy of you."

She was deeply ashamed of her former prejudice against her guardian, for not only had he demonstrated an interest in her welfare and provided solace, he also was a more objective advisor than her overly judgmental mother.

Rising, she said, "I don't deserve that commendation, sir, for I've not been the sort of daughter you ought to have had."

He cupped her cheek. "All these years I strove so hard to win your affection that I must have chased it away. What's past is past, so long as you now know you can always come to me with your problems. I'll always do whatever I can to ensure your happiness. You have my word."

Even in a state of delirious excitement, Annis didn't forget to apply her cowslip lotion before going to bed that night. If Sir Edwin had admitted to her stepfather that he wanted to marry her, something she still had difficulty accepting, it was imperative that she get rid of her freckles as soon as possible. Achieving a more genteel appearance was suddenly a matter of supreme urgency, and in order to derive the greatest benefit from the concoction she bathed her cheeks a second time.

4

"These hangings are entirely too dark for this room," Edwin pronounced while fingering a sun-faded damask curtain. "They should have been replaced when I first came here."

His housekeeper hunched her shoulders diffidently
and lisped through the great gap in her front teeth,
"S'all I take 'em down, then? If I've got strength
enough for it—my back plagues me something fierce
today."

"Never mind, it can wait until after I'm—" Recon-
sidering his words, Edwin chose not to inform her of
his marital aspirations and merely said, "It needn't be
done immediately."

He turned away from the window to study the room
with newly critical eyes. It was gloomily masculine in
its appointments and excessively cluttered, the antithe-
sis of the cheerful simplicity of the parlor at Orchard
Place. His ancestors' ancient fowling pieces, however
decorative, rightfully belonged in the gun room, and
he would never miss the framed painting of a battle
scene between opposing armies. Would Annis like that
stuffed pheasant in the glass case? Edwin wasn't at all
sure he cared for it much. And he definitely intended
to remove the rack of antlers hanging on the wall,
adorned with cobwebs spun by generations of spiders.
The trophies, so dear to his great-uncle, had no meaning for him and would have still less for his future
bride.

"Send for some village girls to come in," he told
his elderly retainer. "Get as many of them as you need
for a very thorough cleaning of the house, from garret
to cellar."

"Aye, sir." The housekeeper merely bobbed her
head, for her arthritic legs prevented her from curtsying, something she hadn't been able to do since long
before Edwin had taken possession of his inheritance.

A few minutes after her departure, Garth Corston
entered the parlor, a strip of linen wrapped around
his head. This was his first day out of bed, and he
stated forthrightly that he meant to make the most
of it.

"You said we could ride to Dartmoor," he reminded Edwin.

"I know, but I can't go there today. I've so much to accomplish in too short a time—that is, I've given the servants several things to do and I feel I ought to be here to supervise. What's your opinion of this?" Edwin picked up a bust of a laurel-wreathed gentleman who was missing most of his nose.

"Isn't he someone famous? Caesar, or some other blasted Roman? There was a chap just like him in the pater's study. He fetched quite a good price at the sale."

"What sale?"

Garth chewed his lower lip, his face unnaturally flushed. "Before we left the London house, my parents sold off a few articles to save having to move them. Pictures, furniture, that sort of thing."

"I wish I could do the same," Edwin commented dryly. "Not that I think anyone would buy a moth-eaten pheasant behind glass. Or a threadbare rug," he added, frowning down at the one beneath his boots.

"Oh, you'd be surprised," said his friend airily. "But why should you want to be rid of them?"

"The house needs refurbishing" was the extent of Edwin's explanation.

Garth narrowed his eyes in suspicion. "It ain't for me that you're banishing the pheasant. I'll wager this has something to do with a female."

Finding himself backed into a corner, Edwin did not quite deny the truth of it. "Until I'm able to discuss my intentions with the lady, I prefer not to speak of them to anyone else."

"You're thinking of marriage? Not to that wench who came here t'other day—the smuggler's daughter?" Garth was patently horrified. "Good God, man, where are your wits? You act as though *you're* the one who took a blow to the head!"

"I'm sorry if you dislike it," said Edwin, striving to keep his temper in check.

His visitor strode about the room, jaw tightly clenched. "You were Lizzie's suitor. She'll be most distressed—my parents, too," he muttered. "I cannot believe you'd be such a fool over a girl like that. Bed her if you must—I'd do the same if I were you—but don't ruin your life by marrying the slut."

Edwin's hand curled itself into a fist. "I won't listen to that kind of talk, Garth. Apologize—now."

"For what? I've committed no crime by calling her what she is, which has been obvious to me since that night at the inn. Didn't you see how she was looking at you, her eyes all soft and her lashes fluttering?"

"I'm still waiting for your apology."

"Oh, I'm sorry, never doubt it. Sorry that you're numb-brained enough to be taken in by a schemer like that one. Why, I'll wager she's lain with half the lads in this part of the shire, your own groom included."

"That's quite enough," Edwin barked. "I've no wish to come to blows with you while you're still a guest in my house, but if you don't guard your tongue . . ." He left his threat hanging ominously between them.

"Perhaps I should leave Harbourne Court."

Edwin wasted no time in seizing upon this half-hearted suggestion. "Yes, that would probably be for the best," he said sternly.

"But—" Garth stared back at him in dismay, but evidently he understood that there was nothing more to be said. "I'll begin packing now," he said, and stalked out of the room.

The midday sun cast its warming rays across the barton at Orchard Place. Annis, crossing the farmyard with a pail of milk, paused to lift her face to the sky, careless of any damage to her complexion.

The surrounding orchards, fully in bloom, were a breathtaking sight now that each tree was surrounded by a nimbus of palest pink. The sounds of springtime were everywhere. The most prominent came from the baby birds nested in the eaves of the outbuildings, whose shrieks drowned out the faint hum of the bees darting from the flower-laden trees to the row of skeps behind the apple house.

In the afternoon Edwin would come, Annis assured herself. In the years ahead, whenever she looked back upon the day of their engagement she could remember it as utterly perfect, one of bright sunshine and an endless vista of apple blossoms.

Hearing hoofbeats and wheels in the yard, she set down her pail and peeked hopefully around the corner of the building where the apple carts were emptied at harvest time. A gig drawn by Sir Edwin's leggy gray horse had halted nearby. Mr. Corston held the reins, a white bandage visible beneath his cocked hat.

"Miss Kelland," he greeted her, climbing down from the vehicle. "The very person I came to see."

Mistrusting his broad smile, Annis squared her shoulders. "I have no desire to see you—or speak to you—ever again."

"Even though I come from Harbourne Court with news of its master?"

Not wishing to be observed in his company, she reluctantly led him to the rear of the cider house, deserted at this season.

"I'm here on an errand of mercy," he began, "because I thought of a way I can help you. Much as I'd like to, I can no longer ignore Eddie's apparent infatuation with you, despite his prior commitment to my sister. If you cherish dreams of becoming Lady Page, I'm willing to make them a reality." Moving closer to her, he added, "But I'll expect a substantial reward in exchange for my efforts."

"Even if I had anything to give you, Mr. Corston, I wouldn't."

His low chuckle was far from pleasant. "What a little liar you are, Annis Kelland—and a persistent one. There's no use denying the existence of the hidden gold, so you may as well tell me where it is. Better still, show me. I need the money. You want Eddie. And we both know his fortune far exceeds whatever paltry sum your father may have left you. Don't be a fool over this."

"You are the foolish one," Annis retorted, her eyes glistening with anger. "What you suggest is as despicable as it is impossible. Begone, sir—I've no time to waste upon you."

His hand shot out and gripped her arm. "Not so fast. You expect to wed Sir Edwin Page without my help, do you? I could just as easily spoil whatever chance you have of winning him if I told him that I'd had you—you know what I mean. And I can make him believe me; don't think I can't!"

She twisted about, desperate to break free of his cruel grasp. "Release me, else I shall scream!"

"Go ahead. And when your parents come rushing to save you, I'll tell them about the many times we've lain together. Once at the inn in Dartmouth, and also while you visited Harbourne Court the other day. And again just now, in the shade of the apple trees."

Her breath came in short, erratic bursts. "You wouldn't dare! My stepfather will murder you!"

Pulling her closer, he contradicted her by saying, "At worst he would demand that I marry you, and I'd have to flee the shire. But not before spreading the sordid tale of our liaison."

Feeling his hot breath on her cheek, Annis wrenched away. Fortunately a weapon was at hand—a long wooden pole that leaned against the wall of the cider house. In her desperation, she realized that it could be used for something other than knocking ripe apples out of the trees.

Seizing it, she pointed it at him and warned, "Keep your distance."

Apparently unconcerned, he let out a braying laugh and lunged at her.

Annis swung the pole, first using it to deliver a hard blow to his upper arm, then employing it as a prod. She drove him around the side of the building and into the stableyard, ceasing her attack only when he backed into a mounting block and lost his footing.

"Arrogant bitch," he grunted, scrambling toward the gig. "You'll pay for this. I'll see to it that Eddie does marry Lizzie—that'll teach you to hit an injured man."

He hastily gathered up the reins and wasted no time in escaping from Orchard Place.

Shocked and shaken by her own violence, Annis dropped the pole.

Instinctively seeking a familiar refuge, she picked up her skirts and ran through the orchard, weaving between the blossoming trees. But she knew she had no hope of solitude or meditation when she found her stepfather standing at the base of her special tree, glaring up at a flame-breasted robin perched on an outer branch.

"This cheeky fellow seems to think *he* owns our Dundridge's Glory," the squire greeted her.

"Make him go away," Annis begged him. "They're such unlucky birds."

"Come now, you're too sharp to believe in all of your mother's superstitions," he chided.

Summoning a hollow laugh, she acknowledged that her luck couldn't possibly get any worse.

"Now that's a puzzler indeed, for at breakfast you were all smiles and sighs."

She gave him a pithy account of her most recent encounter with Garth Corston and was pleased to discover that he shared her vehement opinion of the young man's character and his threats.

"After he has blackened my reputation, Sir Edwin will be done with me," she concluded miserably. "And I'll never be able to recover his esteem once I've lost it."

Breaking off a thoughtful silence, the squire said, "If this young rascal is so intent on making trouble, you had better go to that cousin of mine in Totnes. Now hear me out, Annis, before you refuse. Besides getting you out of Corston's way, being with Myra will do you a world of good. Before much longer you're going to be the mistress of a great house, and she knows everything about choosing servants, entertaining guests, mixing with the gentry.''

"But if I run away, I can't defend myself against Mr. Corston's falsehoods.''

"Never fear, I'll make sure Sir Edwin knows where you've gone and why. I don't doubt it will be even more convenient for him to call upon you at Myra's house for a week or so—Harbourne Court is nearer to Totnes than it is to Orchard Place.''

"Not by much," she pointed out. Thinking it over, however, she saw no reason to oppose his suggestion. "I'll go if you believe I should.''

"I do. By the time you see your young gentleman again, I'll have convinced him that his friend's tales are naught but vengeful slander.''

Venting her frustration, Annis wailed, "Oh, I do wish he had come today, instead of Mr. Corston! This watching and waiting is too difficult to bear for much longer.''

"I know," he said sympathetically, "but your affairs will be settled to your satisfaction within a very short time. I'll go and tell your mother that you must be off to Totnes before sundown. And I must go down to the cellar to find a cask of my apple brandy to send to Myra. I daresay she's used up the last one I sent her.''

Watching him walk toward the house, Annis suddenly remembered the pail of milk she'd abandoned outside the dairy. When she went back to fetch it, she discovered that the kitchen cats had tipped it over onto its side and were lapping up the last drops of milk, most of which had seeped into the earth. That robin, she thought glumly, had definitely been a harbinger of ill fortune.

Late in the day, when thick, dark clouds began to obscure the earlier brightness of the afternoon, Annis set out for Totnes. The boxlike trunk containing her finest garments was strapped to the pony's back, as was the small round keg of spirits that Squire Dundridge was sending his cousin. The baggage, though not particularly heavy, nonetheless prevented Annis from maintaining a fast pace, and she doubted that she'd reach the town before the rain began. From the rapidly graying skies and the way Pippin snorted and twitched his ears, she knew that showers were inevitable.

As she rode past Sir Edwin's estate, she stared longingly at the distant manor house, just visible through a screen of trees. The temptation to stop there was irresistible, but did she dare?

Yes, she answered herself fiercely, she had to see Edwin, if for no other reason than to refute Garth Corston's vicious lies. Guiding Pippin between the ivy-hung pedestals that marked the entrance to the estate, she swatted his rump with her willow switch and forced him to pick up his heavy feet more quickly.

The stableboy Bart, who took charge of the pony upon her arrival, bobbed his curly head in affirmation when she asked if his master was at home. "Aye, and proper busy he is," was the reply he gave.

Annis very nearly fled upon learning this, but if Edwin heard she'd been there he would surely wonder why she'd left without seeing him.

She crossed the lawn, a carpet of green dotted with gay yellow celandines and white oxeye daisies. The front door flew open at her approach, startling her, and the man she loved beyond reason invited her to come inside.

"I saw you from the parlor window," he said, stepping aside to permit her entrance. "This is an unexpected pleasure."

"I'm on my way to Totnes," she blurted.

He ushered her to the parlor, which was in a pitiable state of disarray. "Pray excuse the appearance of this room. The business of imposing order can be a messy one, I've discovered."

Annis walked up to the elaborately carved mantel to examine it, then turned to say, "The last time I was here I saw just enough of Harbourne Court to convince me that it is as beautiful as I'd always imagined." Why was she babbling so idiotically?

I'm glad you like the house. I've grown fond of it myself, though it does lack one important thing. A mistress." Reaching for her hand, he led her over to the window and pointed to a stand of flowering trees whose branches were being whipped by the wind. "Tell me what you think of my orchard. It's not as large or as fine as yours, but it does produce excellent fruit—or will if we can keep the bullfinches from eating all the blossoms. The squire tells me that most of my trees are an old Devonshire variety, the Red Quarrenden."

"A good sort for both cooking and eating," she said, nodding sagely. "But the land is partly responsible for the quality—the finer the soil, the sweeter the apples." She fell silent when the first raindrops struck the windowpanes.

"Close though Totnes is, you cannot ride there now," Edwin told her. "Stay and share my dinner."

"What will Mr. Corston think?"

"He's gone. He borrowed my gig and departed this morning, and he won't be coming back."

Annis refrained from commenting on what she regarded as a fortunate reprieve. It was unlikely that Garth Corston had returned to Harbourne Court after his visit to Orchard Place, which meant he hadn't been able to spout his lies to Edwin.

"When are you expected in town?" he asked.

"At no particular time. Miss Dundridge, my stepfather's cousin, wasn't forewarned about my visit. Even so, I mustn't linger."

"I don't know about you," he murmured, his lips close to her ear, "but I hope the storm won't subside too soon. For I have something very important to ask you, Annis Kelland, and if you give the right answer I'll be even more reluctant to let you leave me."

She looked away from the window and found him gazing at her intently.

"This house and the orchard, and all my other worldly goods can be yours—including that stuffed pheasant in the glass case, which I've not yet consigned to the attic. But if you want them, you must take me as well. Would that be too severe a hardship for you?"

"I think not." She smiled back at him. "To be sure, you're the best of the lot."

"Flatterer," he accused, fingering her cheek. "I suspect it's the pheasant that decided you."

Annis placed one hand upon his chest and confided, "I wanted to be your wife long before I knew about your silly pheasant."

"Ah, Annis," he sighed, his mouth hovering near hers, "you do me great honor."

5

The sound of deep breathing roused Annis from her slumber, and when the feather mattress suddenly shifted beneath the heavier weight of another body she was startled into full consciousness. The realization that she was lying naked in a bed beside Sir Edwin Page reminded her of how they had come to be there, of the night before and everything that they had said—and done.

Her lover slept on, unaware of her scrutiny. She decided that he was no less handsome when his chestnut locks were tousled, or with dark whiskers shadowing his strong jaw and chin.

Her promise to become his wife had earned her

many tender kisses and avowals of devotion, and her elation had been so great that she'd scarcely been able to eat a morsel of the meal they had later shared. The storm had not abated, nor had Edwin seemed eager to send her to Totnes in his carriage, so she had let him overcome her reservations and had consented to stay the night.

When he'd eventually escorted her upstairs to a guest bedchamber, she had received further proof of his regard. Reluctantly leaving her behind, Edwin had proceeded slowly down the dark corridor to his own room. Annis, dizzy with desire, saw him come to a sudden and immediate halt. He'd spun around for a long, searching look during which time had seemed to stand still, and when he had walked back to her she'd understood what would happen next.

Her overwhelming need to become entirely his had been heightened by his previous kisses and caresses, to the point that she was eager to discover what his lovemaking would be like. And having experienced the wonder and beauty and mystery of it, she felt no shame or regret, only joy.

Murmuring unintelligibly, Edwin clutched a strand of her hair, which was spread between their pillows. "Annis."

He was awake now, gazing at her with warm, drowsy eyes, and his smile was one she would remember forever.

"We should send for the parson straightaway, then you wouldn't ever have to leave."

She struggled to sit up, covering herself with the sheet.

Snatching it away, he said, "Let me look at you. Last night it was so dark, and I was too enraptured to think of lighting candles."

She blushed all over as he examined her, wishing for his sake that she was beautiful; and she couldn't help worrying that her complexion wasn't fashionably fair. But he'd seemed to like her body sufficiently well, for he had often placed his hands and even his lips upon her breasts, a form of appreciation that was most gratifying.

His fingers trailed across her shoulder. "You've got freckles here, too—a few very light ones."

Annis had never really noticed them. "In time they'll fade away to nothing," she assured him. "I've been using a lotion made from cowslips, and washing my face in water distilled from elderflowers."

"You don't need to. I *like* your freckles. Every one of them."

"Edwin?" There was a catch in her voice.

His hand, warm and comforting, cupped her cheek. "What is it? Are you sorry you stayed?"

"Oh, no. Country folk don't believe it's wrong for a couple to share a bed, if they've already pledged to marry. But you're used to gentry ways, and I'm afraid you might think worse of me for lying with you before our wedding."

He pulled her closer, saying, "I wanted you to, Annis. For so long I've doubted that I could win you— all these weeks you've been so aloof, so distant."

"Because I didn't want you to guess how much I fancied you," she confessed, hiding her face against his chest. "I was afraid you'd try to take advantage." After a brief pause, she wondered aloud, "What will people think when they find out what we've done?"

"No one is going to. It will be our secret."

Shaking her head, she said, "Not if the stableboy spreads it about that Pippin boarded here."

"Dawn won't break for another hour yet, so you and your pony can be on your way long before Bart leaves his bed."

"But the bedclothes are so mussed, and—"

"Be easy, I'll take care that all signs of your presence are removed."

His kiss distracted her from her concerns, but as his strong arms enclosed her she reminded him breathlessly, "Edwin, I dare not linger." She made a token attempt to disengage herself, only to find that she was trapped by the thickly muscled leg he'd flung across hers.

"You can't go yet," he declared in a voice thick with need.

She sank back against the mattress willingly, welcoming his eager embrace. The delicious weight of him, the heat of his skin, the feel of his hands as they traced her curves—all were a marvel to her, new and mysterious and wildly exciting. Soon he was making her gasp with delight, and just when she was all but delirious with sensation she felt him enter her, slowly and with infinite care.

His fire teased and tantalized her, and before it consumed her altogether she let out a little cry, the only way she knew to express her awe at what he had done to her. And then she was melting, and it was too late to save herself from the unknown and wholly unexpected result of giving herself up to this man, body and soul.

"My own Annis," he murmured into her neck as the tension left him and he sank against her.

"Dear Edwin." She flattened her damp palms against his back as though to hold him there forever.

They dressed as quickly as they could, handing each other the various garments they had removed with similar urgency many hours earlier.

"Don't bother tidying up," he said, "if you mean to be gone before my servants begin to stir. Will you be at Totnes Fair on Monday?"

"I can arrange to be."

"We'll meet there, at the enclosure where horses are bought and sold."

Silently they descended the great oaken staircase, wincing at every creak from the ancient wood, and crept furtively to the stable. In no time at all Edwin had Pippin ready and had strapped the trunk and the single cask behind the sidesaddle.

"What's this?" he asked, rapping his knuckles against the side of the wooden keg.

"Brandy," she replied.

Afterwards, while riding along the twisting country road, she worried that her candor might have given him a false impression. She would have been wiser to explain that the liquor she was carrying was the squire's present to his cousin, and she regretted her failure to clarify that it had come from the cellar at Orchard Place and not off a smuggling vessel from France.

Miss Myra Dundridge, a middle-aged spinster, welcomed her unexpected guest with a flattering degree of enthusiasm, and the news of an impending marriage threw her into ecstasy.

"I was slightly acquainted with the late baronet, your Sir Edwin's great-uncle," she said one day when teaching Annis how to lay the table for a dinner party. "Rather a gruff old gentleman, and inclined to show his pride. He always came to town in his chaise, though Harbourne Court is a scant three miles away, but I've noticed that his nephew chooses to ride. Quite a handsome young man, and such fine horses he keeps!"

Annis nodded, her smile broadening when it occurred to her that in future she would be able to ride the easy-paced bay mare whenever she pleased. "He is coming to the fair to buy more," she informed her hostess, "and he expects me to meet him there. Are you planning to go?"

"Oh, yes," Miss Dundridge replied. "And I know you will also. It's never too soon to begin looking about for suitable servants, and many will come to town on Monday seeking new places. Sir Edwin being a bachelor, his stables are likely better staffed than his house. You'll want at least five women—how many has he now?"

"I cannot say," Annis admitted, "but probably not

so many. He has told me that his housekeeper is quite old and infirm."

"Best pension her off; that's my advice. I suppose there's no manservant, either. Well, that can easily be remedied." After studying the placement of the silver utensils, porcelain plates, and crystal goblets, Miss Dundridge nodded briskly. "Now, my dear, come and see what I have done, and then you must try and copy the arrangement yourself. As mistress of Harbourne Court, you want to be able to direct your servants properly."

Ever mindful of her lack of qualifications for becoming a baronet's lady, Annis paid close attention to all of Miss Dundridge's instructions, however tedious. She must never give Edwin cause to regret choosing her for his bride, nor could she allow herself to be ruled, as her mother was, by a terror of inadvertently disgracing her husband at a social function. The rules laid down by her preceptress might seem unnecessarily rigid but they were easily learned, and in her more optimistic moments she felt confident of becoming a truly great lady.

On Monday the sky was overcast but the rains had ceased, and hordes of town and country folk congregated at the fair. Annis parted from Miss Dundridge at a clothmaker's stall and went directly to the horse paddock, but neither Edwin nor his grooms were to be found in the crowd of farmers and dealers. She waited for over an hour, prey to a growing fear that his absence was due to an accident or illness.

Unless, came the panicked thought, he'd never intended to meet her at all.

In the afternoon, as she and Miss Dundridge wearily traversed the town's clean and well-paved streets, she confided her unease.

"My dear Annis," that lady replied, "you needn't be so alarmed. You've told me that Sir Edwin is quite busy putting his house in better order, and I daresay he simply forgot that the fair would be today. No doubt he'll call upon you tomorrow to apologize and plead for forgiveness. Why, we may even find a message waiting for us at home."

But Annis received no explanatory note accounting for Edwin's failure to meet her. Although her family and her hostess expected her to stay for several days more, she made up her mind to return to Orchard Place by way of Harbourne Court, without delay.

After bidding Miss Dundridge a fond and grateful farewell, she set out toward the south gate of the town and was soon following the road that would take her to the Harbourne River. Looking westward, she noted that the sky had cleared and the faint patch of blue on the horizon was rapidly turning pink with the setting of the sun.

As she neared her future home, she was overtaken by a traveling carriage drawn by four panting horses lathered with sweat. They swept past her, splattering mud in their wake, and to her astonishment they entered the ivy-hung gates of Harbourne Court.

Eager to know who could be visiting Edwin at this late hour, Annis guided Pippin to a cluster of trees. She dismounted, and when she'd wrapped the reins around a slender sapling she sought a clearer vantage point.

The coachman had drawn up in the forecourt and Edwin was opening the carriage door himself. A young lady climbed out, and even from a great distance Annis could see that her attire was extremely modish and probably very costly. She seemed very happy to see Edwin, who evidently reciprocated her delight.

Her knees gave way and she sank to the ground beside a patch of gorse. For a long time after the couple vanished inside the house she sat there, too stunned to move but not too horrified to comprehend this disaster.

All of her dreams of marrying Edwin and living happily with him in the great Elizabethan mansion

were dead. Garth Corston hadn't been able to destroy
them with his spite, but they couldn't survive the ill-
timed arrival of his sister—and there could be no
doubt it was she.

Annis knew that Edwin would want to see her again,
probably not tomorrow or the next day, but eventually. He would seek her out for the purpose of telling
her that a prior commitment prevented him from fulfilling his earlier promise to make her his wife, and
thus he could save himself from what his world would
surely regard as a misalliance. Even now he was probably comparing her to Miss Corston, whose birth and
breeding more closely matched his. Then he would
think back to the night at the Castle Inn in Dartmouth
and recall her reckless and unladylike behavior. The
brandy keg she'd carried to Totnes would certainly
raise additional doubts about her character, reminding
him that her father had gone to prison for receiving
and transporting contraband.

Annis couldn't imagine that he'd deliberately and
ruthlessly set out to seduce and then abandon her. No
man could be so false—or so predatory. Perhaps he'd
honestly believed himself to be free to offer marriage
because he'd had a quarrel or misunderstanding with
Miss Corston, whose arrival on the scene meant that
their rift was only temporary.

How right her mother had been! Edwin was indeed
fulfilling that ominous prophecy that he would break
her heart. And yet her stepfather hadn't been entirely
wrong about him, either—he was also responsible for
an unimagined if transitory happiness.

"Miss Kelland?"

She crept out of the thicket and found that in the
act of spying she'd been spied upon herself, by Captain Harper of the Excise Service.

"Why are you hiding there?" he asked suspiciously.
"Come out so I can see you. And if you're armed,
you'd better throw down your weapon."

Her lover had just been lost to her, but even so,

Annis couldn't help but be amused as the officer stalked toward her purposefully, his bearing stiff and his face set in forbidding lines.

His eyes narrowed when he repeated, "Why were you lurking among the furze bushes? Have you concealed something?"

Again she was inclined to laugh—the accusation was too absurd. "No, Captain Harper. I was riding by and I—I paused to admire the view of Harbourne Court." She hoped he would overlook her brief hesitation. "And I haven't seen any smugglers," she added on a defiant note. "Arrest me if you must. It won't be the worst thing to happen to me this day."

"I'm not going to arrest you," he said testily. "If you're bound for Orchard Place, I'll ride with you—it's on my way to Harbertonford."

He helped her to mount her pony with more impatience than gallantry, and together they followed the winding, hedge-lined roadway. Strangely, his company was not distasteful to Annis, and she was rather grateful to him for serving as a distraction. In future she would have a surfeit of solitude in which to reflect upon her sorrows.

"I expect you've been at the fair," he said as they rode side by side. "I wanted to go myself but was told to spend the entire day at the Bay Horse."

With a pang, she remembered Edwin's lovely mare.

"It's the worst tavern in Totnes for dealing in smuggled liquors," he continued.

"Is it really? I didn't know."

To her surprise, he actually chuckled. "I'll wager your father did. I've always been thankful his heyday was over long before I joined the Excise. By all accounts he was a slippery fellow, and a clever one."

Annis detected a grudging respect in his tone, enough to raise her sagging spirits ever so slightly.

" 'Twill be a clear night," he predicted, "and tomorrow is likely to be dry."

His ability to read the sky impressed her, countrywoman that she was. Curious about her enigmatic escort, she asked, "Are you a native of Devonshire, Captain?"

"Nay, I'm Somerset born. As is Sir Edwin Page." His speculative glance was as unwelcome as his allusion to the baronet, and he prevented her from introducing a less sensitive topic of conversation by adding, "I don't suppose you'll want to tell me the real reason you were spying upon his house."

"I meant no harm by it."

"He's your sweetheart, isn't he? I guessed it the day we met on the road to Dartmouth, when I accused you of transporting contraband and he defended you so forcefully."

Annis, letting her mind wander back to that mild April afternoon, recalled her anger at the gentleman riding beside her and her mortification when Edwin had appeared upon the scene.

"He's a good sort," the captain went on. "He and the squire are among the few landowners in this district who won't condone or support the free-trading. But neither do they lay information against their neighbors, and while it hampers my ability to carry out my duties, I can't help but admire them for that."

When they came to Orchard Place, Annis parted from him with a cordiality that she would never have guessed she could display toward a representative of his hated profession. Her animosity had faded to the point that she could even feel sympathy for one whose work was as difficult and dangerous as it was unpopular. All too often she'd experienced the loneliness and despair that resulted from being an object of notoriety.

She led Pippin through the deserted barton. It was the dinner hour; the orchard laborers and stableboys had already abandoned their daily tasks. In her exhausted and highly emotional state, she was glad no one was around to witness her return.

She removed her sidesaddle and the cloth beneath it and rubbed Pippin down before going to the feed box to measure out some oats. As she passed along the row of stalls, the cart horses pressed their noses against the rails, seeking attention.

After she had latched the storeroom door, she heard a noise coming from a stall that had long been empty. Going over to investigate, she was amazed to find it occupied, and by a bay mare familiar to her.

"How did you come to be here?" she whispered, stroking the smooth muzzle. She reached into her pail for a handful of oats and presented it to the mare.

Intent upon solving the mystery, she made her way to the house. Led to the dining room by the sound of voices, she discovered her stepfather in the act of carving a roasted spring lamb.

"What are you doing home so soon?" Mrs. Dundridge cried. "We didn't expect you back from Totnes before the week's end."

"I left early."

"Were Myra's ladyship lessons so tiresome?" the squire asked teasingly.

She couldn't yet tell him that the lessons had been unnecessary after all, having already decided to delay her explanations until she had fully accepted the misfortune that was making her feel so wretched. Addressing her stepfather, she asked, "Why is Sir Edwin's bay horse in our stable?"

He set down his carving knife and two-pronged fork. "Because she belongs to you now. I bought her as a gift, after Sir Edwin told me how well you liked her. 'Twas a conspiracy between us, to surprise you. I fetched her from him earlier today."

"I'm sorry if I've spoiled the surprise by coming home too soon. It was very generous of you, sir. She's a lovely creature." And also a constant reminder of an unendurable loss, Annis thought bleakly.

"Do sit down," Mrs. Dundridge invited her. "You look as if you need some food."

"I'm not hungry." The aroma of cooked meat and potatoes was not sufficient to revive her flagging appe-

tite. "I'll go up to my room now, if you'll excuse me."
She started for the door, then turned back to say to
the squire, "I hope we can ride together tomorrow."

"Aye, 'twould be my pleasure," he replied, delighted by her friendly overture.

In the privacy of her own bedchamber, with the door
safely shut, she was finally able to release the distress
she'd been holding back so stoically ever since she'd
seen Miss Corston's dainty foot cross the threshold of
Harbourne Court.

At least, she told herself as the tears slipped down
her cheeks, her parents would never forsake her. She was
assured of her mother's love whether or not she married,
and she'd learned that her stepfather could be a source of
wise and helpful counsel. And if she should turn out to be
with child as a result of her night with Edwin, she could
trust them both to shield her from the scandal. No one
else need know about it. She could go away—to her
grandfather in Brixham, or to one of her aunts near Exeter, for they weren't likely to judge her too harshly. Com-
pared to the crimes Jem Kelland had been charged with
and imprisoned for, his daughter's fall from grace and its
possible consequences would seem no great catastrophe.
Like many a girl before her, she'd put too much faith
in enticing promises and sweet caresses, but her relatives
wouldn't let her spend the rest of her days pining.

Crossing to the washstand, she bathed her damp
cheeks. As she reached for a linen towel, she spied
the bottle of elderflower water that she and her
mother had distilled—an age ago, it seemed to her
now. Her hand moved toward it, then fell back, then
reached out again. She would continue using her concoction, and afterwards she'd apply the cowslip lotion
to her face. But from that moment on she'd be doing
it to please herself, and no one else.

"And how are your parents?" Edwin asked Elizabeth Corston, who occupied the only uncluttered chair
in his madly disarranged parlor.

"Well enough, I suppose," she answered. "They must have been startled to read the note I left behind informing them of my visit to Devonshire. Garth instructed me to say nothing beforehand, or give a reason for the journey. But how could I, when his letter failed to explain why I must come here in such haste and secrecy, and without my maid? He deserves a scold for treating me so shabbily. Where is he?"

"By now he has probably reached Torquay, where his yacht has been moored these three weeks."

She bounded up from the chair. "Torquay? But he ordered me to meet him *here*. How long ago did he leave you? And why?"

Edwin could have given her the most probable answer but thought it best not to add to her shock by voicing his suspicions. It was obvious to him that Garth had sent for Elizabeth after his departure in order that she would be compromised by staying at Harbourne Court unchaperoned. He'd made a blatant attempt to force Edwin's hand—at his sister's expense.

Hoping to alleviate the young woman's dismay, he swallowed his outrage on her behalf and said as soothingly as he could, "Garth may have forgotten that he asked you to come. He departed in haste, and rather unexpectedly."

"How typical of him. I honestly don't know what I should do now," she said helplessly.

"It's quite simple. I'll direct you to the most comfortable and respectable inn at Totnes, and tomorrow you can return to Lyme Regis. As you can plainly see, my house is in no fit state for receiving company, and even if it were, I'm fairly certain that your parents wouldn't approve of your staying here."

With a charming smile she said, "Indeed they wouldn't."

Having settled the matter between them in this amiable fashion, they began exchanging news of mutual friends. Miss Corston apologized for her dearth of in-

formation and explained it by saying she'd lived very
quietly of late.

"But I assume you will return to town for the Season," said Edwin, "and in no time will be acquainted
with all the current gossip. I hope to travel there myself this summer. I'm to be married soon, and I'd like
to show my bride all the wonders that you, a Lon-
doner, take for granted. I warn you, I depend upon
your advice on which sights will most appeal to
Annis."

"What a pretty name," Elizabeth commented. "I
wish I might meet her. But surely you've heard that
my family no longer has a house in town. Didn't Garth
tell you?"

Edwin shook his head.

"Father couldn't afford to keep up our former style
of life—that's why we removed to Lyme. He suffered
financial reverses, and then when Garth told him how
much he'd lost at cards he sold off the contents of the
house as well."

"I'm sorry, I didn't know."

"I rather like the change," she said with apparent
unconcern, "unlike my mother who misses the opera
and the fashionable assemblies. Garth cannot abide
Lyme, which is too provincial for his tastes."

Edwin pitied her, although she seemed undaunted
by the changes in her situation. Despite having broken
off his budding attachment to her at a very early stage,
he still liked Elizabeth immensely and continued to
regard her as his friend—a much better one than
Garth had turned out to be.

"My brother is still sunk in debt," she confided.
"Father demanded that he give up the yacht; they had
a fearful argument and Garth sailed away the very
next day. I don't mind telling you I've been concerned—he's so reckless, and I fear his desperate need
of money may lead him into greater trouble."

Edwin was disgusted by this revelation, but it explained a great deal about the motive for Garth's visit.

Rather than curtailing his own expensive pleasures, the selfish young man had expected to restore the Corston coffers by marrying his sister off to a wealthy baronet. And he also must have coveted Jam Kelland's mythical chest of gold, which accounted for his curiosity about Annis.

Elizabeth Corston soon declared her readiness to begin her journey to Totnes, and Edwin sent an order to his stables to have his fastest horses harnessed to the seldom-used chaise, of which his great-uncle had been so proud.

When he handed the young woman into the vehicle, she squeezed his fingers gratefully and said, "I can't help envying you, Edwin. I'd like to be married myself, to a certain gentleman in Lyme, but he won't easily win my father's consent. He hasn't got a title or a fortune. I don't care, of course, but you know how my parents are," she concluded forlornly.

"They'll come around I'm sure."

He would have liked to travel with her, for he needed to see Annis so he could explain what had prevented him from meeting her at the fair. Regretfully he acknowledged to himself the folly of escorting an unchaperoned Elizabeth Corston to a Totnes lodging house in his own closed carriage at dusk. That would be playing into Garth's hand.

His longing to see Annis soon had him reminiscing about their glorious night together. Her instincts had compensated for her lack of experience in lovemaking, and he'd been delighted by her eagerness, her warmth, her pleasure. Impatient for another chance to explore the delights of a shared bed, he hoped they could be married very soon.

It was amazing, Edwin reflected, what a single kiss at harvest time could lead to.

Edwin found her seated high in her apple tree, an open book upon her lap. The blossoms were beginning to drop, and the pale petals drifted to the ground as silently and beautifully as snowflakes.

"Annis."

She responded to his call by glancing down, but he read no welcome in her face.

"I'm awfully sorry I was absent from the fair yesterday," he began, "but I suppose you know the reason by now. It couldn't be helped. Your stepfather came to collect the bay mare, and I couldn't tell him I had plans to meet you for fear he might guess that you'd stopped at Harbourne Court on your way to Totnes. He stayed with me longer than I expected, to look over my orchard, and—"

"It doesn't matter," she said, her voice distant and devoid of all expression.

Her demeanor was not what he'd anticipated—she seemed more despondent than angry. "I'd intended to ride to Totnes as soon as we concluded our business, but before I could a visitor arrived, and by the time she left—"

"She?"

He'd never heard a single pronoun invested with so much disdain.

"Elizabeth Corston. She was looking for her brother—poor girl, he threw her into the devil of a scrape. What's more, his extravagant ways contributed to their father's ruin, and I suspect the financial situation is very grave indeed. Garth can go hang, for all I care, but before he does I hope he'll be sensible enough to sell his yacht and provide his sister with a dowry. She has a suitor in Lyme and hopes to marry him, but—"

"She does? How do you know?"

"That's what she told me when we parted. How I wish Garth had never taken it into his head to come to Devonshire—it made trouble for everyone. Mostly me, and at a time when I would rather have devoted my full attention to you."

Her next comment was inaudible, she was seated so far above him.

In exasperation, he said, "Annis, come down here so I can converse with you properly, or I shall have a stiff neck. Besides, there are things I want to say that I'd rather not shout."

She required no further incentive to descend from her perch, and he hadn't long to wait before she was standing before him, her face prettily flushed and her eyes bright.

"Now *I* shall have the stiff neck," she said. "Why must you be so very tall?"

Placing his hands upon her hips, he drew her closer. "It can't be helped, so you'll have to accustom yourself. We've some unfinished business that ought to be settled at once. How soon can we be wed? If you wish it, I'll travel to Exeter to consult the dean of the cathedral about obtaining a special license so we needn't wait another three weeks for the banns."

"My mother says May weddings are unlucky," she informed him regretfully.

"Very well, ours will be in June. But it must be early in the month. Promise?"

"The very first day," she agreed, twining her arms about his neck.

This fervent answer made him smile. He reached for the branch directly above their heads and plucked a blossom, one of the few still intact, and presented it to her with a loving look. "By tomorrow the rest of the flowers will have dropped, and your bower won't look so lovely as it does now."

"But soon the leaves will come in, and eventually the fruit. Before we know it, we'll be celebrating another harvest home."

"And I shall bring my wife back to this sacred place, and kiss her as passionately as I did last autumn."

Annis tucked his gift into her hair. "You needn't wait so long. Do it now," she commanded.

Edwin derived considerable pleasure from obliging her.

Violets Are Blue

❦

by Karen Harper

1

Baltimore, April 6, 1835

Although the silent house still clung to death, the breeze smelled of spring. Ignoring the morning mist, Violet McClellan thrust her head farther out her bedroom window. No, she could not bear to weed through Mother's old trunks and bandboxes in the dim, dusty attic right now. She was going out.

She shoved her deep-brimmed bonnet over her upswept topknot of thick black hair and pulled her three-tiered rain cape over her mauve morning gown. "Irene," she called down the hall to the young housekeeper her mother had taken in from the Presbyterian orphanage, "I'm going out for a walk! To see if Mr. Marton engraved Mother's tombstone yet. Since you had to stay here the day of the funeral, you could come along!"

The red-haired sixteen-year-old appeared at the hall door, feather duster in hand. "I was just remembering, Miss Violet, your mother said you mustn't shout, but ring for me before orders or requests."

"I know," Violet said, grabbing her embroidered reticule from the bureau and stuffing her gloves in it.

"But you did say you'd like to see the grave without the people there. It's barely sprinkling out, so come on then."

"Thought you said we'd right up the attic this morning, miss."

"Later," Violet assured her and reached out to flick the feathers in the duster. "Don't tell me you think that bird in the hand is worth more than seeing real ones in the bush outside."

The puzzled look on the girl's long freckled face suggested she did not catch Violet's drollery. But if she had, Violet thought, she probably would have suggested it be "bridled a wee bit" in the exact tone Mother would have used. Even though she'd been bedridden at the end, Mrs. Lilian McClellan's strong Scots personality had managed to make quite an impression on Irene in the six months the girl had been with them. But for the first time since the laying out and funeral here in the house, Irene smiled.

"Like to pay my respects at the mistress's resting place, Miss Violet. And be a companion to you so you don't just go walking out alone again, neither."

More echoes of Mother, Violet thought sadly. She missed her so much she almost missed her scoldings, she thought as they set out from the narrow brick townhouse that had been her home from birth. She loved to walk and set a good pace, down East Lombard Street, then uphill toward the church burying ground. In her twenty-nine years, she had come to know the city well. From the time she was eight, when the British came to burn it but were turned away, she had felt protective and downright proud of the cobble- and stone-paved streets, the red-brick houses and white church steeples, and the proliferation of fashionable shops and theaters.

But mostly she loved the great wooden ships laden with exotic goods that came and went from the harbor wharves—ships that for his own tragic reason, her father had never allowed her to set foot on. But now that Mother was gone too, someday, somehow, she would sail out on one of them. Then whatever lay beyond the gray, misty shoals of the Patapsco River—like life—would not just keep slipping by.

"I say, Miss Violet, these cobbles are slippery, so perhaps we shouldn't walk so fast."

"I'm afraid you are old beyond your years, Irene. And I'd rather you call me Violet, really, now that it's just you and I in the house."

"Wouldn't mind, I guess, but what will Mr. Baxter and his sisters say?"

"You must learn not to worry about what others will say, not if you think you're doing what is right. We shall fret over what the Baxters say only if I should ever marry into their family. And I don't see that on the horizon, despite how dear Reed Baxter has always been and what Mother may have hoped."

"Oh, but she didn't hope that," the girl declared. "Told me plain that as clever, kindly, and stable as your Mr. Baxter was, that 'less you wanted children 'fore you're much older, it might be just as well you *didn't* give him your hand. Just the way she put it not a month ago, the very day her fever climbed sky-high again . . ."

Irene continued to reminisce, but Violet's mind snagged upon those last words about possibly giving her longtime friend Reed Baxter her hand. Her hand, but so much more, too: her whole body, her life, her future.

Yet what Violet clung to was that apparently Mother had said it might be just as well if she did *not* wed Reed. Perhaps the fever had made her slightly strange that day, for Mother had always seemed to favor him. Could Violet have simply assumed she would want her to wed him—assumed so because Mother was so opinionated about so much else? Assumed so because there were no other suitors on the horizon? And why had her mother confided her deep feelings to a young servant girl and not to her own daughter? Could she

have lived with Lily McClellan for all these years,
nursed her for these last three, and not have known
how she felt about Reed? But she'd been so close to
Mother. She had known her so very well!

"I'm real glad it's a pretty place." Irene's voice interrupted her agonizings.

"What? Oh, the burying ground. Yes, it is."

They walked along the waist-high brick wall toward
the iron gate. Within, tree limbs blushed yellow-green
with the promise of leaves. Robins hopped, cocked
their gray heads, and darted to pull up their wriggling
breakfast from the damp turf. Canary-colored forsythia bushes, ruby japonica, and white bridal wreath
dotted the rain-slicked grass and peeked from behind
headstones and crypts. To Violet, each bush seemed
a separate bloom set against greenery to make one
huge bouquet of the burying ground—of all of spring-
struck Baltimore.

"Still, I do wish," she observed, "they wouldn't cut
everything back so much here. It should be natural,
even wilder here, like the wooded ridges up by Jones
Falls. But I suppose the church elders would rise from
their graves and haunt the gardeners if the plots
weren't well disciplined and severely trimmed, just as
they want all of us to be."

"Oh, Miss—I mean Violet, how you do put things
sometimes!"

They passed through the big brick archway and
slipped through the iron gate, which stood ajar. Suddenly, a tall man in a black rain cape swept toward
them from nowhere. He bumped Violet's shoulder to
bounce her back a step. He swung his walking stick
away as if he would strike her with it, though perhaps
it was to avoid just that. Irene squealed and jumped
away; Violet gasped. The man—his rain cape made
him seem more like a dark, swooping raven—reached
out quick, hard hands to steady Violet by her shoulders, then set her back.

"Sorry, ladies," he said, but his voice came out cold

and angry. His top hat half obscured dark slits of eyes; his collar came to his square chin. But between those partial masks, Violet saw a scowling slash of mouth. He muttered "Sorry," again, his deep voice reaching out for her as his hands had. Pulling his brim lower as if he might mean to tip his hat, he spun away in a swirl of sleek cape. His boot heels spit gravel at them. Silently, they stared at him until he disappeared through the iron gate, swinging it closed behind him with a metallic clang.

"Mercy me!" Irene cried. "That gentleman's got a burr under his saddle. Must have been near running and hardly looking where he was going."

"Perhaps we should give him the benefit of the doubt and excuse his poor manners, considering where we are," Violet said, her usually strong voice shaky. "He could have recently lost someone dear to him, and was visiting her grave." She was somehow certain he had been here to visit the eternal resting place of a woman. "Come on then, Irene. We'll not let him ruin our good memories."

But as they approached the McClellan plot, a cold cloak of qualms that went deeper than her actual annoyance at the man or mourning for her mother enveloped Violet. The beauty of the day no longer distracted nor comforted her. That man's brusqueness— a black bitterness she sensed in him—chilled her with foreboding as they stood over the twin tombstones of her parents.

And there at the rain-shiny foot of her mother's monument with the newly incised words *LILIAN JACKSON McCLELLAN, b. June 22, 1783, d. April 1, 1835*, lay a sturdy stem bearing waxy white lilies the likes of which Violet had never seen.

"Oh, what grand flowers," Irene said. "Wherever did you get them?"

"I didn't leave them here. They weren't here yesterday. I've never seen ones so . . . exotic."

Violet stooped to lift the big blooms in her hands.

The five trumpet-shaped flowers flourished fresh and strong on their single thick stem, from which glossy green leaves arched like saber points. Golden stamens laden with yellow dust peered from their deep throats. The fragrance was not overwhelmingly sweet but was very pervasive.

"I'll wager Mr. Baxter or one of his sisters brought them," Irene said, as if to answer the unasked question.

"Yes, that's it. On the way home we shall stop by and thank him. Of course someone in the flower business could get such an unusual kind."

"Pity for such pretty things to die here."

"But somehow just right, too." Violet replaced the burst of blooms reverently. "Lilies," she whispered to herself. "Lilies for Lily Jackson McClellan."

When the shop boy went to fetch him, Violet watched Reed hurry out of the backroom cubbyhole that served as his office in his family's flower shop just off the busy Marsh Market. His bright smile warmed her as always, and his clear green eyes were sincerely concerned as he took her hands to greet her. Reed was five years younger, but their piano and flute duets at church and in family circles had made them fast friends years ago. Though the Baxter business was retail and wholesale flowers, Reed now looked more the part of bookkeeper, hastily wiping ink from his fingers onto his detachable canvas cuffs and linen coatee.

"What a fine surprise!" he told Violet. "I was going to call this evening, maybe bring Samantha and Ellen along to cheer you."

"I just stopped by to thank you for the lilies on Mother's grave. They're exquisite."

A look of puzzlement crossed his fine features. He brushed a wisp of chestnut hair back from his high forehead before he shook his head. "I'd like to accept the credit, but it wasn't I—nor my sisters either, Violet, I'm certain of it."

"A shock of five glossy white lilies," she prompted.

"Then I'm sure it wasn't us nor anyone else who gets flowers at Baxter's," he explained. He tucked her hand in the crook of her arm as they strolled the aisle of potted plants and basins of cut flowers. He steered her away from Irene, who bent over varied blooms, sniffing at them so loudly it sounded as if she had a cold.

"Violet, what you are describing sounds like the Bermuda lilies—some call them Easter or resurrection flowers. We haven't yet imported them, though we hope to. The only lilies we've had in the last few years are those yellow-orange ones we call tiger lilies, and that's in May. So I guess you have a bit of a mystery on your hands," he added with a shrug.

"Bermuda lilies, probably brought in by someone by ship," she repeated, considering her clues.

"I can see the mental wheels turning," Reed said and squeezed her arm. "You want to hop a ship to Bermuda right now. Father said he's seen fields of those lilies there, growing wild. They'd fetch a pretty penny here, so maybe we should try again to bring them in, their bulbs at least. But Violet, remember *our* dream voyage," he demanded, lowering his voice and turning his back on the busy shop as if to shut everyone else out.

"Which one?"

"That we take a ship—all of us, perhaps, like one big family—to London and attend every concert hall and theater there. Soon, when Father doesn't need me so much here and the church can find the proper pianist to cover my absence and Ellen is finished with her schooling and . . . ."

"And when Samantha can decide which of her avid beaux to wed and then has children and gets them properly reared and finished with their schooling, and when I can find the money, and when, when, when," she went on, tapping his arm with her free hand. "Pipe dreams, Reed—in my case, flute dreams, our flights of fantasy. I tell you, we've as much chance of seeing the

concert halls of London as we have of becoming famous musicians ourselves."

When she gently disengaged her arm, he tugged her
back by both hands. "Don't say that, Violet. We will
get there and our dreams will come true—maybe
sooner than you think. After your proper period of
mourning, we can really talk about making things happen. I'm just grateful that Irene is living with you, or
you'd simply have to move in with us right now."

She realized it was the closest Reed had ever come
to a marriage proposal—and not much of one at that.
She shook her head, but did not argue. Not only was
there no room for her in the crowded Baxter household, but that would only confirm that Reed saw her
as another sister. She wanted to tell him that her life
must be hers now, but suddenly she simply yearned
to go home. She longed for time alone to consider
who might have left the flowers, to sift through things
in the attic, and to remember her mother without
Reed and his kindly, lively sisters about. And she
wanted to ponder that dark stranger in the cemetery.

"You are not to worry a bit about me, Reed, and
I shall see you Wednesday evening at rehearsal. Perhaps if we practice very hard, we will get another rave
notice in the newspaper," she teased, referring to the
article that had been done after their Handel concert.
She tilted her head to accept a kiss on her cheek,
though over Reed's shoulder she saw Irene's eyes
grow big as teacups at the familiar display in public.
Perhaps the one regret Violet had about Baltimore
was that reputation ruled. It had hurt her mother, but
Violet had vowed never to allow it to hurt her.

"Then you'll let me know if you have any need of
us, and we'll be there in a trice," Reed insisted.

"Yes, of course," she said, but she suddenly realized
that, beyond being her friend and fellow musician, she
really had no need for this dear man at all. Not a
deep, woman's need, which she had once been so sure
would bloom in her for him someday. She turned away

and shooed Irene out ahead of her. They were just beyond the door when Reed caught up with them, placing a nosegay of her favorite spring daffodils and perfumed purple hyacinths in her hands.

She thanked him again and remarked on the beauty and fragrance of the bouquet. But the truth was, they did not look half so alluring nor smell nearly so seductive as those lilies lying in the rain on the cemetery's sodden ground.

It was nearly nightfall when Violet discovered not answers to her mystery, but rather questions to deepen her dilemma. In a trunk her mother had stored in the attic, an old, dust-shrouded, hump-backed one shoved far back under the steep slant of eaves, she found a perfectly preserved and evidently unused *trousseau* of dusty-smelling, old-fashioned garments—definitely for a marriage trip. In the bottom of that trunk, pressed between pages of her mother's family Bible, which Violet had never seen before, were the remains of single flowers of various types—each with a vellum card attached by a ribbon. On each card in faded but bold masculine handwriting was a brief message. She knew immediately, though she could not read the words by the dim light, that the hand and signature were not those of her father, Michael McClellan.

Violet took one of the flowers—a faded red rose— to the dormer window to read its note in the remaining daylight. Some of the outer petals flaked away as she read the words: *June 22, 1810. Captain of my heart, yet another year apart. Still love blooms fresh as a rose. Eternally, Jon.*

A chill feathered up Violet's spine and made the hair on the nape of her neck prickle. Her stomach cartwheeled. Her mother had been twenty-seven years old when she received this and long wed. She hefted the big Bible in her arms to take its secrets downstairs to the privacy of her father's library.

*   *   *

Both of Violet's parents had suffered tragedies in their younger years. Michael McClellan, as a boy of sixteen, had lost his parents and two brothers en route to the new country from County Clare, Ireland when their ship, the *Mary Bridget,* foundered in a storm and sank. Only thirty of the one hundred eighty-four aboard were saved. Michael did not thank the Virgin Mary nor St. Patrick for his deliverance. Perhaps he dared to blame them, for he never set foot in a Catholic church nor on a ship's deck again. Thus, Violet was reared in her mother's Presbyterian faith and was forbidden to get near any ship, even one tethered to the dock.

As for her mother, as proper a lady as ever was— or so Violet had thought—she had another cross to bear. Lily Jackson's father had been the notorious "Black Jack" Jackson, who had made the first of his easy-come, easy-go fortunes during the Revolution, running the British blockade and racking up massive profits from "fellow patriots." Lily, though she adored her father, in deference to her husband's wishes never went near the docks that were the lifeblood of Baltimore, though in her youth she had loved ships and the sea.

Instead, as if in penance for her father's sin of subsequently speculating with the British, the young Mrs. McClellan turned to charitable works, collected imported French porcelain, kept house, and reared her daughter. The small McClellan home was Lily's inheritance from her father's last going, going, gone fortune before his death—one, they said, made on wagering on other people's fortunes.

At any rate, Black Jack's romantic but *roué* reputation and the fact that Lily's Irish husband was a lowly bookkeeper at the British-owned Mackie and Sons Shipping kept the beautiful Lily McClellan out of Baltimore's fashionable, patriot-proud drawing rooms. Perhaps, some whispered, it was Lily's father's reputation that left her no choice but to wed a down-and-out Irish immigrant. But her lack of acceptance in Baltimore society kept her at home with her family, and that—as far as Violet had known—had always seemed to be enough for her.

Over the years, Michael McClellan had been a devoted husband and father, who never traveled farther than the outskirts of Baltimore. He was always happiest at his desk in his library after a long day's work, amid his books, with his jot of Irish rye at his elbow and his occasional jigs he played on his pennywhistle—or listening to his only child practice her flute.

Now, at that desk seven years after his death, his daughter sat stunned, with her head in her hands and the evidence of her mother's three-decade secret love affair spread before her. As she had read the various verses and seen the array of flowers, she had been swigging the remains of her father's last bottle of rye.

"Blue blazes!" Violet swore his favorite oath, which he'd never so much as whispered in his wife's presence. Violet took her glass and wove her way over to the hand-cut, gilt-framed silhouette of her mother's profile hanging in its place of honor over the mantel.

"Mother, who is this Jon?" she demanded, shaking her fist and slopping rye down her arm. " 'Eternal love?' Father thought he knew you! I thought I did, too! But I didn't, not at all! He left the flowers on your grave today, didn't he, your 'Eternally Jon'? And I'm going to find him and find out all about you!"

In the black of her mother's silhouette, Violet saw again the form of the dark stranger. He'd seemed younger than this Jon should be, but she hadn't really seen his face. Had he known who she was—recognized her as Lily's daughter? Was that why he'd been so brusque and tried to flee? Had he returned from the sea—Bermuda—and just discovered his beloved's death? His deep voice reached out for her again; she could almost hear him reading these lover's notes of the years, almost feel his powerful hands on her again as they had no doubt once held her mother, the woman whom she—she and Father—had thought they knew.

"How could you?" she cried. She raced to the desk, bumping her knee, and smashed the old dried rose lying there with her fist. It flattened, puffing out pieces and dust.

A knock on the door, followed by a twist of the doorknob, made Violet jump. She shook her head to clear it. The room had grown dim; the single whale oil lamp on the desk guttered low.

"Violet, did I hear you shouting?" said a muffled voice through the locked door.

"I was just talking to myself, Irene. I'm fine. Go to bed."

"*Back* to bed, you mean. It's nigh on midnight, you know."

"I lost track of time. I'm going to bed soon. Go on, then."

Evidently, Irene went. But it was dawn before Violet locked the Bible away and trudged upstairs. She did not even get in bed, but washed her face and took powdered charcoal in water for her headache. She dragged her bounteous black hair up into a topknot and changed her clothes. Then, even before breakfast, she slipped out and headed for the burying ground again.

That day, the mysterious visitor to her mother's grave had been there before her. A second spike of pristine lilies lay against the stone to join the other, slightly limp one. Violet inquired of the gardeners if they had seen anyone early—a man in an old-fashioned black cape? No one—nothing unusual, they said, eyeing her strangely. But at least, she thought, perhaps the new lilies meant the phantom visitor would come tomorrow, too.

The next morning, Violet left the house even earlier, all in gray so she could secrete herself behind the pale stone crypts some little distance past the McClellan site. Yesterday she had looked from different vantage points and realized she might be spotted if she hid any closer. Today she had to wait until the old caretaker unlocked the gate. He too stared at her suspiciously before he recognized her and said he thought the Handel concert she'd played with the church pianist was lovely. She supposed now it would soon be all over the congregation that her mother's death had so unhinged the spinster McClellan that she was lurking about her grave at all hours.

Waiting in this solemn, solitary place set her to agonizing again. How could one's daily life entwine with that of one you loved—your own flesh and blood— and yet you never really knew them? Perhaps she didn't even know herself anymore, didn't know what she wanted to do with her life. Should she pursue security—a duet in marriage as well as in music—with Reed Baxter, even if she didn't really love him? Would sharing his life change her feelings? Her mother had evidently had two loves, and here she would probably never have even one!

Every muscle in her tightened when she heard the hollow echo of the clanging gate just as the sun rose high enough to send sharp shadows across the dewy grass. She crouched behind the crypt and counted to ten before she dared to look over it. Yes! A man, *the* man, though the black cape was gone. Yes, moving quickly toward her mother's grave.

Stooping, she emerged from behind her shelter. His head disappeared for a moment as he evidently bent to leave the flower. But he did not stand to ponder, pray, or agonize at the grave as she had imagined, so she did not have time to creep up on him. He turned abruptly and strode away.

Violet broke into a little run, but her legs shook and her heart beat hard. He was moving away so fast on those long legs, not taking the paths but cutting straight toward the gate.

Fearing that if she called out he might flee, she

picked up her skirts and ran, darting between and around stones. But one headstone lay flat; she stubbed her toe, tripped, tumbled. She heard the metal gate clang.

Without brushing herself off or examining grass stains or dew marks, she got up and ran again, silently cursing her painful toe, the man, even her mother. The stranger was heading north, back to the city, swinging his walking stick. She had to see his face, stop him, confront and accuse him. Despite the stitch in her side, she ran harder, panting. A half a block ahead, he turned up busy Light Street. A businessman, heading to his law office or countinghouse, she thought. If he were a trader, he would have turned toward the wharves. Then too, the theaters were up this way. An actor, someone who came and went with certain plays perhaps, so she would not recognize him as someone from town. Yes, a thespian with that deep voice, who had met her mother years ago, a master of disguises, a seducer of people's imaginations . . . and of her mother.

People stared at her as she ran. Unfortunately, her minister, the Reverend Mr. Forbes, passed her and called after her, but she did not stop. She bounced off several people, gasping an apology as she rushed on. And then, ahead, the man stopped to buy a newspaper from a boy hawking them on the corner of Redwood, just under the hanging sign of the Fountain Inn.

"You, sir!" she cried as he turned away again, though several men stared her way. "You there. Stop!"

He turned toward her at last. His was not a classically handsome face, but intense, compelling. It registered surprise, then anger. So he must know who she was!

"We have no business," he insisted, holding up gloved palms to halt her when she hurried closer. "Be on your way, as I am."

"My name is Miss Violet McClellan. I want to talk

with you! Jon, stop!" she dared as he made a move to cross the busy street to elude her among people, horses, carts, and calashes.

At that, he stepped back and faced her squarely. "My name is not Jon." He crossed his arms and walking stick across his broad chest. "I fear you have mistaken me for someone else."

He stood a good half-foot taller than she; his top hat and span of shoulders blocked out sun and sky. He still glowered at her, but she did not waver.

"Whatever your name, sir, I need to speak with you. You have been placing flowers on my mother's grave, and I'd like to know why."

"Why, indeed!" he shouted, so loudly that she stepped back. But he dared to seize her arm and propel her out of the flow of pedestrians, nearly pressing her against the door of the inn. "I admit, she certainly doesn't deserve them," he went on. "I know you're her daughter. I saw you when they buried her."

"What? I demand to know who you are, or I shall summon the authorities!"

He snorted derisively and glanced upward as if for heavenly assistance. When she tried to shake off his hand, he yanked open the door to the inn and pulled her inside after him. She landed a kick to his shins and attempted to pull away to run back out. Yet his firm hold on her arm restrained her. She had not considered a private physical confrontation, yet anger fueled her strength. Before she could strike him, he seized her wrist, then suddenly loosed her. With arms crossed over his chest again, he leaned against the door, pushing it shut behind him.

"If you must know, Miss 'Violence' McClellan, my name is not Jon. I am acting for one named Jon, who, I regret to say, greatly admired your mother once. As it was long ago and they have been long parted, let us follow their lead."

"I—I just learned of this recently. But I have found notes and pressed flowers signed 'Eternally Jon,' dated over many years—not just long ago. This has all been such a shock."

"Indeed," he said, frowning at her. She blinked up at him in the shaft of sun that flooded through the fan-shaped skylight over the door. He seemed to waver now, as if he were struggling with himself. He removed his hat at last. His ebony hair was curly, whereas hers was board-straight; his was tinged with silver at the temples, while hers was so black it shone almost blue in the sun. The outside corners of his eyes were faintly lined, but she saw how much younger he was than her mother's Jon could have been. His eyes were a cloudy gray, as she had always imagined the measureless ocean would look from the rolling deck of an outward-bound ship. The right side of his mouth twitched downward as he brazenly studied her too.

And then, just as she decided she must demand again that he tell her all, he said, "You must forgive me, Miss McClellan, for several things. Especially for saying that you have the most incredible eyes I have ever seen. That shade of lavender—did your people name you—did she, Lilian Jackson McClellan, name you for that? It is obvious to me you were not named Violet because you are the shrinking sort—not you."

Those words and his intense, assessing stare completely disarmed her. She suddenly felt so aware of herself: of her no doubt hoydenish, disheveled appearance after her tumble to the grass and her run through town chasing a strange man; of her face blushing hotly now, though that was so unlike her. She sucked in a startled breath, much too loud.

"Then you will explain things to me?" she asked.

"What I know. If you will afterwards let it—and me—be. Will you?"

"It seems I have no choice if I wish to hear your story. Yes, then I will leave you alone."

She thought she heard him whisper "Alas" as he stepped away to unblock the door. But he did not lead her out into the street. Instead he motioned her into the common room of the inn, where she saw two men setting up the tables for the day.

"Mr. Stone. Ah—the usual, for two instead of one today?" the taller man asked, as, flatware and pewter plates in hand, they both stared at Violet. Behind Mr. Stone's back, she had begun to smooth her skirt and shove stray tresses back under her bonnet brim, but at their perusal she stopped.

"That will be fine," her host said and slid a barrel-backed chair out then in for her, as if they met for private, intimate, unchaperoned breakfasts every day. Yet thrusting all of that aside, her trembling hands clasped in her lap, Violet sat ramrod straight and stared at the man across the narrow table.

2

By late afternoon, Nathan Stone thought he had walked his anger off enough to go home and speak in a civil manner to his father. He went in the front door before the butler could answer and took the carpeted steps up to the second floor of the mansion two at a time. He did not stop at his own bedroom, but continued up to his father's private realm on the third floor, his feet thudding on the wooden steps.

He was glad to see his father was alone, without his butler, Grayson, who also acted as his valet—but was more friend than servant. Tossing his coat and hat over a chair, he faced the older man he so resembled, though his father had blue eyes and the deep bronze of perpetual sun and wind on his face from years at sea. Jonathan Stone, his captain's hat tilted at a jaunty angle on his silver head, rolled his wheeled chair toward his son, across the wide expanse of floor.

"I must say I heard you coming, Nate. Sit down, or

can you still not abide my company since I asked you for one little favor?"

"One *little* favor?" Nathan demanded, suddenly glad to be back in the thick of their earlier argument. "Did you really think I wouldn't guess you'd been unfaithful to my mother for years when you asked me to meet the ship and then take those flowers to that woman's grave three mornings straight? You only admitted your longtime *affaire de coeur* after I told you I happened to see her funeral procession when I visited my own mother's resting place. You know, your wife's grave—the one without flowers," he added.

"I have sent flowers to your mother's grave before. And I only asked you to take the remembrance to Mrs. McClellan's until Grayson recovers from his chest cold. If you'd said no, I swear I would have crawled downstairs and gotten myself there somehow. As I said before," he added, and hit his fist on the arm of his chair, "I thought—man to man—I could trust you to understand, but I see you don't get one damned, blasted bit of it."

"Don't I? I'm thirty-four, Father, a man who's lived all over Europe, a widower, and I can't understand that my father loved another woman all the years his wife was faithful to him? I've seen the ways of the world, though I admit it's tough to accept them in my own father. But I didn't come here to debate all this again. I just thought you ought to know that your *paramour's* daughter waylaid me uptown and demanded to know everything."

"What the deuce? Lily's daughter Violet? Really?"

When Nathan glimpsed a smug smile on his father's face, he strode away and hunched a shoulder against one of the long windows from which his father spent hours surveying harbor traffic with his telescope. The fifty-eight-year-old ship owner and former sea captain had become a self-imposed recluse these last five years after a snapped mizzenmast crushed his legs in a storm. And now, just for these three months before Nathan

left for his latest foreign assignment, he had come
home to spend some rich hours with the man—and
gotten mired in this mess.

"Yes, it really was your Lily's daughter—in the
flesh," Nathan said, his voice quiet now as he pictured
again the creamy skin of her alert, avid face, her
shapely female form, and the beguiling *dishabille* of
her garments, like some ravished, ravishing wood-
land nymph.

"And?" his father prompted.

"When Violet McClellan saw the flowers, she hid
in the cemetery and followed me. She'd already found
a packet of *billets-doux* you'd sent her mother over
the years. I told her what little I knew and made her
vow to leave it at that—and leave us alone."

"What does she look like? I haven't seen her for
years. When I was in port I sometimes used to sit in
the back pew of the Presbyterian church and watch
the both of them. The girl was as skinny as her flute,
her face all huge pale-purple eyes."

"She's not skinny anymore. And her eyes—yes, I
noticed." He still frowned out the window, as if he
could not bear to look at the older man. "Would you
believe that she chased me, kicked me, and demanded
to know all about this—this grand passion of yours?
And all I could do was think I was going to drown in
those eyes."

"Spoken like a man there may yet be some hope
for," his father muttered. "You've been so obsessed
with your blasted career, I wasn't sure."

Nathan turned and walked toward him, then leaned
back against the edge of the big desk, with its navigational instruments and stack of charts. "You're one to
talk, Father, as ambitious as you always were." Changing his mind about leaning casually, he rose again to
his full height. "And I'm following in your footsteps,
about to reach the pinnacle of my career, further my
own fortune, and serve my country—even if not in the
same calling you did."

"Then listen to some advice from one who learned too little too late, my boy. Who will you leave the fortune to? Who will you share your cares with at the end of the day in one of those trading houses in China so far from home? Your pride in self, love of duty and country will be cold comfort then, I promise you."

"The point is, Father, I moved here for the months before I sailed so I could share things with you, and we are doing such a damn poor job of that."

"My point is that even here you drive yourself too hard and allow yourself no rest. You don't stop to enjoy life—the little daily things that really matter when you look back on life. Have some friends in for dinner, take a lady to the theater, cultivate people or flowers—something besides your damned business accounts and perfecting the scribbles and gibberish of the Chinese language!"

"Cultivate the outside world, as you have lately, you mean, walling yourself in here like a monk?"

"My heyday is past, Nate, but the prime of your life lies ahead! When I'm dead and gone, who else will care what happens to you and your precious career but your high-and-mighty employers, and they can replace you in a week. As I said before, I regret again that I've distressed you with this sort of homecoming. I loved your mother, son, and stayed away from Lily Jackson McClellan because I respected both her and your mother."

"How could you have loved or respected Mother if you loved the other woman first—and through all those years?"

"I can't explain it to myself, let alone to you," Jonathan Stone said quietly, tipping his hat back and closing his eyes. "It was just that Lily was a woman I could never stop loving, could never forget—even when I sailed away time after time, even when things did not work out for us, even when we each had our own mate and child."

"It wasn't just that she was married to someone else then?"

"No," the old man whispered. For the first time since Nathan had been home, his father sounded old and tired. When he opened his eyes, Nathan saw they were watery behind his spectacles. Suddenly, he wanted to touch his father's shoulder, to hug him like a little boy would, but he stiffly stood his ground. His father turned his chair away and rolled it toward the bunk he'd built in the wall, much like in a captain's cabin of a ship.

"It's a long story, Nate. But I guess I owe its telling to you and the girl, since you've both become so involved—with me and her mother, I mean, not with each other."

"The girl. Violet McClellan?"

"Invite and escort her to the house this evening after supper, won't you? I know where she lives, if you didn't think to inquire." Jonathan Stone adroitly hefted himself into bed with his powerful arms, did a half roll, reached down to arrange his legs, then lay staring up at the wooden ceiling above his narrow bed. He removed his spectacles, lay them on his chest, and pulled his hat down over his eyes, as if that final command ended their conversation.

"I told you I made her promise to stay away," Nathan said.

"Then," came the muffled words, "I will honor your wishes on that, if you can't face her or don't wish to see her again. I know you are one to make your own decisions. I certainly wasn't suggesting anything would come of your knowing her."

The strangest thought flicked through Nathan's mind, but he immediately discarded it. How far-fetched to even consider that his father would have set this up—risked giving up his secrets, risked this argument on top of all their other ones, just because perhaps he wanted to see the daughter of his long-lost love. Ridiculous. He had left the choice up to him about whether she came here or not.

"If you want—if she will agree, I'll bring her," he said as he gathered his things. He hurried downstairs, surprised he had agreed so readily when he still wanted to argue. But he was curious about how it had begun—and ended—between Lily and his father. And though he hated to admit it, he wanted very badly to see the unshrinking Violet again, and entirely for his own reasons.

Nathan Stone had lived abroad, escorted wealthy, elegant women to grand events at *châteaus* and *palazzi,* and courted and adored one he'd married and lost to consumption. Yet he felt as nervous as a schoolboy when he left his horse and chaise in the street and rang the bell at the East Lombard Street townhouse to see Violet McClellan. The place seemed squeezed in among the larger, grander houses, a shirttail relation in the neighborhood. Yet there was something sturdy and defiant about it, just like its mistress.

A thin, red-haired girl answered the door. Hardly hiding her surprise and curiosity, she put him in the dim parlor to wait and scurried upstairs with his calling card. He in turn was surprised that Violet appeared almost instantly. She was attired in a deep blue day dress, her ebony hair parted in the center with many wayward tendrils and a tousled topknot. Many women looked plain that way, but the casual coiffure emphasized her fine skin, heart-shaped face, and those stunning eyes. Facing her in this cozy little room, he felt he had tumbled into a domestic, intimate moment, the charm and power of which he had almost forgotten.

"I thought we agreed we had parted permanently," she began. "Oh, I didn't mean that as a rebuff. Please sit, Mr. Stone." She indicated a chair just across a tiny table from the chair she took, though there was a much more comfortable-looking settee; he sat down, leaning a bit forward with his hands on his walking stick between his feet.

"I spoke with my father and he expressed a desire— a willingness—to tell both of us our parents' story. After our rough beginning today—the way you re- acted with anger—I didn't know how you would feel about any of this, but I thought I owed it to you to ask." He could not believe he was stumbling over his own native language when he could speak three foreign ones better than most Americans could ever hope to.

"That is kind of you both. I did not think you kind at first, but perhaps you were just angry at your fa- ther, too."

He nodded, hesitant to share his still-raw feelings with this woman, however much they shared this expe- rience of parental perfidy. Besides, he was used to European women, who made an art of emotional hide- and-seek, not to new acquaintances of the opposite sex who were so honest and direct about sentiments. Even the women of Boston, where he'd lived the last year, guarded at all costs their emotions—if not their opinions. Her forgiving him for his earlier brusqueness, even for his reticence to tell her anything over the tense breakfast they had shared, touched him deeply.

"Yes, I was furious," he admitted. "I had just found out about it before I bumped into you that first morn- ing in the cemetery."

She leaned forward as if she would reach out to touch his hand on his walking stick, or even to pat his knee. "I do understand," she whispered. "It will take me but a moment to be ready."

"If you'd like to bring your lady's maid or a servant, that would be fine," he added hastily, amazed at her trust. And for a woman to say she would be ready in a trice when called upon so suddenly—unheard of.

"I have but Irene, whom you have met. You see," she said as she stood, "I am not Black Jack Jackson's granddaughter for nothing. I used to think Mother was not like him—bold and brazen enough to break rules—

but I have learned the error of that belief. And, if I must, I shall yet proudly own up to their rebel's blood in me—even in the little things."

When she hurried out, Nathan sat stock-still with his mouth open in total enchantment, until he recalled how his father had been snared by that rebel blood. He shook his head as if to cast off a spell and, frowning, stood to pace the small room until she came down to join him.

Although Nathan Stone had told her that his father was now a ships' owner and retired sea captain, the size and grand interior of the brick mansion on tree-lined, fashionable Fayette Street awed Violet.

"My mother used to entertain a great deal—my father, too, when he was home," he explained as the butler led them formally up the sweeping central staircase from a tiled foyer graced with a large chandelier. In the wide hall, and in every room into which Violet caught a glimpse, stood the ornately carved and lacquered furniture of China, set off by brass dragons, suspended gongs, and shelves of vibrant porcelain.

Nathan had explained to her in the carriage that his father would receive them on the third floor, in what had once been a ballroom, where he had lived since his accident so that his wheeled chair had no barriers of doorways or stairs. But she had not been prepared for the fact that the large open area looked just the way her mother had described the captain's cabin of a seagoing vessel. Flags and signal pennants were strung along two ceiling beams like drying laundry; two smiling bare-breasted wooden female figureheads in flowing wooden garments dominated corners amid ship's models and bells, charts, and coiled ropes.

"Oh, my," Violet said after introductions. "It's almost as if you're at sea up here—though, I regret, I've never been there myself, Mr. Stone."

"Won't you call me Captain? And, though he evidently has not given you his permission yet, Nathan or Nate will do for the younger Mr. Stone, right, son?"

"Of course," Nathan said, but his quick scowl at his father did not reassure her he meant it.

"Now, you say you've never been to sea?" the captain asked, indicating she and his son should sit in the hoop-back chairs facing his wheeled chair across a low wooden table, where a navigational chart seemed to serve as a tablecloth.

"I've never even been on a ship," she explained. "My father did not wish it, and there was nowhere to go on one, anyway."

"Nate's going clear to China on one in June."

"Oh, China? Now that's an adventure, and an exotic one!"

She did not want to like the captain—her mother's "Eternally Jon." She had meant to remain judgmental, even aloof, however much curiosity burned in her about him and his son. But she could not help but be drawn into their lives, as the older man gave her a tour of what he called his crow's nest and talked about places he had visited, places Nathan had actually lived.

"I'd be happy to arrange a tour for you of one of my three ships," the captain said later, with a pointed glare at his son. "But two are out and one is being repaired—the newest one, *Bold Venture,* on which Nate's going to the Orient."

"I suppose since she's never seen a ship close-up," Nathan put in, "even one in dry dock would be a step up."

"Thank you, but there's no need," she said hastily, feeling snagged on silent saber points between the two men. "I plan to go to England soon enough with some friends. Besides, maybe I would not even have sea legs."

"I'd give anything for any kind of legs," the captain muttered as the butler entered to serve cakes and coffee.

Over their little repast, the captain began to reminisce about Violet's grandfather, Black Jack; once again, Nathan sat silent, apparently just taking it—and her, whom he studied both avidly and subtly—in. And then finally, without warning, the moment Violet was certain that Nathan as well as she had awaited arrived.

"It was when your mother was visiting one of Black Jack's ships one day, docked at McEldery's Wharf— as a matter of fact on her sixteenth birthday—that I first saw her," the captain said, his eyes growing doubly glassy behind his spectacles. "There she was, more beautiful than any woman I'd ever seen, laughing and hanging over the rail like an angel from heaven, with her dark hair blowing. You resemble her in some ways, you know," he told Violet. "Don't take this wrong, but when you walked in, it was almost like seeing a ghost at first; but I see you are your own woman."

"As I am alone in the world now, Captain, I try to be. My mother and I share birthdays on June 22, though, so I guess that was the day you met her in 1799."

"It was indeed, so long ago and yet so fresh—fragrant—in my mind. Anyhow, after that chance meeting, though her mother sometimes watched her like a hawk and her father often had hired men who waited outside shops for her, we managed to . . . to see each other. I was twenty-two then, my father's first mate and aching to have my own ship at my command. She had a friend who sometimes covered for us, though I can tell you nothing untoward happened between us. However young and eager we were, I loved her too much for that."

When his pause stretched out and Nathan shifted in his chair to recross his long legs, Violet asked quietly, "And her parents discovered it and broke it off?"

"No. When I proposed to Lily and she accepted my suit, it was not Black Jack who objected, but Seth Stone."

"Grandfather?" Nathan put in.

"Because she was Black Jack's daughter," Violet added.

"Yes to both of you. And yet it went much deeper

than that. Seth Stone was a clever man, but a hard one too. He demanded absolute allegiance on his ships and in his family—certainly from the son who would inherit his business. He did not forbid us to wed, but said only that if I wanted the captaincy of the *Dauntless,* I must wait to announce any betrothal plans until I returned from my first captain's voyage to Liverpool. But once I was there, his agents had me sail to Le Havre, then to Madrid. I wrote Lily, but it seems— through my father's devices, I later learned—the letters were not delivered. Rather, she was told that I had accepted a voyage to the Sandwich Isles and to China immediately after I returned to Baltimore, after having been away for over a year by then. Not hearing from me, feeling betrayed as she later explained, Lily Jackson wed your father, Miss McClellan."

Violet felt her anger at her mother—even at this man she wanted so to dislike—gradually ebb. "I'm sorry for you," she said sincerely, even as his own son sat as still as a wooden figurehead.

"Thank you, my dear. It doesn't exonerate me for losing her, of course. I was overly ambitious to sail. I very much desired to go to the Far East, where new markets were opening, new challenges awaited. Mine was one of the first fast ships to trade there when the lucrative China trade began," he added proudly.

"So when you were home in port," Nathan asked, his tone so harsh in comparison to the captain's softer voice, "you carried on a liaison with Violet's mother over the years?"

"If you call those flowers I sent on her birthday every year carrying on a liaison, Nate. No, though I admired and loved her from afar—and perhaps, since she kept the things, she still cared for me—we never so much as spoke, but once, briefly and nervously, when we met by pure chance outside a store on Albe-marle Street about ten years ago. Rather, she became my ideal of love—the perfect but elusive woman, just outside my grasp."

They all sat silent at that. Violet's empty coffee cup trembled in her hand; surprised she still held it, she dinged it a bit too loudly when she set it in its saucer. To love so deeply all those years, she thought, and to deny themselves each other ... to remain faithful to their spouses ... to pay for Seth Stone's treachery or cruel circumstances ... or for the captain's youthful ambitions. Her sense of security was shaken still more.

"I understand now," Violet whispered, while Nathan only cleared his throat. "So many years to love and yet not live that love ..."

"Life takes strange turns," the captain said. "And when two lives entwine and the chance for happiness—the commitment, the union of lives—is not made then but delayed, disaster and loss ensue. So—I didn't mean to preach at you two. It's not your problem or your life, but I did want both of you to understand."

"Thank you," Violet said, and leaned over to take his hand. "For loving my mother with honor. And for sharing your advice."

As she and Nathan took their leave from the old man, she thought about her dear friend Reed. She was appalled to realize that for the first time ever she had forgotten their duet rehearsal at church tonight. He would no doubt go to the house to see what had happened, and what would Irene tell him? But she pondered the fact that their lives were entwined, and if he proposed marriage, that would be her moment to seize happiness and make a commitment to him. And if she let that moment slip away, would she regret it and grieve forever?

But she forgot Reed as Nathan accompanied her downstairs. She was so aware of his hand pressing hers through their gloves as he helped her into the chaise, of his strong thigh so close to hers on the horsehair seat.

"I really would like to show you the *Bold Venture*," he said as he took the reins.

"The ship in dry dock?"

"Yes, at the Fells Point shipyard. They've almost repaired a hole beneath her waterline that the pumps could barely keep up with. Maybe we'll be there to see her relaunched."

"Relaunched for the second chance at a 'bold venture,' " she said, trying to sound clever and calm, however awed and excited she felt about his invitation. "The chance to take you clear to China! I hope you'll tell me all about it."

"Before I go or after I return?" he asked, snapping the reins to send the horse on its way. "I'll be gone for at least three years."

"Three years!" was all she said, but inside she cried, *an eternity*!

The sun shone and the wind whipped clear and clean as they arrived early the next afternoon at the teeming shipyards and wharves overlooking the harbor at Fells Point. Nathan pointed out vessels from Santo Domingo, Buenos Aires, Cape Horn, Bengal, Calcutta, Canton, Liverpool, London, and Bermuda. Chandlers and tattoo shops, taverns, warehouses, building sheds, and rooming houses lined the waterfront. Men of all descriptions, of several skin colors, were everywhere; she saw not one other woman. Yet the sights, the sounds, the smells—even the slightly forbidden nature of it—she savored it all.

"Oh, she's beautiful!" Violet cried when Nathan pointed out the *Bold Venture,* sitting in a big wooden cradle in the midst of hovering horse-powered derricks and yardhands with mallets, drills, long brushes, and barrels of tar.

"Yes, even when not under sail, she is that," he agreed and smiled. His eyes lit, sparking a fire she felt clear down in the pit of her belly. "Besides being replanked in one spot," he explained, "her deck's being reseamed, and she'll be partly rerigged too. But it looks like she's almost ready for a launch. Let's go aboard."

He introduced Violet to Captain Murdock and First Mate Wyley, the latter then accompanying them on a belowdecks tour. She was amazed at the narrow companionways and the boxlike cabins and the sweep of the sleek decks. As they waited for the late afternoon relaunch of the vessel, Nathan explained the workers' tasks. He steadied her arm to help her walk the deck planks, newly reseamed with tar-soaked hemp, which the men called caulkers, jammed and pounded in the cracks. Leaks could mean danger or disaster on the monthslong rough round-the-Horn and trans-Pacific crossing to China.

Violet marveled at the well-worn rich mahogany of the rails and the bleached white wood of the decks, the polished brasswork winking in the sun, the tree-tall masts, the spars, shrouds, and web of rigging above them. The sails were being repaired elsewhere, but puffy clouds in the sea-blue sky overhead made her feel as if they might set out for Canton right now, together.

"I wager she flies like a bird," she told Nathan as they stood at the rail near the prow.

"They call them clipper ships because they've clipped days, even weeks off long runs," he explained so proudly he might have been the captain himself. "In eight minutes, she can go from bare sticks to full sails and fourteen knots when she's given her head."

"I can tell you love sailing. Why didn't you follow in your father's footsteps, as he did his?"

"I wanted," he said through lips no longer bent in the hint of a smile, "to be my own man. Not to have to *kowtow*—that means bow down in Chinese—to family tradition or my father and grandfather. They say men of the sea are restless, but I was always more so. I craved new challenges, faces, tasks, places. Even more variety than I'd ever see commanding my own ship."

"But even knowing you so briefly, I think you have commanded your own ship—even if not one of wood and canvas. Your life must have been so fascinating!"

And so Violet McClellan, who had never set foot on the deck of so much as a dry-docked ship before, became beguiled by the story of Nathan Stone's adventurous life. He described distant lands, exotic customs, and far-flung assignments for foreign trading firms. She learned he had even visited China before. But what she discovered most of all was that he could become animated, as excited as a child, when she had thought him at first to be so stern and stoic.

"Since the massive British East India Company lost its monopoly on trade in China last year," he went on, "the Orient is finally, for the first time, really open to Americans. Three United States trading companies are getting in the race to export Chinese goods. The Boston firm in which I'm a partner, Russell and Company, thinks the sky's the limit, so I've been learning Chinese and will take my place at their trading post there—called a factory or *kohung.* And really, I'll be benefiting doubly from this new endeavor, since my family's ships will be carrying some of the bounty back to America."

"Yes, I can see the sky's the limit," she echoed, finally making herself look away from his avid expression, up at the bare forest of masts and spars again. "It's only too bad you lost your wife and have to go all that way alone."

"You sound like my father," he told her, his voice becoming taut again. "I would *never* have taken this assignment if I were wed, for women aren't allowed in *Kwangchow,* the Chinese name for Canton. Caucasians are closely watched and regulated. They call us *qwai-lo,* foreign devils, so that speaks volumes about their real attitude toward us. The Westerners who are married keep their wives and families in the Portuguese colony of Macao and see them only infrequently. That's a three-day journey from Canton in hired, guarded boats through some rough territory. No, I'd never put a woman through the grueling trip over and all the hardships and separations."

Their eyes locked and held; they seemed not to breathe for a moment. She felt so drawn to him, as if she could tilt right into his arms, despite his obstinate expression. She wondered if he might be recalling what their parents had gone through—hardships and separations, as he said. He studied her so intently she felt a hot flush creep up from her collar to heat her throat, cheeks, and ear tips.

"There is no wife to put through all that, so it's a moot point anyway," he added, still staring so she felt like a butterfly pinned to cotton under glass. She nodded quickly before jerking her head to look away at the bustling waterfront.

They lingered as the final preparations were made to relaunch the *Bold Venture.* The mallet men gathered below to loosen the cradle blocks to free the ship; the towboat stood by in the water. Violet and Nathan strolled to the stern, where he pointed out the wooden rudder brace that would keep the steering mechanism from breaking off in the sudden impact of water. With the captain and first mate, they went to brace themselves against the wheelhouse to counteract the tilting slide of the great vessel.

Beneath their feet, they could hear and feel the mallet men releasing the ship. Keelblocks clattered free. When the weight of the ship fell onto the cradle, Violet's stomach seemed to drop away. Piles of beams built along the hull's underbelly rolled along another greased layer. Born anew from her wooden womb, the *Bold Venture* groaned as she settled into the slick trough and picked up speed.

"Now we're moving!" Nathan cried, grinning like a boy.

Everyone on deck, Violet included, cheered wildly as the rumbling ride went on and on to plunge the stern faster toward the water. Violet felt shaken, shivery—wonderfully so. She shrieked in mingled joy and excitement, as if she were going to sea to face such a fine future of her own.

"Brace yourself!" Nathan cried, and grabbed her by the arms.

The huge stern smacked the wall of water; the entire vessel shook them in bumping, listing jolts. It threw Violet into Nathan's hard embrace; he pulled her to him. Instead of jumping back, she held tight. Her belly and legs pressed to his as he took their weight against the wheelhouse again and again; her hoops and petticoats whooshed her full skirts back and she felt crisp air swoop up her stockinged legs. When, grasping the rails, the captain and first mate hurried off to their duties, Nathan continued to crush her to him.

"*Oomph!*" she cried. He seemed to swallow her breath of surprise and jubilation as his mouth took hers. Her bonnet bounced back and danced by its ribbons. He shifted his weight and slanted his head to settle closer into the caress and kiss.

For Violet McClellan, the entire world might as well have jolted and smacked into the sea. Winds of longing capsized the sails of her senses. Desire swamped her poise. She clung closer to him; she parted her lips and kissed him too, however much her head spun as she felt a relentless rocking clear down into the depths of her stomach.

"Ah—sorry!" Nathan whispered at last when he set her back, looking soul-struck himself. "It's—tradition to kiss a lady when a ship is launched."

"If it's tradition," she said breathlessly, "don't be sorry." She was wobbly on her feet so she still clung to his strong forearms, and he held to her elbows to steady her. His gaze captured hers; she felt she could pitch into his embrace again, even though the deck somewhere below her feet had probably steadied now.

Fortunately, she thought, Nathan Stone did not seem one bit sorry he'd grabbed and kissed her. He looked ravenous—and not for the light supper she had promised him at her house afterwards.

"I—ah," he hesitated, before saying in a rush, "didn't really mean it that way, that I was sorry."

He cleared his throat and shook his head. "And I've overlooked something. We'll have to walk a ways through that raucous waterfront area to get the chaise after they tow us down the docks for the new rigging and sails. The dock—well, it's no place for a lady."

"I won't be afraid with you," she assured him as they strolled slowly to the rail while she fumbled to retie her bonnet. "Besides, I don't think it's fair that some of the most thrilling places in the world are not for women, including this waterfront and your *kohung* in *Kwangchow*! And I won't *kowtow* to anyone who says different!"

His firm lips parted slightly. He stared at her, luminous-eyed. She assumed it was because she had remembered three Chinese words he had used but once to her. Still, she hoped he stared for another reason too, because she could not bear to take her eyes from him for one moment either—not even to look out over the harbor or turn to the first mate, who came up to offer them a mug of beer.

They lifted their drinks to toast the launching of the *Bold Venture*. This ship might take Nathan Stone away from her, she thought, but at least it—and the wasted years of their parents' blighted love—had helped to bring the two of them together.

3

In the moments, hours, and days of that soft springtime, Violet McClellan fell in love with Nathan Stone. She did not announce it to the world or even tell him so. Perhaps he could see it anyway, because it was, for her, like the thrilling, life-jarring ride of a drydocked ship sliding to meet the sea.

In the evenings that April and May, they walked and talked and spent many an hour with Nathan's father. The men taught her to play Chinese checkers and *mah-jongg*. Nathan showed her how to eat rice and Oriental dishes with chopsticks, and they laughed themselves sore until she mastered it.

When the captain turned in and they went downstairs to the drawing room, Nathan read poetry to her in Chinese, a language so strange sounding but alluring to her ears. His sobriquet for her was *tabu-yuen*, a sweet dessert. But it was such small, simple glimpses of his sweetness she treasured, for he had buried it beneath layers of brusqueness and burning ambition— and brooding anger whenever his father tried to give him advice.

Sometimes after supper at the mansion, Violet played the flute for him and the captain. She thought the music sounded different in that house so elegantly adorned with exotic Eastern imports and bedecked with seagoing memorabilia. Her melodies swelled and soared rather than seeming small and restrained as they had in the chambers of her home. It even sounded better than in church, where the large congregation and Reed's splendid piano skills seemed to mute both her tender and triumphant tones. She wondered if her music would fly fully free on the deck of a ship, surrounded by vast skies and rolling waves....

She sang and taught the Stones her father's Irish jigs and sad, sentimental ballads. Nathan favored the lively, bouncing songs, but—and she understood why—the captain loved songs of loss like "Danny Boy."

Other evenings she and Nathan went out to concerts, lectures, and entertainments at the Holiday Theater. Yet they could not wait for each to end so they could talk and kiss and caress in the carriage while he took her home. Other days they picnicked, hiked the hills, strolled and shopped, rode about town, and downed enough cups of fashionable wine punch at both the Fountain and Indian Queen inns to launch another ship.

And always, whatever they did, part of their delight was in making the next day's plans together. In doing so, even for little jaunts, they expanded their joy by anticipating the next hours and days. It was as if they were mapping out great, elaborate strategies for finding or founding entire new civilizations. Above all, it kept them from thinking too far ahead.

They attended her church, too, though at first Violet regretted she had suggested it, however politely Reed's family greeted Nathan when introduced. After the service, she and Nathan visited their mothers' graves and left flowers both places, on behalf of themselves and the captain. Violet saw there was yet some barrier between the men that kept them from truly being at ease in each other's presence. She felt sorry for them, facing a separation so soon. But as the *Bold Venture*'s departure date neared, she grieved as well for her own looming separation from the man she loved.

Violet stood now at her bedroom window in a shaft of sunlight, waiting for Nathan to call on her for an outing. She suddenly recalled another of the brief notes her mother's "Eternally Jon" had sent with a flower, this one a starlike aster that disappeared to dust when she touched it: *The stars may fall, the sun decay, but firm as heaven, my love shall stay. Eternally, Jon.*

She gripped both hands on the window latch and leaned her chin on them, trying to calm herself with deep breaths of June air. Perhaps there was no truth in "eternally"—in love remaining—for Nathan would soon leave her as surely as his father had left her mother.

"The stars may fall, the sun decay, but still he will be on his way," she whispered her own version of the little verse. In less than three weeks all this would be over, and would she be rejoicing or grieving then that she had loved and lost him?

"Violet! He's here, Nathan's here!" Irene's excited voice floated up the stairs. "And he won't tell me where he's taking you, neither!"

Despite her dire dilemma, Violet had to smile at how the girl had changed. Violet's mother never would have let a servant shout upstairs to announce a visitor, or call "her betters" by their given names, or mingle in a familiar way with a guest. But Irene knew things were different now. The house and its habits had become Violet's at last—just when she would gladly toss it all into the sea for a grueling, dangerous voyage to China.

Nathan's surprise was to take her down to the little fishing village at the tip of Ferry Bar, just southeast of town. Seagulls wheeled noisily overhead, seemingly scolding the busy humans cluttering their shoreline. The oyster season was ending, so people were scraping out their final feast with dredges and iron rakes. Crab season was underway, so fishermen were stringing trotlines for the prized, soft-shelled crustaceans for Baltimore's famous gumbos, cakes, and chowders. Boats farther offshore trawled for shad and herring.

In the village itself, lining a single stony street, ramshackle whitewashed cottages and boat sheds huddled together, seemingly held in place against the elements by tangles of morning glory vines. Even this far back from the water, Violet thought the scene picturesque, for blue and white violets sprinkled the knoll of grass where Nathan halted the horse next to a peeling picket fence tilted askew by the wind.

"Mother loved violets," she murmured, more to herself than him.

"I never would have guessed," he replied as he climbed down to wrap the reins around the fence, then reached up for her. "Painted plates with violets in the house, her daughter's name—even the eye color she chose for you," he teased. "See, a few clues and I can surmise a great deal."

"And what shall I surmise about this day, since you brought our picnic this time and wouldn't tell me where we were going?" she asked. She knew she sounded a bit testy, but tides of foreboding and melancholy had been lapping at her composure today. "This place looks lovely and busy, but are you tired of my dinners or the places we make plans to visit together?"

He held her suspended against him before he lifted her down, letting her slide slowly against him. He stepped close to block her in against the chaise. "I never tire of you or your food or the places we plan to go together," he whispered, tipping her chin up with a curled index finger. "I thought you'd like it here. We're going to search for crabs, and I have a friend who will steam them for us. Is that all right? Are you all right today?"

"Of course."

"Have I missed something? Violet, just tell me. One of the most wonderful things about us—you—is that I can rely on you not to hold back or play games that waste time, thank heavens, as we have precious little of it."

"That's right," she said, and tried to pull away. He gently hauled her back. Captured, tapping her foot, she heaved a huge sigh. "So please," she added, looking up at him, "allow my fussing over little daily plans, as we have no big future ones to take my attentions."

She sidestepped and started away yet again, but he caught her arm and swung her back. "We can have. Despite the fact I'm leaving, we can have. We'll talk about it. I want to. Do you want to leave now and discuss—"

"Nate, lad!" a man's voice boomed out so close they both jumped. "You're a wee bit late. Thought you'd never get here. And this is the bonny lass you told me of, eh? But her eyes are the hue of my favorite wild heather, not just garden-variety lavender," the sun-burnished, white-haired old man rambled on while surveying Violet thoroughly.

She was not annoyed. He cut a rakish, romantic figure with that swagger, a lilting brogue, bare feet, and a gold ring in one ear like some latter-day pirate. She smiled at him as they shook hands.

"Violet," Nathan said, still holding her elbow tightly as if she would bolt again, "this is my father's favorite retired first mate, Hamish MacGregor, called Ham. Ham, Miss Violet McClellan, but I'm not sure we'll be staying now."

"Of course we will," Violet said. After all, she told herself, Nathan had told this man she was *his* bonny lass and had evidently described her through a lover's eyes. And he had more or less promised there were serious plans to be made, so wasn't anything possible? She was so excited she could have flown down to pluck those crabs right out of the water bare-handed.

"I've never caught my own soft-shelled crabs before," she told Ham, fully intending her next emphasized words for Nathan too, *"but I love a good adventure."*

"Then best take off your shoes and stockings too, and hike up your skirts, lass," Ham told her with a wink back over his shoulder as he led them down toward the shore. "See, an old man can give a lass bawdy advice, Nate lad, and get away with it too!"

Roaring a laugh, Ham MacGregor playfully punched Nathan in his belly. Nathan feinted a return blow and grinned guiltily at her. She smiled at them both, and her heart sang louder than the cries of the gulls.

Later, having gasped or laughed at every old sea-salt story Ham could recall, sated with crab, beaten biscuits and jam, coffee and strawberries, Violet sat barefoot next to Nathan on the stoop of Ham's cottage. When the old man went off to check his trotlines again, silent at last, they watched the water, empty now of all but one distant ship and Ham's busy silhouette on the shore.

"I wish I had far-flung tales like that to tell," she said, letting sand sift through her fingers like an hourglass.

"They're far-flung all right. Probably half of them weren't even true," he said with a shake of his tousled head as he leaned back against his side of the door frame, watching her.

"But such wonderful adventures and places. You and the captain have had experiences like that too, but I can tell only everyday ones of *terra firma* Baltimore."

"You'll take an ocean voyage someday. I'll see to it, if you can just be patient, my *tabu-yuen.*"

"And how patient would that be?"

He sighed deeply, not meeting her eyes. "Obviously, three years at least."

She clenched her hand so tight the sand bit into her palms before she threw it down at their bare feet. An answer to her prayers, but not all she had hoped for. He wanted her—he did mean that, didn't he? As a wife? But not for years, for he intended to leave her. She wanted both to exult by whirling in wild circles like a child and to grieve by throwing herself on the sand and stones and howling in a fit of temper.

"Violet, I do want us to have a future," he said, and took her hand in his. "But with my obligations, you must understand it can't be now. If you could see yourself caring enough to wait for me ..."

"Yes, but what if you never come back? What if something happens, like it did to—you know?"

"What happened to them is completely different!" he insisted. "I just feel I cannot make a full commitment—marriage, a betrothal even—when I'm leaving for so long. It wouldn't be fair to you."

"Indeed it would not!"

"Then you don't care ... deeply enough ... you won't wait?"

"Nathan, I care so deeply that I will be waiting for your appearance, your voice, your touch the rest of my life, even if I never see you again. But to wait with no assurances, to wait for a man who doesn't care enough for me in turn to alter his plans or take me with him—"

"Take you? I can't! I've explained all that."

"I'm not afraid. I would love every moment of it. I'll stay at Macao if I must. If we're to be together someday, I should go with you now. Why waste precious time? Your father said we need to seize a chance for happiness and commitment, or disaster can ensue."

"He was talking about himself and your mother, Violet. And all my life he's said a lot of things that don't apply to me—to us. However, I see you've been listening to him and not to me," he said and loosed her hands to lean down and seize one of her bare ankles in a hard, warm grip. "So just let me tell you a little more about why you cannot go with me." He surprised her further by grasping the arch of her foot with his other hand.

"Even in Macao," he went on, frowning, his intense face so close to hers, "the Chinese greatly outnumber the Caucasians. And do you know what the Chinese would think of a beautiful, graceful, strong, lively woman like you? They would think you are ugly, a real *qwai-lo,* for one thing because you have what they believe are big, vulgar, obscene feet instead of the desired three-inch golden lilies."

"Obscene? Golden lilies? What?"

"They bind the feet of their female infants and break and turn the toes and bones under to deform the feet into tiny stumps. It's years of torment, and in adulthood the women totter about as if crippled."

"No—"

"Yes!" He loosed her foot and reached for her shoulders to give her a hard little shake. "The more dependent women are on the men, the more desirable.

It's not the place for any woman, let alone one like you."

"The feet—that's horrible. They must be convinced to change."

"Change?" he cried, and snorted derisively. "You've missed my point. They've done it for centuries and cannot stomach mingling with any of us bigfeet ugly 'round eyes,' who are so stupid and crude we don't have their ways. They wouldn't open up *Kwangchow* or change at all if they weren't in need of trade—and didn't have Western gunboats staring down their throats to force them to it."

"But those huge national political problems can't alter how we feel, so—"

"There's much worse I won't go into now. You see, in wanting to go with me—the voyage can be hell too—and wanting to be there with me, you don't know what you're asking. Their culture is advanced and brilliant in many ways that I admire deeply. But it's backward and brutal—damned dangerous—in others."

"I suppose the Western cultures are too, and—"

"All right, I guess you need to hear more. Many of their people are opium addicts, and the Chinese government blames us foreign importers for that. The whole situation is so tense that the *kohungs* fear we might be sitting on a powder keg with who knows what sort of bloody rebellion or war in the offing. Violet, they strangle and behead their own criminals in China, so what might they do to foreigners they could overwhelm if given the chance? That's one of the reasons the rewards now are great for those willing to take the risk to live there. I have made that decision for myself, but I *will not* expose the woman I love to any of that!"

She gaped at him. If he had meant to shock her about the China that produced the lovely, delicate poetry and porcelain, he had succeeded. Yet he had frightened her more with his reasoning of why they could not be together.

With each breath he both bolstered and broke her, gave and took away. He loved her but would not take her. He wanted to protect her, but in doing so must desert her. And he did not declare he loved her in a—a loving way, but as a reason they could not be together! He did not believe that she was strong enough to take the bad with the good, that she could face the different and the dangerous to be with him. Why couldn't he see that she would not be afraid if he took her, but rather only if he left her behind? For if he did, she was certain that somehow she would lose him for all eternity.

"You said there is a colony of Western women in Macao," she said, fighting to keep calm despite arguments and emotions roiling inside her. Her voice trembled. "And I'm not one of those European women or Boston beauties you've no doubt been used to who would have been deeply offended by—unfortunate Chinese customs. I might be named Violet, but I'm no hothouse flower!"

"I know you're not," he said, pulling her to her feet and hard against him in the fading light in the doorway. "I'll think it all over, but whatever we decide, you cannot go with me—and I'm committed there."

She bit her tongue, hoping some future victory could come from this. But she remembered that Captain Stone had warned her more than once that Nathan was wedded to his ambition above all else. Was that why he and his father did not quite get on—not because they were different, but so alike? At least she had no intention of being like her mother, left behind to languish—no, not even for the consolation prize of wedding another man and having his child to love. Not even if ever afterwards this man she adored vowed *Eternally, Nathan* and sent her flowers until the day the world ended.

"I want to marry Violet, but it would not be right," Nathan blurted out to his father over breakfast the next week.

Captain Stone's newspaper rustled as he crumpled it to the table, barely missing his scrambled eggs and coffee. "Hallelujah! But what in the devil do you mean, it wouldn't be right?"

"To marry her and leave her. It's either that or give her a ring and ask her to wait, which she has, more or less, already rejected. And I'm not certain once I ... lived with her, even briefly, I could bear to go."

"This gets better and better. You know, you could take her with y—"

"Of course, you would get to that. The two of you sound like echoes sometimes, you know!"

"No, I didn't know. You mean she's taken to saying *damn, blasted,* and *devil take it*?"

"This is serious, Father," he said, scraping his chair back from the table so fast it almost toppled. He strode to the windows to scowl out at the sky, for rain clouds threatened and he wanted to take Violet to their favorite place near Jones Falls to propose.

"What I'm trying to tell you is that I won't take her to China, and you know the litany of reasons as well as I." He fought to calm himself as he turned and strode back. "But, I wanted to ask you, if she'll wed me before I leave, would you be willing to have her live here while I'm away? I know she must remind you of what you lost once—Lily. I see how you study Violet's face sometimes."

"Of course she could live here," Jon Stone declared. "I would be honored—and damned relieved to have you married to such a wonderful woman, even if you are half a world away. And Nate, if I watch Violet, it's to read what she feels for you, and I'd dare to say she's loved you almost from the first."

Nathan leaned stiff-armed on the table and shook his head. "Did you plan all this from the beginning, when you had me drag her here to be told the tale of loyal, lost love?"

"Do you think I'd play Cupid, my boy? You did that for yourself. But you'll also play the fool if you sacrifice years away from her, now that you've found her—if you really love her."

"If? Why are you always judging me, trying to push me this way and that? You've told me that Grandfather's trying to control you ruined your life, and you still try to control me."

"You haven't listened, have you? *I'm* the one who ruined my life—when it came to being too ambitious and losing Lily Jackson, at least—not my father. Just as you now have the opportunity to ruin your own. But I think things are looking up—as you said, if she'll have you," he added, removing his spectacles and polishing them on his napkin.

"The thing with Violet is that she is strong-willed—in a different way from women I've known before—so I'm giving her the choice."

"The choice?"

"Of a betrothal with a wedding after I return, or a wedding before I go, though the latter would give us only a quick week or so together. She knows she can't go with me, so those are our only options. Well?"

"Who am I to dare to advise you? Besides, either way it's me who will benefit from her charm and company these next long years, not you," his father concluded as he replaced his spectacles, rescued his newspaper, and flapped it open again.

Nathan frowned down at his own untouched plate of food, realizing that though his father had ended up agreeing with him for the first time lately, he still felt he had lost another battle. But today, surely, the war with Violet would be won.

"Well, aren't we being daring today, with a storm threatening and all?" Violet teased Nathan as she unpacked their picnic lunch and began to spread things onto the carriage blanket on the grass.

The wooded area around Jones Falls had a lofty hillside view of city and harbor. Although in Baltimore a falls meant simply a sturdy stream, there was a waterfall nearby and a humpbacked bridge they'd crossed to reach this secluded spot they loved. Sometimes, despite the too brief months of their courtship, it seemed to Violet that she had been savoring and hoarding moments and memories with Nathan for years—even decades, for her heart was full.

"I predict that rain cloud is going right around us, and the sun will shine," Nathan said with a taut smile. "Besides, it's a day for taking risks, my *tabu-yuen.*"

"Sweet talk will get you everywhere." She laughed and pelted him with a biscuit. As if that were his cue, Nathan reached for her, pulled, and tumbled her across the blanket into his arms.

They kissed each other breathless before he set her back and helped her to sit up again. "I feel like a boy who can't keep a secret any longer," he told her, fumbling in his inner waistcoat pocket. "I have a ring—if you will accept it. And it is up to you whether it's a betrothal or a wedding ring."

She stared at him wide-eyed, then dropped her gaze to the delicate gold ring he plucked from a velvet nest in a small box. Her pulse pounded; it was the moment she had hoped for, and he was giving her a choice. But to have him—to be his wife—that was what she wanted. The sooner the better.

His hands trembled as he extended the beautiful ring toward her. As if the whole world applauded, the leaves over them began to thrash in the increasing wind.

"Violet, I need and love you very much!"

Free yourself from care and ever dare to know I love you, danced through Violet's mind—words from her mother's poems.

When she stared amazed at him—for it was the first time he had ever directly declared his love—he said, "Violet, you know of my great admiration and respect for you. Will you do me the honor of pledging me your love as I do to you?"

"Yes. Oh, yes! And thank you for the choice. You've come to see that a wedding is the best?"

"Yes. Yes, I—"

She hurled herself against him, hugging, kissing. He laughed triumphantly, she thought, but she saw tears gild his eyes. They were both shaking as he guided the ring onto her finger.

"We'll try it on for size, and then I'll keep it until the ceremony," he whispered. "Look, a perfect fit."

"Yes, both of our lives fitting together, you'll see!" she promised, and hugged him hard again.

Violet ignored the rumble of distant thunder. Her life had been shaken, turned upside down, and had come out perfectly. She was going to marry this man; she was going to China with him so they could build a new life together. Whatever the obstacles or dangers, they would conquer them together!

"I hope you'll want to move in with Father," he was saying, his lips pressed to the blowing hair at her temple. "He's thrilled, needless to say. We'll be married as soon as possible, to give us some time together here—a week at least—before I sail."

"What?" she demanded, pulling back from his embrace. "You said a wedding. I made it clear that you could not just leave me. I thought a betrothal would mean I would wait—stay here—but a wedding . . ."

A frown crushed his strong features as he now held her at arm's length. "That's why I gave you the choice. If we're betrothed, the wedding can be when I return. But if we're married, we'd at least have a week. However hard it would be to part then, we'd have—"

"We'd have proved we don't really want to be together! That you need me only enough for a week, not enough to take me along. That you don't believe I'm dedicated to going with you. That your idea of love is separation and possible loss!"

"Violet, you're letting what happened between our parents color everything again!" he argued, as the first big drops of rain began to plop around them. "Your idea of love is risking something dire happening to you, and I told you time and again, I won't have that. I won't take a chance at losing you permanently by taking you!"

"Then I can't have this—have you," she insisted, and twisted the ring from her finger to press it in his big palm.

"Then we'll be betrothed," he said, his voice reasonable, maddeningly calm, as she began to grab their things from the blanket. "Violet, I have been my own man too long, and I won't be dictated to by anyone— you or my father—who think they know what's best for me. I have seen China, and you have not."

"But your father's seen it too, and he evidently thinks I could go. That is what you just implied, that he thinks you should take me."

"He saw it years ago, before things were so tense there."

"Then let me put ... put it this way," she stammered as she jammed the last of the things into the basket and slammed the lid down. "I cannot respect nor admire—however much I love him—a man who takes himself into such a dangerous world just to satisfy his own ambitions, to feed his fortune, when he could be hurt or killed, and deprive the woman he supposedly loves of his presence for the rest of her life!"

She stood and, lugging the basket, started away toward the bridge in the thickening rain. Nathan ran after her and grabbed the blanket. He swung her around and took the basket from her to drop it on the ground and pull her into his arms. He kissed her hard and long, until a crash of thunder made them jump apart.

"Come on—shelter," he shouted, taking their things in his other hand, practically dragging her.

"Why bother?" she demanded, yanking away and smacking her palms on her wet skirt. "You'll go into deepest, darkest China, which might explode at any minute, so why fear a little lightning strike or the falling tree that could crush us, or—"

"Damn it!" he roared and hauled her under the overhanging roof of an abandoned gristmill. His face was wet; his thick lashes spiked together while water dripped off his nose and chin.

In the mess they'd made of things, she thought, this storm suited them both. The agony of loss drowned her. He was going without her. She wanted to throw herself against him and beg him not to, but she was angry too. Most of all, she feared she would give in to one of his choices—both of which perhaps showed he loved her, but not enough to not leave her.

"I cannot," she said, forcing herself to utter the words, "become either betrothed or married to a man who could take me with him—at least to Macao—but will not."

"Then I can only hope you will wait for me and reconsider my sincere offer upon my return," he responded, his voice suddenly as stilted and stern as she had heard it that day she chased him through the streets of Baltimore to catch him—to begin this precious, impossible quest. They stood a few feet apart, sodden, arms crossed, glaring at each other. The rains came harder, water rushing in a torrent off the sloped roof, spinning the wheel in the rising current.

"You're determined," he accused, shaking a stiff index finger at her, "to end up like your mother after all, married to the wrong man!"

"I am determined *not* to end up like her," she insisted, "left behind by the man she loved, who gave her not himself but a parade of flowers that are as dead as all they could have shared . . ."

Her determined voice broke on a sob as she turned away from him. Grateful that the thunder rumbled more distantly over the hills, she ran out into the lessening rain, across the bridge, and back to the carriage ahead of him.

4

Though Violet tried to keep busy the last two weeks before Nathan would sail, she thought only of him—of them. And whether she played the flute in church or gave a concert at the orphanage where Irene had once lived—even if she endeavored to play the lightest, happiest of melodies—her tunes, her feet, her spirits dragged.

Too often, in accompaniment to her inner thoughts and music, she heard, like doomsday bells, words of one of the notes which "Eternally Jon" had once sent to her mother. The message that taunted her today, while awaiting Nathan's final visit, was, *Tho far away from thee I roam, forget you I will never, for deepest joys this life affords are centered in you ever.*

"He's coming down the street, Violet—walking, not riding today!" Irene poked her head in the drawing room as the doorbell jangled. "A man like Nathan Stone, I'd wait for him forever, I tell you that!"

"You have been telling me that, Irene. Just let him in and bid him farewell, as I'll show him out myself later."

Through the door, which stood ajar, she could hear the girl wishing Nathan a safe voyage and return. Violet closed her eyes for one moment to let his deep, distant tones wash over and through her. Today they chilled not warmed her. How silent, how somber the house would be without his voice, even if she invited friends in, gave music parties, took in other girls like Irene, gave flute lessons—the myriad things she planned to do during the next three years. But still she whispered, "The deepest joys that life affords are centered in you ever."

When he entered, he gave her a quick peck on her cheek and, as he had lately, managed to avoid looking long into her eyes. They chatted about the warm, windy weather—yes, fine for sailing, they agreed. Since their argument at Jones Falls, he had been here twice, both difficult visits with renewed disagreements crashing into the same impossible impasse.

Now he tugged his shirt cuffs down from under his coat sleeves and sat stiffly on one end of the settee while she perched on the other. They faced forward, turning only their necks, not their bodies. Their quick conversation fell to a stilted silence before he cleared his throat and spoke again.

"Violet, thank you for seeing me this last day."

"I believe I will see you every day you are away," she told him. She was surprised the words tumbled out, but she had always—sometimes to her detriment—said what she thought to this man. He had seemed to accept and admire that, so she was not changing now. The trouble was, he would not change either, and that had doomed them.

When he looked quizzically at her, she explained, "I mean, see you in my mind's eye, my memories—happy ones above all, I assure you."

"And will you see me in your hopes and dreams for the future?" He leaned closer on the settee, so they turned slightly toward each other.

"I don't know now. Perhaps."

"Then I will be so bold as to leave this with you. For safekeeping. For a promise."

He fumbled in his inner waistcoat pocket and again produced the ring. "Wait," he said, "before you protest, hear me out. If this cannot be a wedding or betrothal ring for us, please accept it as a vow of my undying devotion while we are apart. I will come back, and should you then be of a mind—"

"And where will you be headed for then? The steppes of Russia, which are too cold and snowy for me? Deepest Africa, where serpents and headhunters lurk and it is entirely too hot, a place where a lady would sweat? The distant moon, where it will be too barren for a woman or where the man in the moon won't let you bring a wife for fear of feminine lunacy?"

He looked shocked at her outburst. "I'm sorry you are bitter, my *tabu-yuen.* I did that to you, and I am sorry. You're no doubt thinking it is *not* better to have loved and lost than never to have loved at all."

"I'm thinking we're supposed to learn from the mistakes of others and we—you—have not."

"I'll not argue that again. Do you know what Father said today? Besides telling me I'm dead wrong, of course. He said he used to think he had all the answers to life, but then he learned he didn't even have the questions."

"That sounds like him. A pity you think you're so different and that admitting your similarities would mean you can't be your own man."

"I promised myself we would not argue today, Violet. But as for Father, he's missed you lately, as I shall while I'm gone."

"Oh, I will be able to call on *him,* and play the flute for *him.* I enjoy his company and he, after all, will be within reach."

She noted her subtle needling struck its mark whereas her blatant outburst had not. The little frown lines deepened above his nose; his already ruddy color darkened. Still he did not lose control of himself, when she so much wished he would.

"I will write, Violet," he said, his voice taut.

"I'm not sure I could bear that, Nathan. I'd feel I must press your letters in the pages of some musty book and store them in some dusty old trunk in the attic."

"Will you at least," he began, and slid closer to open his hand to her, "take this ring and keep it for me—to remember that I love you?"

She took the ring, hot from his palm where he'd clasped it. Closing her fingers around it, she slowly lifted her fist to his chin as if she would strike him. She had meant to drop the ring right back into his

lap, but she could not. All her anger, and defiance
ebbed. He took her hand, opened it, and kissed her
fingertips, then her damp palm where she held the
ring. He leaned toward her, nearly into her, then
pulled her to him.

Though she did not want to capitulate or cry, she
clung to him desperately as hot tears squeezed from
her eyes. She matched him frenzied kiss for kiss. At
last he set her gently back.

"You could watch the *Venture* sail with Father—
through his telescope from the house, I mean," he
said, pressing his lips to her temple, where his ragged
breathing heated her skin and rustled her hair. "I
couldn't bear it if you were really there at the dock."

"You should know by now," she said, pulling back
slightly to stare up at him, "I don't like to do things
from a distance. I intend to be there, Nathan Stone.
You won't take that away from me, too."

His lips a taut line, he nodded, stood, and drew her
up, full-length against him. He kissed her hard again,
then pulled away with a rasping gasp almost like a sob.

"Violet, I will be back for you, if you will wait. I
don't expect you to, of course, but I will be back.
However much you think I'm deserting you, I too will
have you with me every moment, waking or sleeping,
no matter what . . ."

He hurried from the room, closing the door with
the same finality with which he had banged the grave-
yard gate the first day she saw him. She rushed to the
front window and yanked the draperies apart, pressing
her nose to the glass, but he was gone. And then, she
knew why he had run. At the last, he had almost asked
her to go with him.

She jumped at Irene's voice. "He's gone so soon,
Violet?"

"Yes," she choked out. "Gone so soon."

It took Violet's last shreds of courage and bravado
to see the *Bold Venture* sail the next morning. But she

had decided, even though she was losing her chance for a fine future with Nathan, that she was not going to let life just go by as she might have before she met him. She had plans to keep her days full and fulfilling. However painful it might be, she intended to continue her friendship with his father. She would give more concerts, offer flute lessons to help others and earn extra money. She would donate more time and funds to the church orphanage, but also keep some back to take a trip herself to see the world—a little of it, at least. When she would go, where, with whom—those decisions she would make to get through the years without Nathan.

With Irene in tow, she arrived at McEldery's Wharf nearly at the last minute in order to avoid another personal farewell to him. She could not have borne that on or near the ship. She might lose her control and run aboard, chaining herself to a mast, or sneak on and stow away. In the desperation of her thoughts recently, all those options seemed entirely reasonable. As they walked the cobbled wharf, she steeled herself not to shout up, "Please don't leave me! I love you! I love you!" if she saw him at the rail.

Unfortunately, as if in time with her steps, her favorite of her mother's "Eternally Jon" notes tormented her, that childlike, haunting chant: *Roses are red, violets are blue, lilies are fair, and I love you.*

"Which ship is it?" Irene asked, her eyes darting everywhere. "*Oooh,* what a smell!" Their nostrils flared to take in the sharp mingled scents of bags and barrels of imported goods lining the wharf or being loaded on wagons: coffee, chocolates, Jamaica rum, and fish of all sorts.

"That ship there," Violet said, picking it out immediately. The *Venture* looked sleek but sturdy and ready for the sea. Its sails, even furled, made the vessel seem so much taller than she remembered. They walked closer, craning their necks to look up at the many men aboard. Deckhands leaned over with ropes, and sailors hung in the rigging. But Nathan was nowhere in sight in the frenzied preparations to depart.

Ships actually had to back out of the harbor here and come around in the river before heading out; Captain Stone had taught her that in one of his various through-the-telescope lessons from his loft on Fayette Street. Violet pivoted now to discover she could not see his rooftop from the dock. Surely he must be watching, but she would have to stand on a ship's gangplank or deck to have the right vantage. She sighed and turned back—and saw Nathan staring at her over the railing along the *Venture*'s prow.

In the booming noise of shouted orders, anchor chains rattling through hawseholes, the gangplank scraping up and away, they could not even shout a farewell. Yet they waved as her heart cried out to him: "Violet is blue, but she loves you. Eternally, Violet."

He was daring to smile—perhaps to make her feel brave, or just so she could remember him that way, or because he was eager for his fine adventure. She bit her lower lip hard to keep from crying. That and her stiff face muscles kept her from smiling at him in return.

The anchor weighed, a single sail hoisted, the big vessel slipped away from the wharf. Some fools cheered lustily at its departure. She could not bear to see it disappear, with him and without her aboard.

"Come on, Irene," she said and steered the girl away. "Mother's gone and Nathan, too. We've got a whole new life to live."

For once Irene knew not to scold or even ask a question. Violet set a fierce pace away from the wharf, refusing to look back. But as they turned onto Light Street, Reed Baxter caught up with them and took Violet's arm.

"Oh, Reed! Whatever are you doing here now?"

"I must admit I was watching you, following behind this morning. Even though you brought Irene, you shouldn't be down here."

"As you can see, we were perfectly safe."

He squared his shoulders. "Some may not care enough to stay about to protect you, but I will always be here for you. And if you're wondering how I knew,"—he looked sheepish and Irene fidgeted—"I imposed upon Irene to tell me when he was leaving and that, thank God, you were not going with him at the last minute to that heathen place. I just want the best for you, Violet, and always have. Irene, think you can go on home from here and I'll walk Violet back?"

"Oh, yes, sure, Mr. Baxter," she said, and seemed glad enough to escape.

"I know she called your beau by his first name," Reed said, his voice even more accusing now. "I know you both cared for him. But he's gone, and all this has made me do some thinking."

Violet started to walk again, slowly. Reed took her elbow to escort her across the cobbled street and up to the wooden walkway on the other side.

"It's made me do a great deal of thinking too, Reed."

"Good. I've been a complete dunderhead not to make my feelings—my *honest* feelings—known before, but I was so busy. And we seemed comfortable in our deepening friendship. I thought it was assumed ... that we were kind of promised, I guess. I am hopeful I am at least partly the reason for your refusal to marry or become betrothed to Mr. Stone. So I will put forward my suit, my proposal, if you'll have me, Violet. I've tried to bide my time, until you decided what you wanted."

She stopped and they stepped out of pedestrian traffic into the entryway of a tobacco shop. The sharp smell reached out to curl around them. She recalled again Captain Stone's words about seizing the opportunity for commitment, or separation and sadness could follow.

"Reed, I am so grateful for your continued friendship and kindnesses. But you see, I have decided what

I want. And that is that if I can't have the man I love,
Nathan Stone, then however close you and I have been,
I must be on my own, even if that means being with-
out a husband or child."

"But that's crazy! You don't mean that. You won't
when you get over him. You're just distraught. I've
tried to be so patient and understanding these last few
months, and will be yet again. I just haven't given you
enough time. If we live in your house when we marry,
I'll have money for a wedding trip to England, and
Father will take care of the business while we're away.
I won't give up on us, Violet! We need to be together."

She stared into his dear, impassioned face. This man
was offering her a fine future, everything that Nathan
had denied her. Security, understanding, unity, and a
bold venture to sail out to see some of the world. He
even got on with his father. Could not the music of
her and Reed's lives be as strong and sweet as the
duets they had long played together? He, like her father, would be content and eternally loyal.

But he was not Nathan Stone. And if she took her
second choice, as her mother had, she deserved to end
up with dried memories pressed in pages of a never-
opened book hidden in the dim attic. And then she
would be unfaithful, at least in her heart, not only to
her husband but to herself.

"I'm sorry, Reed," she began in a whisper, her voice
growing stronger as she spoke. "You deserve a woman
who can love you as more than a friend. And no—"
she added, and lifted her hand as if to stop his next
protest, "time would not change my mind. Although
no enduring promises passed between Nathan Stone
and me, I will have no other man. Now, please don't
see me home as I have somewhere else I must go."

"Violet!" he called after her in a ravaged, frenzied
voice. But he did not follow. She felt she had stabbed
him with that sharp refusal, but she could not regret
she had been honest. She quickened her steps, heading

uphill away from the harbor, away from what might have been.

Nathan watched the roofs and hills, the very harbor of home, shrink and slip away. Suddenly exhausted, he rubbed his eyes with thumb and index finger. Going to sea, especially to face a new challenge, usually invigorated him. But he had slept poorly for days—weeks—and not at all last night. Lying awake, he had fought the fierce urge to ride to Violet's door and pound it down. He would tell her he was brave enough to take her with him, come hell or high water—or come admitting something fearful to himself.

It was not just that his father had been right about some things, but that Violet had been, too. Not that he resented, even feared, his father's strength and power over him anymore, for in his maturing love for the man, he was coming to accept now that he could be both like and unlike him. How he wished he'd been able to tell him that this morning when they parted.

But what he was really fleeing was the simple fact that he resented, even feared to admit, that he had found a woman with strength of spirit to match his own. And that, however he had clung to the riggings of control, she had turned the set sails of his carefully planned life upside down!

"Mr. Stone. Mr. Stone! Captain says," First Mate Wyley called up to Nathan, "you want to take a turn at the wheel while we're still in the river?"

Since his family owned this vessel, the crew was always willing to please him. "No, thanks, not right now!" he called down, cupping his hands around his mouth in the stiff breeze. They were out into the broad reach of river and would then enter the Chesapeake Bay, and too soon after that slip beyond the reach of land, country, continents. And beyond reach of Violet for years, perhaps forever, he mourned.

In the wind through the shrouds, he heard her voice again—not calling him, but convincing him. She was a clipper, like this vessel able to plunge into storms or swelling seas and keep going. She did not need to be coddled, but had love and courage enough for them both. He heard again her last words to him, before he'd left her house yesterday: "Don't you know I don't like to do things from a distance? I intend to be there, Nathan Stone." Be there. Yes, she was. Firmly planted in his heart, his hopes, but not his arms or life, and that was his fault. And now it was too late.

But again, he heard his father's voice. "Who will you share your cares with at the end of the day? Your pride in self, love of duty and country will be cold comfort then, I promise you!"

Nathan hunched his shoulders against the breeze, though it was warm enough here in midmorning, still cradled as they were by the big bay before the open depths loomed eternally wide and deep. He grabbed for the rail to steady himself as realization racked him.

He ran across the gently tilting deck, trying to get his sea legs. "Captain Murdock!" he shouted as he approached the wheelhouse. "Captain!"

"Decide you'd take a turn at steering 'fore the going gets rough?" the man asked.

"Yes," Nathan told him with a decisive nod. "Exactly that!"

Violet walked so fast uphill that the calves of her legs hurt and she got a stitch in her side before she even turned onto Fayette Street. The Stones' butler, Grayson, opened the door almost immediately when she rang the bell.

"I'd like to see the captain, please," she told him, quite out of breath. "With Nathan gone, I thought he'd need some cheering."

"Sure enough, he does, Miss McClellan, and he didn't want it from me," the elderly, immaculately attired man said with a shake of his grizzled head. "June 22, 1835 is not going to be a date he'll want to remember in that daily ship's log he keeps."

Violet shook her head as she followed him up the flights of stairs. How could it have slipped by her that today was her birthday—hers and Mother's? And the very day, years ago, that Jonathan Stone first beheld his Lily leaning over the rail of a ship, much as she would always think of Nathan now. She was thirty today, but suddenly she felt one hundred and thirty.

"Violet, my dear, how good of you to come!" Captain Stone called to her from under the bank of windows overlooking the harbor. "I take it you saw the departure in person, as Nathan said you would?"

"Yes, unfortunately." She hurried to him and took his outstretched hands. "It was not easy, but I had to do it."

"Your credo in life, I believe," he said, loosing her hands. His steely blue eyes, magnified behind his spectacles, were sad. "Well, we've lost him for a while, but in a way, even if you get busy with your other life again, I've almost gained a daughter. I only pray, my dear, it will someday be a daughter-in-law. I've just been sitting here staring out and thinking how many invisible but impossible barriers, like all these layers of glass," he added, tapping his spectacles and the eyepiece of the telescope, "still separate me from my boy."

"I am so sorry—for both of us," she whispered, and bent to kiss him on the cheek before stepping back. She bumped her skirts against the edge of his desk and turned to see what she had disturbed—just his navigational map of the South China Sea and the newspaper clipping on top of it. At once she recognized it was the article that had been done on her and Reed's concert last year at church. It had praised their music and included brief descriptions of them—"the comely, talented Miss Violet McClellan, aged twenty-nine, daughter of Mrs. Michael McClellan."

It struck Violet that perhaps the captain had done some orchestration of his own to get her and Nathan together. Was it more than curiosity and conscience-cleansing that motivated the old man to invite her to the house that first night? She had wondered more than once why he had not found someone else to deliver those so-called Bermuda or resurrection lilies to her mother's grave so Nathan would never know of his father's secret love. Had the wily sea captain baited a hook with flowers for her, and then used her for bait, hoping she would in turn catch his son? Of course he had desired to make Nathan happy—and make him stay here. But had "Eternally Jon" also hoped his pain of loss could be eased if his son could wed his Lily's daughter? Perhaps she would ask the captain someday, but not today.

"And what new traffic is sailing *into* Baltimore today?" she asked, trying to keep her voice light. She bent to look through the telescope, turning the end of the scope to focus it for her own eyes as he had taught her. Rows of rooftops and a forest of masts and rigging jumped at her, and beyond, one ship—a sleek clipper—cutting in toward, not out from, McEldery's Wharf.

"There's a beauty of a clipper coming in," she told the captain. "She looks a lot like the *Venture*. Can she be one of your other ones?"

"Not for weeks, but I'll be able to name her by the set of her sails," he said and moved his wheeled chair closer to take a look.

She stood aside as he fiddled with the eyepiece and the barrel. And then she saw with her naked eye, even before he spoke, sails blooming big above the familiar vessel as it nosed into its same berth along the wharf.

"Victory at sea!" the captain shouted, and then she knew.

She hugged him hard and ran for the stairs. His hurrahing followed her; as she skidded around the last flight down, she thought she heard him shouting for Grayson and a carriage, but she could not wait for that.

It was easier running downhill, though she had to

be careful her feet did not skid out from under her. Like that day she had chased Nathan from the burying ground, she ran around people, bounced off a few, shouting back broken apologies as she tore on. Yes, she told herself, gasping for breath—for whatever reason, the ship had returned, and she would chase Nathan clear across the sea, to China, to the farthest reaches of the world, endlessly if she must.

As she ran down the cobbled wharf, holding up her hems, trying not to turn her ankle, she saw the ship's familiar figurehead and nameplate on the prow. The gangplank scraped and thudded down. She felt every bit the rebel, Black Jack's granddaughter indeed, as she just laughed at some raucous dockhand's comment shouted her way and ignored a bawdy suggestion or two. Nothing would stop her now. Her mother should have argued, should have run down here to stop or meet her "Eternally Jon's" ship. Years of living together should have been their mementos, not dried flowers and pretty poems! But she and Nathan would make up for all that.

She saw him hurrying down the gangplank. When he spotted her, he waited not one moment more to cup his hands and shout through the din, "Violet! Violet, marry me now and come with me forever!"

They rushed together, kissed fiercely to the cheers and cries of strangers. When they broke the kiss, they both spoke at once.

"I'll send someone up to fetch Irene to pack for me, as I'm not letting you out of my sight again, not until China; but there I'll be waiting for you just three days and not three years away!"

"I'll send someone for your minister to marry us," he said. "We may have to live frugally for a while, as I bribed the captain a month's salary to turn back."

"I think your father will settle that with him. I believe he's a much cleverer man than you've ever guessed."

They turned to look over their shoulders at the rat-

tle of the familiar Stone family carriage coming through
the crowd. The captain had sent it down for them,
she thought.

But Jonathan Stone had surprised her yet again.
They both gaped up into the slant of sun to see the
captain himself leaning from the carriage window,
waving, still hurrahing. When the carriage jolted to a
halt, Nathan reached up to grasp his father's hand,
then she put her smaller one on top of theirs before
Nathan kissed her again so hard her ears rang.

Adding their voices to the captain's, the officers and
crew leaning over the rail of the *Bold Venture* yelled
and whooped, urging them on. But they needed no
urging. This moment marked, Violet thought through
a haze of happiness, the closing of her life's previous
pages. But better yet, it was the opening of fresh ones,
fragrant and blooming with the precious promise of
many tomorrows.